"Just his lips,"
Iliani promised herself.

"I'll cease this madness once I touch his lips."

Still she hesitated. Her hesitation had nothing to do with losing her nerve. It was anticipation, pure and unadulterated. Reaching out slowly, ignoring the slight tremor of her fingers, Iliani lightly skimmed her fingertips over Alaex's firm but, as true as she assumed, soft lips. Once satiated some small amount, her curiosity, instead of curtailing itself as she had promised, unleashed fully, and Iliani found herself touching the rest of his face as well. She even ran her fingers through his slightly curly hair and over his darker and coarser beard.

Iliani was acting instinctively, and she was unaware that she leaned in closer to Alaex and that her lips had parted. Neither did she know that her nostrils had flared slightly as if she were trying to learn him through scent as well as touch.

She was unaware of all these things; however, Alaex was not.

The Inheritance

ANTOINETTE WRIGHTON

POCKET BOOKS

New York   London   Toronto   Sydney   Tokyo   Singapore

This book is a work of fiction. Names, characters, places and incidents are products of the author's imagination or are used fictitiously. Any resemblance to actual events or locales or persons, living or dead, is entirely coincidental.

An *Original* Publication of POCKET BOOKS

POCKET BOOKS, a division of Simon & Schuster Inc.
1230 Avenue of the Americas, New York, NY 10020

ISBN: 1-4165-0189-4

This Pocket Books paperback printing May 2004

10 9 8 7 6 5 4 3 2 1

POCKET and colophon are registered trademarks of Simon & Schuster Inc.

Cover art by Mitzura Salgian

Printed in the U.S.A.

For my own special "inheritances"—

To my brother James for the gift of past memories and the untold treasure of new beginnings . . .

and

To my brother- and sister-in-law, Ted and Karen Mason. I don't have the words to express what your support and encouragement have meant to me. Thank you with all my heart for being there.

The Inheritance

→ Prologue ←

"You have waited long enough, Alaex."

The voice in his head, a perfect replica of one that he hadn't heard in thirteen long years, startled him and he nearly missed the opening of the sheath for his sword. He bit back the oath that sprang to his lips. His recovery had been swift, true, but not swift enough. The sting and feel of blood trickling down his right thumb told him so.

Alaex was grateful for the approaching darkness that shielded his blunder from the casual observer. He pressed his forefinger across the wound in a bid to slow the blood, not stem the pain. The sting of the wound was already forgotten, overshadowed by the faint echo of what had ultimately caused it. Although he knew the futility of it, he could not quench the desire to turn and see whether Aeric of Fontwyn, whose voice he had heard clearly in his head, was there.

Troubled not just by what he had heard, but by a pervading restless discontentment, he left the camp and the sounds of celebration of victory. Today Alfred, king of all English-speaking people not under subjugation of

1

the Danes, as one scribe had described him, had resoundingly defeated Haesten and his great army.

Alaex smiled grimly. If there remained any doubters as to Alfred's kingship and worthiness, after today there would not be. Tales always grew in the rendering, but this one would need no exaggeration to make it great. The fervor of the celebration around him—of which he should have been a part but was not—said that what had been done would never be forgotten.

Despite the merrymaking all around him, or maybe because of it, no one marked his passing or tried to detain him. As he passed noiselessly through the camp, Alaex accepted that he was more than a mystery to the soldiers, and at this time of joy his austere presence might not be appreciated. He also recognized that it was within his power to change their opinion. All it would take was for him to break a near lifelong pattern of keeping his own counsel and rarely speaking.

His sigh made a long wisp of steam before him as he realized that knowing this solved little. He would have to do something, and with not having made the attempt to be more conversant before, Alaex admitted he was at a loss how to proceed. 'Twas much like knowing a place existed, but being unable to find it without a map. He saw the ease and sometimes camaraderie between other lieutenants and their men, and there were times when he envied it. What he could not see was a way for him to bring that about himself. His men respected him, true, and they were loyal. But Alaex would not wager his last coin that they understood him better than anyone else.

He leaned back against the stout trunk of a tree some distance from the encampment and looked out over the men, not really seeing them or their activity, his thoughts elsewhere. A sudden chill breeze swept through him, as if it sensed and echoed his colder thought that he did not need to focus on them to see them. He saw them always; he felt he always would. Too many battles—losses and victories—had ensured that.

Alaex shivered slightly, although he really didn't feel

the cold—at least not from the outside. The numbing sensation he felt in his bones had little to do with the elements and much to do with the images of countless battles which, owing to too many years, were no longer distinct mental entities. Instead they now overlapped and coalesced in his mind to form one long, interminable encounter. It seemed war in one form or another was all he knew and had ever known, and he was weary of it beyond telling.

This time, kind, intelligent, deep blue eyes appeared along with the voice, supplanting the images of the horror of war in his mind's eye. "Then 'tis time."

Alaex's hands clenched into fists. "Why now? Why now, Aeric?" His thoughts were so tortured he did not know if he spoke aloud or if he asked the question of the memory springing forth in his mind.

Silence answered him. It was as if having succeeded in turning his attention to the topic Alaex had been avoiding, the voice was now willing to maintain its peace. However, Alaex didn't need the whispered reminder that he had procrastinated. He knew he should have long since returned. Yet something had kept him from it. He refused to think that the something might be cowardice. Certainly he who had stood beside Alfred as they battled invading Vikings had no fear of an oath vowed long ago? Nevertheless the unfamiliar clenching of his insides and the suspicious moisture trickling down his spine when he considered what awaited him belied his claim of bravery.

Discarding that uncomfortable realization, he tried to view the situation with disciplined calm, and his mind froze into blank nothingness, making him recognize that that in itself was the difficulty. This was no battle where strategy—charge, countercharge, feint, or tactical retreat—or superior strength could decide its outcome. This was unknown territory for him. He was not a man of few words, but one whose preference was toward none at all. Expressions of almost any sort were difficult for him. It could be said that from the point of a sword, he had the grace of a scholar. It might be decided by the thrust and parry of shield and lance that he had the wisdom of a sage. But he knew with certainty that what was before him was different and unlike the cold familiarity of war—at least not the sort of warfare to which he was accustomed.

"You do not celebrate."

The quietly spoken statement did not unsettle him. Even lost in thought as he was, Alaex still had heard the soft footfall of the man he had followed, served, and respected the past thirteen years.

Alaex turned to face Alfred of Wessex, who to him still looked the same as he had the first time he had seen him—commanding in stature, burgeoning with wisdom, and overflowing with kindness. Alfred had the distinction of being one of the few men in Alaex's acquaintance whom he held high in esteem. Another was Aeric of Fontwyn, but as at the moment thinking of Aeric brought discomfort, he focused instead on the king.

"Nay, sire."

Alaex could feel the piercing intensity of the king's stare through the gathering dusk. It did not make him uncomfortable as it would some. He waited to see what was on his mind.

"On the morrow, we all return to our hearths. What of you? Does the thought please you, Alaex?"

Alaex's lips quirked slightly. "Aye, sire."

Alfred smiled kindly, and even in the increasing darkness Alaex could see the king's genuine fondness for him, not only in his eyes but in the gesture.

The seconds moved silently past and Alfred's smile grew. "As ever, a man of few words. Tell me, Alaex, what plans have you after this? Do you finally return to Fontwyn Hall?"

Startled, Alaex hid his surprise at Alfred's question. It was eerily similar to his own unsettling thoughts. " 'Twas my thought when Your Majesty approached. I need turn my attention to that place and a long-spoken oath."

Alfred smiled again. He knew what an effort it had

taken for Alaex to reveal that much. He would press him no further. Nor would he comment on or inquire about the shadows, which he was certain had nothing to do with the growing dusk, lengthening the usually clear, bright blue eyes of his trusted lieutenant.

"Peace be with you, Alaex," he said solemnly after studying him a few moments longer. "After these last years we all crave it, but I know of no one who needs it more." With those sincerely uttered words, Alfred turned to leave. He didn't expect an answer and Alaex didn't disappoint him by giving one.

If but Alfred could have known, Alaex was already occupied with answering another voice, a voice that now existed only in the distant past and the turbulent vestige of memory.

"Cease your torture, Aeric! You have won the day. 'Tis only my hope that once there, you guide me through what must be done. Rest easy, old teacher. I ignore the oath no longer. I am going home."

Chapter

➤ 1 ◄

There should have been more joy.

Iliani was ashamed to think it, but the thought persisted nonetheless. There *should* have been more joy. Today was her wedding day, and although her marriage was arranged, it was to a man she had known all her life. In fact, since she was five years old, his family had raised her. His mother had become hers. His father had been like a father to her.

Iliani could barely remember her own father, and although she respected the woman who had given her life, she had no recollection of her whatsoever. How could she? Her mother had died while bearing her. She had never known the gentleness of her touch, the depth of her wisdom, or the warmth of her love. For some time while growing up, that had bothered her. Then she had come to accept it merely as something that was, and beyond her ability to change.

Her father belonged to a slightly different category. She did have a few memories of him—hazy ones with the passage of so much time, but no less cherished. Besides, she looked like him—or so she had been told.

Staring now into the looking glass, Iliani tried to form an image of how a man with her features would appear—and failed abysmally. Her face was too oval. It was hard to imagine a man with that feature. Her eyebrows were arched in smooth lines of slashing black. She could well picture him with dark eyebrows, but would they curve so? Her eyes were dark blue, closer to violet actually, fringed with lashes that looked like the soot left over after a fire died. Iliani tried to imagine her father with eyes like that (she had been told their color was the same), but she couldn't quite make the image solidify. About the only thing she could picture them having in common was thick, raven-wing black, curly hair. His undoubtedly would have been better kept than hers as he was bound to have worn it shorter than her waist-length tresses.

Iliani continued to stare at herself and had to resist the childish urge to stick out her tongue at her reflection. She had tried many times to bring forth an image of her father, and each time she had failed. It was frustrating. Unlike with her mother, she had seen and known her father, yet she couldn't call his face to mind. Perhaps it was too long ago. She didn't know why she still bothered. Edouard, her father's friend and her guardian since her fifth year, had tried to dissuade her attempts at recollection. He had said it was part of the faraway past and would only bring her pain. He loved her, and although he did not want to take her father's place, he did not want to see her hurt. Iliani had been touched. She hadn't wanted to hurt Edouard and it was obvious that her attempts at remembrance did. So instead of ceasing her efforts, she simply ceased telling him of them. For the first time, however, she considered that he might be right. Maybe too much time had passed.

The last time she had seen her father she was five years old. She was nearly nineteen now and a lady—one who was about to become a wife. Defiantly she stuck out her chin, determined to concentrate on that fact and how happy it should make her, and not on some half-remembered, half-formed image.

Suddenly Iliani gasped. Whether it was a trick of the sunlight against the glass or her defiant gesture that made her imagine that for a fleeting instant she had captured the image of the man whose memory was so dear to her, she didn't know. But it had been there, and it was bittersweet.

The smile that came to her full, sensuous, naturally red lips was soft, curving to reveal even white teeth. Perhaps that was the one trait she shared with her sire: stubborn defiance. Leaning closer to the glass she added, "And a strong chin."

"Where is the joy, Father?" she asked aloud, her smile diminishing as her original concern returned. "Am I wrong to expect it? Eadwina says it will come." All traces of the smile disappeared. "Father, I love her dearly, but 'twixt us two, we both know that she lacks the brain God gave a goose. I am not sure I can trust what she says."

She sighed, a frown marring her brow. "Edouard, he is different, Papa. He is strong, as strong as I have always thought you would have been. He has raised me, loved me. I could not feel more his daughter. In truth, Papa, he is the reason I did not dissent in marrying Cam. My first reaction was that it was unthinkable! How could I marry a man I had looked on as a brother? I told Edouard that. That was when he told me that 'twas your wish also. By doing this, I will be pleasing you both. Is that all the joy and happiness to be found in this?"

Iliani rose from the table where she had sat brushing, or rather, attempting to brush the curls from her unruly hair. She was not ill at ease with having a one-sided, audible conversation with herself. She had done so many times. It soothed her. It made problems seem smaller and solutions clearer. She grimaced as she remembered trying to talk to Edouard's wife, Eadwina, about her feelings.

Eadwina, sweet woman that she was, had cavalierly

put it off to nerves, telling her that everything else would come with time. She had gone on in that birdlike voice of hers to say that her own marriage had been arranged and that until the day of the wedding she had never seen Edouard. After all, she had chirped, Iliani *knew* her betrothed. She had grown up with him. What was there to fear?

Precisely. "What was there to fear?" Iliani echoed. Was fear the reason for her growing discomfort? Did she merely fear what lay ahead or was this something more?

Iliani did not need to peer into the looking glass to know that her reflection would show a face clouded with worry and eyes shadowed with doubt.

" 'Tis foolishness! Nerves, as Eadwina claimed!" she muttered fiercely. And if she mentally flinched to be taking the advice of a woman who, though kind, had once thought there was more than one moon, the one she left behind and the one before her, Iliani ignored it. " 'Tis no more, no less. Did not Eadwina tell me that all brides are affected thus? Is not Eadwina like a mother? Edouard, a father? They are my family. Something for which I have always longed and never had. Marriage to Cam will only make the bond stronger."

"Yer pardon, lady?"

An embarrassed flush tinged Iliani's skin. As soothing as she found her conversations, she knew they disconcerted others. Cedra, Iliani's maidservant, had entered unheard, carrying her wedding dress, and had stopped to stare in confusion at the sight of her lady pacing hard and talking to herself.

The girl looked frightened witless. Seeing that, Iliani blushed all the more.

" 'Tis naught, Cedra," she said quickly, seeking to distract her. "I merely spoke a thought aloud."

When the servant's brow did not clear, Iliani changed the subject. "Where is the lady Eadwina?"

Cedra's expression eased slightly. "Do ye want for me to fetch her, lady? Are ye faring poorly?"

Iliani took a deep breath. Her thoughts were too much

in disarray to see Eadwina. "Nay. I only wanted to know where she was. She said she would attend me."

Cedra turned away to lay the pristine white garment on the bed. She was at the door before Iliani could stop her.

"I shall bring her here, lady, and she can help ye, most sure."

"Wait! I did not—" But Iliani could have saved her breath. The door shut on the rest of her words and she had no doubt that when it opened again, Eadwina would come chattering through it.

Iliani sighed and a begrudging smile lit her face as she recalled Cedra's rapid exit and her hurried words. She could guess what sort of help Cedra thought she needed, and it had nothing to do with helping her to dress for her wedding.

She looked at the white gown on the bed, a rueful expression on her face. So much for distractions. It wasn't surprising, then, when a few moments later she heard Eadwina talking to Cedra as they came down the hall. Iliani clasped her hands together, prayed for patience, and waited quietly. There was naught for it now.

The door burst open without the benefit of a knock, and Iliani, although frustrated, could not help the smile that crossed her face as she viewed the plump woman coming toward her.

"Darling, are you well? Cedra," Eadwina said, nodding her brown head toward the servant, "seems to think something amiss. I told her 'twas naught. Just as I told you 'twas naught and naught it is. Naught but nerves. You are nervous, are you not? Did I not tell you to expect that? I did. I remember distinctly doing so." Eadwina took a brief pause, her green gaze falling on Iliani's clothing. The pause was over.

"Why are you not dressed? Oh, because Cedra only just brought your gown. I ken. In any event, no time to dawdle. None at all. Come here, dear, let me brush your hair. Did you . . . ? Well, aye, I can see you tried, but well, let's do it again anyway. I tell you, Iliani, as much of a chore as this tangled mane has been, I will miss this. I will miss mothering you—and Cam, too, of course, but he is a boy and you are a girl and 'tis a difference and all that. Still, I shall miss you both." Eadwina sighed and began to brush Iliani's thick black hair.

From the corner of her eye, Iliani caught Cedra's movements and cast a quick glance at her to see that the woman was now studiously attending her duties. The determined look on her face said she was going to do what she wanted and ignore them both, and that she would count herself fortunate if Eadwina and Iliani returned the courtesy. At that thought, a sparkle lit Iliani's eyes and her lips twitched.

Eadwina, who had been staring at her with pursed lips, relaxed her mouth and smiled. "See there! Did I not tell you you would feel better? 'Tis a miracle, that. Weddings have a way of making you feel up and down. One minute you are anxious, the next happy. See there, Cedra," Eadwina called, and Iliani almost laughed at the near comical chagrin on the maid's face. "Come here, girl," she ordered as Cedra hung back hesitatingly. "See the happiness on your lady's face."

By the time Cedra approached, Eadwina was on to a new thought, giving the girl no time to respond, had that been her intention.

"Did I not say 'twas so? It was the very same, I tell you, with me and my sweet Edouard. He was more nervous than I," she chirped on as if confiding something. "Why, the man scarce said a word. I had to do all the talking. Can you believe it? Believe it or no, 'tis truth. Cam's just like his father. He barely speaks also. They so enjoy it when I do, and I do, you know, because they enjoy it . . ."

Iliani shut her eyes and tried to drown out the sound of Eadwina's voice. She tried instead to concentrate on the soothing strokes of the brush through her hair.

An answer to the dilemma of her unsettled emotions was no nearer her grasp than before, but as she had always been logical, she just reviewed the facts. The fact was she loved no one else. Edouard, Eadwina, and Cam were all the family she had and she did love them. Lourds Keep had been her home for most of her life and would be more so after today. Marriage to Cam would also give her what she wanted in the way of providing her with children. There would be no foster link there. They would be hers and she would love them with a passion that surpassed anything.

So what if there was no joy springing from the happiness of marrying one you loved? Iliani knew with all her heart that with those things she had just considered, there could be if not joy, then at least contentment. Seen in that light, there was nothing but good to come of this.

When she opened her eyes again, Eadwina was still talking and Cedra had gone about her other duties—or had taken protective flight. Then Iliani noticed the unusual silence and her eyes met Eadwina's green ones in the glass.

"What is it, Eadwina? What is wrong?"

To her surprise, tears glittered in Eadwina's eyes, and her voice, though still high, was roughened with accompanying emotion. "'Tis only you are so lovely, m'dear. I see the beautiful bride you will be and the lovely children you will bear. My happiness has no limits in spite of the fact that unlike most mothers, I feel as if I am losing both son and daughter."

Iliani was shocked not only at the emotion in Eadwina's voice, but at the words themselves. They were so un-Eadwina-like.

"I know I came to help you with your toilette, but I find myself overcome. Can you manage the rest on your own?"

For once, she waited for an answer, and Iliani nodded.

"Good. Then I shall leave you to dress. Call for Edouard when you are ready. I shall be below attending to our guests."

As usual, when in Eadwina's presence, Iliani could say nothing. However, what was unusual was that this time she had not been overwhelmed by the woman's constant chatter. She had been overwhelmed by her love.

An hour later, Iliani stood above the main hall watching the crush of guests below. She looked around for Edouard but could not find him in the crowd. She didn't see Eadwina either, but she did see Cam standing in a corner, the ever-present Namin at his side.

While Cam watched the guests, Iliani watched him. He was tall, well-muscled, yet slender, and she had the opinion he would remain so, for he looked exactly as Edouard did and even now Edouard had no fat around his middle. Cam's hair was light brown like his mother's, but his dark brown eyes were a mirror of his father's. Next to Namin—who was at least a head or two shorter, with pale brown eyes that were much too close together, giving him the look of an eager ferret and a build that bordered on lank—Cam was an impressive figure. Iliani did not need to be told that many maidens would give much to be in her position, marrying into a powerful family and getting such a pleasant-looking man. Yet she felt their envy was misplaced. Looks were no man's measure—or woman's, for that matter.

Eyeing Cam closely now, Iliani ignored his appearance and concentrated on his demeanor. He stood stiffly as if he were angry. Iliani might have understood dismay, but anger? What had he to be angry about?

Iliani had just begun to wonder if her confusion was leading her to see what was not there, when a furtive movement at Cam's side caught her attention. Namin was once again speaking, and it was clear that despite the obvious hesitance in his manner, Cam had little liking for whatever it was his friend was saying. As Iliani watched, any thought she had about being mistaken about Cam's mood was erased when she saw Namin, still speaking, move away nervously. Namin always looked nervous when Cam was angry.

There had been many times in their childhood, times

which Iliani wished to heaven she had not recalled just before her wedding, that she had seen Cam win an argument not with words, but with fists. Poor Namin had received more than his share of blows. Although Iliani had not liked, and still did not particularly care for, Cam's friend, she had felt compassion for him and had intervened on Namin's behalf from time to time. For his part, Cam had always been remorseful after one of his explosive episodes, and although his actions had been less than admirable, Iliani, by focusing on his other, more pleasing traits, had always forgiven him. Cam could be charming when he chose. At those times, it was more than easy to overlook his little flaws—it was easy to forget he had them.

Looking back at him, Iliani could see that whatever Namin had said, he had averted the worst of Cam's temper, and she smiled. Perhaps Namin was not as light in the head as she had thought. Momentary humor aside, she still felt saddened that Cam's behavior was at times less than desirable, and again she wished that she had not chosen this time to remember that. It was time to see the good in him. He had always been wonderful to her, Iliani reminded herself defensively, trying to avoid any thought that might sound remotely disloyal to a member of the family that had raised her and made every attempt to make her one of their own.

As always, Iliani's overwhelming sense of gratitude for Edouard and his family asserted itself, making her feel slightly ashamed for any ill thoughts she had. They had reared her, loved her, and they deserved more than her churlish and traitorous lack of thankfulness just because she quested for an elusive feeling of joy that she was not sure even existed. Even now their only thought was for her, to give her what she had been denied all her life: a real family. It was unfair of her to chide their son, even if only in her mind. Flaws could be found in anyone, and in that *she* was certainly no exception. And no one deserved to have his shortcomings listed and enumerated only to be found wanting—especially by the woman he was about to marry, and one who already owed more than could ever be repaid.

"There you are!"

The voice behind her startled her, and Iliani nearly jumped. She turned to face Eadwina, trying to smooth the remnants of guilt and concern from her face.

Iliani need not have made the effort. Eadwina went on without taking account of her expression.

"'Tis not seeming for the bride to spy on those who have come for the festivity of her own wedding." She had lowered her voice and Iliani smiled again in true amusement, knowing Eadwina was about to scold. When she had been a child, Eadwina had always lowered her voice when admonishing, even when they were alone as they were now. "Besides, Iliani, 'tis really rude to stare. What if someone saw you? Why, just think of what they would think! They might be moved to think I have not reared you properly. Come, come! Let's go down to the hall and greet them fittingly. Honestly! I am surely surprised at you. Why, you used to do this as a child—especially when you first arrived. The first days here, you didn't say a word, not to me, not to Edouard—to anyone. However, you *would* sit yourself in the gaps of the gallery above the hall and watch what went below. I saw you but I never told Edouard. Nay, never. That, with your silence, would have distressed him greatly. When your watching continued even after you began to speak, I thought *he* might think I was not rearing you properly, but after a time you stopped. And here now, nearly a wedded woman, I find you still doing it! I say! Come meet your guests face-to-face as an adult and . . . not—"

Eadwina's tirade ground to a discordant halt and her hand clenched on Iliani's upper arm as her round face whitened. Whereas her nearly ceaseless chatter had not concerned Iliani, her alarmed expression had done so instantly.

"Eadwina, what is it?" Instead of waiting for an answer, Iliani turned back to the guests, having noted that the eerie silence that gripped Eadwina seemed to have a hold on them also.

No one moved. Cam, Namin, one and all stared at the hall's entryway. As Iliani turned to see what everyone else saw, Eadwina seemed to return to life. In a voice Iliani had never heard from her before, she said, "Now is not the time, dear. Let us go to your room. Plenty enough time to go down later. Aye, plenty," she whispered, nodding distractedly.

As Eadwina spoke she propelled Iliani from view and down the corridor to her room. But it was too late. Iliani had seen him.

A new guest had arrived, but it did not seem that he had come to enjoy the food and wine or even the gossip as the others had. How was it possible that one man could make you feel besieged? Iliani did not know the answer to that; she just knew this one did.

From that brief glance she knew she would never forget how he looked, what his stance seemed to say. As Eadwina closed the door to her room and hurried down the gallery muttering that she must find Edouard, Iliani knew she hadn't misjudged the man standing silently below. This guest had come for none of the things the others had. This one seemed to have come for war.

Chapter

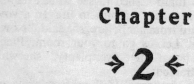

The silence seemed obscene after the previous merriment, offensive and complete. Nothing breached it. Everyone sat in quiet expectancy, waiting to see who could or would make the first move.

Alaex watched the people around him, all halted in varying degrees of eating and drinking. Originally he had felt the urge to laugh at them and their wide-eyed stares, but that impulse had been fleeting. It lasted as long as it took him to realize that this was a wedding feast, and it was no stretch of wit to say whose. That unpleasant surprise and the immediate rush of anger singing in his blood kept him where he was. He entered no farther. He merely waited.

It was into this frozen assembly that Edouard entered, alerted by the silence that something was terribly wrong. But he was unprepared for what he saw. When he recognized the tall, silent figure by the door, he wanted to howl in frustration; he wanted to grimace in lamentation; but most of all, he wanted to grab the ancient sword of his forefathers from the wall and run the man through. It didn't matter what Alaex wanted, Edouard did not want to give him the chance to speak. Alaex's presence sowed dissent and he was not foolish enough to think that his appearance here, now, would be any different. Nay, it did not bode at all well. He was positive that Alaex would not approve of his son marrying Iliani, and Edouard heartily cursed his friend, long since dead, for giving this man the right to approve or disapprove. It was galling to know that the only reason Iliani was at Lourds Keep was because Alaex allowed it. Aeric had given him that right, legally making him guardian to her *and* her estate.

Although Alaex had never exercised the right, should he ever choose, he could remove Iliani from Edouard's care and there would be naught to do but accept it. Edouard had lived with that fear for years, and although Alaex did not seem inclined to have the girl about, that did not mean he could not change his mind. Most certainly he might, once he discerned what was transpiring and that no one had bothered to inform him.

Edouard frantically sought a way to salvage the situation. He knew of the rumors, and his heart sank as he accepted that Alaex probably did also. But rumor was all it was. Cam was not as they claimed. He was not mean, dishonest, or, even worse, a coward. Alaex had no right to object to this marriage based on lies spoken by jealous fools.

Thinking of his son, he turned his eyes abruptly to see what Cam was doing and found him as frozen—more so if that were possible—as the others. Quickly putting from his mind what his son's lack of action might imply and certainly how others might see it, Edouard turned his attention—and berated himself for momentarily allowing it to wander—back to their unexpected guest. Very aware that all eyes, even those of his son, had turned to him, Edouard squared his shoulders and approached Alaex as if he were an honored guest and not the instrument by which he was certain that the dreams of a lifetime were about to be cindered into ash.

"Alaex."

A nod was his response.

" 'Twas good of you to come. We did not expect you."

Finally Alaex spoke, his voice deep and quiet, yet carrying. None of his anger showed. "That is clear as I was not invited. What goes on here?"

Edouard's smile was forced. "A wedding celebration."

Alaex's pale blue eyes narrowing between the protection of a noseguard asked what his lips did not.

Edouard cleared his throat. "My son Cam, whom you know," he replied hoarsely, waving in the general direction of where he had last seen his son, and praying he was still there, "and, and Iliani, your ward."

Rage blasted from Alaex's eyes in waves, and as a purely reflexive result his hand lightly grazed the hilt of his sword. If he had looked hostile before, it was nothing compared with his expression now.

A few of the ladies close enough to see that threatening action promptly fainted. In the ensuing tense quiet, no one doubted that bloodshed would be avoided. Edouard himself found his thoughts moving to regret that he did not have a sword, although he doubted the benefit the weapon would bring.

To most of his guests, this man was more myth than reality. Edouard knew differently. He had on occasion seen him wield that wicked-looking sword, which he now caressed so naturally, with such efficiency and dexterity that the thing seemed to have a life of its own. Even sheathed, it sang of power and lethality.

"I want to see her." Alaex was implacable. Identification of who it was he wanted to see was as unnecessary as his adding the word "now."

Summoning a courage he didn't know he possessed, Edouard tried to delay. "The girl is preparing for her wedding. She did not know . . ." He swallowed heavily. "That is, she is not expecting . . . ." His words died for want of a diplomatic ending.

Alaex, for his part, was back to waiting. He would say no more. He could not. The rage within was too great. It fed on his guilt as he realized what his delay had almost wrought. His rage—and guilt—was the only reason he'd allowed Edouard's lame attempt to stall him. It would not be wise to see Iliani for the first time in years in such a state. He knew little of women, and of Iliani not at all, but common sense said she would not appreciate his coming to her with blood-splattered clothes and sword—especially if the blood he wore belonged to the man who she thought had provided for her all these years. He was no fool. Iliani would obviously feel more than passing affection for these people, while he knew he would be fortunate if she even remembered him.

It was these things that checked his anger—these facts, and the news he brought. He did not want to compound its impact with violence. Iliani, as had a few of the women in this room, might decide that fainting would be the best course.

However, despite his forbearance, his patience was not endless and he was no longer willing to stand there and be the object of Edouard's and his guests' gawking. Their stares, a unique mixture of cowardice, awe, and disdain, did not appease his temper.

Alaex's jaw clenched tightly and his eyes conveyed the message that it would be most unwise of Edouard to make him ask again.

"I shall fetch her anon," Edouard mumbled hastily, and turned to leave.

"Wait," Alaex commanded. Although his senses screamed at turning his back on any in this room, he suddenly realized that because of what he had to say, it was better not to see Iliani here. "Take me to her."

Edouard gulped. "But she is . . . I told you."

Alaex took a step toward him and Edouard quieted; however, Cam chose this time to speak.

"Father, I must protest!" he cried, striding forward and evading Namin's restraining hand. "'Tis my be-trothed!"

Blue eyes turned to him and Cam froze again. He had not known it was possible for eyes to be so cold and lifeless, and yet so filled with promise.

"Is she?" Alaex asked softly.

"But, of course—"

"Time will reveal." Alaex dismissed him and although he directed his words to Edouard, he kept his eyes on Cam. "My lord?"

"This way," Edouard mumbled. Now was not the time for conflict. He hoped the hasty glance he sent to Cam revealed that, for it seemed his son looked as murderous as he had ever seen him.

Alaex walked silently behind him and his silence was amazing considering the amount of armament he wore. When they disappeared from view of the main hall, he heard the resumption of noise, although it was subdued. Still he listened. The excited babble did not concern him. What he strained to hear was the sound of footfalls behind him or the sharp, nearly noiseless hum of a blade heading for his back. One in his profession did not have a lengthy career if one did not learn early to detect the very sound and smell of treachery. This place reeked of it.

So hard was he straining to identify all sounds that he barely noted Edouard stopping before a stout wooden door.

"She is within." Again Edouard hesitated. "I ask . . . I beg of you to allow me to speak to her first."

"For what purpose? Have you knowledge of what I wish to discuss?"

"Nay, Alaex, but—"

"Then 'tis useless to try to prepare another for something you know not. Announce us."

Seeing that further talk or delay was useless and that Alaex had no intention of sharing his aims, Edouard knocked and called out, "Iliani, 'tis I, Edouard. May I enter?"

The door was opened quickly as if the person on the other side was anxiously waiting, and Edouard found himself face-to-face with the girl he had raised since her father's death thirteen years before. Even having seen

22

her every day, he was startled by her comeliness, and again his heart sank as it awaited the loss to come. The moment he had dreaded so long was here. It had to be so. There could be no other reason for Alaex's presence, ill-timed or not. The only question remaining in Edouard's mind was vague wondering at the effect her loveliness was having on the man of stone behind him. It was then he saw Iliani's bright gaze move over his shoulder to take note of the man herself.

Iliani was mesmerized by the tall, silent man whom she had glimpsed so briefly before. He was more fear-some up close, but she forced herself not to panic. She sensed he almost looked for it. That quiet expectancy and the fact that Edouard had brought him here to her door wore at her resolve to remain calm. Her composure was further threatened by the inscrutability of his ex-pression and the fear she sensed in Edouard.

Pulling her eyes away from those of the enigmatic and frightening stranger, Iliani turned back to Edouard. "You wished to see me?"

Edouard nodded, then corrected himself. "We wished to see you. Iliani, this is Alaex of—"

"Alaex will suffice. May we enter, lady?"

Iliani's eyes flew back to his. His words were a question, but he wasn't asking. With those few words, he impressed his will upon her, and although Iliani began to shake her head in an instinctive denial of his request, she also stepped aside without realizing she was doing it.

Unperturbed by her contradicting actions, both men entered. Once inside, Alaex turned to Edouard. "You may wait for me below stairs. I need not remind you of the lady's safety."

"Nay, Alaex, but—"

"Enough!"

Iliani looked from one man to the other and she thought she saw Edouard pale. His alarm fed hers.

"Milord, please. I know not what you wish, but can he remain?"

"Nay."

There was no room for dissent and Iliani sensed that repetition of the request would not be appreciated. For an instant she thought his refusal was subtle revenge for her reluctance to allow him entrance into her room, but as she looked into his eyes she saw implacability but not pettiness. He was merely a man accustomed to being obeyed without question. The very hardness in his tone—whether from choice or circumstance, Iliani could not determine—said so.

Looking over to see Edouard clench his fists, she decided the source of his hardened tone did not matter. Iliani wanted to go to Edouard and comfort him, but as had happened a moment ago at the door, her desire lost the conflict with her action. Some primal instinct warned her that going to Edouard would not be wise. Instead she watched silently as Edouard unclenched his fists, smiled faintly at her, and then left the room.

Loyal anger on Edouard's behalf caused Iliani to turn hot eyes toward Alaex. She deeply regretted the moment of cowardice that had kept her from Edouard's side. Who was this man that he could enter her life and within minutes impel her to his will? His likes and dislikes?

Heated words surged to her lips and died just as suddenly as Iliani was taken off guard by his expression. Was it her imagination, or did the man of iron before her relax a bit when the door shut? He still looked stiff enough to break with a slight amount of pressure, but somehow he seemed different. The difference didn't put her at ease, but it had remarkably blunted her anger.

"You wanted to speak to me, milord?" she prompted, hoping he would state his piece and go.

Alaex leisurely looked around the room. Even in the casual perusal, his eyes marked the shadows and recesses—places where one might lurk—and the heavy tapestries that hung upon the walls that might conceal a hidden passageway. Finally his gaze came back to rest on the small woman in front of him.

She seemed almost childlike to him, so tiny was she in

stature—or maybe it was only that he was so large. Her head reached only midway to his chest, and that thought made him frown. What few women there had been in his life had been made of much heartier stuff. He had seen sterner-looking flowers than this woman.

Alaex was so deep in his thoughts that he didn't notice—a rarity for him—the effect his frown and prolonged silence were having on Iliani. It was only when she had backed nearly to the door that he realized what was happening.

Quick anger at himself for his distraction caused his voice to be sharp. "Do not."

Iliani swallowed. Usually she was not so timid, but this man terrified her. He was huge—larger than either Edouard or Cam, and they were the biggest men she knew. They were both nearly six feet. He seemed to be at least a head or two taller than that. Again she took note of his size. Surely it was just the battle gear he wore that gave him such width. As if those things weren't intimidating enough, he gave off a coldness she had never felt before—at least in anything living. Iliani could not stop the outrageous thought that should she touch him—something she would never do—his hands would feel like shards of ice. She was not superstitious but there was something about him that told her that his entrance in her life would be about as calming as a winter storm—and about as warm. It didn't help that he still wore his battle garb, even his helm, which while giving protection added to the aura of ferociousness. However, she didn't need to see his face to know that this was not a man to alienate. Her first glimpse of him when she stood on the gallery had brought a feeling of unreasonable terror, and warning bells had begun to peal in her head with increasing fervor. Now the sound was a deafening roar. Suddenly her lips went dry, and as her tongue darted out to lick them, Iliani realized that he had not answered her question. She needed to know why he was here. It was the only way to beat back her unexplained, growing hysteria. Somehow by his mere presence Iliani felt threatened, as if his appearance in her life was something not just to be wary of, but to be terrified of and avoided at all cost.

Doing her best to shy away from those disturbing thoughts, she repeated, "You wished to speak to me?"

His answer was not what she expected. "You do not remember me." Again his question had the ring of statement to it.

"Should I, milord?"

Iliani read his surprise. "We have met. I knew your father."

Not knowing what to say to that, Iliani waited. She barely remembered her father, but the faint memories she did have did not match with his knowing such a person. Edouard had told her that her father had been a scholar, a gentle man of peace, and she herself vaguely remembered a faceless man bent over parchment, whose tunic and fingers seemed to be always stained with dark ink. Her father had loved learning and books, not war and weapons. Had he not named her after that ancient Greek city of Troy, at one time called Ilion? Could a man such as that have dealings with one such as this, as Alaex's statement seemed to imply? She did not think it possible. Her father's face might be clouded in the mists of memory, but she did not need a face to remember the man.

Without knowing it, Iliani shook her head. Nay, there could not have been room in her father's life for a man like Alaex.

"You do not believe that."

He seemed to accept her disbelief too easily, and that made Iliani feel slightly unbalanced. She resolved more than ever to tread with care. She had already assessed that he would not bear contradiction well, and since she still did not know what he wanted, giving offense was not the course to take.

"Nay, milord," she began, only to halt when his eyes narrowed in a clear warning that said, "Do not lie to me." She tried again. " 'Tis only hard to reconcile with what I recall of my father."

Alaex's lips twisted into a smile. It was not smooth or fluid, and made Iliani think the muscles in his face were unused to such a movement.

"Aeric was an extraordinary man. 'Twas an honor, the greatest of my life, to know him. 'Tis because of him I am here."

Iliani did not like the feelings those cryptic words caused. Without warning, before he said anything else, she was overcome with a fearful urge to see his face.

"Milord, will you take off your helm?" Her voice roughened with anxiety that she hoped wasn't apparent to him, unaware that it reflected brightly in her violet eyes.

The slight twist left Alaex's lips and he wondered briefly how much of her growing fear was due to her remembering him or what she had been told of him. Years of discipline made him swallow a grimace caused by the realization that he could not say which version would be more favorable.

"Is it possible that you are beginning to remember?" he asked in a slow, mocking voice, unreasonably angered by the thought that she might believe the stories circulating about him. Alaex didn't wait for her to answer. Reaching up, he removed his helm to reveal dark blond hair and even darker brows over piercing ice blue eyes. His nose was high and sharp—whether by birth or from many years in the helm, Iliani could not tell. His lips would have been fuller and more shapely had he not held his mouth so tightly, and the square of his chin resembled steel. When he turned aside from her intense scrutiny, Iliani thought he might have been embarrassed, and she was just disregarding that thought as nonsense when she saw the scar and her breath caught sharply.

Iliani knew then who he was. It now seemed that on some instinctive level she had known even before seeing that legendary smooth-curved scar that ran from his right brow and disappeared into the smartly clipped beard he wore. There was only one man known to have such an identifying mark. It was said that after he received it he still had slain the man who gave it, and countless others. She had also heard that during that same battle it was the image of his fierce, blood-soaked face while he dealt destruction to the enemy that had rallied his men and caused them to take the day against overwhelming odds.

Here was the legend come to life. Aye, she knew of him. His fame was renowned, so much so that it bordered on myth. Some men revered him; others feared him. However, regardless of their reaction, there was not one who had not heard of him. It was said that he nearly single-handedly helped Alfred beat back the Danish advance. This was not just Alaex, as Edouard had called him, but *Alaex the Destroyer*.

She no longer cared whether her fear was visible to him. Her voice was extremely thin. "Your concern with me, milord?" she asked, not bothering to confirm his taunt that she remembered him. It was obvious. Any fool could tell from the amount of shaking she was doing that she knew precisely who he was.

"Your concern, milord?" she asked again, when he only stared. Her voice was breathless and rising. Iliani took a deep breath and tried for a calmer tone. "As you know, 'tis the day of my wedding and I have not only a bridegroom, but several guests waiting below."

Some unfathomable urge had pushed her to say that, as if it could be a pitiful shield against the weapon of this man's sheer presence. The moment the words were out, Iliani knew she had made her first real mistake.

That got a response from him. Alaex shook his head slowly. "I think not."

"Why is that, milord?"

For a second Iliani thought she saw fire in his eyes, but whatever she saw was quickly enveloped by the coldness there. Her nerves were stretched to the screaming point when he finally replied.

"Because even one of Edouard's *power*"—although he did not sneer the word his sarcasm was evident—"cannot arrange a wedding for one already wed."

Iliani frowned, momentarily forgetting her fear. "I do not understand."

"Do you not? Consider it but a moment and you will."

"Me? *I* am married?" she squeaked incredulously when his meaning became clear. "To whom?"

Alaex's blue eyes were totally devoid of emotion. "To me."

Then what he had feared would happen, did. Iliani crumpled in a dainty mass at his feet.

Chapter

➤ 3 ◆

Berating himself sharply, Alaex leaned down to pick up the small form in front of him. He had seen it coming. He had known she was going to faint. Her eyes had grown huge and her skin had gone pale. Still he had done nothing.

Idiot! He had thought an unemotional declaration best, but in truth he had not known how to do it otherwise. Tender emotions were not only foreign to him, he doubted they existed in him at all. Contrary to what others thought, he did not hate; he just did not know how to love. Wanting things to be different would not make it so. How could one show what one had never seen? Should love come and land on his shoulder, he feared he would not know it for what it was. With harshness he knew no difficulty. He recognized it in all its forms and it knew him equally well. It was only the gentler emotions that seemed to evade him.

Alaex had sensed Edouard's expectation when Iliani had revealed herself, and he knew his reaction to her beauty, or his *lack* of reaction, would probably add kindling to the fire of his reputation, of being coldly unaffected by things that overwhelmed other men. He saw her comeliness—Lord, how could he not? He was not sightless. But her beauty was not all he had seen when he looked upon her. He had seen an intelligence, kindness, and sensitivity that had intrigued him more than her loveliness. It was not difficult after admitting a lack of such qualities in oneself to be fascinated when faced with them so openly in another.

Too many years of war had made him forget that life could offer gentler things such as what he had seen in Iliani's eyes. Those things beckoned him more than physical beauty ever could. No one would believe it, but he was not unlike other men in his craving for the softer things. He was merely uncertain whether he could attain his desires.

As Alaex laid Iliani gently on the bed, he admitted that his doubt as to whether he knew how to find peace with her or make her happy with him had been a large part of the reason he had procrastinated so long in returning. He had been avoiding his fear, and after one look at her face he knew his fear had not been unfounded. Just one look, and feelings he was uncomfortable with and doubts he had thought long since squashed surfaced, and he didn't like it.

Alaex didn't know if his dislike was a shield to help him stave off his doubts or a bulwark to hold back the intense surge of feeling brought on merely by looking at Iliani. All he knew for certain was that until now, no one had made him feel these things.

Abruptly Alaex stood, pulling his arms away from her as if her slender body had become a flame. He focused not on his reaction to her, but on her needing his help. Calling for someone was unthinkable, but he was at a loss as to what he should do next. Aye, there were a few times in his memory when a few spleenless men had fainted before a battle, but he could hardly do to Iliani what he had done to them. First, there was no nearby cold lake to dunk her in, and second, there was no large bucket present to dash water in her face. In either event, he didn't think Iliani would care much for his ministration.

It was then he spotted the washbasin and ewer. With fluid, silent steps he went to them, poured the last of the water into the basin from the ewer, and dampened the cloth beside them. As he eased down beside Iliani on the bed, he naturally moved the massive sword to the side and he leaned over and began to wipe her face as gently as he knew how.

Alaex almost smiled when a few short seconds later she began to moan, moving her head from side to side. He thought he heard her mumble, "Nay, it cannot be," and if those were the words she uttered, he knew exactly what it was she thought could not be—that she belonged to him.

His heart beat hard, thick strokes at the thought that she did indeed belong to him and at this form of rejection so sincere that it came from the depths of a mind not fully alert. He grimaced. He knew he was no maiden's dream. Knowing at least partially what Iliani found so lacking, Alaex's hand absently touched the scar on the side of his face, tracing its curve. It was ironic, but when he had received the wound his only thought was that it could have been worse. He had been grateful to be alive. Since then he had had several occasions to rethink that view. The scar seemed to have become all he was. It was assuredly what everyone saw, as if it was a manifestation of what he was. He was flawed. His holding the scar as of little account only marked more severely his lack of commonality. Everyone else was concerned with his appearance, worried by a mark left from the mere tearing of flesh; he was concerned for his soul and the marks left there from a tearing of spirit. It was there that scarring was the most repugnant. Those scars just were not visible to others, but they went deeper, leaving him not just uncomfortable with the emotions others seemed to take for granted, but with the deep-set and implacable conviction that like physical scar tissue, what lay beneath was dead. There were no feelings.

Looking down at Iliani, whose head moved more vigorously as she came closer and closer to consciousness, he had never regretted that truth more. Perhaps he *had* done her a disservice by coming back. Maybe despite her father's wishes, he should not have. Maybe it would have been better for all had that blade that nearly cost him his eye cost him his life instead. Perhaps that was what Aeric had hoped.

No sooner had the thought formed than Alaex was swamped with shame. Aeric's blue eyes appeared before him chastising him and bringing him from the unprecedented lapse into self-pity.

Never had Alaex known such kindness, openness, and acceptance. Aeric had truly been a man above men. He saw not one's birth or appearance, but one's worth. He strove for good in men and tried hard to teach Alaex to bypass the evil.

The faint twist of his lips that Iliani would have called his almost-smile appeared. Even Aeric had had to admit defeat in his efforts to teach Alaex to think of most, if not all, men as good. Alaex had seen too much of the real world by the time he met Aeric. At fourteen he had seen more than most men three times his age. He didn't have to be told the world was an ugly place; he knew it firsthand. It was a lesson he learned at the hands of parents who deserted him either before he was old enough to know who they were, or later when he was still too young to know that they had no right. The lesson was reinforced through the years by those who thought themselves either his equal or his better.

Again the almost-smile appeared. If people feared him now, they would have run screaming had they encountered the wild young man Aeric had known. But Aeric had been different. He had seen beneath the savageness and the grime. To this day, Alaex didn't like to think of what Aeric saw. His pride, the only common possession of those rich and poor, would not allow it. However, his pride did not creak under the heartfelt gratitude he had for Aeric, even years after the man's death.

Aeric had made him learn—despite Alaex's vehement wishes to the contrary. When Alaex had taunted him by saying that even *nobles* did not read, Aeric had smoothly returned, "Because one man is wrong, should another be also? If they ran their destriers from a mountain peak to crash to the rocks below, would you also? Learning is not about coming to know what is popular; it is coming to know what is right." That had made sense to Alaex. Besides, Aeric had promised to feed him in exchange for his willingness to be taught.

Now Alaex could see the absurdity in that, but when one had been fourteen and regular food had been scarce . . . Well, at the time he'd thought it a fair exchange. The irony was that the more he learned, the more bitter he became. One day in a rage he had screamed at Aeric that he wanted to learn no more. These things did not belong to him. They were not for him. What good was it to know the names of the stars if one could never reach them? Aeric had encouraged patience, and by this time Alaex had grown as used to relying on Aeric as he ever could on anyone.

He shook his head at the memories that were bittersweet and looked back on Iliani's face. Alaex realized that her head was no longer thrashing to and fro.

"Open your eyes, lady. I know you have recovered."

Without opening her eyes, Iliani moaned. "I was hoping you and this entire situation would be gone or that it was some sort of nightmare." She opened her eyes. "I can see it was not." Normally Iliani would never have spoken so rudely to another, but this situation had shaken her. "Why?"

Alaex knew she was asking why her father would do such a thing, and for the second time he overlooked the deep insult in her words. Truly her reaction was not surprising. Had he not asked Aeric the same thing?

They had been arguing—a fairly common occurrence between them despite Alaex's grudging and growing respect for him. This particular argument had taken place after Alaex had been under Aeric's tutelage for five years, and although after all that time they still argued intensely, the burning rage within Alaex had been tamped back. He had always feared its resurgence, but Aeric had made him see that his mind was stronger. His rage had been controlled; it no longer controlled him. So when he had asked the question Iliani had just posed, there was intensity and curiosity in his tone, but strangely no heat.

Aeric had told him then that although he loved his daughter as nothing else in the world, Alaex had become the son of his heart. Iliani's mother had died bearing her. With her death so too had his heart died. Yet Aeric was not bitter. He had informed Alaex that the richness of the years with her were filled with beautiful memories to last him the years without her. Besides, he had his precious Iliani and God had brought Alaex to him. Did he need more? But that, he had said, was not the reason he wished them to wed.

He knew his contemporaries saw him as foolish, more interested in books and bygone eras than the present and the legacy of the future. His absolute disinterest in war—more specifically, war against the Danes—only increased their belief of his strangeness.

Even now Alaex could see the sadness that had haunted Aeric's eyes as he had said it was not that he did not notice these things or care, it was only that too much time and blood had already been wasted in pursuing them. Still, that did not blind him to the present and the danger it presented, a danger from which he wanted very much to protect his daughter. Alaex was that protection. The fact that he had survived his circumstances so well and had become only stronger had made Aeric know Alaex was the man for his daughter. He had said that although he would wish it otherwise, the world was not for men such as he; but he hoped that with what Alaex was and what he had learned, he would find his way better. Thus, so would Iliani.

Aeric had not demanded; he had asked. As humbled then as he still was now by what Aeric had seen in men and had wanted from him, Alaex had promised. And although he had known that Aeric trusted his oath, Aeric himself had insisted that the deed be done immediately.

When Alaex had asked Aeric to wait, Aeric had replied that time was an enemy to all and he did not feel himself to be the mighty exception. He wanted to see this, his most treasured wish, take place before he met his end.

Although all others saw him as eccentric, Aeric had not lacked a formidable power of his own. Special permission had been obtained and he, Alaex of no name, had become husband to a lively five-year-old girl.

Pulling himself again from the past, Alaex wondered, as he had many times since, if Aeric had known he was going to die a short five months after the ceremony. The burning pain Alaex still felt at Aeric's passing was lessened only by the fact that he had done the one thing Aeric had ever asked of him.

Focusing on the dark violet eyes—eyes so like her father's—that studied him intently, Alaex finally answered, "Because he wished it so."

Iliani, who had begun to think there would be no answer coming for her question, sat up and backed away from him. Alaex saw the protest in her eyes before she spoke in a clipped, nearly emotionless voice.

"I do not believe you. Where is your proof? Where is the proof that my father did this thing to me?"

Alaex pulled a parchment from his mail. He was about to hand it to her when he hesitated, asking, "Can you read?"

Iliani's nod was stiff. "Edouard—although he did not approve—honored my father's wish in this."

Alaex put the document in her hand. As Iliani read it, she was thankful to be on the bed, as her bones seemed to melt in reaction. She had seen other things her father had written, and this looked very much like his writing. Behind the letter in her father's hand was the special writ

3 6

that acknowledged, sanctioned, and validated her marriage to Alaex at the tender age of five.

Silently she gave the papers back to him, making no denial of what she had just seen. The documents looked indisputably authentic. Her voice sounded unnatural as she said, "I know who you are."

Alaex did not so much as blink at the swift conversation change. Whereas strain was evident in her voice, his in turn was smooth, deep, and melodious as he returned, "So do I."

"Do you mock me?" Iliani asked angrily.

"'Twas not my intent. What would be the purpose?"

Puzzled and startled by his controlled, pragmatic tone, Iliani studied his expression to find a hint of other answers there, and then gave up in dismay when it revealed nothing. Fleetingly it occurred to her that he might be adopting his stoic attitude in a bid to convince her of the truth of his words and thus stem her rejection. If that was so, he was failing miserably. His seemingly unshakable calm, which Iliani began to see was real and no ploy at all, did not ease her mind into full acceptance that she was his wife and had been since before her father died. Instead it increased her need for fervent denial despite his proffered proof.

Alaex offered her nothing more than those words written long ago, as if he lacked the knowledge or insight that for her even to *begin* the process of acceptance, she needed so much more. It was that lack, volubly expressed by the very calm that emanated from him in maddening waves, which pushed Iliani toward the calculated hysteria she felt building within.

All of the images she had of him, built and maintained by years of rumor, clamored in her head. Her violet eyes clashed momentarily with the unbending will in his blue ones, and Iliani felt the edge of hysteria move closer.

"You are the one they call the Destroyer," Iliani said, hoping her voice was as emotionless as his expression.

There was no reply, and her calm slipped further.

" 'Tis said you wreak destruction and desolation on whomever you encounter. Is it now my turn?" Her words were a defiant challenge as Iliani tried to hold on to her fragile control. They were also uttered in the hope that he would say anything to deny the ugly rumors.

Alaex, for his part, again felt an unfamiliar clenching in his chest that she believed the stupidity that passed as myth, but he didn't know he needed to defend it. So again he said nothing.

Iliani's discomfort grew. "You do not deny these things."

"There are certain things not worth denying," he answered cryptically.

"Are you proud, then, of what you do?" Iliani asked incredulously, not inclined at the moment to decipher coded messages as even more of her hard-won control eroded. She was trying to goad him into revealing something more—such as why he was there. If those documents were to be believed, she had been his wife all this time. Why was he there now? But then her heart froze as she answered her own question.

She had been about to marry another man.

Iliani shuddered at the awful consequences had he not appeared, even while she briefly wondered if he would go away if she promised him she would not marry Cam or anyone else. A quick glance at the depth of his ice blue eyes told her he would not.

She was cornered. Iliani felt the brittle bonds holding her hysteria in check crack. "Why won't you answer me?"

Although she knew he could see her mounting agitation, Iliani no longer cared. Putting forth a brave front was not important anymore. Saving herself by whatever means available was. Besides, in the few moments she had known Alaex, she knew he would not react to her lack of control the way other men would. Her observation was proven when he lifted his shoulders in a shrug both fluid and unperturbed.

"Of what use are words that will not be believed? I have no *written* proof of what I will say."

The bite beneath his words made her pause. So, he was not totally impervious to what was happening, Iliani thought. She knew then that he resented her disbelief, but she did not care. Did he truly think she would meekly accept this marriage? Nay, she did not care that she had pricked him. Conversely, that small chink in his emotional armor did what her determination had not. It pushed back the hysteria that had menaced her from the time Alaex had entered her room and it brought her a moment of satisfaction.

"Of what use are words or feelings, milord? Does neither concern you? 'Tis my life we toy with."

" 'Tis mine as well."

With just those few words, he managed to dissipate her calm and her brief satisfaction. For the first time in her life, Iliani felt the urge to strike someone as Alaex resumed his silent stare without elaboration of his few terse words. Just when she felt she would scream with frustration, he spoke, and again his words were not what she expected.

"Why does my profession occupy so much of your thoughts?"

Iliani frowned at this switch in conversation. "Profession?" she echoed blankly, almost having forgotten her previous statement as to his identity. "Is that what you call what you do?"

Again there was no answer, and it occurred to Iliani that Alaex was not going to respond. It was becoming apparent to her that he was thrifty with his words and he did not answer what he deemed obvious. Taking a deep, soothing breath, she rephrased her question.

"How can you call it a profession? You take from those weaker—"

"I do not."

Grinding her teeth, Iliani went on as if he had not interrupted. "You extract a dear cost from those who at

times cannot afford it—and all for gain, and at no cost to yourself."

Alaex's eyes hardened. "The cost is dear to me: it is my life."

"It means the lives of those involved also."

"That risk is theirs to take."

"It is not theirs!" Iliani screeched, her control all but gone, and no longer thinking of his fighting the Danes for price, but of her father and his promising her to him.

She saw fleeting confusion in his eyes. Striving again for calm, Iliani continued in a softer tone, adding lamely, "Were it not for men such as you, many lives would be spared because others would give up causes that are lost."

Alaex's confusion did not dissipate. "A thing of value to a man is not a lost cause. He wants it, at times above all else."

"You cannot always have what you want," Iliani replied with frustrated bitterness. "Men should learn to accept that."

Finally Alaex understood. It was not what he did. His profession, as repugnant as war was becoming to him, was not the issue. She might not approve of what he did, but that was not the source of her rejection. Her objection was being married to him.

With eyes of understanding, he now looked deeply into hers. He saw her fear of him, but even more, the proof of his thoughts—her defiance of their marriage. Without intent, Alaex's eyes hardened more and what little softness there was in his face disappeared.

Before Iliani's disbelieving eyes, his face became a mask, as cold and lifeless as hewn stone. She didn't tremble at his words, which were uttered quietly. She trembled because of the fierceness with which he said them.

"Nay. I never have. I never will."

His soft tone terrified her. With those few cold words, she was finally, inescapably forced to acceptance, an acceptance so terrifying that it coldly banked every ounce of encroaching hysteria. She was his wife and there was no changing that. What were the words—"'Til death do us part"?

Swallowing heavily and casting another quick glance back to Alaex's set features, Iliani feared that the man who claimed her as his wife would attempt to defy even death to gain what he deemed his.

Chapter

→4←

"What do we do now, milord?"

"My name is Alaex." He didn't add that Iliani should use it, but she understood what he meant. She nodded.

"What do we do, Alaex?"

Iliani saw he was pleased. She, however, found no pleasure in this or anything else said or done since this man had blown into her life. His next words were no exception.

"We leave."

Iliani shook her head, thinking she could not have heard aright. "Pardon?"

Alaex sighed. He knew she had heard him; there was no possibility she didn't. It would be better for them both if his wife understood that he detested repeating himself, especially when it was obvious that it was unnecessary.

"I ken it has been many years since last we saw each other. Your memories of me—if you have any at all— are probably vague. We do not know each other; therefore, we need to learn. A first lesson for you is that I dislike repeating myself."

Iliani stared at him unblinking, again unable to believe what she heard. She opened her mouth, ready to ask him to repeat himself, then closed it just as abruptly, knowing her ears had not played her falsely. In the wake of that knowledge came anger. It was so sudden and strong it left her fear of him shriveled and dried beneath it. So he disliked repeating himself? Wasn't that just too blasted bad! He had come for her. She had not sought him. Now he dared lecture like a put-upon tutor?

While Iliani began to struggle beneath the weight of her anger and the situation, Alaex was silently congratulating himself for his forbearance and tact until he noticed the change in Iliani. He knew before her eyes began to flash that her words would not be to his liking.

"Am I now supposed to apologize?"

Alaex's jaw tightened, but Iliani went on boldly. "Since we are exchanging lessons, *Alaex,* let me say that *I* dislike this entire situation. What think you of that?"

Iliani was so furious she didn't notice the loosening of his jaw or the look of surprised admiration that came to his eyes. She was too enraged to see the muted sparkle in his pale blue eyes. She didn't, however, miss the twitch his lips made.

"Don't you dare laugh at me!"

Alaex's surprise grew, for he was taken aback by his instinctive reaction. The urge to laugh was a rare feeling indeed. He could only credit it to the fact that he was finding the woman who was his wife to be a surprise—not an unpleasant one. She had courage and fire. He could even understand her ire, a quality that when controlled he found admirable. Alaex had hated it when he saw fear in her eyes. He might not know what he wanted from her and their marriage, but he knew he didn't want that. And from the furious look Iliani was giving him, he didn't think he was going to get it. She looked ready to launch herself at him.

That amused feeling was back again, only this time it was stronger. Mentally shaking his head, not understanding himself or his reactions, he took refuge in dryness.

"You seem to have gotten over your fear of me quickly enough."

Iliani paused, considered his words, and found them true. Realizing that Alaex awaited some sort of response, she sighed and said lamely, " 'Twould seem so."

"Good."

"Nay, Alaex. There is naught good about any of this. Our problem is still there, only the solution is lacking. You may think it otherwise, but leaving is not a solution."

Alaex looked hard at her. "I did not claim it to be. You asked not for a solution but for an action. We *are* leaving."

Iliani slid off the bed. She knew she couldn't get away from him, but she needed to distance herself from the disapproval she knew would come from the next words.

"Nay, Alaex," she repeated, her tone soft but implacable. "I cannot go with you."

The only evidence of his disapproval was in the narrowing of his eyes. "Cannot or will not?" Alaex shook his head. "It does not matter. I did not give you a choice."

Iliani's anger returned. " 'Twas not yours to give."

In that instant Alaex rethought his previous opinion of admiration for her fire. "I am your husband."

"Only on parchment! Can you not see that is not enough? 'Tis not binding! You wed a five-year-old girl! Thirteen years have passed. When I last saw you I was but ten and that encounter lasted scarce an hour. I can understand why you would not have told me then. I was a child. But why did you wait so long? Nearly nine years have passed, and not one word. Why now?"

Alaex looked away from her for a moment. He had an answer for her question; he just did not want to give it. He did not want to think of it. The reasons changed nothing.

"It matters little, nay, not at all, the reasons. What was

has not been changed by the time passing. You are my wife."

"But do you want me to be?" Iliani countered softly, reading his angry confusion and gaining slim hope.

Alaex rose abruptly from the bed. "You try my patience—something I never possessed in abundance—with your ceaseless questions."

Hope died. "Ah," Iliani snapped. "Another lesson learned."

Nay, he definitely did not like her fire. Perhaps a little fear was not a bad thing. A fearful woman would have left with him without protest. This one was fighting him sword and dagger and Alaex found it more tedious than all the battles he had experienced put together. He took a deep breath.

"You are my wife. We leave here in less than an hour, be you prepared for it or not."

To his amazement she smiled. It was beautiful, transforming her face and making him wish he knew how to return it—until he heard her contradict him a third time.

"Nay, Alaex. I am not your wife. I am your bride if anything, and even that fact is open to speech. Ours is no marriage. Most definitely 'twas never consummated. It can be undone as easily as 'twas done, probably easier."

Father in heaven, but the urge to strike her was great. Or even better, he wanted to give her shield and sword and challenge her. At least then he would see the blows ere they struck him with such painful ferociousness. Alaex could not believe he had talked, nay, argued—something else he had never done—this long with her.

So their marriage was invalid because it lacked consummation? he thought grimly. That was easily corrected.

Any satisfaction Iliani felt at her continued defiance disappeared as she watched his eyes darken. Some inner instinct which had been regrettably silent before told her she had crossed a dangerous border. With nauseating clarity Iliani realized that her fear of him was not totally gone. It was fear tightening her jaw and drying her tongue as she watched him casually unhook his sword belt. The bow he wore at his back was released and the short dagger in his belt was placed aside. When he reached down to loosen his cross garters, Iliani knew her anxiety was not misplaced as she read his intentions.

She would have dashed to the door then, but mute fear and the loud warning in his eyes held her still. He had removed his mail and undertunic when she realized that he was only one man, and one in unfriendly territory. What could he do? Those below were her allies, not his.

Breaking free of his hypnotic gaze, Iliani ran for the door only to be stopped not by a cold hand, but by a colder voice that asked, "Do you really want all here to die for your foolishness?"

An inner voice, one Iliani wasn't sure she could trust, said to keep going. It said his words were an empty threat. After all, he had removed his battle gear. Edouard and the others could subdue him before he had the chance to don it again.

Iliani took another step.

"Or do you think I will die and so end your dilemma?"

Iliani would not have thought it possible, but his voice had gotten colder. It was not just the temperature of it; it was the contempt in it. She ignored that. It didn't matter what he thought of her. However, his words evoked an image harder to disregard. Did she want him dead? Nay, she was not that callous, regardless of the circumstance. Despite her attempts to stave off the feeling, she was becoming ashamed that she had even thought to bring Edouard, Cam, and the others into this. They would have come to her aid, and Alaex was right: someone would have died.

Without turning she said, "I wish for *no one's* death. Neither do I wish to be raped."

He was silent awhile. "What you wish for is a lost cause. Why not learn to accept that?"

Inadvertently Alaex repeated her own words and they

stung. Iliani swung around ready to hurl herself at him for his mockery. She froze.

Everything he had removed he had replaced. She had not heard him move. Iliani blinked several times. Either her eyes or her mind were playing tricks on her, she thought, still refusing to believe what she saw. But she knew that neither was. She *had* seen him remove his gear. He was just much more adept at putting it on. That alone told her something of him.

Suddenly Iliani felt despondent and out of her depth. She looked away from his piercing stare, and her voice was soft and desolate. "I beg of you, please do not do this."

Alaex watched her dejected expression and felt something clench in his chest. Again he surprised himself by being gentle, when a moment ago gentleness was the furthest thing from his thoughts. "Do not do what?"

"Take me here," Iliani whispered.

Alaex frowned, not bothering to point out that he could little do that since he had replaced his battle gear. Instead he concentrated on the meaning behind her words.

"Does the place truly matter?"

Iliani's eyes slammed back to his. She did not flinch away from his hard gaze. "If it must be done, then, aye. The place matters. This place has been my home. Here I have always felt safe and protected, loved. It would be unbearable to be violated here."

Now Alaex looked away. His voice was drawn when he repeated, "Violated? You would see my . . . our . . . the consummation of marriage vows as a violation?"

Iliani hardened her heart. It was not pain she heard in his voice. "You speak of vows? What vows? 'Tis insanity to expect me to honor vows I cannot even recall making."

When Alaex's eyes returned to hers, the expression in them was sharp and flat. "Very well, then. You do not recall your vows. Does the memory of your father fail you as well?"

"What has he—?"

"Everything!"

Iliani was taken aback by the volume of his voice. She had the feeling that he never yelled or raised his voice.

"'Twas your father's wish, not mine, that we wed. I wanted it then no more than you do now. I asked that we wait. 'Twas he who pressed me. I could not refuse. So, madam," he ground out, angry at himself for allowing her to make him angry yet again, "if you have grievance over this, I suggest you wait until next you meet him if you think such a thing possible, and ask your questions of him."

"Why could you not refuse?"

To Iliani's amazement, Alaex visibly started at her question. Then his expression closed and his eyes hardened in a way that was terrible to see.

"You may see it otherwise because of the consequence to you, but the reasons I could not refuse were a private matter between your father and me and are none of your concern."

Neither his words nor his expression left her room to doubt that the subject was firmly closed. From the vehemence of his tone, Iliani gained the impression that even Alaex himself did not entertain that thought often, and when he did it was not pleasant.

So where did that leave her? Married to a man she did not want. A man who by his own mouth admitted he did not want her. The only person who could provide some sense of order was her father, and he was dead.

Iliani took a deep breath. "Your pardon if I trespassed, but can you at least tell me why my father did this? I would not have thought this to be his wish."

"Why?" Alaex asked coldly. He was tired of her endless contempt. *Oh, Aeric, what have you done?*

Without thinking, Iliani said, "Because Edouard said . . ." The instant surge of fire blazing hotly in his eyes stopped her.

"Nay, do not stop. Tell me what Edouard said." The ice in his voice was at variance with the fire in his eyes.

48

Iliani again felt a resurgence of fear—not just of Alaex, but of the situation, for it finally occurred to her that someone had lied. It could not have been her father's wish that she marry both Cam and Alaex. That had been her father's handwriting on the documents Alaex showed her—at least she thought it was. That would mean Alaex spoke truly. But that was impossible. Edouard would not have lied. Alaex might, but never Edouard. Perhaps Edouard had misunderstood. One thing was evident and that was that he had not known of her marriage to Alaex. He would never have tried to wed her to Cam had he known.

These thoughts warred in Iliani's mind, and the one thing she needed—time to think—was the one luxury she did not have. Slowly she said, "My father must have discussed a similar thing with Edouard."

"Is that what Edouard says?"

Iliani did not miss his contempt. "Edouard was my father's friend! He raised me! 'Twould only be natural that I be considered as a wife for his son. Edouard did not need to say it. I am certain that such a conversation took place, but if 'tis reassurance you seek, we can discuss it with him," she said, hoping for a confrontation, not to find an answer to his question but hers.

"If I do, then what?"

Iliani looked at him blankly.

"What do you then, madam?" Alaex asked. "Do you come with me quietly?"

It felt as if a trap was closing around her. "Naught will have changed," Iliani said, trying to stall. "Our marriage can still be dis—"

The almost-smile was there again. "I think not."

"Why?"

"Have you no ken as to how long we have been closed in together?" he asked, pointing out something that had not occurred to her. "Do you truly think that given my reputation, any of the several witnesses below believe you still a maid?"

Alaex gave a bitter humorless laugh and Iliani envied

him that much. Laughter of any sort was beyond her as she accepted the truth of his statement and its consequences. No one would believe anything else. Any man who would have thought to have her would now see her as used, soiled.

The trap closed around her and rage the likes of which she had never felt poured through her, burning away restraint. Before Iliani was aware she did it, she lunged at Alaex, striking him repeatedly across the chest.

For a moment Alaex was too stunned to do anything. Never—battles aside—in his memory could he recall being personally attacked. And by a woman. If the situation were not so dire, he would have laughed in true amusement. Instead he reached out and caught Iliani's fists, which were turning bright red from banging against his mail. He cursed himself for not stopping her sooner. The only person being hurt by her outburst was her.

"Enough!" he said firmly, giving her a shake to pierce through her rage.

"Nay! Nay!" Iliani screamed. " 'Tis not enough! 'Twill never be enough. How can you do this? How can you so calmly destroy my life? I asked if 'twas my turn. I see now it is. How can you?" She raised tear-bright eyes to his. "How can you?" she repeated, but this time her voice was weak with defeat. "Have you no feelings? Do you not care?"

Alaex looked deeply into the violet eyes swimming with tears and pain, and again he questioned Aeric's judgment. This could not have been what he intended.

"I gave my word." He knew as he said the words that they were not enough.

Iliani's eyes narrowed. That was it? He gave his word? "I did not give mine."

His pale gaze became implacable. "We cover the same road and I tire of it. Nay, you did not give your word, but your father gave it for you. Were he alive he could tell you so himself. He is not. Were he alive he would choose a man for you himself. He has already done so. You would respect it then. You must respect it now. Come," he said, releasing one of her fists and heading for the door.

Resistance was futile. He walked along as if he were not pulling another person behind him. They were in the gallery above the hall when Iliani stopped struggling and became aware of the deafening quiet below. It seemed that everyone listened to hear what passed above stairs. They would all stare at her with either pity or knowledge and Iliani didn't know which she would find more abhorrent.

"Alaex, please," she whispered desperately. "I will respect my father's wishes. Only do not do this. Please."

Alaex stopped and turned to her. He looked into her eyes a long time. Finally he said, "Your word?"

"Alaex—"

"Your word?"

"'Tis not as simple—"

"Your word."

Iliani's eyes dropped from his. "I give you my word," she whispered in a lifeless voice.

Immediately Alaex dropped her hand and turned to go down the gallery, and in that moment Iliani truly hated him. Yet hate or no, she found she was really Aeric's daughter. She had given her word. She would keep it.

Chapter

The next hour was a blurred nightmare.

Iliani watched Edouard come rushing forward to meet Alaex, and then after a few terse words—and she knew without the benefit of hearing what those words were—she watched Edouard whiten. He did not reach for the papers Alaex held out to him but stared at them as if they were vipers. He shook his head in denial of the need to read the documents, and Alaex returned them to his mail.

Although white-faced, Edouard kept his composure, and Iliani admired him for it. However, when he called Cam to his side and spoke quietly to him, Cam did not react nearly as well.

There was no good face to put on it. Everyone knew that something was wrong, just as they also knew that Alaex had spent the last half hour in Iliani's bedroom. Nevertheless, Cam's reaction destroyed any doubt lingering in their minds.

While Alaex stood stoically, Cam ranted and raved and finally challenged him. Iliani turned away when Edouard began to plead with Alaex to ignore it, saying his son was overwrought and a challenge would solve nothing. Iliani was Alaex's wife and everyone accepted and respected that.

Cam, who was being restrained by Namin and three other men, ranted, "Nay! I do not! Why do you simper before him, Father? He is but one."

Edouard roared, "You will be silent! There are others here for whom to have a concern. You show your ignorance, Cam. Have you not looked beyond the doors to see his army there? He is no fool! He came prepared. And we cannot, no matter how we wish it otherwise, fight a man for his own wife!"

Iliani turned back at Edouard's words. An army? Alaex had brought an army? A chill flitted down her spine as she recalled him asking her if she wanted all here to die. It wasn't a threat. It was fact. He hadn't been trying to influence her by means of his ferocious reputation. Nay, he had been warning her.

She looked from Edouard to Alaex, who still said nothing. It was Cam who pulled her attention with his words.

"Let me go," he snapped. "I will do naught." When the men reluctantly freed him he said to Alaex, "She may be your wife now, but she can just as easily become your widow. 'Tis not over. I vow it." He stormed out, and the pregnant silence he left behind was unbroken until Edouard said, "Forgive him, Alaex. 'Twas but disappointment that made him speak thus. Surely you understand. His disappointment is keen, as is ours. He will do naught."

Alaex, who had replaced his helm and had remained silent throughout the entire horrifying scene, now looked down on Edouard. Iliani did not need to be near him to see his anger. Even across the distance she felt it.

"See that he does not, Edouard. 'Twould cause me no undue pain to end the life that you have paid me to protect these many years." His words caused a shocked ripple among the guests. "That protection," he continued, "ends today. Warn him that should he cross my path, I will not ask why he is there."

Iliani did not remain to hear any more. She went back to her room and began systematically to gather her clothes—nothing else. She did not want to bring souvenirs of this life. It would only make her new one that much more difficult.

Too soon she was done and standing below to say good-bye to Edouard and Eadwina who, although tearful, was thankfully silent.

"Well, Daughter," Edouard said softly, his eyes suspiciously moist, "I had planned to say good-bye today in any event, only not in this manner. I shall miss you. Should you ever need me, I am here." He kissed her gently on the forehead and then turned away.

Iliani felt the burn of tears in her own eyes and could not hold them back when Eadwina took her in her arms and said, "I do not know what to say. Well, aye, I do." Eadwina pulled back and smiled, her round face brightening. "Do not stand in draughts. Cover yourself in rain. Do not burn his food. Men don't like that, they—"

"Eadwina!" Edouard shouted, and Iliani knew the depth of his distress, never having heard him use a tone like that with his wife before.

Eadwina flinched and Iliani was speechless as she watched more tears roll down her plump face. Then Eadwina's expression changed slightly and she said to her husband, " 'Twas what *I* had planned to say. Iliani still needs to hear it, and perhaps if we are kind to him he'll allow us to visit, will you not?" she added hopefully, directing this last to Alaex.

Iliani cast an apprehensive glance at Alaex's set features and prayed that he would say nothing to hurt the kind woman. True, Eadwina could rant on, and usually she was fascinated by things of little or no value, but she meant well. There was not a mean thought in her head or heart.

Alaex just stared perplexedly at Eadwina as she asked again, her green eyes pleading, "Please say you will."

To Iliani's amazement and seemingly to his as well, Alaex replied, "She is no prisoner, madam."

"See there, Edouard," Eadwina squealed, giving her husband a glance that said she knew something he did not, before turning back to beam at Alaex. She looked so childishly happy that Iliani wanted to smile, but instead she watched in astonishment as Alaex bowed slightly to her.

Then he looked to her. "Ready?" he asked quietly, ignoring the blue-violet fire sparkling behind the tears. It was clear he expected a scathing retort, but Iliani only nodded jerkily.

They were outside when she asked, "Would you hold a moment? I need to find Cam. We should not part like this. It should not be this way between us."

Unreasonably Alaex became angered. The thought occurred to him that she hadn't cared how things were between them, but for that mewling coward she wanted to set things aright. He knew his reasoning was not sound, but the rage was there nonetheless. His jaw hardened and Iliani had her answer before he said it.

"Nay."

"Why? There is naught he can do," she said with bitter sarcasm. "You have won the day. All accept that I am your wife."

Alaex's eyes bored through her. "Have they? Has he? Have you?"

Iliani looked away, aware that her lack of response, which in itself was one, caused him to stiffen further.

"There is my answer," he said tautly. "I have given you yours."

Before Iliani knew it she was seated on a destrier, surrounded by an army of strangers, riding through the gathering dusk. While she could ignore the strangers around her, she could not elude the fact that the strangest one of all was the man seated behind her—her husband.

Chapter

→ 6 ←

Iliani had been with her husband two days. Two days of silence. Two days of riding. Two days of not knowing where they were going. Although she hadn't been to Fontwyn Hall in years, Iliani did not think it took two days to get there from Lourds Keep. Yet she was not speaking to Alaex, so how could she ask? The lout! He knew she was not talking to him, so he wasn't offering the information. He knew she wanted to know. He had come upon her when she had been subtly trying to question one of his men. When the man had stammered and turned away, Iliani had known that Alaex stood behind her. When she turned she found she was not mistaken. Her only error was in miscalculating how close he stood. The heat from his body pulsed over her.

Iliani had to look up to see his face, and despite his inscrutable expression she knew he waited for her to repeat her question. For a moment she had considered it, but then she thought she'd detected a flicker of amusement in his eyes. Her pride had ignited and with it the fuse to her stubbornness. She had walked away calmly, not giving in to the urge to stomp in frustration. But oh, how she had wanted to.

That had been yesterday, and even thinking of it now, Iliani wanted to gnash her teeth. The man was driving her insane. He was so infuriating and always so close. It seemed she felt his presence even when he was not there. Iliani was beginning to think he stayed near purposely, just to irritate her. She didn't know how he knew his nearness bothered her, but she sensed that he knew and that was why he continued to hover over her.

He was behaving like a child, she thought waspishly as she watched him speak to one of his men on the far side of the camp. When he felt her gaze and glanced up, Iliani raised her chin and looked swiftly away, ignoring the realization that *her* behavior would not win an award for maturity either. Stubbornly she held her assertion that their situation was Alaex's fault alone. He was the one being unreasonable, and Iliani refused to share any of the blame.

Blame or no, by day four, Iliani could take it no longer.

"Are you ever going to tell me where we are going?" she snapped as they rode along in front of his men.

Alaex coughed and his voice sounded a bit strangled when he said, "I merely waited for the question."

Iliani had a feeling he was laughing at her, but she didn't turn to confirm her suspicion. If she saw proof of it she knew she would explode with rage.

"If you knew I wanted to know, why did you not just tell me?" she asked tightly.

Again the cough. "I only enjoyed the silence."

Iliani tensed like a drawn bow. She was about to make a scathing retort when he said, "To Alfred."

That sidetracked her as she was sure it was supposed to. "Alfred?"

"Aye, the king."

"Why?"

"I need to speak with him on a matter of some importance."

Iliani waited for him to elaborate. It was only when they had traveled another mile that she realized that he was not going to do so.

"Alaex?"

"Aye?"

"I am not slow of wit."

Behind her, Iliani could almost feel him frown. This time she did turn to face him. Her instincts were correct; he was frowning. She took a second to marvel at how rapidly she was coming to know his reactions before her gaze connected solidly with his.

Finally Alaex said, "I do not recall insulting your intelligence."

"Oh?" Muted fire sparked in her eyes. "You tell me you must see the king and when I ask why, you say 'tis gravely important. You must think me stupid if you don't think I would know that much. Since I doubt Alfred claims you as kin, and I have not heard that there existed an extraordinary bond between you, I would have to assume that *any* business with the king is important. I doubt he would see you otherwise. Did you really think saying the matter was of some importance was an answer to my question?"

Iliani thought she controlled her anger quite well, but it now threatened to overflow as Alaex quietly stared at her.

"Well?"

"I concede your point."

"You concede my . . ." Iliani did not know which was greater, her frustration or her anger.

Alaex sighed, giving her the impression that he, too, might be frustrated. "What would you have me say? That I prefer not to mention my reason for seeing the king? That 'tis naught of your affair?" His voice was not loud but it carried an unmistakable edge.

Iliani did not know what to say to that. Without another word she faced front and stared out over his mount's ears. What could she say? That that was the rudest way anyone had ever been considerate of her?

Unexpectedly the humor of it struck her and she began to laugh. Iliani could feel Alaex looking at her strangely, but she did not care. When she sobered, Alaex asked in a voice as dry as an autumn leaf, "There was something in all this to amuse you?"

Iliani looked back at him and smiled, fighting the impulse to laugh again at his growing confusion. "Aye, Alaex, there was."

He stiffened. "I see none."

Her smile widened. "Now there's an obvious truth."

Alaex became more rigid. "Do you laugh at me, Wife?"

There was a mischievous glint in the blue-violet eyes that met his. "Do you never laugh, Husband?"

The moment the words were out, Iliani regretted them. Why had she called him husband? True, he was her husband. That was clear. It didn't need saying— especially by her, especially in that way. Those words had sounded almost normal in a situation that was the most abnormal of her life.

For some reason, her embarrassment soothed his mood. There was no overt sign, but as before, Iliani sensed it. His posture unbent a little—about as much as she expected Alaex's posture could unbend. When she met his calm blue eyes again, Iliani could see the faint challenge in them. Ignoring his taunt, Iliani looked forward again, determined to say nothing else. Silence was definitely best around her husband.

"Alaex! I did not think to see you again so speedily."

"Nor I, sire. Things were not as I expected."

Alfred glanced from Alaex's set face to that of the beautiful young woman standing beside him. In a thrice he understood.

"This then is your ward, Aeric's daughter," he said gazing directly at Iliani. "Finally we meet again. I have not seen you since you were a child. 'Tis a pleasure, my lady."

After casting a curious glance at Alaex, Iliani bowed and smiled. "You knew my father, sire?"

"Aye. 'Twas a pleasure incomparable," Alfred said, his pleasure unmistakable and obvious. "'Tis rare indeed that one finds a man with a mind such as his."

Iliani did not reply, hoping she didn't offend, but not knowing what to say. Surprisingly Alfred understood. He nodded, then said, "But I go on and you, I am certain, can scarce remember him."

Iliani smiled. "That is true, Your Majesty."

The king's smile was wide and warm. "You need only gaze at your reflection. You are his image."

"I have been told thus," Iliani said quietly, and this time it was Alaex who filled the silence.

"She is not just my ward, sire, but my wife."

Alfred's eyes snapped back to Alaex. "He did it, then? Aeric had mentioned he was considering a contract for his daughter, but I did not know that ere his death he had had time to see the matter settled."

"Aye, he did. He was most insistent," Alaex said stiffly.

Iliani stared from one to the other and a small, previously unacknowledged hope shriveled and died in her chest. Alfred was *bretwalda,* the king of all English-speaking people. There was no question he would not be involved in something less than honorable. Everything Iliani had ever heard of him told her so. And even if she had not heard of him, just looking into his dark eyes she could see his integrity and honesty.

Without thinking, she broke into their conversation. "You knew of my father's wish that I wed Alaex?"

More was revealed in her tone than the simple query. Alfred's eyes were serious as they looked into hers, and he wondered what was passing there. He could not say that Aeric called Alaex by name as the man to whom he wished his daughter to wed, but he knew that that was what Iliani was asking him to confirm or deny. There was a confused question of hope in her eyes that said that whether he said yea or nay she would not be satisfied. Nevertheless he could only answer truthfully.

"Milady, your father did not call for Alaex by name, but I knew of his fondness for him and thus am not surprised." Looking deeper into her violet eyes, he saw fear mingle with the confusion. Briefly he wondered if Alaex was aware of it. If the grimmer set to his former lieutenant's features were any indication, then he was.

Alfred was certain neither knew what their expressions revealed, and despite not knowing everything, he wanted to ease the strain he sensed between them. It wasn't just for Aeric and the fondness he had felt for him. Nor was it entirely because of the trapped, haunted look in the eyes of his friend's daughter. His main reason for wanting to help was because of the studied stoic expression on Alaex's face. For some reason, that said to Alfred greater than anything else that Alaex was more affected by his wife's reaction than he seemed or even wanted to be.

"Please sit," he said calmly to them both, gesturing to two chairs that sat below his.

Alaex waved his arm for Iliani to precede him, and after they were all seated Alfred, trying not to repeat that Aeric's choice had been unnamed, said, "Aye, Iliani, I knew of Aeric's wish in these matters. At the time, I did not know your husband as well as I have come to know him since. In any event, let me say that I find your father's reasoning sound and this turn of events excellent."

Iliani could feel no anger at the king's blatant attempt to soothe the tense situation. She could not, nor would she ever, accuse him of lying, but his own honesty had already compelled him to say that Aeric had not named Alaex as the man he wished her to wed. Now the king was simply trying to make a bad situation better. That was an act of kindness, an ineffective one, but one over which she could not become angry. She cast a surreptitious glance at Alaex to see how he was receiving the king's words. Despite the understanding of him she thought she'd gained, this time she could discern nothing in his inscrutable expression. Turning her attention fully to the king, Iliani asked, "If I may, sire, when did my father make his desires known to you?"

Alfred's expression altered. "Trying to put together the ultimate truth, lady? Surely Alaex told you."

His expression was just bland enough for Iliani to know she had given offense. She hastened to repair any damage. "I do not mean to offend, sire. If I have done so, I deeply apologize."

The look on the king's face smoothed. "No offense was taken, and—" He glanced briefly at Alaex to see his reactions to their interchange, and seeing slightly more than Iliani had, Alfred went on. "—given all, understandable." His pause was short. "Aeric mentioned it a few months before his death. I thought it a mere casual exchange and later put it from my mind. You will allow?"

Considering that the last several years of his kingship had been spent battling the relentless tide of Viking invasions, Iliani did. Why should he remember such a conversation that had naught to do with him personally? It seemed to Iliani as she looked around the drafty, wooden, high-beamed structure that Alfred called home that even the things pertaining to him had been left unattended. There was a constant wind blowing through the cracks in the double doors of the manor, making the tapestries on the wall ripple. Upon closer scrutiny of those tapestries, Iliani saw that they were unlike the ones that adorned Edouard's home.

Instantly she was ashamed. Of course Edouard's home might be more elaborate. The king and men like Alaex had been fighting so that it could be. Guilt at her thoughts made her nod more curtly than she normally would have, and Iliani had the awkward impression that Alfred, as his eyes quickly scanned where hers had just been, sensed her thoughts. When he smiled, an action that should have put her at her ease, her discomfort increased.

His words didn't relieve her discomfort, either. "I ken you do not recall any of this; nevertheless, 'tis your duty to stand behind your father's wishes."

"I understand the demands of duty," Iliani answered, wanting to say that duty was not the issue. The issue was whether she was truly doing what her father wanted.

"Good," Alfred replied, ignoring the implication in her words. Then to Alaex, "And speaking of a father's wish, what of Brita?"

Alaex paused for a moment; yet, when he answered, his voice, while clipped, was resolute. "That situation is the same. She is my ward still."

"It has been five years," Alfred replied, looking at Alaex consideringly.

"I know that well, sire."

"Does *she* know?" Alfred asked pointedly, nearly wanting to laugh at the slightly confused and uncomfortable expression on Alaex's face. Clearly his former lieutenant had no liking for this conversation, but Alfred would not relent. It was not mere curiosity prompting him, and it was greater than a desire to see Alaex finally happy. He needed peace in the regions Alaex held, and there was no quicker way to erode peace than internal strife. While it was true they had defeated the Danes, Alfred was ever wary, ever vigilant. Personal discomfort could not be a consideration in his decisions with his men. Mentally, he grimaced as he thought of the way he had lived for several years when the fighting was its fiercest, and he knew that personal discomfort had not been a consideration even for himself.

Alaex's words brought Alfred back from thoughts of that unpleasant time when he, the ruler of Wessex, had lacked what could be called a home.

"I do not know, but it matters little. That has naught to do with this."

Although Alaex's words were strong and reassuring,

Alfred still looked as if he disagreed with his assessment. However, after a quick glance at Iliani, who was watching them and listening silently to their conversation, he decided to take Alaex's word for it.

"I suppose it does not." The last vestige of concern left his voice as he added, "I have no doubt you will execute your duty to all concerned."

Alaex, knowing a little of the king's concerns, took no offense at Alfred's unusual interest. "Have I not always?" he responded quietly. "In this there is no difference. 'Tis the truth 'tis why I am here. I came for your acknowledgment. As Aeric is dead, the validity of the marriage may be questioned. With your open acknowledgment, no one can dispute the union, nor can any other have expectations. Your word speaks louder than one beyond the grave and with more power than the written document."

If Alfred thought Alaex made a specific reference, he ignored it as he had Iliani's. "You have it," he said unhesitatingly, and Iliani, who had been about to ask about the woman Brita whom both Alaex and Alfred knew, but about whom Alaex seemed strangely reluctant to speak, forgot about her completely. Now, instead of voicing a query she had to clamp her lips together to keep from objecting.

Alaex's head moved slightly in her direction, and Iliani knew he had been aware that she wanted to object; however, he said nothing more than "My thanks" to Alfred, who inclined his head. "Here are the documents that Aeric had drawn."

Alfred reached out to take them even as he said, " 'Tis no need for this. Even had I not known firsthand of Aeric's desire for the marriage, I knew beyond a doubt of his fondness and pride in you. In those times I visited, it fair reeked from him as if he were your sire and not your . . ." Alfred's voice came to a quick halt as he glanced at Alaex's face, which Iliani was surprised to see had tightened into even stronger forbidding lines than usual.

Puzzled, Iliani glanced from Alaex back to the king to see that Alfred was no more comfortable with what had been said—or almost said. He looked away from Alaex's set face to add with seemingly unwarranted vehemence, "I trust your word."

The unexpected tension of the moment did not ease with those words as Alfred casually examined the papers in his hand. It seemed there was something else he wanted to say, but felt it would not be wise. It was then that Iliani noted his gaze shift beyond her shoulder and a look that suspiciously bordered on relief enter his eyes.

"Ealswith. Come, my dear, and meet Aeric's daughter, Iliani. Alaex you know, of course."

Alaex stood to greet the king's wife and Iliani stood and turned also. The queen's arrival forced her to set aside her curiosity over the king's behavior and the suddenly odd and stilted conversation he and Alaex were having. Her increasing discomfort eased once she looked into the woman's eyes. Alfred's wife was gracious and striking—every inch a queen. Her smile was warm and welcoming.

"At last! I have heard much of you, m'dear. The tales of your beauty were not exaggerated." Ealswith's words were not dissimilar to Alfred's first ones, and along with her smile, they lessened the tension.

After a brief bow she said, "Your Majesty is kind."

Ealswith tut-tutted. "I think not." She looked to her husband and then smoothly turned to Alaex. "How goes it with you, Alaex?"

Alaex's smile was fleeting. "As always, Your Majesty."

Ealswith's smile grew at that, and Iliani wondered if she were the only one who noticed that the queen looked ready to burst into laughter. Iliani could not believe what she was seeing. The queen found Alaex amusing?

She was given no time to consider this question, because the queen was gently and inexorably now moving her from the men's presence. Ealswith spoke kindly, and although Iliani did not doubt the queen's sincerity, she knew the gentle and warm chatter was supposed to cover the fact that she was deliberately being led away. That in itself was puzzling. The king could have simply dismissed her instead of making it seem that she and the queen were departing of their own accord. Obviously he wanted to talk privately with Alaex. *So, why this?* Iliani wondered.

It did not take long for her to get an answer. The air between the king and Alaex had been strained enough before Ealswith arrived. It had been tense ever since Alaex had introduced her as his wife. Since that time, Alfred had tried to alleviate the tension. He probably thought that dismissing her when she had questions and clearly wanted to stay would cause more tension.

Ealswith's voice disrupted Iliani's thoughts. "Would you perhaps like a cup of cider? The weather is a bit more than brisk."

Iliani nodded absently, still thinking about the scene with Alaex and Alfred. When she glanced back over her shoulder to see Alaex and the king deep in discussion, she knew her assumptions were correct. The sudden tension that had sprung so unexpectedly between them seemed to have eased with whatever the king was saying, and Iliani saw that now Alaex spoke freely.

It was strange seeing Alaex say so much. Usually he was terse in the extreme. What subject could cause him to break his usual pattern? As Iliani continued to watch them while doing her best to seem interested in what Ealswith was saying, she was aware that while Alaex's tension might have eased, hers had not—especially when Alfred would occasionally look at her and then back to Alaex. She was certain their discussion centered on her, or at the very least, her and Alaex's marriage.

And Iliani was not wrong.

As Alfred watched his wife lead Iliani away, he said, "Well Alaex, I am as pleased about this union as I know Aeric was and would be were he here. But our feelings account for naught. What of you? What think you of your bride, Alaex? Nay, do not turn. She watches."

Casually, Alaex turned only his eyes to where Iliani stood beside the queen. As Alfred had said, she stared, then catching his glance she looked away and pretended to listen to what Ealswith was saying. Alaex knew it was mere pretense. The queen had been diplomatic, but it had been obvious—at least to him—that she had answered Alfred's unspoken need for privacy. He had wondered if Iliani noticed. Now he was certain she had.

Alaex looked away from his wife and answered the king. "Truly I do not know, sire. I have been with her only four days."

Alfred nodded. "But married so much longer if I understand these documents correctly." He did not need Alaex's assent. The papers were clear.

"I hardly think that signifies. We are strangers to one another."

" 'Twill not be so for long. Marriage is the speediest way to become familiar."

Alfred allowed his statement to linger, and when Alaex said nothing, the warm smile that Alfred saved for a precious few appeared. "Fret not, Alaex. All will be well. Do not allow your quest for answers to cloud the true issue."

"And what is that, sire?"

Alfred sighed. "That above all else, Aeric wanted happiness for you both. He felt it could be achieved. Knowing you and after having seen her again, I doubt it not."

"Would that I had your certainty, Your Majesty."

"I am certain of it," Alfred said strongly and clearly.

Alaex's smile was little more than a twisting of his lips. Humor was reflected in his eyes even less. "The lady was about to marry another when I appeared to collect her."

Years of dealing with unsettling news stood Alfred in good stead. "Is that so?" he asked without a flicker of surprise.

"Aye."

"Do you wish to speak of it?"

Alaex shrugged. "'Tis not much else to tell, sire. She was about to wed Cam, the son of Edouard. Had I not returned when I did . . ." Alaex did not finish, and completion was not necessary.

"Cam?" Alfred asked with studied nonchalance. Both Edouard and Cam would have been astounded to know that Alfred had heard of him.

Even days after the fact, Alaex could feel his blood heat at the thought. "Aye, Cam."

His anger was not lost on Alfred; however, Alaex missed the king's pleased expression.

"Of course, it can be said in their favor that neither he nor his father knew of Aeric's wishes."

Alaex nodded curtly, causing Alfred's amusement to grow. "What of the lady? How took she all these occurrences?"

For the first time since Alfred had known him, Alaex's face lacked its characteristic inscrutability. Chagrin was etched upon his hard features as if placed there by a sculptor's tool.

"Not well."

A hearty chuckle was Alfred's initial response. "Why do I ken that to be vast understatement?" he asked, looking over to where Iliani and Ealswith were watching his grandson play. Although they seemed to be engrossed in the youngster's antics—he was sure Ealswith was—he was just as positive that Iliani was not. When she met his eyes briefly and then colored and looked away, he chuckled again.

"What now, Alaex?"

Alaex shrugged and he, too, looked at Iliani and then away. "I do not know. We leave here for Fontwyn. Once there"—Alaex shrugged again—"I do not know."

"Why not do what any couple newly wedded would do—even though you are not?" Alfred asked softly.

Piercing blue eyes latched onto Alfred's dark ones. "With what has passed, sire, I think that unlikely."

"Why not?" Alfred returned. "She is a maid—a comely one at that, more than comely—and you are a man. I have seen more than one woman give you the eye. There is no reason why your wife will not, provided you put yourself in her eye's path."

Alaex didn't reply, but Alfred was not deterred. "Surely you do not find her lacking?"

A hungry expression in Alaex's eyes was fleeting but clear. Thinking it wise not to comment on it, Alfred said quietly, "I have never known a situation to be beyond you. I cannot believe this is the exception."

Alfred did not expect an answer; therefore, he was stunned when Alaex said in a voice deep and distant, "After the decisive battle against Haesten's army, I knew 'twas time to turn my thoughts to that of another battle, albeit of a different sort. Yet in my mind no plan formed; there was just a hollow space where thought should be. 'Twas the most unique experience of my life, until I met my bride. Now that blankness seems to be a constant state. Normal, sire?" Alaex made a dry sound that should have been a laugh. "If I ever knew what that was, I know it even less now."

Alfred was silent a long time. These were the most words he had ever heard Alaex speak, and they were the first that gave a glimpse of the troubled man within. It was this insight that suddenly gave Alfred a clue what to say next.

"Alaex, how does one win a war?"

Alaex was startled by the question. "Your pardon, sire?"

Alfred smiled. "I asked how one wins a war."

"Through a series of battles."

"Does one envision the outcome or the events?"

Alaex frowned. "The outcome," he said slowly, clearly unable to follow Alfred's reasoning. "To think of the events can lead to defeat."

Alfred's smile grew. "Can you not see the similarity? You have tried to envision the events. Do not, Son. Set your goals to achieve a desired outcome. Then pursue them one battle at a time."

The confused look left Alaex's eyes.

"I see you ken my point."

Alaex nodded slowly. "Aye, sire. 'Tis only I never saw it in that way before."

"There is no other way to see it. The conflict between man and woman is the oldest form of war," Alfred said. "So wage it a day at a time, a goal at a time, and all else will settle itself. Do not forfeit the war ere the first battle begins." Again Alfred laughed. "I would wager my hard-won kingdom that you have yet to kiss the lass."

Alaex said nothing and again the king chuckled. "I yield, Alaex. I will not ask if 'tis your want. What man would not, and you are the man with the right. A word of advice, though, not from your king but from a man who loves his wife and would want the same joy for you, his once and still trusted lieutenant and friend. Do not wait too long in the exercising of that right. Having seen the horror of war in close range, you and I both know that this world holds too little joy. Do not delay. Every moment you do is one less of that precious element."

Chapter

What is Fontwyn Hall like?"

If Alaex was surprised to hear Iliani's voice after her
prolonged silence, he gave no sign. They had left Alfred's
fortress three days before and if her silence had held a bit
longer, her query would have been unnecessary. She
would see Fontwyn Hall for herself. He answered her as
if her question were a normal continuation of casual
conversation.

"'Tis a house, large, not too unlike any other."

Iliani sighed. As usual even when Alaex spoke, he said
little. She had tired of waiting for him to speak, to tell
her what he and Alfred had discussed so earnestly. So
she had decided to engage him in conversation that
would, she had hoped, lead to an opportunity to broach
it. A conversation about Fontwyn seemed innocent
enough, although in truth she had no curiosity about the
place of her birth. She had not seen it since she was a
child and she was in no great rush to see it now. She felt
an underlying, unnamed dread the nearer they got to
Fontwyn, and Iliani could only assume it was the circumstances under which she was returning. Trying to

put her worries aside, she renewed her efforts to engage Alaex in conversation.

"When was the last time you saw it?"

"Three years ago."

"Oh."

Alaex nearly smiled. He was beginning to know his bride. Iliani did not want to discuss her home. He knew that. What he didn't know was what she really wanted to discuss. If he did, he would have opened the discussion himself. Iliani, he knew, would be more than capable of carrying it from there.

"One battle at a time, Alaex." Alfred's advice played itself in his mind.

Alaex cleared his throat. "Is there aught the matter?"

Iliani, shocked by his uncoerced speech, turned rapidly—too rapidly—to face him and nearly lost her seat. Only Alaex's quick reflexes kept her from falling buttocks first to the ground.

"Easy, Bear," he soothed his destrier, which was already skittish under the unaccustomed added weight. He patted the horse's neck with one hand and clutched Iliani with the other. When the horse quieted, Alaex looked down at her.

"What is the matter with you?" His tone was filled with unmistakable censure.

Iliani, who already felt foolish, bristled. "There is naught the matter with me that would not be relieved with but a little assistance from you."

Alaex frowned down at her and stopped his destrier, signaling for his men to continue. "Will you tell me what that means?"

Iliani waited for the last soldier to pass. When they were alone, she raised hot eyes to his. "If you intend to speak but once every thousand years, you should give warning so as those of us who do it a bit more often will not be startled."

Her explanation confused him, a now familiar feeling. Alaex had been confused since he'd collected his wife, and she had given him no indication that that status was going to change. He was beginning to think that if he ever understood her, it would be cause for alarm.

"Iliani," he said, startling her further by using her name. Iliani could not recall his using it before despite his tacit command that she use his. "I spoke as much as you did. I thought silence was your preference."

"And if it was not?"

"I asked if aught was the matter," he reminded pointedly.

"And?"

His frown deepened. "And?" he repeated, feeling stupid and not liking the feeling at all. "If there is more, speak it."

Iliani's bark of laughter was slicing. "Famous words from a man who barely speaks!"

Deciding to concentrate on one discomfort at a time, Alaex took a moment to wonder at the sudden increased heat of the day and to consider if the others were as uncomfortable beneath it as he. Then it was his turn to nearly lose his seat as he realized it was not the sun's intensity causing his increased warmth, but Iliani's verbal jabs. That awareness was as incredible as it was irritating. He who had stood incalculable taunts, insults, and the like was now becoming affected by the sharp-edged tongue of the woman to whom he was wed.

He looked at her thoughtfully, wondering dispassionately if Aeric ever beat her. Immediately he discarded the thought. No, Aeric hadn't lived long enough. When he'd first taken Alaex in, Iliani had been only a babe. Seeing the glitter in her eyes, Alaex felt a totally new kind of remorse at Aeric's death. Perhaps had he lived still or even had he lived longer, his daughter would not be so sharp-tongued. Aeric would not have stood for it; he wouldn't have liked it. Alaex knew he didn't.

Still it was not too late to do something about her tongue's sharpness, Alaex thought, deciding that as her

husband he could beat her. However, despite the pleasurable satisfaction that thought briefly brought, he recognized sheer bluster when he heard it, and his life was
complicated enough without the additional problem of
fooling himself.

"See what I mean?" Iliani snapped, and this time
when the thought occurred to him to subdue her, it was
stronger.

Alaex took a deep breath. "Nay, I do not and I think
neither do you. Were I not speaking, could we be having
this argument? By the by," he said, not hiding his
lessening patience, "if we must argue, please tell me the
cause."

Iliani clenched her teeth. "You are the cause."

"I have done nothing."

"There's a truth: done nothing, said nothing. Do you
realize that we are married—in the most intimate relationship possible—and we have never had a real conversation?"

Alaex stiffened, feeling unjustly accused. "I have
tried."

Iliani made another tauntingly hollow laugh, and
Alaex decided that he definitely hated that. "What is the
point of conversation?" he asked defensively.

"That you can ask tells me too much. I know naught of
you, at least nothing worth knowing. I do not know what
you think or know of me, yet we are bound for life and
expected to build a future. You see nothing wrong with
this?" Her tone dared him to contradict her.

One battle at a time? He should have taken Alfred
more literally. Strangely he wasn't angry anymore. He
saw her point. The question now was how to break a
lifelong pattern. He didn't see an answer to that.

"What do you want to know?" he asked softly.

Iliani's harsh, "Stop that!" took them both unaware.
The frown was back between Alaex's dark golden brows.

"Woman, are you daft?"

Iliani smoothed her features, trying not to let her own

amazement at her reaction show. "Nay, but most assuredly you are trying to make me so. You have to stop
saying the unexpected."

The moment the words were out of her mouth, Iliani
regretted them. They rang hypocritical even to her ears.
Had she not just said the unexpected?

Alaex did not miss the hypocrisy. His jaw tightened
tellingly. "If I speak the unexpected and that disconcerts
you, then I need not speak at all. Ah, I forget," he
continued harshly, "you like silence no better. I did not
know there was such an art to conversing. Why do I not
just wait for you to tell me what I should say and when I
should either say it or be silent? Is that your preference?"

Iliani sighed, understanding his ire and seeing her
blame in it. "I apologize, Alaex. All I wanted was to talk
to you, to get to know you better and stabilize my life to
some measure."

Alaex nodded briefly. "I gave you the opportunity to
ask me what you wanted."

Her remorse vanished and her gaze was direct and
unwavering. "This conversation is beginning to have an
uncomfortable familiarity. You have told me you dislike
repeating yourself. Clearly you do not object to making
others do that which you so hate. I know I have said this
before, but no matter, I will say it again. If you knew
what I wanted, why would you make me ask?" Iliani
wasn't sure, but she thought she saw a hint of increased
color in his cheeks.

"Perhaps because I hoped to avoid the question."

"Why?"

Alaex's jaw set. "Because 'tis highly personal. Despite
your being my wife, we do not know each other well
enough to speak of all things with ease."

Iliani flinched slightly. "Blunt but true. I take it then
that I should not ask about what you and the king
spoke?"

The darkening of his expression was enough. She
didn't need his quiet "I would prefer not."

"I see. And of course, we should make allowances for *your* preferences." It was unnecessary for her to add that her desires had been given no such treatment.

Iliani looked away and was quiet a few moments. "It will not succeed, you know," she finally said softly. "This thing between us. Is there no other way?"

Alaex was silent, but Iliani was not unsettled. His silences no longer disturbed her; she was finding his words, and her reactions to those words, a much larger cause for concern. When he finally spoke, Iliani could feel his hollowness. It did not help that it was a pitiful reflection of her own emptiness.

"Nay. I think not. We both are bound by words spoken to each other and to another." Without waiting for her to reply, he sank his heels into his horse's side, increasing their pace to overtake his men.

As they rode along, Iliani thought of their situation and what Alaex had said. She knew the "another" to whom he referred was her father. He was the unseen force that bound her more firmly to the man behind her than the king's blessing and recognition of their marriage or even the vows themselves.

For the first time in her memory, her thoughts of her father were not kind. Again Iliani wondered how he could have done something like this to her. While she could barely remember him, those few fleeting images she had had not given her cause to think him mentally unfit or cruel. So then, why this? Had he thought this would be a good thing? It was all too confusing.

Bit by bit, Iliani examined what little she knew of her father. He had been, by all accounts, kind and gentle and good. Could such a man have bequeathed such an inheritance on his daughter? Nay, her heart cried in fervent rebellion. The few memories she had of her father she could not bear to taint with thoughts of his possible cruelty. He had loved her. Of that she was certain. That had to be her unshakable conviction. That, then, was the place from which to start.

A stinging pain in her palms made Iliani aware that

her hands were clenched. Slowly she opened her hands, and not wanting to alert Alaex to her inner turmoil, she expelled a gentle breath and tried to regain control of herself.

The moment of desperation subsided by slow degrees and Iliani once again thought of possible motives for her father's decision. Her unrest eased a bit more as she recalled the memory of something Edouard had once told her. Her father had had some sort of heart ailment. It had been the thing that caused his untimely end. Perhaps because of his precarious health he had known he would not live to see her raised. In that event he would most likely have wanted to see to her welfare and future. He would have wanted to know she was protected. Being a loving father, that would have been his primary goal. He would not have thought of the man Alaex would become—or maybe more specifically, the man Alaex hid from him—nor naturally would he have seen him from a woman's view. Certainly Aeric would not have considered him too hard. He would have seen that hardness as strength. His terseness he would have attributed to inner fortitude, the ability to keep his own counsel, something men prized and Iliani still did not understand. And certainly his looks would have been no concern, because Aeric would never see him in that way.

In fairness to her father, Iliani had to admit that she didn't *see* Alaex in that way either. True, she was aware of his features, but after cursorily noting that he had the requisite parts, she had not made a feminine evaluation. From the time he had barged into her life, she had viewed him only through the scales of fear or aversion, and these reactions were based solely on what she had heard of him. The fear was gone, but that was all she could say. That day in her room when he had removed his helm, she had been so overwhelmed by him and then his news, the only thing that signified from that disastrous event was the identifying scar. Surely it wasn't as hideous as she remembered.

A warning that it might be dangerous to pursue this

line of thought sounded in her mind, but it was too late. Her curiosity was fully aroused. Just what color *were* his eyes? Were they truly the cold blue she remembered?

Ignoring the instinct which grew stronger and cried out to her that she was about to tread on uncertain territory, Iliani allowed her curiosity free rein. Oblivious to the last line of Alaex's men whom they had overtaken, she turned to study Alaex's face.

To say that Alaex was surprised would have barely tapped into his reaction. He didn't recognize her look; he *felt* it. It was as if her hands caressed him instead of her eyes. Without realizing it, he stopped his horse and again his men moved ahead. Neither he nor Iliani noticed the knowing and approving smiles on a few of their faces.

Iliani was wrestling with disbelief and trying to discern when Alaex had become so appealing. She had been with him nearly a week. How could she not have noticed? As for the scar—all she could think now was, what scar? That mark did naught to diminish his attraction. Whether it was a trick of her mind before or now, his eyes were blue, but not the cold blue she had previously assumed. While Iliani would never describe them as warm, they were not the lifeless waste she had imagined before. The dark blond arches above them were the same up close, only now she noted his lashes were extremely long, so long that they curled on the ends. His nose was straight—minus the helm—and his cheekbones were high and sculpted. But his lips, certainly they had not looked like that before. They were not a mean angry line cut into his face. They were full and sensuous, and Iliani supposed they would be soft to touch.

O, Iliani, she admonished herself, *you really are going to have to stop thinking things that spur you to the corresponding action.* However, again the warning came too late. As she had known it would, the thought demanded manifestation and now she wanted to touch him. She wanted to touch him, so badly the desire bordered on need.

Just his lips, she promised herself. *I'll cease this madness once I touch his lips.*

Still she hesitated. Her hesitation had nothing to do with losing her nerve. It was anticipation, pure and unadulterated. Reaching out slowly, ignoring the slight tremor of her fingers, Iliani lightly skimmed her fingertips over Alaex's firm but soft lips. Instead of stopping herself as she had promised, her curiosity got the best of her, and Iliani found herself touching the rest of his face as well. She even ran her fingers through his slightly curly hair and over his darker and coarser beard.

Iliani was acting instinctively and she was unaware that she leaned in closer to Alaex and that her lips had parted. Neither did she know that her nostrils had flared slightly as if she were trying to learn him through scent as well as touch.

She was unaware of all these things. However, Alaex was not.

Watching her face while feeling her hands upon him, Alaex was hit with the keenest, most explosive desire he had ever felt. It wasn't her beauty, although he had long since admitted that she had that in abundance. One didn't react to beauty on this level. It was her expression, as if she were in the awe of discovery; it was her eyes, which seemed to want to drink him in; it was her lips, which seemed to beg for his kiss; but most of all, it was the delicate flare of her nostrils, which gave evidence of her hunger, a hunger it seemed she wanted him to appease.

Neither was reacting consciously anymore. Slowly Alaex lowered his head to hers, surprised, despite the hunger he'd seen, when Iliani did not pull away. When their lips met, everything seemed to still—Alaex, Iliani, the birds on the wing, even the wind in the leaves.

Alaex had never known such quiet contentment. It was like coming near a warm hearth after enduring long unprotected months in the cold. When their lips met, the lonely howling within him for once was silent. For Iliani, her emotions had frozen at first contact, only to come riotously alive. There was color everywhere in a world that moments ago had been only shades of gray. Her emotions were careening so wildly that she could not identify or define them.

When Alaex groaned, a sound that came from the depths of his chest, Iliani felt it because she was pressed closely against him. Suddenly through the wonder of his kiss, Iliani noticed other things: his hands' fevered motions across her back, on her neck, in her hair. The intensity of it all was too much. These emotions were too strangely new, dousing her awakening passion.

Another revelation to stem her growing ardor was Alaex's seeming desperation. Iliani could understand why she could be so moved. It was her first taste of passion, her first kiss. But Alaex? Surely it was not so for him, and she was not conceited enough to think that her untutored innocence could drive a man to this kind of yearning.

Iliani pulled away abruptly. She couldn't bear to see his face then, so she buried hers in his chest. She needed to think, and she prayed that Alaex wouldn't try to kiss her again. He didn't. He only held her close in a gesture Iliani now found as intimate as kissing and he made a sound similar to an arrogant chuckle.

Suspecting the source of his amusement did much to help clear her head, and her first lucid thought was wonder at how things had come to this. She had not intended to kiss him. Until that moment she'd had no idea what desire was, had no notion it could flare so powerfully, so unexpectedly. That her first taste of such a shattering emotion should come from a man she wasn't sure she could trust . . .

Iliani's entire body tightened and then she shivered.

"Cold?" Alaex asked softly, a new note of gentleness in his voice.

"Nay," Iliani forced herself to mumble through her tightly constricted throat. His tenderness made her uncomfortable, raising a feeling of guilt, and for once she was glad of his tendency not to discuss things overmuch.

She was struggling too heavily under the weight of her discovery.

She *didn't* trust him. Her father's part in this charade she could understand and forgive, although forgiving was harder than understanding. What were Alaex's motives? Why would he bind himself to a five-year-old child?

Iliani strained to remember all she had ever heard of him. He was an orphan, at least she thought he might be. Quite possibly he was a bastard also; she wasn't sure. Somehow she didn't think that her father would bind her to a bastard, but that fact would not have disturbed her. A person could not help the circumstances of his birth.

Rapidly putting that thought from her mind, she went on to what else she knew of him. Her father had taken him in when he was fourteen. That piece of information had come from Edouard. He had told her that a long time ago. The rest of what she knew was just battle rumors, cold enough to chill her blood. At the time they were told she had barely listened, and now she barely wanted to remember.

The feeling of desperation was returning. The few facts she had were practically no facts at all. Not one of them would supply the answer as to why he would marry in such a way. Iliani knew that asking Alaex would yield no real answer, if he answered at all. If she had learned anything about him, it was that he hated any queries about his honor. To ask him what was his recompense for marrying her would not exactly put him or his honor in a flattering light.

That left her back at the beginning. The only person able to give her any insight was her father, and he was incapable of answering.

Alaex's deep voice startled her. "You asked of Fontwyn Hall. See it there in the distance."

Iliani looked to where he indicated and saw her first glimpse of her home in thirteen years. Edouard had never brought her back. It had been painful for him. And Iliani had never requested it. At first she had not thought of it; then the desire had not been there. She had wanted to solidify her link with Edouard and his family because they were all the family she had. Aside from trying to remember her father, seeing the place where she was born and had lived the first five years of her life had had no appeal for her.

Looking now at the unusual structure of the place that had been her home—it was stone instead of wood—Iliani realized why it held no appeal all these years. It was because it held no memories for her. No warmth, no sharing. Its only points of renown were that her father had died there, and the recently learned fact that she had been married there. In the past, the first reason was not one for which to return. At present, the second fact was not one to make her look to the place with anticipation. These things aside, she would admit to a casual fascination with the structure.

It was huge, larger than Edouard's manor. Although both buildings had two floors, that was their only similarity. Lourds Keep, where she had grown up, was predominately wood. This place was entirely stone, giving it a sturdy appearance. It seemed to have been standing since the time of the Romans, and Iliani would not have been surprised if it had. The stone was a soft gray, which looked as if it might once have been white save for time and the elements. Its windows were double arched and narrow, making it appear that the house squinted down upon the surrounding area. Other than its size and substance, the hall offered nothing else remarkable. There were no other people about, and that fact caused dread to grow in Iliani's heart.

Despite the coolness of the late winter's day, there should have been some activity. There always had been at Lourds Keep.

Pulling herself upright, Iliani decided then to stop making unfair comparisons. Lourds Keep was not Fontwyn Hall. Lourds Keep was no longer home. Fontwyn Hall was. The sooner she accepted that, the sooner she would find some ration of peace. It was useless to torture herself with heartrending comparisons and unanswerable questions.

Knowing that Alaex waited for her reaction, Iliani said, "'Tis different."

That was not the answer he was expecting. He gave no verbal indication of it, but Iliani was sure. She sensed his disappointment with her tacit response.

Alaex looked down at her briefly before looking back to the hall in the distance. "So it is."

They rode silently for the next few moments, Iliani lost in thought and Alaex chiding himself for his. It was ridiculous to want her to be excited about Fontwyn. He reminded himself of how young she had been when she was last there. Perhaps she had no reason for warmth toward this place. With him, it was different.

For years, particularly when the horror of war had been too severe, he had thought longingly of Fontwyn and the quiet, peaceful days he had spent with Aeric. Childishly, he had been afraid that somehow the place he recalled in his mind would be changed, and he could not halt the leap of excited pleasure in his heart when he saw it had not. That and the kiss he and Iliani had shared moments ago made him greatly anticipate their first evening at Fontwyn. Now, after another quick glance at her face, he wasn't so sure.

The silence was uninterrupted as they filed through the massive iron and stone gate and were in the outer bailey. Alaex leapt to the ground and Iliani remained seated on the horse, looking about.

The stone of the place seemed more cold and forbidding up close, and still there was no one about either to greet or assist them. She was about to question Alaex when he called out, "Jon!"

Immediately a tall, burly man wearing nearly as many weapons as Alaex came forward. Iliani could tell nothing of this man's features because he wore his helm.

"Alaex?" he responded in the deepest voice she had ever heard. It seemed to rumble from the depths of his feet.

"Alert all that we are here. Tell them we expect little tonight, but on the morrow to be prepared to resume all duties as we are staying."

Alaex continued to speak to Jon, but his eyes were on Iliani. "Tell them the lord and his lady have come home."

Chapter

⇒ 8 ⇐

Iliani could not suppress the shudder that went through her at his words. They seemed so final, so irrevocable. Alaex's eyes narrowed at her reaction. When he reached up to lift her down from Bear's back, she could not meet his chilled stare. Instead her gaze settled on the column of his strong throat. She could feel his piercing look on the top of her head, willing her to look at him, but Iliani stubbornly refused. She didn't look then, nor moments later, when a handful of the hall's servants gathered around them.

Alaex moved away and Iliani released a sigh. Keeping her eyes averted from the open curiosity of the few servants watching her, Iliani examined the hall and the grounds. It was not just different as she had told Alaex. Up close, despite her initial perception of its coldness, it had transformed from a huge, characterless structure to something unique and truly beautiful. It looked not only pleasing to the eye but able to withstand attack, as if the original builder had been able to foresee the marauding menace of the future: the Vikings. Yet for all its sturdy appearance, the hall seemed to exude a certain sense of vulnerability, almost as if it were incomplete without its occupants.

Iliani shook her head at such fanciful nonsense; however, the thought would not leave. There was an aura of sadness and weakness about the place that contrasted highly with its apparent sturdiness.

"Iliani?"

Iliani turned to Alaex, immediately understanding from the tone of his voice that it was not the first time he had called her. "Aye?" she answered, avoiding his eyes and ignoring the disapproval in his voice.

Alaex studied her face for a few minutes before he glanced down to the hand he had extended to her. If he noticed her hesitance in taking it he said nothing, but when Iliani tried to draw her hand back after a moment, his grip tightened and his words became clipped.

"These few servants here are those who remain at all times at the hall. Arthur," he said pointing to a white-haired yet curiously unwrinkled elderly man, who for his apparent age looked to be as vital and solid as the house in which he served.

Iliani's eyes met the deep hazel ones of the servant and she nodded slightly. His wife, Gwyn, a robust woman with gray-streaked, dark brown hair that was exactly the same shade as her eyes, barely looked at her. Their children, Harold, Berne, and Lucy, had red hair that varied in hues, making Iliani assume that their father's hair must have been some shade of red before it turned white. These children, like their parents, avoided Iliani's eyes.

Their enigmatic reaction, compounded by Alaex's tense presence, wearied Iliani. There were just too many strange things going on in her life. Giving up any thought of ease with Alaex, Iliani could only hope that she mistook Arthur and his family's reserve. In any case, recalcitrant servants were the least of her worries.

"Lucy will be your maidservant." At Alaex's abrupt announcement, Iliani forgot her resolve to avoid looking directly at him.

There was a triumphant light in Alaex's eyes as he tenaciously held her gaze while his eyes sought answers to unasked questions. He had known this would happen.

Iliani had, too, and she had feared her reaction. As had happened on the road, she was mesmerized by the pale blue depths of his gaze. Also as had happened on the road, she forgot everything and everyone.

Whether he approved of what he saw, Iliani could not tell. The edge was gone from his voice when he asked, "Is that to your liking?"

Iliani felt like a complete fool. She was not about to tell him she couldn't recall what he'd said, so she nodded.

"Good." Then she was staring at his profile as he turned back to the servants. " 'Twas good of you to come out at no notice. Your diligence is to your credit. You may go."

The servants stared as incredulously at this speech as did Iliani. Did he just thank them? Is that what she had heard—gratitude? As much as Iliani admired Edouard for his mildness and even-tempered nature, she had never heard him thank a servant. A servant did his job, no more or less. What was there to thank? Of course, disobedience had to be addressed, but obedience was ignored as it was expected.

She still had not gotten over her amazement when the five walked away and Alaex turned to her. "You seem unsettled," he remarked, noting her shock but mistaking its source. "Was there another you wished to attend you?"

"Nay," she replied absently. She knew of no one else to act as a maid. The only personal servant she had ever had was Cedra, and she was left behind at Lourds Keep. Although Lucy looked a little older than Cedra and definitely older than Iliani's eighteen years, she seemed capable if somewhat reluctant. "You thanked them," she blurted in explanation, unable to get past that remarkable deed.

Alaex started. "Should I not have? They were here

when I did not request it. Thanks should always be issued when someone does the unasked."

Iliani stared at him. "But they are servants."

Alaex's jaw tightened. Was this something she learned from Edouard, or was that barb aimed at his lack of true nobility? Whichever it was, he didn't like it. "I see," he said curtly. "They are servants, and therefore unworthy of gratitude as another would be."

His words put her on the defensive. That hadn't been what she meant at all. "I did not intend it that way," she said tightly.

The silence lengthened, and as it grew so did Iliani's discomfort. She did not fully understand what had caused yet another confrontation between them, so Iliani tried for what she hoped would be a neutral topic.

"How long have Arthur and his family been here?"

"Since before you were born."

Another surprise. "Then they know me?"

Alaex stared. "I would say so," he answered slowly, his irritation ebbing in the face of her obvious unease. "What ails you?"

Iliani looked at him and then away. He had already asked her if she were daft. The answer to his last question would remove any doubt from his mind, because even as it echoed in her own thoughts, *she* thought it sounded insane. She sighed in defeat. There was nothing for it.

"'Tis only the expression on their faces and the looks in their eyes. It made me uncomfortable."

Alaex frowned. "In what way?"

At first Iliani considered not answering; then she discarded that as futile and stupid. Alaex was not going to let the subject drop until he had his answers.

"In the beginning they just stared as if they were trying to see something." She paused for breath and then rushed on. "Then they seemed to withdraw as if what they saw was not to their liking."

Iliani was not watching Alaex, so she missed the

transformation of his frown into a smile that, even had she seen it, she would have had no way of knowing was a rare one for him. It was a smile of true amusement, complete with an accompanying twinkle in his pale blue eyes.

Alaex himself was surprised at his reaction, especially in light of the harsh irritation he had felt a moment ago. Few things genuinely amused him, and he usually did not fluctuate from one emotional extreme to the other— at least he hadn't until he collected his bride. Iliani had sounded like a little girl—the one he had known years ago. The same little girl who had looked up at him with beseeching innocent eyes and had told him she had no idea how her father's ink had gotten on his only clean undertunic, even though that same ink stained her hands, the front of her gown, and the tops of her shoes.

Focusing again on Iliani, his smile faded, but the warmth it had brought did not. He felt slightly ill at ease, but he ignored it. Strange that he could ignore his discomfort but not hers.

"They are most likely only trying to match the five-year-old hellion they knew to the woman who stands before them."

If her day took one more unexpected twist, Iliani felt that she would scream hysterically. Regardless of how she wanted to deny it, Alaex had just *teased* her. Her eyes snapped to his, and for the second time that day she thought she detected a rise in his color. The world righted from its bizarre angle, leaving her with a sudden urge to laugh—an urge she repressed. If Alaex had begun to shuffle from one foot to the other, it couldn't have been more clear that he was unused to playing the role of consoler. Iliani did not want to embarrass him further, yet she could not allow his kindness to pass unmarked. What was it he had said? "Thanks should always be issued when someone does the unasked."

Iliani did not try to examine her feelings or rationalize them. Enough of that had already been done. Using the hand he still held firmly clasped in his, she pulled him down to her. When his head was within reach, she kissed him softly and whispered, "Thank you."

Astonished, Alaex released her hand, and as she was suffering a bit from the unsettling riot of her own thoughts, Iliani used that momentary freedom to slip away from him and enter her new home.

Chapter

➔ 9 ←

For all the strain of the evening meal and after, the quiet moment of accord in the outer yard might have been an image generated from an overactive imagination rather than reality. Iliani's mood plummeted abruptly the moment she stepped into Fontwyn Hall and no memory, not even a flicker of one, stirred. It should have been momentous. She was returning to her home after all. Yet as Iliani stared around the huge well-appointed hall, she felt neither welcome nor rejection. It was not home, just a place where she was expected to live.

As if those disappointing feelings were not weighty enough, Iliani also felt the near-embarrassing anticipation of everyone around her. She was a bride returning home with a triumphant groom. This was their first night in the "new" home. It seemed that the servants conveniently forgot the circumstances surrounding her and Alaex's marriage. She could not; those circumstances were a formidable barrier. She had almost married another man; she had had no knowledge of her marriage to Alaex; and the greatest hindrance of all, she could not accept him as her husband though he had "proof."

Then there was the tapestry. Arthur had brought it to the main hall. After receiving a slight nod from Alaex, he had proceeded to hang it, telling one and all that Aeric had commissioned it long ago. Despite the dust that clouded it, the picture of the tapestry was clear. Its weaving told the tale of a wedding that was the cause of great joy. In its center was a strong blond warrior and a dark-haired maiden. The identity of the maiden was unmistakable: she had dark locks and violet-colored eyes.

All eyes had turned to her, and not knowing what else to say, Iliani had mumbled, " 'Tis lovely. Who made it?" Arthur had answered that his wife Gwyn had. She had a particular talent for such work, he had added with an inoffensive lack of modesty.

Iliani had dropped her eyes and Alaex remained silent while the hall filled with the boisterous cheers of his men. Their cheering had lasted so long that Iliani was afraid that the walls, which had already stood for eons, might now crumble beneath the tremors.

The servants had been more reserved in their good-will, although their pleasure was obvious. It was during all this that Iliani had stolen a glance at Alaex and found his usual inscrutable mask gone. The intense heat in his blue gaze seared her.

Even thinking of it now, while she sat in the rapidly cooling water of her bath, it seemed to heat the water anew. It was a great mystery to her how a face that was otherwise so expressionless could emit such heat, such hunger. The mere memory of his face frightened her. No, Iliani admitted, that was untrue. It was waiting for him to come to her that terrified her, and the situation had no solution. She did not want the wait to end in his arrival, and she couldn't stand the wait itself.

Unknowingly, she asked of her father a question similar to Alaex's when he had first come to collect her. "Oh, Father, what have you done?"

Heedlessly, Iliani ran the cloth over her body, rinsing what was already rinsed as she continued her one-sided conversation with her father. "For a long time, I have wondered if marriage to Cam was your wish, and I had my doubts about that. Now I believe I am faced with proof that it was not your will, but the proof raises more questions than it answers. Alfred cannot name the man you intended, and you are not here to say who speaks the truth or the lie.

"I am lost. I have many questions and few answers. I know only that he will come to me soon, and whether it be your will or not, I do not know if I can be a wife to him in truth."

Iliani sighed, and then she finally felt the coolness of the water. Standing swiftly, she got out of the tub, rubbing herself briskly with the bathing linen in an attempt to become both dry and warm. This done, she donned a light chamber robe and sat down in the middle of the massive bed she had been told had seen her birth, and began the difficult task of brushing her hair. Lucy had been there to aid her, but after the unconcealed expectation throughout the meal, Iliani had felt uncomfortable under the maid's stares and had asked her to leave. Alaex would be joining her soon and she was nervous enough without Lucy's stares adding to it.

She pulled a little too hard on a tangle in her hair and winced as the hair was pinched from her scalp. With quiet determination, Iliani laid the brush down. Baldness certainly was not going to help. What would help, she had no idea. There was no help, no answers, and no time. Alaex would be here soon.

Unable to sit and wait any longer, Iliani stood, not knowing what she was to do or where she was to go. However, further consideration was not necessary, because at that moment Alaex quietly entered the room.

When he shut the door behind him, it was as if he repeated his words to Jon that the lord and his lady were home, and along with the memory of the words came the return of the feelings they had aroused. Iliani's heart lurched and her feelings swirled tumultuously, ill-defined and unclear. It was too much, and Iliani knew that if Alaex took but one step, the hysteria that never felt far off would unleash, snapping her nerves.

But he did nothing.

Taut minutes passed as they stared at each other. Alaex's eyes moved over her from head to toe. He missed nothing—not the terrified confusion in her eyes, the intensity with which she bit her bottom lip, the agitated rise and fall of her breasts, or the way her hands opened and closed spasmodically. Fleetingly he wondered if Iliani knew what her face and body revealed, but he wisely kept his thoughts to himself. Her look caused a familiar battle instinct to surge to life within him, and he knew he had to proceed cautiously. His wife's fear was nearly palpable, and as Alaex had come to think of their relationship in terms of warfare, he knew that she was feeling panicked and trapped. One or the other emotion was manageable. The two together made the adversary dangerously unpredictable. Alaex knew he had to gentle her, and he searched rapidly for a way to do that.

Gradually he pushed away from the door, slowing his movements more when he saw Iliani's eyes widen. He walked to the far side of the bed, leaving its width between them. His breath came a little easier as Iliani relaxed slightly. Again he found himself wanting to smile at her open reaction. The bed was no obstacle to him, but its bulk seemed to ease her. Not knowing what to say and realizing that the tension had been reduced but was far from relieved, Alaex began the systematic removal of his battle gear. He was down to the soft chainse he wore beneath his tunic when Iliani spoke, and although he did not turn to face her, he knew from the sound of her words that she had not moved from her spot.

"Why did you not tell me I was your ward?"

Alaex paused. Of all the things he expected her to want to discuss, this was not one. He shrugged. "It seemed best."

"For whom?"

"For everyone."

"Why was that?" Her voice was curious, not angry.

Alaex sighed, wondering how much he could tell her. If her nervous stance and glances were an indication, not much.

"My life, as well you know, has not been one of peace. There are men—unscrupulous sorts—who would have used your relationship to me to gain their ends."

Iliani had to think about that a moment, as the connection was not readily apparent. Then it became clear.

"Because of your closeness to the king?"

Again Alaex paused, but this time he turned to see her, surprised by the quickness of her mind. Seeing this, he was glad he had said no more. This new insight also put him on warning for future discussions with her.

Finally he answered. "Aye, there was that."

"Did Edouard know?" Iliani asked, only to answer her own question before he had the opportunity. "Of course he did. He paid for your services to protect Cam." She raised curious eyes to his. "Why did you do that? 'Tis clear you have no liking for him."

Alaex couldn't help but smile. Here at last was Aeric's daughter. He had the feeling that if he stood before her a few moments more, she would be telling him even more startling facts that he did and did not want to hear.

Iliani was momentarily sidetracked by the pleasantness of his unexpected smile. Although seeming more natural, this smile made her more uncomfortable than his others.

"Why do you smile?" she asked, needing an answer that might help her to understand her contradictory reaction.

Instead of answering, Alaex countered with his own question. "What makes you think I do not like Cam?"

Undisturbed that he avoided her question, Iliani returned promptly, "You have just confirmed it."

"How have I done that?"

"I did not call a name, I only said 'you have no liking

95

for him.' I could have been speaking of Edouard. Besides, I was there when Cam threatened you. I heard your response. 'Twas obvious you two do not meet as friends."

Alaex hoped he hid his shock. So she had seen and heard that exchange between him and Cam. He had thought she was packing. He had not wanted her to know of his problems with Cam. The situation was distressing enough. He didn't want her to worry about what would inevitably occur when he and Cam met again.

Becoming impatient with his brooding silence, Iliani said, "You have not answered my question."

With an effort, Alaex pulled his mind away from the future conflict with Cam to the present one with Iliani. "Which question?" he asked, and when she frowned, he clarified, "You asked two. Why did I protect Cam and why was I smiling."

Iliani wanted to rub her temples to ease away the sudden ache. She always felt as if she were swimming upstream when she spoke to Alaex. Deciding that she didn't care why he smiled—in truth, she had forgotten she asked—she said, "The first."

"Because you were there," Alaex returned.

For some indefinable reason, the ache in Iliani's head moved to her stomach. The simple intensity with which he said the words made her nervous fear return more strongly than ever. Her heart began to speed, her tongue dried, and her hands began to moisten.

Normally she would ask what he meant by that, but instead she licked her lips and looked away from his intense gaze. He was an extremely complicated man. What had just happened? One minute they were talking and then the next . . . they were still talking, but it felt different.

Alaex, for his part, was having no difficulty. He recognized sexual tension, and although he, too, was a bit surprised at its sudden appearance, he did not want to see it die. At the moment he wanted nothing more than to take Iliani in his arms, as his mind replayed the image of her seated on the horse in front of him just before she'd touched his face and they'd kissed. He saw her in the outer yard, pulling him down for her kiss. He had been so shocked that he'd remained bent until Jon came over and asked if his back ailed him and whether he needed assistance to stand.

Alaex had been too befuddled to be embarrassed then, and embarrassment was far from what he was feeling now. He ached to hold her in his arms again. His eyes fell to the brush on the bed, and inspiration struck.

Gently, Alaex, gently, he warned himself. It would do little good if he were to scare her and she bolted.

"Where is Lucy?" he asked, as if only just noting the woman's absence.

"I sent her away," Iliani answered, confused at this abrupt change of conversation.

Alaex leaned over and casually picked up the brush from the bed. Not knowing how next to proceed and not wanting in ignorance to say something foolish, he decided on the direct approach.

"May I?" he asked, waving the brush toward her hair.

Iliani blushed, but saw no ulterior intent in his steady gaze. Perhaps from his limited experience, he did not know that a man brushing a woman's hair was an intimate, personal act.

Keeping his expression neutral, Alaex took advantage of her hesitation. Before Iliani knew what happened, she was seated on the floor before the fire with Alaex kneeling behind her, methodically and soothingly removing the tangles from her hair.

The strokes felt so good, so relaxing that Iliani absently sighed with pleasure. Alaex maintained his silence, gently nudging her head to the side for better access, and Iliani moved it willingly. Her eyes closed as she enjoyed the feeling of his hand following the brush through the thick black mass of her hair.

Suddenly Iliani's eyes flew open. That was not his

hand. Before she could protest, Alaex's lips found the sensitive spot behind her ears that she had not known existed and he murmured, "Both you and your hair smell pretty."

The words weren't flowery, but Iliani couldn't deny their sincerity. Despite that, though, she opened her mouth to ask him to stop. At that instant, she felt his tongue tickle the pulse in her neck. Her eyes closed again and instead of a demand that he cease, she heard a throaty whisper she couldn't recognize as her own voice say, "Thank you."

Alaex responded with a soft, seductive laugh. When his lips caressed her neck, all pretense at hair brushing stopped.

Iliani heard the solid thud of the brush as it hit the floor, and was quickly overwhelmed by the sensation of Alaex's arms closing around her. As she felt the heat of bare muscled chest against her back, Iliani wondered when he had had the chance to remove his chainse. Yet the pleasure swamping her at the contact made her quickly discard such musings. His lips on her neck and his hand on her br—

When she opened her eyes and looked down, the sight of Alaex's strong bronzed hands kneading her breasts arrested her breath. She was frozen. She looked around for her robe, not bothering to try to discern just when he had removed it.

Alaex shifted suddenly and Iliani found herself lying on her back. The fire burning in the hearth was nothing compared to the blaze in his eyes.

"Alaex," Iliani began shakily, more horrified than she had ever been in her life.

His name was enough. The fire was gone, but his passion, so violently aroused, died slower. Alaex closed his eyes, effectively hiding his expression from her. His nostrils flared as he fought for control.

Iliani watched his mute struggle with fascination, never realizing what a close thing it was. Alaex lost the battle just as she came to her senses and was about to use the moment as an opportunity to escape his overwhelming nearness. Without opening his eyes, he lowered his head and his lips unerringly found hers. Groaning inwardly, Iliani felt her will once again become his.

She had never felt anything like his kiss, had not known that such an element existed. His lips stirred both fire and ice within her, and when she realized that his tongue's insistent caress was a bid for entry into her mouth, Iliani thought she would die from the intensity of emotion.

With this kiss, though, Alaex made his first tactical mistake since entering the room. It was the very potency of it that brought back Iliani's anxiousness, then her denial, and finally her fear.

Iliani grabbed the sides of his face and began to push away while she thrashed her own head back and forth. Even lost as Alaex was in the tempest of his own emotional storm, he would have to have been dead not to know that it was renewed rejection and not passion stirring her movements.

Slowly he lifted his head. This time he looked down into her eyes and Iliani was able to see passion and confusion warring for dominance. The passion she tried to ignore, bowing to its recently learned power. The confusion she could understand. It was certainly a large part of what she herself felt.

Things had gotten out of control and she had no idea how. It was unthinkable to allow this madness to continue.

"We cannot do this, Alaex."

"Why not?"

Iliani bit her bottom lip as she tried to think of a way to make him understand. Things were moving too rapidly. She needed time. Iliani looked away, needing to be free from the enveloping heat of his gaze. Absently her fingers began to trace his scar while she searched for the right words.

No words were necessary. Without looking at him, Iliani could feel him growing cold. When she looked back at him, what her hands and body felt, her eyes confirmed. Alaex was coldly furious.

Leaving her lying on the floor, he silently and slowly got to his feet. When he looked at her, Iliani thought his eyes resembled chips of blue ice.

"Do not struggle to find gentle words, milady," Alaex bit out sarcastically.

His attack stunned her and Iliani was unable to hide her reaction to the accuracy of his words. "How did you—"

"Suffice it to say that this is a scene I have played before," he interrupted bitterly. "As I am sure you can find naught new to say, I will relieve you of the burden of trying." His hand started for his scar, and it seemed as if he exerted every fiber of his will so as not to complete the telling action.

Understanding dawned and Iliani surged to her feet. "You think my reaction is because of your scar?"

Alaex's eyes blazed, but he tightened his lips and said nothing.

Through the heat of his anger, Iliani thought she detected hurt. Aside from the fact that his assessment was not flattering to either of them—it painted her as shallow and him as lacking—it was untrue.

"Alaex," she began, touching his arm gently, overtaken by the inexplicable impulse to soothe away the hurt she knew he was feeling. "My feelings have nothing to do with your scar. 'Tis just that I have not yet adjusted to being your wife. This is all new." She shook her head in frustration. "I do not understand . . . so much," she finished lamely. She had been about to tell him that she still did not understand his part in their marriage, and that, even worse, until she did she could not trust him. Had he coerced her father into allowing the marriage? Edouard, who had raised her and been her father's lifelong friend, had said Aeric's wishes were otherwise. Where was truth in all this? Iliani needed to know that before she could allow herself to trust him, but how could she tell him that? Already his stance was threatening, and in confirmation of his rage, when he spoke his words were chilling.

"You do not understand what?" he asked with deceptive silkiness.

Iliani was no fool. She shut her mouth, hoping silence would calm the mounting tension. Although she was not one to lie—she hated dishonesty—she was ashamed to admit that she was tempted. Quickly she rejected the idea and it was not entirely due to her integrity. For some reason, Alaex seemed able to detect when she was not telling him everything. His rage now seemed so great that a lie would probably make him lose control. Silence was best.

Tense moments passed as he watched her with an unblinking, unnerving, hawklike stare. Iliani could barely stand it. She was about to break under the stress when he spoke.

"'Twould seem my honor is in question," he said with shocking accuracy in a voice so cold that to Iliani, it bordered on inhuman. "However, 'tis a small consequence. 'Twas not to you my word was given. Nevertheless, fulfillment of that word only goes so far and 'twould seem we have reached that limit. Believe this or not, as you will. Coming for you fulfilled my word. I will come no further. I vow to you that if there are any more advances to be made, 'twill be by you."

"I do not understand," Iliani said softly, surprised she could speak at all, so intimidated was she by the violence emanating from him in waves.

Alaex could feel his anger grow, and each word he bit out was clipped. "Plainly put, madam: if this marriage is ever to be consummated, you will come to me. 'Twill be your desire that brings such an act about. I will not come to you before then." The fire in his eyes rekindled, but this time it was not sparked by passion. "I neither want nor desire a fearful girl in my arms. 'Tis a woman I want beside me in my life and beneath me in my bed. A woman whose trembling is born of desire and joy, not fear and distrust. So—" With a vicious swipe he picked up his chainse from the floor. "Solve your mysteries without me. I have had enough. When you find your answers, let me know or not, as is your wont. I no longer care. Though it has never been my choice, futility is no stranger to me." His eyes seemed to bore through her. "I wish you well in the arms of its cold comfort."

Chapter

→ 10 ←

I gave the monies to the serf—this man, Milord Alaex,"
the man said, waving to the serf who stood beside him.
"He was to give it to my wife. I was distracted by other
duties and had no wish to keep such an amount on my
person. 'Twas only later when with my wife that I
discovered the money had not been delivered to her. The
man denies it and therefore, not wanting to take matters
upon myself, I brought him to you."

The freeman Deric ended his speech and waited
quietly. The serf whom he had accused stood meekly,
head bent, and saying nothing.

Iliani looked from one to the other and then to Alaex.
She was not the only one looking to him. Everyone
waited to see what he would do. This was a serious
matter, the most serious concern to need Alaex's judgment since they had returned to Fontwyn one month
ago.

The serf, Gaelin, had been accused of theft, an extremely serious crime. He could lose his hand, or worse,
his life. Yet the man had no proof. It was his word
against that of a freeman, a tenant. It did not look good

for him. Everyone knew that against any other above his station, a serf's word was worth far less than the patch of earth upon which he stood. How Alaex handled this would set an important precedent.

Looking again at Gaelin, Iliani was moved with pity. She couldn't condone stealing, but neither did she want to see the strapping man maimed or killed. For all his size, he was known to be kindhearted and soft-spoken. Still, stealing was stealing.

"I applaud your not taking matters upon yourself," Alaex said after staring at Deric for a long time. "That would have been most unwise. No one—" He seared everyone present—knights, tenants, and serfs—with his gaze. "—has the authority to act in my name unless I specifically grant that right. As I have not—" His eyes moved back to Deric. "—then you acted wisely, setting a fine example for others."

Deric stood taller and his chest expanded. Gaelin, Iliani noted, seemed to shrink in comparison.

"I knew you would be just—a man among men, that's what I tells my Gert," Deric said, pointing to his wife, a somewhat large woman with small black eyes and a knot of stringy black hair upon her head. For the first time since the proceedings began, the woman's face had lost its forbidding expression and she actually smiled, transforming her face almost to prettiness. When she felt her lord's eyes upon her, Gert giggled—a most startling sound from a woman of her proportions—and quickly hid behind a meaty hand the missing tooth such an act revealed.

Alaex turned his attention to Gaelin, who still stood silently. "Have you naught to say, man?"

Gaelin did not raise his head. "Nay, milord, except—"

"I am here!" Alaex interrupted sharply. "And when you speak to me, you look at me, not the dirt."

Slowly Gaelin raised his head and Iliani wondered how it was possible for a man to be looking straight ahead and still seem to be cowering. It seemed forever before the serf's eyes met Alaex's.

"That is better," Alaex said less sharply. "Save your staring at the dirt for when it is warranted, such as when you till the earth. You were about to tell me something?"

Gaelin swallowed. He almost dropped his eyes from Alaex's and seemed at the last moment to remember what he had been told.

"I have naught to say, milord, that I have not said before. True, I worked the land where he lives. But he did not give the money to me."

"Did anyone see this?"

Gaelin shook his head. He swallowed heavily again and Iliani wished that Alaex would just pronounce a speedy judgment. The man seemed tortured already. Deric, on the other hand, looked smug. He knew his word would be taken. That is, he knew that until Alaex turned to him.

"Was there anyone else to see what you claim you did?"

"Did, milord?" Deric stuttered. It clearly had not occurred to him that he would need to present a witness. "My wife—"

"Was not there, sir, as you yourself have already stated," Alaex said abruptly. "Good woman," he continued to Gert, leaving Deric alone for a moment. "Did you ask your husband for the monies or did he mention the funds to you?"

Gert flushed at suddenly being the center of everyone's attention. Nervously she smoothed her dirty apron and ran her hands over her gown, which didn't seem that much cleaner. She looked in confusion to her husband. Before that one could speak, Alaex warned, "I have asked the question, not he. You will answer me and look at me when doing so."

"Nay, milord—I mean I—you see, 'twas me."

Alaex's sigh was loud and Gert got hold of herself, realizing that she really hadn't answered her lord at all.

She squared her shoulders and said a bit loudly, "I asked him."

It was much like watching a tourney. One minute everyone watched Alaex; the next, they turned to see the person with whom he spoke. Now they all turned back to him. Most had puzzled looks on their faces and Iliani understood their confusion. What was taking Alaex so long? What did it matter if Deric asked his wife or if she asked him? The money and the sheep were gone. Deric admitted selling it and the man to whom he sold it agreed that the amount of money Deric said he had given Gaelin was the amount he paid for the sheep.

"We seem to have a problem here," Alaex said thoughtfully. "A crime has been committed, as monies are missing. However, we have no witnesses for one or the other." He seemed to hesitate as if giving his words great consideration. "Therefore, integrity must be the deciding factor. I know that for some, that would make the answer clear. I admit freely, it is not so for me. Someone lies," Alaex said with an edge to his voice.

His gaze focused again on Gaelin, and although the man still seemed to cringe he met Alaex's stare. "That to me is as unacceptable as thievery." Abruptly Alaex shifted his hard stare from Gaelin to Deric. "Justice must be swift. If a thief may lose the hand with which he stole, then 'tis fitting that a liar lose the tongue with which he lied. Do not believe that I think truth comes solely because of a man's station. Lying knows no station and is the great equalizer of men. All that is needed for it is imperfection and a tongue. And since these things all men possess . . ." Alaex let the words trail off.

Iliani was beginning to wonder what was happening, when she noticed something unusual. Gaelin seemed to be standing taller, more erect. His eyes shone and he did not tremble. Deric, on the other hand, seemed to be unraveling beneath Alaex's stare and words.

"Milord, I—I think I might—I have not lied," he said uneasily, "but I think I might be mistaken."

"Oh?" Alaex asked quietly. "About what might you be mistaken?"

"I—I may have lost the money. That's it! I recall now. I came across a friendly game of chance, and although 'twas my intent to give the serf the money to take to my wife, I lost it in a game."

Iliani was stunned. She looked to Alaex and wondered if he had known all along that Deric lied. Iliani did not stare at her husband long, for Deric was still speaking, except he babbled nearly incoherently.

"I did not wish to face my wife, milord."

"'Twas your preference to face me instead?" The question was dangerously soft.

Deric couldn't seem to find his tongue, or perhaps he feared that wagging it more would certainly cause him to lose it. Instead he lowered his eyes and Iliani was not surprised to see that he shook.

Shock and curiosity were on everyone's face. Shock at what had almost happened, and curiosity to see how the new lord would handle this new development. No one questioned his ability. After all, he seemed to be handling things well so far.

"Your confession, as it was," Alaex said sarcastically, "has saved your tongue. However, there is the other— that of the sheep and the monies from it. You cannot steal from yourself; therefore, there is no crime. Nevertheless, your wife might see it otherwise. Since your harm was to her and your family, I leave it to that good woman to exact your punishment. I am sure she can see to it that you are properly chastened. You are dismissed."

Iliani could not believe it. That was it? Deric's wife could punish him? What sort of justice was that?

Then when she glanced again to the sturdy-looking Gert, Iliani swallowed a chuckle, seeing the bend of Alaex's mind and questioning his "mercy."

There was a low buzz of conversation as Deric and Gert and the others finally left the hall. Iliani and Alaex were alone and she stared at him as confused now as she had been on the night they first arrived and he had thanked the servants. Bewildered or not, Iliani wanted to talk to him. They hadn't truly talked since that disastrous first night, and this seemed an excellent opportunity to rectify that. She wanted to tell him that she admired his insight and wisdom, but as she struggled to form the words, Alaex inclined his head and, without a word to her, left the hall.

Iliani stared after him, thinking over what she had seen and heard. It took her a while to notice that she was not alone as she had assumed.

A few servants were going about their tasks and they, too, spared a glance to the door where Alaex had left. But there was no confusion in their eyes. Their eyes shone with pride and loyalty. Wondering uncomfortably whether she had looked that way moments before, Iliani silently slipped upstairs to her room, unmindful that as she passed, the servants' eyes moved from the hall door to watch her progress up the stairs.

Days later, Iliani was no longer oblivious to the servants' stares, but as usual when she looked up from her needlework, everyone else seemed to be looking at— nay, absorbed in—something else. She should be accustomed to it, but she wasn't. Ever since that day when Alaex had sat in judgment—even before then, but especially after that—the servants stared at her as if she were a curiosity. Her *husband* had done much in the way of helping them to think that.

Blackguard! Iliani thought while viciously stabbing the needle through the cloth in her hand. Alaex had done exactly what he said he would. He went about as if naught were wrong in his world.

Actually, Iliani thought sullenly, laying in her lap the tunic she embroidered, there *was* naught wrong with his world. Hers was still reeling from the shock of his unexpected entrance and she was no closer to setting it aright than she had been when she first arrived at

Fontwyn. The only difference between then and now was the state of her nerves. Her nerves were beginning to fray under the relentless air of expectation that permeated the hall. It was as if everyone waited, from the soldiers at arms to Arthur and his family, to the hens in the roosts.

Iliani did not know how they knew, but the passionless state of their marriage—despite Alaex sleeping beside her every night since their return—was no secret. The knowledge was in their stares when she chanced to catch one. Knowledge, and veiled accusation. The underlying consensus seemed to place the blame at her feet. Of course, no one said anything, but a sightless person would have seen it. Their actions expressed it. All their sympathies were with Alaex. To their minds, Alaex was honoring her father's wishes; she was not. He was being patient; she was being difficult. Some of the servants remembered him and he them; Iliani recalled no one and nothing about the place.

Fontwyn had long been without a master, and Alaex, though hard, was fair. He had raised the serfs to a sense of equality. Not as far as stations in life were concerned, but in integrity. He had proven that in the case of Deric and Gaelin. And even Iliani had to admit that from that day forward, things had changed.

Fontwyn, although apparently well run before, now hummed with a dedicated vibrancy. Work was done more efficiently, and not just requested work. Chores that could have been postponed or were not needed at the time were done, and even had she not seen it in their eyes, Iliani knew that one and all were pledged to Alaex. All except her.

Is it any wonder they side with him? she thought, resuming her embroidery with another vicious jab at the unoffending cloth. Nay, it would be no great stretch of intellect to see why he had their loyalties and that they therefore watched for a change in her. She wanted to scream at them that one act of justice did not make someone perfect, but she held her tongue and pretended not to notice the accusation in their glances.

The strain was wearying, though, and Iliani bristled under a combination of her own sense of guilt and the indignation she felt that all assumed her to be at fault. It had to be assumption, for she knew Alaex would have said nothing to them. In truth, he was the only one behaving with a degree of normalcy, and although Iliani knew she was being irrational, and that she shouldn't be irritated by it, she was.

Despite what she had viewed of him with others, her part in his life was not so easily reconciled. It was common for a man to behave better toward his land and those who worked the land than toward his wife. Sometimes on a good day a wife's worth came somewhere beneath that of a good steed.

Distractedly Iliani jabbed again at the stitchery in her lap and flinched when the sharp needle pierced the tip of her forefinger. Wincing, she pulled her hand from the cloth to examine the damage, thinking it was no less than she deserved for her viperish thoughts. She had learned enough about Alaex to know that he did not think the way most men did.

An unexpected voice from behind her nearly caused her to drop the tunic. "Milady would perhaps like my mother to complete the stitchery?"

Iliani caught the material before it slid to the ground, pressed her thumb against the prick in her finger, and turned to face Lucy. She couldn't be sure, but it looked as if the woman was holding back a smile.

"That will not be necessary," Iliani said, a little more harshly than she intended. Immediately she regretted her tone. Although she knew Lucy and the other servants probably would not have believed it, she had never spoken to a servant so brusquely. Hadn't she recently admired Alaex because he was of a similar disposition?

Casting a quick look at Lucy, Iliani read the regret on the woman's face that she had said anything at all. In that moment, she again saw herself being compared to Alaex and once again found lacking.

She had no time to consider why that disturbed her.

Lucy bowed and turned to leave, and Iliani, driven to make amends or balance the woman's opinion of her—she couldn't tell which—said, "I am sorry, Lucy. That moment was not one of my best."

Lucy stiffened in surprise. When she swung back to face her mistress, her eyes were searching. Knowing that she could put a stop to it, Iliani did nothing and was rewarded with a tentative smile from the woman.

" 'Twas naught, milady."

It was Iliani's turn to smile. Lucy's hesitant warmth made her realize just how little of that quality there was in her life, and how desperately she missed it. She was loath to let it go.

"Do you share your mother's talent with needle and thread?"

"I do not think so, milady," Lucy said shyly, "but Papa says I do." She took a few steps back toward Iliani, openly studying her.

As had happened before, Iliani allowed Lucy's searching glance, understanding the reason behind the look. She hoped that the servant would recognize her sincere attempt to soothe her feelings. Iliani knew that no one here knew aught of her save she was the old lord's daughter and the new lord's wife.

With the turbulence of her life in the past month, Iliani had not cared, nor had she tried to change their perceptions. However, that one moment of tentative warmth from Lucy—perhaps in combination with her own depressing thoughts about her circumstance—made Iliani know that her entire existence did not have to be so sterile.

Thinking of her life in that particular way made her recall Alaex's words about life's futility and his leaving her to its cold comfort. Then, Iliani had not known how right he would prove to be, and now she wanted only to change what she could of her existence. The situation with Alaex was beyond her control. Her difficulty with Lucy and the other servants was not.

Forcing herself to keep a neutral expression despite

her increasing awkwardness, Iliani waited to see what Lucy would do next. True, she wanted warmth and acceptance, but those things could not be forced, only earned.

When Lucy's face broke into a smile, Iliani again returned it, delighted with this one small victory. She didn't even mind the remaining slight hesitation in the maid's voice.

"Mama said that was her best work," Lucy said, pointing to the tapestry behind Iliani.

Iliani looked over her shoulder to the tapestry of the great wedding. She studied it silently while Lucy continued. "Papa says Mama creates miracles with a needle and thread. He says there is naught she sees that she cannot recreate."

Although Iliani knew Lucy would misunderstand it, her only response was a noncommittal. "Oh." She was not irritated. It was just that her wedding or anything to do with it was not her best subject. She hoped Lucy would change the topic before what little progress she felt she'd made was wasted.

"I recall how nervous she was when Milord Alaex asked it be made . . ." Lucy's voice faded at the expression on Iliani's face. "What is it, milady?"

Iliani's eyes had fastened onto the maid's and her face had gone pale. "What did you say?" she asked in a strained voice.

"Milord Alaex asked it done," Lucy replied diffidently. "Milady, what—"

Lucy could have saved her effort. Iliani neither heard nor cared that the servant was still speaking to her. She was at the stairs when, without turning, she called back sharply, "Please ask my husband to come to me, Lucy."

Without breaking her stride, Iliani mounted the stairs, feeling nearly crippled beneath the weight of her fury. She gave no consideration to the bewildered servant she left behind. Her entire being was focused on what she had learned and what it meant. Yet another lie.

Lucy, for her part, watched her mistress's stiff back until it was gone from view. As Iliani had assumed, they *were* all expectant, and even without knowing the reason for her mistress's upset, Lucy knew that no one should yet expel his breath in relief. If the lady's words and posture were any indication, the wait for harmony between the lord and his wife was going to be a long one.

Alaex had received Iliani's summons, and although he could gauge his wife's mood from all that Lucy didn't say, he saw no need to stop his practice to answer it. Therefore, it was well past noon before he entered their bedchamber. He assumed that since she had made no appearance at the midday meal she was still closeted there. He was correct. Knowing that Iliani had heard him enter, Alaex said nothing, using the time to study her.

Iliani's back was blade straight and about as stiff. His wife held her hands clasped together in front of her and her gaze was fixed on something in the distance. She seemed completely absorbed in thought, holding herself rigidly in a quest for control.

Having made that assessment, he braced himself and asked, "You wished to see me?"

Iliani had not thought it possible for her anger to increase, but those few words were the fuse igniting her rage. Her hands gripped each other tighter and it was only the pain she caused herself that made her lessen her grip. The pain also provided a frail measure of control.

"What day is it?"

Nay, this is definitely not going to go well, Alaex thought to himself while frowning over her unexpected and icy response.

Iliani turned then and Alaex saw that ice was in her eyes as well. "You have forgotten, too?" she asked with frosty sweetness. "No wonder. We both have aged considerably since I made my request."

Putting aside his half-acknowledged hope that Iliani

had asked him there to set things aright between them, Alaex felt his heart sink. His disappointment was his fault. He should have known better.

So this was to be the way of it. So be it. He sighed. "Regardless of the time that has passed, I am here."

Those weren't the wisest words to use. Alaex watched in astonishment as her body lurched slightly as if it instinctively wanted to pounce upon him and attack. Her pulling back spoke of last-moment self-control. If he weren't angry himself, he would have found that amusing. However, his own dark thoughts and Iliani's expression let him know that there was little cause for amusement.

"You wanted something?" He rephrased his original query.

Iliani reclenched her hands. "Aye. I *want* something. I want the truth!" She took a deep breath to calm and fortify herself. "What I want is for everyone to stop lying to me. I think I have told you this before: 'tis with my life that these games are played."

Needing to calm his own rapidly blooming anger, Alaex hesitated to answer, and instead watched her as he leaned back against the door. Considering his rage, he was able to say with remarkable blandness, "I take it I am among the 'everyone' you wish to stop lying to you. Could we stretch it to say I am *all* of the everyone?"

His words and stance were carefully insouciant, masking his reaction to the issue that was most important to Iliani. She was about to lose control when something in his eyes made her pause. What his words and body concealed his eyes blared, and finally Iliani took note of his anger.

Her consideration lasted a second. "Aye," she said bluntly, then added coldly, "the 'great equalizer' that attacks all imperfect men who have tongues." She didn't try to hide her disgust, and most of it was self-directed as she recalled her naïveté. She had been impressed when he had said that.

Alaex studied the crown of the hilt of his sword with

undue fascination, noting the large crack that ran its width and irrelevantly thinking he should have had it repaired by now. To his wife he asked softly, "And what is it I have lied about?"

"You tell me!" Iliani shot back. "I do not know the quantity. Have they all been lies, Alaex? You said my father wanted us to wed. You showed me 'proof.' Upon my arrival here you showed me a tapestry that he had commissioned which was, I supposed, further proof of your claim. But I have learned that he did not commission it at all! You did!" Tears of anger and confusion coursed freely down her face. "Are you so lacking in honor as to lie over a dead man's bones to achieve your ends?"

Iliani gasped the instant the words left her lips, knowing she had gone too far. She regretted them but could not take them back now that they had been spoken and lay between them like an ugly wound. She had only wanted answers, which she was certain now, if the look on his face was any indication, she wasn't going to receive.

Alaex's face had whitened and even his eyes seemed to have paled apace with the darkening of the rage in his blood. He didn't need to speak to tell Iliani that no one, male or female, had ever spoken to him thus. Regret was insignificant and not an issue. True, the offender would have felt remorse, but the time remaining to them would not have been enough to express it. His head throbbed as he tried to gain control of his anger.

Iliani silently watched him. Never before had she been the object of such fury. Even knowing that he had li—misrepresented the facts, she amended to herself, she felt the need to assuage some of his anger, and that was before she heard the loud snap.

It was difficult to say whose gaze held more surprise, hers or his, as they both looked at his hand to see the snapped-off hilt of his sword in it and the blade now hanging irretrievably in the sheath.

Alaex seemed to recover first. He raised blazing eyes to

her, and before he spoke Iliani was apologizing. "I'm sorry. 'Tis only—"

"Enough!" he said, and while Iliani had been expecting a shout, this near murmur was more terrifying. Reflexively she took a protective step back. Alaex looked as if he wanted to grab her but knew it would be supremely imprudent. He looked disgusted with her, as if he could barely abide the sight of her.

Alaex took a step toward her and Iliani shrank back. Her recoiling from him reawakened his sanity. Seizing the tiny sliver of sense granted to him, he turned to leave.

Until the instant he turned his back on her, Iliani was unaware that she had held her breath. Yet just as she was about to expel it in a relieved "O," the door, which was upright one second, was lying flat on the floor in the next as the force with which he opened it released the hinges.

Alaex left without looking back to see what damage he had wrought, stepping over the door and disappearing from Iliani's disbelieving gaze. Iliani collapsed to the floor, certain she had never seen anything like that before and praying harder than she ever had for anything in her life that she never see such a thing again.

Iliani didn't know how long she sat on the floor. The hall grew dark and what few sounds she heard were muted as if they were made by accident.

Her eyes focused and her heart jumped in her throat as she heard footsteps approaching. Thinking it might be Alaex, Iliani thought to jump up before he saw her in such an ignoble position. Then she thought, let him come and see. She didn't care.

Iliani didn't look up when she heard the footsteps stop in the doorway, or rather the place where the door used to be. As the steps came closer, it registered briefly that it was a servant's shoe she saw, and that if she had any pride at all she would rise. Yet she did nothing. The feeling of apathy was too soothing, and Iliani was not about to pierce it for something as inconsequential as pride.

"Oh, lady," she heard a sympathetic voice she recognized as Arthur's say above her. Hands strengthened by days of long and hard work were unusually gentle as they lifted her to her feet and then laid her in her bed. Still Iliani did nothing but stare. She could do no more. When Arthur gently pulled the covers over her, she didn't acknowledge his kindness or actions by so much as a blink.

The silence was interrupted only as Arthur struggled to stand the door as best it could in its place to give her a measure of privacy. Looking sorrowfully back at her, Arthur thought he had never seen such a sad sight. If she were his daughter, he'd have taken her in his arms, but as she was not, that was unthinkable. It was on the far side of enough that he had taken her in his arms to put her in the bed. He could do naught else. There was no one else to assist her. After viewing the lord's rage, the servants feared going near her. Those who did not fear blamed her for their master's unhappiness. Either one or the other kept them from approaching her. Only Arthur dared to come to see how she fared.

He heard a small wounded sound. His lady's eyes were closed now but he knew she didn't sleep. The tears on her face told him that.

As Arthur squeezed through the small opening where the door could not come fully to its rest, he glanced back quickly to the lady lying still and silent except for the tears flowing down her cheeks.

Nay, he repeated to himself, she was not asleep. No one who was asleep cried like that.

Chapter

⇥ 11 ⇤

Alaex was ashamed. As he rode Bear fiercely through Fontwyn's forests he didn't know what fed his fevered pace—the height of his rage or the depth of his shame.

He had never lost control like that in his life. That he should do so against a woman and one who was his wife only doubled his disgrace. At least he had left before he had struck her, and even that had been a close thing. He could not understand the reason for his monumental rage.

Although a month had passed, he knew Iliani still rebelled against the idea of being his wife—his bride, he amended, remembering Iliani's distinction. Aye, she was no wife, and despite the fact that his vow to wait until she sought to make it otherwise now rang hollow in his ears, he had all intentions of keeping it. He would not touch her until she came to him. And according to his caustic calculations, based on today's lunacy, that should be four days after never. Why had he not just told her that Aeric had wanted the tapestry done, but having died before he could order it, he had had it done for him?

Alaex's thoughts came full circle, causing him again to

wonder why he'd reacted so violently. He should be capable of ignoring her words regardless of their insult. He had certainly been accused of worse and it had left him unaffected. Where then was the control—the only part of that myth of his reputation that was true—that he had honed to an impenetrable force? True, he had recognized that his skin had become steadily thinner since their arrival at Fontwyn. He had also conceded that he saw no relief for either himself or their situation. He had thought he was handling the situation well and that none of his irascibility with it showed. Now he was uncertain. Perhaps the anger he felt at her lying beside him unaffected night after night as if he were contemptible or, worse, a eunuch had not been pushed back as far as he had thought.

So where is the control? Alaex taunted himself with that question again. An ugly laugh came from his throat as his mind formed an unwilling answer. If he were but to look, once Iliani unclenched her dainty palm he would find the crumbled remains of his control there.

As illogical as his mind found that reply, his heart knew he couldn't fight it. Had not his self-control been cracking steadily beneath her softly delivered barbs alternated with those moments of unguarded, yet reluctant, admiration he had glimpsed in her eyes? Between moments such as those in his days and the barren torments of his nights, his wife was effectively lacerating his control.

He recalled with self-derision the first time he had seen a look of respect in her eyes. His reaction of hopeful disbelief had been totally irrational and he had castigated himself as a fool. Upon his next viewing of it, his reaction was different, although to his mind no less foolish. He would have grown wings on his back and flown with the falcons if he had thought that it would make that look come and stay in her eyes.

Alaex sighed, seeing their situation as greater than impossible. It was hopeless. Trying to focus on something else, he became aware of things around him, the darkness and density of the forest behind him and the blown state of his horse. The beast was lathered and snorted great gulps of air. He hadn't realized he had ridden so hard and for so long. Giving the command for Bear to halt and taking a moment to orient himself, Alaex accepted the fact that the ride back was going to be even longer. He couldn't push the horse any further. It was ready to drop, and if he killed his own horse he knew that his control would snap altogether. He was still on his own land, so the danger was minimal and he was in no great rush to return to the hall, his cool wife, and their colder bed.

Half an hour into his trek back, Alaex decided that Bear had cooled enough. He was about to mount the horse when a foreign sound at odds with commonplace night noises reached his ears. Instinct came alive warning him of the need to move cautiously. There was someone else there ahead of him. What suspicions Alaex had were confirmed when Bear began to prance in agitation, a sure sign that he scented someone unfamiliar.

Very aware of his own solitude, Alaex quieted the horse and again cursed the lack of control that had led him to this. He breathed with relief that Bear no longer snorted and gasped restlessly, because in the still of the night the sound surely would have carried. Reaching into the small satchel tied to his saddle, Alaex pulled out four lengths of soft cloth. Quickly he tied the cloths to Bear's hooves to muffle any sound the horse might make. Satisfied with that, he led the horse stealthily ahead, carefully watching the path as best as the dark allowed for twigs, branches, or dried leaves that would alert to his approach.

Alaex knew whoever was there had to be outlaws of some sort, because tenants and villeins would not be this far from the hall and protection. Ever since the Viking attacks and Alfred's instructions to fortify towns, the manors or halls had become the nucleus and no one dared to venture far. Seclusion made one too susceptible to Viking attack. Since tenants and villeins could be ruled out and Alaex knew he had not assigned any men to this area such that they would need to set camp, that left only outlaws.

Either these men were brazen in their courage or they were fools, he thought acidly, unable to believe the fire he saw glowing cheerily in their midst. It was either of the choices he'd just thought or they had assumed that no one would detect it so far from the hall. Normally no one would have been this far to see them and their fire. The forest was dense and vision extremely limited at night. Had he not had a fight with his wife, neither would he. At last, Alaex thought caustically, something good from that event.

As Alaex drew closer, he saw a few men sitting around the fire, and although the one on the far side seemed familiar, he could not make out enough of his features to identify him. The man appeared to be suffering from the dropping temperature, and he kept trying to get closer and closer to the flame. It would not take much more for him to be in the fire, burning like the wood it consumed. It was this that caused his companion to speak.

"Namin, go any further and the fire will feast on your backside." With the exception of the one called Namin, everyone chuckled at this dry statement.

Even from the distance Alaex could see that this man called Namin seemed more concerned about other things. His terse words confirmed Alaex's intuition.

"Were I you, I would worry less about my backside and more about your tongue, which will get us killed should it lead to our discovery."

The tart statement was ignored. "Nervous, Namin?"

Namin nodded. "Discovery would not be favorably seen by any—our leader or the master of these lands. Owing to either consequence, neither would I."

"Where did he— What was that?" asked the man who had teased Namin.

Four pairs of eyes scanned the surrounding area, sweeping over the place where Alaex stood among the trees. With his control once more firmly in place, Alaex knew he needed to stand perfectly still. They thought only that they heard something. Should he try to leave, the chances were greater that he would make a noise and they would be able to find him. Ordinarily that would not have disturbed him, but he finally remembered that his sword was useless, its hilt having been snapped. Those thoughts and the fact that the man Namin seemed familiar to him gave him pause.

Alaex had seen that man before; he was positive of it. When he stared back at the camp, his gaze focused solely on Namin as he tried to force himself to remember from where it was he knew him. He hoped the man would say something else, but even as they eased back, satisfied that they heard nothing save the ordinary, their faces were watchful.

Knowing they would say nothing further, Alaex decided to ride for the hall before they came upon him. Whether they would know him to be the master of the land he did not know, but he did not want to answer that question when he was defenseless.

Keeping his eyes on them and backing Bear away, he waited until he was several yards away before jumping on the horse's back to ride swiftly for home.

"Alaex, there is a party approaching." Jon had to repeat himself before Alaex responded.

"Party?" he asked distantly. It wasn't so much that Alaex didn't hear him, but Jon's stance was not one of alarm and Alaex's thoughts were still centered on his late-night discovery. It had been to no avail to ride with a few of his men back to the spot where he'd seen the outlaws. Either they were migratory and sheer chance had brought him to them or somehow, despite his and his men's stealth, they had heard their approach. In any case, they had left. Were it not for their hastily discarded campsite with a fire that still smoldered in spots, Alaex would have thought they had never been there.

"Aye," Jon said, disrupting his thoughts again. "Six to

ten riders. No swords drawn. They approach leisurely. We have not released the gates."

"Good," Alaex replied, giving the matter at hand his full attention. It was not wise to be put at ease by mere appearances or numbers great or small. Many who had underestimated one or the other were no longer there to tell of it.

"Where is my wife?"

For a moment Alaex couldn't believe his eyes as Jon, one of his fiercest warriors and whom Alaex had begun to think impervious to everything, flushed slightly. "She, uhm." Jon coughed uncomfortably. "She has not come down yet."

Alaex stared at him a moment longer, his surprise growing as Jon shifted slightly, clearly uncomfortable with the reference to Iliani. Alaex was aware that everyone knew of their argument. How could they not when the door still needed rehinging, and after scowling at all who dared come into his view, he had ridden off viciously? To his mind, though, that still was not enough to explain Jon's behavior. In fact, now that he thought about it, it had been unusually quiet this morn and he had seen less of the people than he ever had since his arrival. Reluctantly Alaex conceded that his continued scowling this morning—although for a different reason—probably had not eased his people.

Here again was a new situation for him. Usually no one was able to tell his thoughts regardless of their content.

Yet the knowing look in Jon's eyes brought him up short as he realized that the man was reading his every expression. *This has to stop!* Gathering himself, Alaex schooled his features and said to Jon, "When she leaves, have the door repaired. For the nonce let us see who comes."

Alaex had just given the order for the gates to be opened when the sound of hoofbeats was heard. Without pause the entourage clamored through the gates, and as they came to a stop, Alaex searched their faces to see if any were of the few he had glimpsed yestereve. There were none.

When the front riders parted, he found himself staring at a woman, and by discerning her identity two mysteries were solved. He knew where he had seen Namin before and who the leader of the men was. It was also no stretch of intellect to discern why the leader would not wish to be discovered.

"Lady Eadwina," he said by way of greeting.

The smile she gave him was totally out of proportion with what he would have expected to receive from Edouard's wife and Cam's mother. The quick thought that this was not a casual visit, which probably would not have occurred to him had he not chanced across her son's encampment, sharpened his gaze.

Eadwina did not miss that action, but in her usual birdlike way misinterpreted it. "You are put off that I did not come sooner," she stated with near comical matter-of-factness and a hint of regret. She left Alaex no opportunity to respond.

"I am so glad to know I was right. I should have come sooner. But really, you could have *asked* me to come, my boy. Then again, nay, you should not. Neither should you have hoped to see me. You are newly married and that takes time. What you and Iliani needed was time and I was right to give it. You may not think it, but even this visit may be too soon. However, I do not want you to be too hopeful. Therefore, I must tell you that I have no intention of staying any length of time—at least not yet. Another time is plenty enough, I say. Don't you agree?"

The blank look in Alaex's face was priceless. He was too stupefied to answer, much less take offense at Jon's sudden bout of coughing and the rest of the men's amused preoccupation with saddle cinches.

Again he realized he would not get the opportunity to respond even if he could think of something to say, as Eadwina turned to Jon.

"Young man, you truly ought not to be out and about with such a cough. I know not what causes it, but I know the morning air can't be good for it. Run along now and see to your rest. Albert won't care."

All expression wiped clear of Jon's face seconds before it changed to an apoplectic shade of red as he realized that she had called Alaex Albert. When he dared to cast a glance to Alaex's face, the expression on it was his undoing. Laughter welled up and in his fierce control of it, he began to cough again.

"See there!" Eadwina rejoined. "I told you." Turning back to Alaex, who hadn't moved since her tirade began, she called out, "You may assist me. Come, come, Albert. 'Tis clear as clear that your man won't go inside until you do. Come on," she prodded when Alaex did nothing but stare.

In a daze Alaex approached her, and setting his hands on her ample waist, he braced himself to take her weight. No sooner had Eadwina's feet hit the ground than her chatter began again.

"What's the matter with you, Albert?" she asked, a slight frown in her brows over Alaex's stunned expression.

"Pardon, milady," one of the men who rode with Eadwina interrupted before Alaex responded or Eadwina continued. "But I believe the Des—"

Abruptly he cut himself off, and the red in his face was not caused by restrained laughter. After a quick glance at Alaex's hard face, the man finished weakly, "His name is *Alaex*, milady."

Eadwina's bright green eyes shifted to Alaex. She didn't look embarrassed, only surprised.

"Alaex?" she asked dubiously. Not waiting for Alaex's curt nod, she went on. "Oh well, if that is what it is. No need to look so shocked. I have met you but once and names elude me from time to time. When you know me longer, you will understand. Everyone else does," she declared with a solemn nod of her dark head.

Alaex doubted he would understand anything of the sort, but he was saved from answering when Eadwina, still watching him intently, said, "You must be wondering at Edouard's absence. Well, I would lie to you and say he could not come, but I do not condone lying. So the truth must do." She sighed. "He would not come. He said he could not, at the least not yet." Unexpectedly Eadwina's face brightened. "I say, 'twould not have been a lie to say he could not, because 'twas what he said. I do feel better now. There! I have not lied and I have not offended. I have not, have I?"

Alaex opened his mouth when Eadwina asked, "Where is Iliani?"

This time he didn't even try to answer.

"Do not say to me she is still abed. You must think I did not rear her properly, but I did, upon my word—that is, if you take the word of a woman, and why should you not? I have just proved I do not lie. Oh! Where was I?" Her lips puckered, then she smiled as she remembered. "Aye, 'tis better than that I raised her. She just needs reminding. We all do. Aye, we do." Eadwina nodded and laughed. "Edouard says that to me all the time. I was hoping you would not have to say it to Iliani, but I guess you do. It must flow in the blood so to speak, because I am sure you know there is no blood between us."

Alaex's ears actually ached. He marveled at the fact that Iliani had escaped becoming like the chattering woman who, while still talking, had moved ahead. Never in his entire life had he seen anything like it. For the first time he felt sympathetic stirrings for Edouard and Cam.

Watching her, he didn't think she knew that he was not beside her. A shadow fell across his face and recognizing it as Jon's, Alaex did not turn.

Jon's voice was as dazed as Alaex's expression. "Have you—?" he asked, the remainder of the question fading into disbelief.

"Never," was Alaex's amazed response.

After a moment or two of staring, they both began walking slowly, following Eadwina to the hall. When Jon spoke again his voice still had not returned to normal.

"What think you of this?"

"Of her being here, or of her?"

Jon's head snapped in his direction, having been with Alaex long enough to understand what he meant by what he didn't say. "Surely you do not think she spies?" he queried disbelievingly.

Alaex shrugged. "Things are not always as they appear." He stared after Eadwina and winced when he saw she was still talking. "Although in this instance, I do not believe so. Since she carries no parchment to set down what she sees, and is not, as she told me, staying past today, where would she keep the information?"

It took Jon a moment to absorb what Alaex meant. He nodded his agreement and followed him to the hall's doors. However, just as Alaex preceded him in, Jon's eyes began to glint. With an act that conveyed their relationship clearer than any words, he clapped Alaex soundly on the back and murmured, "But as you say, things are not always as they appear . . . Albert."

Chapter

→12←

Alaex was in no mood to share Jon's misplaced humor, which only increased when Eadwina turned about and said, "See, he improves already. Be indoors, that's what I say." She looked around the hall admiringly and for an instant, with the exception of Jon's soft chuckles, there was blessed silence.

It did not endure.

"Iliani? Iliani, darling, where are you?"

Servants came running from different parts of the hall and one and all stopped abruptly to stare at the plump woman standing near the new lord, with her hands on her hips. Arthur was among those who came, and as he remembered Eadwina, he came forward.

"Lady Eadwina, may I assist you?"

Eadwina turned and her small mouth formed a pleased and silent "O." From her expression, one could almost expect that she was about to clap her hands in childlike happiness.

"Arthur! Is that you? Why, of course 'tis. Who else would you be?" She smiled. "It has been a while, has it not? Where is your mistress? Tell her I have come."

That the lady was exactly the way Arthur remembered her was evident in that her ramblings did not disconcert him. Yet when he looked over her shoulder to Alaex, who seemed to be caught between annoyance and disbelief, Arthur had to smother a smile as the new lord nodded a dazed permission for him to do as Eadwina requested.

"I will get her, milady," he said smoothly to Eadwina.

His assistance, however, was unnecessary. Iliani had not only heard Eadwina's call but had heard the approach of the riders earlier. She was slowly coming down the stairs, and when Eadwina saw her and held out her plump arms, something Iliani would never have suspected happened. In front of her husband, Jon, Arthur, and the few servants who had not yet returned to their duties, she burst into tears.

Eadwina rushed over to her and held her gently, while Alaex cleared the room with a glance, his expression grim. The only saving grace was that as usual, Eadwina misunderstood.

"Tsk, tsk, Iliani," she scolded softly. " 'Tis naught for tears. I, too, am happy to see you. Come now, cease. What will your husband think?"

That question had the desired effect, making Iliani remember where she was. Slowly she backed out of Eadwina's embrace, only to wish she could crawl back in when she saw the expression in Alaex's eyes. He burned her with that look for a full minute before exiting the hall, leaving her and Eadwina alone.

Hours later, Iliani waved a final good-bye to Eadwina as the woman and her guard rode off, then turned to go back into the hall. She felt calmer, and strangely, Eadwina's unexpected visit was the cause. The woman's mindless chatter had been familiar and soothing, and she was grateful for it. Another reason for Iliani's gratitude to Eadwina was that Alaex had yet to return to the hall, and she knew Eadwina's visit was the cause of that, too. That, and her shameful display of tears, which Eadwina had misunderstood and Alaex had not. Iliani suppressed a twinge of guilt. Alaex's absence gave her time to think.

Their situation was intolerable. Unlike her stubborn refusals before, Iliani was now prepared to accept a measure of the blame whether Alaex accepted his or not. However, blame was not the issue. She was no longer willing to accept her half life. After having waited so long for the chance to have a true family of her own and a real sense of belonging, this circumstance was acutely unbearable.

Sighing deeply, Iliani realized that if she were ever to have any inkling of contentment, let alone a chance at happiness, she would have to make the best of what was and stop pining for what might be. Although she could not see how, perhaps both Edouard and Alaex had been mistaken in her father's desires.

It is possible, she argued vehemently against the remnant of undying skepticism. *In any event, I am married to Alaex and back at Fontwyn. Argue with that!* she thought fiercely, tired of her endless doubt. Her doubts had solved nothing, aided nothing. They had served only to worsen the situation. Since there were no answers and even the questions were unclear, it was time to set the doubts aside.

Despite her fierce determination, Iliani was no fool. Words were just that, words. They did not make for deeds. Doing was always more difficult than mere saying, and with the way Alaex had looked at her before he left, she would indeed be a fool if she didn't recognize it was going to take a lot of doing just to begin mending their relationship.

Iliani mentally squared her shoulders. There was no more room for shrinking back, and by her doubts she had been doing just that. If her suspicions could have been proven, then she would not have had to proceed forward. At the time, proceeding forward with Alaex had been the last thing she had wanted.

A rueful smile crossed her face as she wondered whom she thought to fool with such feeble reasoning. "At the time"? There was a jest! Even in the present, proceeding forward with Alaex would not have been her first choice. A little of the light went out of her smile as she recognized that it was not her first choice, it was her *only* one.

That was a daunting realization and Iliani was nearly dragged under by the weight of her problems. As quickly as her confidence had come it fled, leaving her feeling inadequate to the task before her. She couldn't suppress the sudden feeling that not just her world, but the literal walls of the hall were pressing in on her.

Feeling as if she couldn't breathe, Iliani's only thought was to get away from Fontwyn for a while. She had thought that without Alaex's overwhelming presence she could think clearly, but she was wrong. Even without him there the place was too forbidding and, for her, too condemning.

Moments later, seated on the bay gelding that had been her mount and her pride and joy when she was at Lourds Keep, Iliani took her first free breath in what seemed like weeks. She had barely listened when Eadwina had prattled on about bringing her the horse, but here was an additional cause for gratitude to the woman. The horse was another thing familiar to her and she would be able to ride him without trepidation, leaving her to concentrate on other things—namely, her situation with Alaex.

Already lost in her thoughts, she paid little attention to anyone as she crossed the outer yard, never noting that one and all had stopped to look at her. The only person she noticed was Geoff the gatesman, standing before the iron bars that locked out intruders.

Iliani gave the man a wan smile. "Would you please release the gates for me?" What little smile she had fell from her face with his terse answer.

"Nay, milady."

It took Iliani a moment to comprehend that he was deliberately disobeying her. The thought was so inconceivable that she thought the man had not heard her.

Discarding that—Geoff's answer was negative, not irrelevant—she thought that there might be something wrong with the mechanism.

"Is there aught wrong with the locks?" she asked, already pulling on the reins to return the horse to the stable, certain of his answer. The horse had taken two complete paces when she registered what Geoff had said. Jerking on the reins, Iliani turned back to face Geoff, whose sandy brown hair and dark eyes seemed to darken apace with the reddening of his face.

"What did you say?"

"I, uh, I said, *ahem.*" He cleared his throat. "I said, nay, milady."

With a calm she didn't feel and a return of the sensation of being closed in although she was outdoors, Iliani walked the horse back to him. Her gaze was fiery.

"There is naught wrong with the gate and yet you refuse to open it for me. Why?"

"Because he does not wish to answer to me."

Iliani swung around at the unexpected and menacing sound of her husband's voice. Alaex stood not two yards behind her, his arms folded across his chest, causing his upper muscles to bulge and complete his aggressive demeanor. As he advanced the rest of the way upon them, he nodded curtly to Geoff and the man hastily took his leave. One acerbic glance at the men who were clearly eavesdropping like fishwives in the marketplace and they, too, saw the pressing need to be anyplace but where they were.

Despite the significance of what had just occurred, Iliani did not dismount. She refused to accept that she was a virtual prisoner, that she could not leave this stone fortress. Where she was going was unimportant. What mattered was that wherever it was, she wouldn't be allowed to go. With a combination of anger and frustration, she waited for Alaex to come alongside her, thinking it amazing that before his advent into her life, she had never thought herself to be a violent person. Before her knowledge of her marriage, she had barely raised her voice, let alone wanted to attack anyone. Since becoming aware of her marriage to Alaex, it seemed—particularly as far as her husband was concerned—a normal and familiar feeling to want to hurl herself at him and pound him with her fists.

When Alaex stopped beside her and looked up, Iliani forced herself to unclench her teeth and fists and say to him with heated sweetness, "I do not know why you prefer it thus—that it be you who opens the gates. I would have thought you had greater responsibilities to occupy your days. Alas," she went on with grating mockery, "since you apparently do not, who am I to deny you your little pleasures?" She patted the horse's sleek neck. "Wind Dancer and I shall wait until you have personally opened the gates. We are in no rush."

Alaex wanted to reach up and wipe away the blood he knew should be seeping between the links of his mail. His "sweet" wife was unerring as usual, and she knew how to draw first blood. There were times after talking with her when he felt he should let *her* practice with his men. Surely her ability to wound without weapon was something any warrior would need to know. Hoping his expression revealed nothing, he met Iliani's gaze steadily.

"Geoff only followed my orders," he said, ignoring her tirade.

"Are we perhaps under silent siege?" Iliani taunted.

Blow two, Alaex thought as his eyes narrowed with growing annoyance and the sharpness of her words. "Perhaps my last statement needs clarification," he bit out. "Geoff is not to open the gates."

"To me?"

"To you."

All of Iliani's feigned control evaporated and she exploded. "You cannot be serious!" she charged, the words bursting from her. "Are you telling me that I cannot leave here at all? And for how long is this bit of idiocy to continue?"

"Iliani," Alaex called in a near abstracted tone that,

even through her rage, put her on warning, "I am a patient man, would you not agree?"

Iliani snorted indelicately. "I do not see—"

"I do not press you unduly," Alaex went on as if she had not spoken or had given her assent to his query. "In fact, I leave you to yourself, exercising more patience than any man in this predicament can be expected to possess."

He paused and Iliani stared deeply into his eyes, and the dark threat she read there nearly made her wish to sink her heels in the gelding's sides and ride away in desperation. He looked wild and savage, and worse than that, he exuded unrelenting menace.

"Alaex, what goes on here?" Iliani asked, confused and deciding to be slightly conciliatory while despising the weakness generated in her voice because of what she had seen. "I wanted to clear my head, to think. I was merely going—"

"I know where you were going," he interrupted, and Iliani's confusion grew. Despite her attempt at reasonableness, Alaex seemed angrier than ever.

Iliani wanted to ask him where he thought she was going, but instinct stopped her. She was about to back away when Alaex reached up and grabbed Wind Dancer's reins.

"Did you enjoy your visit with Eadwina?"

Alaex was beginning to truly frighten her. The threat in his eyes intensified and his voice was becoming quieter, icier. In her mind, Iliani was seeing him as he had been just the night before and it made her curse herself for forgetting so quickly and provoking him so rashly. Her pride, however, came to her rescue and it helped to still some of the quaver in her voice.

"Alaex, what is wrong? Please. What is all this talk of patience and Eadwina's visit? And what in heaven's name does my riding beyond the hall's perimeter have to do with it?"

Incredibly his eyes hardened further. "I am not a fool, Iliani! You may have been able to twist Edouard around your delicate fingers, but it will not be so with me. Cease this pretense! For the first time in a moon, you wish to ride and ride beyond Fontwyn's walls. Eadwina comes but cannot stay and Cam is camped not twelve leagues from here! Where do you go to do your thinking, madam?" he spat. "In the arms of the man you loved? By the side of the man with whom you needed to set matters aright so it 'would not be thus' between you?"

Alaex's anger was a palpable thing that seemed to feed upon itself. At least now Iliani understood what fired it. However, understanding aside, she still feared his anger. Yet, most astonishing of all, underneath all those emotions she felt an easing of the tension within her chest. Eadwina had come and Cam was there. The knowledge made everything seem less foreign or insurmountable.

Despite knowing Eadwina's flightiness and Cam's selfishness as well as she did, Iliani still cared for them. She viewed their shortcomings as imperfections and she accepted them. They had always been there for her. It seemed they still were. Some of her loneliness eased, and she could only be happy about that.

The inner calmness she felt spread to her features, and Iliani was oblivious to how her reaction was affecting Alaex. He did not leave her in ignorance for long, as her serene expression made his anger slip its tether.

"I see I had it right," he snarled. "You asked how long and I tell you that the beast beneath you will grow wings and fly before you are allowed to leave this place without me. You have experience with how I feel about keeping my word. I tell you now, on this you have it."

Chapter

➤ 13 ◆

Fool! Alaex thought as he walked away angrily. Had he learned naught from last night's shameful debacle?

Obviously not, Alaex thought with unrelenting self-derision. Within the span of mere hours, he again had allowed Iliani to provoke him into behaving like a raving idiot. Why hadn't he just explained the situation? And why in the name of all that's holy had he not simply let the subject die when she said she'd only wanted to ride?

Nay, not he! Alaex berated himself acerbically. He had had to carry lunacy to new boundaries. It had been like a sickness, both nauseating and uncontrollable. Not only was he losing control, he was losing everything else, including his mind.

"Alaex?"

Although he wanted to ignore the summons, Alaex halted, relieved that it was not Iliani who called to him. He stood tensely, waiting impatiently for Jon to draw near.

When the burly man stood beside him and for long moments said nothing, Alaex, keeping his gaze straight ahead, asked sharply, "Aye?"

It took no great mental strength for Jon to see that Alaex was not in the best of moods, and thus he hesitated before speaking. He wanted to speak gently and not cause Alaex further irritation.

While Alaex waited for Jon to speak, he saw movement from the corner of his eye. Despite his determination, his eyes were drawn to watch Iliani walk her horse back into the stable. When he looked back to Jon and saw that the man had not missed what he had done, Alaex's jaw hardened and his remaining patience came to an abrupt end.

"What is it?" he growled. Normally he never used such a tone with any of his men, especially Jon, and certainly not when the man had not spoken, let alone acted, but Alaex recognized that his behavior was far from normal.

Jon looked into the blue fire of Alaex's gaze and then nervously cleared his throat. For the first time since he had known him, Jon was unsettled in Alaex's presence.

"Practice, Alaex," he finally managed, noting where Alaex's stare had once again shifted. Angry pale blue eyes fixed on him, this time making Jon take a step back.

"Do I have the look of a man who needs to hold a sword in his hand?"

Before this Jon had never thought himself a coward, but the promise of barely suppressed violence in Alaex's eyes made him pause. He chose his words carefully. "Nay. If it were any other than you, I would not waste breath on the subject. Yet you have left it to my charge to ensure that all—even you," he added quickly, "do the required hours of drill. 'Tis only your rule I follow. You have said that a battle does not allow for one's personal state and that a good warrior uses even that to his advantage."

The fire in Alaex's eyes brightened. "I know what I have said," he returned, feeling more the fool than ever when he caught the bend of Jon's thoughts. Belatedly he remembered that all had seen him talk—if one could call it such—with his wife. Now he was going off when he should have been practicing. His men were not stupid. They would have known the reason he did not participate, the same as they knew that he would not have allowed it in them.

Jon was right. Any other man would not be given the warning. Had Jon left him alone, Alaex would have done more than feel as if he had lost yet another argument with his wife; he also would have lost the respect of his men. No leader worth his blade asked something of others he himself was unwilling to do.

Taking several deep breaths, Alaex forced his anger to lessen in slow degrees. He still felt it beating vibrantly within his chest, but now he was controlling it rather than letting it control him. He even managed a weak smile for Jon.

"My thanks, Jon," he said softly and sincerely. "As always, you are the wind at my back."

Jon's face flushing slightly at the unexpected praise helped Alaex to control his anger further. " 'Tis nothing, Alaex," Jon responded gruffly.

"Naught, you say?" Alaex grinned. "Let us see how you feel about your diligence and my gratitude after drills. For your perseverance and competence, you have earned the distinction of being my sparring partner."

Alaex laughed, forgetting his anger completely when he saw the slightly apprehensive look that crossed Jon's face. "I see you regret your tenacity for duty already. Come," he added with another chuckle. "I can assure you that both the day and that feeling are young."

When Iliani dragged herself downstairs for the evening meal, she was met with the hearty laughter and general goodwill of those already seated at Alaex's table. The meal had yet to start. There was nothing unusual in this, for neither Alaex nor Jon had come in.

Iliani had been seated for some time and was beginning to feel a touch of apprehension when neither man appeared. She was just wondering if she should order the meal to begin when the hall's door opened. Iliani was aware of slight yet surprising disappointment when she recognized Jon's huge form in the door. However, neither her disappointment nor her reaction to it had the opportunity to take root, because following close behind Jon was Alaex himself, and he was smiling.

Considering the murderous expression he had worn the last time she had seen him, Iliani had trouble believing what she saw. Earlier his face had been scorched with anger. Now as she surreptitiously studied it as Alaex moved closer, it looked if not happy, then relaxed.

That expression lasted until his eyes met hers. Alaex's smile vanished and his eyes became shuttered. Iliani watched as Jon looked from Alaex to her and back, and then whispered something to Alaex. Whatever he said made Alaex laugh, bringing them to the notice of everyone at the table.

The men looked toward them, and when their gazes rested on Jon in particular, they began to laugh too, although Iliani was positive they couldn't have heard what he said. Thibert, a lean young archer with a crop of black curly hair, hazel eyes, and a square fierce face that was miraculously transformed by his smile, called to Jon.

"The table has never seemed farther, eh, Jon?"

Renewed laughter erupted and again Iliani was puzzled at its source. She saw nothing funny in what Thibert had said. Yet it was clear she was the only person who did not.

"If 'twould not offend Alaex and his lady, perhaps you would prefer to take your meal on the floor with the hounds," yelled another warrior whom Iliani had heard called Ethelward. "This way when you pass out, you haven't far to fall."

This time Iliani did not concentrate on their words. Instead she looked at Jon and noted that although he advanced steadily, he did seem to be moving a bit slower than usual. As Iliani continued to stare, she could see that instead of his ground-eating strides, he seemed to be practically mincing along. Not only were his steps short, they were stiff.

Iliani was immediately curious. The good-natured teasing Jon was receiving had no hint of cruelty in it. On the contrary, every barb seemed to underscore the men's respect and fondness.

Recognizing the lowering emotion of jealousy, Iliani firmly put any self-pitying comparisons from her mind. Instead of allowing the merriment around her to highlight the starkness of her own life, she resolutely decided to enjoy it as best as she was able. That resolution came to an abrupt end in the next few moments.

One of Alfred's men had arrived earlier that afternoon with a missive from the king, and as an urgent response was not requested, Alaex had asked the man to stay. He had seemed fascinated with Fontwyn and all that went on there. Knowing that the report to the king would contain what the man saw as much as what was said, Alaex had given him a loose restraint. However, he had not intended that lax restraint to encompass nearly three skins of wine, which unfortunately turned the man Ethan's exuberance into carelessness.

Ethan was new to Alfred's service and he was young— a fact that was belied by the premature bald spot atop his head. From his overindulgence, that same bald spot was now nearly as red as his nose and he was caught up as much in his cups as the revelry around him. Heedlessly he bellowed, "'Twill be a long while before you again practice with milord, eh, Jon?"

Now the men's laughter was not quite so hearty. It was one thing for them to tease one of their own, but this person, Alfred's man or not, would not be encouraged to do it.

Blissfully unaware of their reactions, Ethan burbled on. "Especially after he's had words with his lady and no sweet actions to lessen his anger to it!"

The silence in the room was painfully intense. It seemed that all actions, even that of breathing, halted.

Through mortified eyes, Iliani watched Jon stiffen even more, and she was certain it was due to rage and not soreness. Alaex froze, his face whitening in fury, and the men had looks on their faces that said they both regretted what they had started, which had led to this, and that it would be their fondest wish to drive a dull blade through Ethan's heart.

It was not the cessation of merriment but the unremitting animosity, for even the servants stared at him with repugnance, which sobered Ethan hurriedly. Too late he realized what he had said and his face paled, and his eyes, after a quick glance at Alaex, sought Iliani's. Although the insult was as much to her as to the lord of Fontwyn, it was to her he made his appeal. Ethan's mind, rapidly clearing from the fog of too much drink, recognized that Iliani would be the only one from whom he could hope to get sympathy.

Iliani did not miss the pleading in the messenger's watery brown eyes, but she was in shock. No one ever mentioned her and Alaex's situation aloud. It was kindly ignored, as one would notice yet ignore the deformity of another. Obviously there was talk, and Ethan had learned of it. But it was starkly clear that he had *not* learned that he should not speak of it.

Feeling closer to his final resting place than he ever wished, Ethan took Iliani's silence for refusal to aid him. He stumbled through an apology in the hopes of appeasing her.

"Milady, I am sorry . . . in error, grievously ashamed . . ." He finally halted, hanging his head in shame, not knowing how to continue.

The oppressive air in the hall was stifling, especially on the heels of the previous laughter and warmth. For that, and as much for the terror she had glimpsed in Ethan's eyes, Iliani subdued the urge to run and hide, which she knew would provide the death knell to any further happy activity and quite possibly to Ethan as well. The atmosphere was so thick she doubted that it would be lightened even if she stayed, but for some reason she felt as if she were to blame for the damage. Ethan had only spoken aloud what everyone knew. He should not be punished for that.

Focusing again on the balding head of the man who was too ashamed to face her, Iliani said dryly, "No need for apology, Ethan." When he looked up at her gratefully, she managed a weak smile. "No offense was taken, and as I am sure you ill like the taste of sole of leather, why not try putting something else in your mouth, like Cook's wonderful venison?" Her comment had enough sting that he should be warned about such folly in the future, and enough kindness to remove the lasting effect of the sting.

Iliani did not know it, but in that instance her esteem mounted in the eyes of more than one of Alaex's men. They knew what she attempted, because Alaex could not seek reprisal against Alfred's man and the man was new to his post. They might be angry, but they knew he had meant no harm. 'Twas just the bad combination of too much inexperience, too much wine, and too little brain. He need not die for it, especially if Alaex would suffer for it. Deciding to aid Iliani in her cause, one or two of them even laughed at her jest, although the sound was weak and hollow.

Alaex, too, recognized what his wife had done and applauded it despite the fact that he was not, as he knew she hoped, going to let the matter die.

"Ethan," he called, using the soft, dangerous tone Iliani had come to fear. "As my wife suggests, venison is always better than leather for putting in one's mouth, but a poor substitute when one must put one's foot to the road—rapidly. Agreed?"

Ethan paled more. "Absolutely, milord. In truth," he stammered on, "I believe I shall forgo its taste to apply my feet immediately."

Without waiting for anything further, he ran from the hall and into the night, leaving Iliani to wonder if he'd stop long enough to saddle his horse. His rapid departure did nothing to lessen the tension. If anything it seemed to increase.

The silence was so complete it seemed to listen, practically begging for someone to break it and thus end its agony. It was mercifully broken by Jon's dry comment.

"With such cheery faces to entice me, is it any wonder that you compete with the hounds for my presence? They are," he said with a large smile, looking around at the men's morose faces, "warmer and friendlier than this group, when the smell is ignored."

"Theirs?" Thibert offered halfheartedly.

"Nay, mine," Jon returned, and was rewarded with rich laughter that covered his equally loud groan as he eased himself into his seat.

Late that night Iliani stared through the arched windows into the impenetrable darkness of the woods beyond Fontwyn. It wasn't the slight chill in the night air that pushed sleep away. Sleep was the last thing on her mind as she waited and tried to convince herself that what was happening was not.

Surely he was coming.

He had come every night before and he had seemed restored to good humor after Ethan's departure. Yet despite her desperate reasoning, as hour chased hour, Iliani knew it was not going to occur.

Determined to ignore the growing truth, Iliani decided to wait awhile longer. She didn't know why she cared, why it was so important that he not stay away. Perhaps it was Ethan's thoughtless words exposing the wretchedness of their relationship. Maybe it was only pride that made her want him there. Maybe she didn't want everyone to think that she was so intolerable that he could no longer bear to sleep beside her. Whatever it was, she was not going to admit that he wasn't coming. He was only detained.

By the time dawn had appeared over the tips of the trees, Iliani finally admitted defeat. For the first time since her return to Fontwyn she had slept—in a manner of speaking—alone. Her disappointment far surpassed the momentary twinge she had felt when he had been delayed at the evening meal, and finally she conceded what she had denied all night. Alaex was not coming.

Chapter

⇥ 14 ⇤

No one with the exception of Lucy, who brought her meals, saw Iliani the next day. Everyone speculated as to the cause. Some projected that despite her witty comeback to Ethan she was too embarrassed by the truth of what he had said to be seen. Others thought, especially after viewing a portion of her and Alaex's furious words earlier and then noting that Alaex did not go to their room, that she hid for that reason. Neither assumption was true. In simple fact, Iliani was asleep.

After waiting all night for Alaex to come, she had spent an additional exhausting hour thinking. That one hour had been more emotionally tearing than all the hours she had spent at Fontwyn Hall.

It would have been too simple to say that what had transpired at the evening meal was the cause. Certainly that incident had not helped, but it was not fully to blame for the unrest of her thoughts and her heart. Iliani had come to the conclusion that those disturbing situations stemmed from her indecision. Indecision, she had concluded, was not only debilitating, it was also painful.

In its own way it was more painful than having made the wrong decision.

Even before the embarrassing scene at supper, she had accepted that she could not continue to exist as she had been with Alaex. And that was what it was—existing. Iliani refused to think of it as living. Living is what people did when they enjoyed some measure of their lives. She enjoyed nothing, and as difficult as it was for her to face, Iliani had wondered if perhaps this sterile existence was of her own doing. True, Alaex was not very approachable, but she had not given him the impression she wanted to be near him.

With acceptance of that, it was easier for her to see that she had the means if not to enhance her life, then to improve it. She had had dreams and goals of her own, one being her desire to have a family. That was still possible if Alaex didn't continue to stay away.

As her thoughts had focused again on Alaex, her inner turmoil had grown, and she had consoled herself with the thought that he couldn't be all bad. He couldn't be and have men, good men, follow him. Iliani was not blind. She recognized the character of Jon, Thibert, and the others. This was without including Alfred's unrestrained praiseworthy opinion. Surely that meant that Alaex was worth considering in an alternative light.

Then there was his activity around Fontwyn. Iliani might not have grown up there, but even she could see that the property and the people prospered under his care. Thinking on it, she had had to concede that it was not the first evidence she had seen of Alaex's benefit.

All those years while no lord had been present, Fontwyn had not gone to ruin. There had actually been something there worth returning to. Certainly his efforts in that regard could not be minimized.

In that agonizing hour before Iliani had permitted herself to seek her rest, she had mercilessly admonished herself to base her opinions on what she saw, not on what she did not see. Using the evidence that was there and not the shadowed conclusions of unanswerable questions, it had been easy to see her mistakes. Bravely she had not shrunk back from her wrong, even asking herself how she would feel if Alaex had judged her not on what she was or even what she lacked, but what he *thought* she lacked. Disliking the answer to that, Iliani had forced herself to accept that that was what she had done.

Once that painful admission was behind her, the task before her seemed only difficult—not impossible. An embarrassed laugh had come to her lips as she tried to imagine Alaex's face when she came to him. He had said that that was what it was going to take, and that was what was going to happen.

It was time for her to make her happiness instead of waiting for it. More than anything else she wanted a child, and while not an expert on the matter, she knew that sleeping apart from her husband was not the way to accomplish it.

In all, it had been an exhausting night and a more exhausting self-inspection. She felt as if her life, which had seemed strangely off course since she discovered her marriage, could now move forward positively. She felt in control to a degree, and recognized that the feeling of not being in control had played a large part in her unhappiness. A soft smile had crossed her face as she acknowledged that control even in one's own life could not be given. It had to be seized.

She was taking control of her life, and to her mind the ride ahead could be no less harrowing than the one behind.

When Iliani finally emerged from her room, it was night. The hall was quiet and dark except for a few torches. Although she felt she knew her way around Fontwyn well enough, she was grateful for the light. She was also grateful to Lucy for bringing her meals. The nervous clenching in the pit of her stomach at what she was about to do would have been unbearable otherwise.

As Iliani moved quietly down the hall to the door of

the room where Alaex was sleeping, she again murmured a quiet "Thank you" to Lucy. When the maid had casually apologized for the delay in bringing her meal because she had an extra room at the far end of the corridor to tidy, Iliani had only nodded. It occurred to her after a moment that Lucy might be trying to tell her something, but as she was unsure whether it was a hint, a warning, or an accusation, Iliani had stood silently waiting.

Staring in unwarranted concentration at the rushes on the floor, Lucy had mumbled, "I offer no excuse, milady. Milord Alaex is an uncommon tidy man. 'Tis only that it was an extra chore." She had looked at Iliani anxiously before darting her eyes elsewhere. "I wanted to explain."

"I understand," Iliani had said softly, then softer still when the woman turned to leave, "Lucy?"

"Milady?" Lucy asked turning back.

"Thank you."

Lucy's smile had been as heartwarming as it was wide, but she had said nothing else, leaving the room quietly. Iliani did not waste time wondering why Lucy had told her what she had, for it did not matter. Whatever the reason, she was grateful to know of Alaex's whereabouts without the embarrassment of asking.

Making her way down the hall, Iliani pushed any remaining negative thoughts and lingering doubts from her mind. Now was not the time for it. All her thoughts had to be on what she wanted to accomplish.

As Iliani opened the door quietly, she released a pent-up breath in relief that it did not squeak, and looked around nervously. With the exception of the fire glowing in the hearth, the room was dark, and Iliani took a moment to acquaint herself with her surroundings. Although she intended to throw herself at her husband, her goal was to be in his arms, not land at his feet in an undignified heap. Her eyes adjusted quickly and made out the blurred outlines of two chairs, a large wooden table, and a stand, which looked to hold a washbasin and cloth. The only other thing of note was the bed.

Once Iliani looked at it, she could not look away. Alaex was sleeping there. She could see his form as he rested above the covers despite the coolness of the night. Grateful for the dark that concealed her reaction, Iliani saw that he was naked. Swallowing heavily and gathering her courage, she moved over to the bed, unaware that Alaex had awakened the instant she had pushed the door open.

He knew immediately who it was and he had relaxed, curious as to what her intentions were. Like the others, he had not seen her since the evening prior. Unlike the others, he had not been able to casually put her from his mind and attend his duties. Throughout the day his thoughts had returned to her. He had known of her embarrassment last evening. For that alone he had wanted to skewer Ethan, or at least the man's thoughtless tongue. As the rest of his men, he too, had been pleased by her response. Yet last night he had been unable to go to their room. Whether it was masculine pride that sent him to seek his rest elsewhere, Alaex did not know. He knew only that if all thought he was not a man in his own bed it could look no worse if he chose to make that bed elsewhere.

Now, as he strained to listen for the soft footsteps that brought her closer to him, Alaex's heart began to beat heavily. Fleetingly considering Iliani's unexpected volatile temper, he wondered if she had come to try to do harm to him, but he quickly discarded that thought. That left only one other. She was coming to him as he had stipulated she should if she wanted the marriage consummated. With greater willpower than Alaex knew he possessed, he quelled the fierce desire to jump up and shout with elation, and instead lay still while Iliani advanced the remainder of the way and looked down on him. He thought it was a wonder she couldn't hear his heart beating, so hard was it pumping.

But Iliani could hear nothing over the beat of her own heart. For a moment or two as she looked down on him she had to hold her breath because it was coming so harsh and fast. She didn't want to disturb him just yet. Taking slow, controlled, silent breaths, she strove to find calm. Overwhelmed at the sight of the male beauty before her, her hand reached out of its own volition. Her fingers shook with greater force the closer they came to the warmth of his muscled skin, and suddenly she jerked her hand back.

It wasn't lack of desire. It had finally occurred to her the folly of unexpectedly touching a warrior when he slept. The consequences might not be pleasant.

Alaex, however, who had been watching her through slitted eyelids, had no idea why she drew back. As finely attuned to her as he was, he had nearly felt her hands' descent. His skin had tingled with anticipation, already experiencing the feathery touch of her soft hands. Then she had drawn back and again it took great effort of will on his part not to groan in disappointment. With his nerves screaming, he waited silently to see what she would do next.

Iliani crossed over to the opposite side of the bed, deciding that if he awoke abruptly, he would be less inclined to become violent should he find her lying before him. Her head had barely pressed the pillow when Alaex swept her into his arms and kissed her fiercely.

At first Iliani thought he was dreaming. As his kiss grew hotter, she amended that thought. Perhaps it was she who dreamed, for it seemed that only in the realm of dreams could anything feel this marvelous. Alaex's lips tutored her. They demanded and gave. His hands on her body felt more like a natural extension of herself than an external force.

In mere moments, he brought Iliani to a fevered desire that so burned her brain and seared her senses that even recalling her own name was beyond her. Her motions, which at first had a slow sensuality as she began the wonderful initiation into passion, were now frantic—much like his.

Iliani proved to be an apt pupil. Soon she was returning Alaex's kisses with an innocent passion that fed his as she couldn't hide, and he didn't miss, the hope that nurtured it. Alaex's rough gentleness made her wonder why she had hesitated so long to seek him out. He had banished all her fear. She wasn't afraid of giving or of his seeming relentless desire to take. The more he took, the more she had to give. Yet instead of feeling emptied, Iliani felt an unsurpassed fullness. It was as if in the taking he gave more than he received.

Her eyes filled with tears as for the first time Iliani glimpsed the true meaning of belonging. It was a wondrous feeling she never wanted to end. It taunted her. It beckoned. She wanted it fulfilled in a way she had never wanted anything in her life. For that feeling alone, she was prepared to give herself to him unreservedly. Such wondrous emotion deserved expression and Iliani experienced the unquenchable need to speak to him. His silent giving was a gift behind which she could hide no longer. However, just as she opened her mouth to tell him what she felt, Alaex's lips found the breast his hand had been caressing, and all coherent thought vanished. In the time it took for him to move from one breast to the other, her words returned, only to flee again beneath his loving assault.

Her hands found the back of his head and without realizing it, Iliani groaned, "Oh, Alaex."

Alaex heard his name, and it was not just her call that raised his head, it was what he heard in it. He was startled to see the sparkle of tears in her eyes.

"Aye, Iliani?"

Once more Iliani's thoughts deserted her as her eyes connected with the tenderness in his. With a gentle and soft finger, she ran her hands over his face, stopping just short of his scar, recalling what had happened the last time she had touched it.

There was a muted chuckle from deep in his chest, and as if he read her thoughts, he grabbed her hand and moved it across the wound. "'Tis naught but dead flesh now. No longer does it hurt me," he whispered, turning to kiss her palm.

Iliani's throat worked. "I know that, but I know, too, that it still has the power to bring you pain."

Alaex's eyes fired and he froze momentarily before giving her an unhurried nod while studying her face and saying slowly, "But never again, I think, from you." Not giving her the chance to answer, he lowered his head and kissed her deeply.

Iliani did not have much experience with kisses, but she would have wagered all she owned that this one was the tenderest any woman had ever received. Again the magic began, but this time its elements were keener, its penetration deeper. In a frenzy of movement, Alaex removed her chamber robe and what his hands had merely touched before his eyes now drank in. Iliani had not known there was as much hunger in the world as she saw in his eyes. She closed her own against the poignancy of it. It was too much. There was no shame in what he made her feel, and no trace of doubt.

"Please, Alaex," she murmured. "Make me your wife in truth."

Alaex needed no further encouragement. Unhesitatingly he rolled atop her and Iliani gasped at the feel of his manhood pressing against her. Again she heard Alaex give the warm and sensuous chuckle that raced through her blood like the smoothest wine.

"There is naught to fear from him," he said and smiled down at Iliani. "He is a little overzealous in his pursuits at times, but he, like all other parts of me, will never harm you."

His banter, unexpected as it was at a time like this, calmed her as Iliani was certain it was meant to do. "I know," she murmured again.

Alaex's smile widened, making Iliani wonder why she had ever thought he didn't know how. "Becoming the much-venerated wise woman, eh?"

Iliani looked away from the brilliance in his eyes and smile. "There is much I do not know, but I have learned much of you. You have been most generous in that respect. I have not. You know little of me."

Wondering at the soberness in her tone, Alaex's first instinct was to ignore it and complete the promise of what they had started. Yet despite his fervent desires, he found he could not.

"What is it you want me to know?" he asked softly, sensing she wanted to tell him something.

The look in Iliani's eyes when she looked back at his was worth the pain of delayed passion.

"I want you to know that I have honor, too. I would never have gone to Cam as you suggested. I would never dishonor you, the memory of my father, or myself in such a way."

Alaex's eyes reflected silent approval and Iliani found the courage to continue. "I have done much thinking, Alaex. I do not know where this marriage will lead. I do not know from what source it has sprung, nor can I guarantee a perfect resolve to these questions. However, I do know beyond a doubt that I want a family. I want a real home. If, as I think, you do also, then we may as well proceed together."

For a moment Alaex looked down at her, cursing himself for not stopping her as his instincts had warned, and marveling that even her gentle words had the ability to wound gravely. Despite the mildness of her tone, her words managed not only to kill every ounce of his passion, but murder his heart as well. It stung his pride unbelievably that she saw him as naught else but a means to attaining a child. As a person, he mattered little. She was willing to make do.

While reeling beneath that enormity, he tried to find acceptable reasons why he should care. He was too angered to discern one. At least, not one he was willing to admit. His *wife,* with her gentle words, had singed his pride enough. There was no way he would admit that his desire for her was spurred by more than honor. So they could "proceed," could they? And still she backhanded his honor. "Not know from where the marriage sprang," was it?

It was too late to exercise any sort of control over his

rage. It was already full-blown. In that instant even Aeric shared a portion of it. Had the man hated him? Was this some sort of insane delayed punishment for seeking to rob him all those years ago? Why else would he wish this woman on him? If not Aeric, then someone was to blame, Alaex thought unreasonably. Never in his life had anyone had the ability to anger and enchant him until he no longer knew whether he came or went.

Iliani had finally recognized his anger, and none of the enchantment was visible. She felt him shrink against her as tangibly as she felt his anger grow. Fear again became a part of what she felt, but somehow she gathered the courage to ask, "What is wrong, Alaex?"

Alaex's eyes narrowed. "I was just wondering who pays you, madam."

Iliani's confused "Pays me for—" was cut off by the laughter she was accustomed to hearing from him. It sounded even harsher after the deep, rich chuckles he'd shared with her before.

"Certainly someone is paying you, and handsomely," Alaex said bitterly. "No one does what you do as well as you do without some recompense. Or is torturing a poor hapless fool payment enough?"

Iliani tried to wiggle away, but he tightened his hold, keeping her fast. "Nay, you go nowhere until you listen to me. Can you be so incredibly naive as to think this was what I wanted?" His hot eyes flashed contemptuously down both their bodies.

"Had I desired only a hollow experience, I could have taken that long ago. I do not want honorable acceptance." Alaex sneered the last as if it were detestable. "No man worth his skin would, and should you find one willing, run far and fast. I do not need your pity, nor do I need your sacrifice. Need of that sort has naught to do with this. I *want* you to want me," he ground out, furious that she pushed him to say it. "Is that understood?"

His eyes bored into hers. "Only now that I have had to say it, I find I do not want it quite so intensely. I think 'twould be a bit of kindness to include myself in that warning I gave earlier. Run fast and far from me, Iliani, because I know not when I have been closer to violence."

Alaex rolled away and lay tautly on his back, his fists clenched at his sides. Iliani did not need a second warning. She fled.

Chapter

⇾ 15 ⇽

The next days after Iliani's disastrous attempt to seduce Alaex were an excruciating ordeal, and a painful pattern was set which became more arduous to endure by the end of each one. Whereas before she had felt that he had ignored the situation existing between them, now it seemed he ignored more than that. Now he ignored her, barely putting in an appearance whenever she was present.

Just when Iliani thought she could scarcely bear any more, something—or rather, someone—occurred that made the difficulty of the previous days seem as pleasant as a lakeside picnic.

It was a week after the embarrassing scene, or, as the only way Iliani could bear to think of it, "the incident" in Alaex's room. One long week in which her emotions had careened from one extreme to the other. First it was fear followed by outrage, which was stalked by anger, which was finally soothed by bewildered acceptance. Iliani would not have thought there was room for so much conflict, but as she quickly and bitterly discovered, when one slept alone and one's husband made sure you did practically everything else in the same state, lack of space was not an issue.

Thinking on it all caused Iliani to sigh, and it seemed that Wind Dancer echoed her feeling. The horse pawed the ground anxiously, and it was only then that Iliani realized how long she had had the horse stand in one spot while she was lost in thought. Her sudden awareness of Wind Dancer's impatience reminded her that he was not the only one she had kept immobile. Casually she glanced back to see how her guard was taking the inactivity.

The six men who were forced to ride with her looked as bored as wood. Iliani nearly smiled at their attempts not to look so, but controlled her impulse. Just because they tried not to look irritated didn't mean they weren't. Laughing at them would not aid the situation. Having recently become aware of her previously unknown ability to drive men—one man in particular—to excessive rage whether that was her intention or not, Iliani was more than careful around Alaex's men. While a lack of safety in their presence was not a problem, it seemed unfair and unnecessary to waste her newfound talent on them, she thought with heavy sarcasm. Nay, she thought bitterly, it was so much better to save it for their leader—when he deigned to be in her company, she amended.

During the first few days of Alaex's withdrawal, Iliani, after she calmed, had realized that she had handled the situation with the finesse of a rampaging boar. Although she saw the justification in Alaex's anger, she still didn't think she deserved his volatile reaction. His rejection had been most painful. Instead of refusing her, they should have talked. However, it was now a week later and Alaex's anger showed no signs of dissipating. It had been so unyielding that he had informed her, through Jon, that he would not accompany her on her rides as he had originally stated he would. Instead a guard was to be provided for her. And so it was.

Feeling the now almost familiar bite of frustration,

Iliani again pulled herself from her thoughts. With a silent determination to salvage what she could of the ride, she looked back over Wind Dancer's neck, patted it, and then gave the horse what it wanted. Iliani had barely applied pressure when Wind Dancer took off in a flurry of hooves on a well-known path through the forest.

Even the sound of the breeze in her ears was not enough to drown out the collective sighs of the men behind her. Whether they were sighing with relief because they were again moving, or sighing with disappointment because they weren't headed back toward the hall, Iliani could not tell.

As Wind Dancer sailed along, his powerful muscles throbbing beneath her, Iliani reveled in the feel and the thrill of the freedom she always felt when she gave the horse its head. This was why she rode. The exhilaration provided an escape, relieving her mind of all else.

They were thundering across a clearing within the forest when Iliani noticed Thibert gaining on her. Usually the men rode behind her, and as the places where they rode, although wooded, were not concealing, Iliani had assumed that they felt she was safe enough. For Thibert to be riding faster and beside her when they were in an open area was puzzling, but not enough to make her stop.

She had a new destination today. Arthur had told her that on the other side of the forest was a valley split by a stream and that the view was breathtaking. His description of lush green land, which in spring would be dotted with wild blooms and parted by crystal blue waters, that now in the last stages of winter frothed with gray crystalline beauty, made her yearn to see it for herself.

Leaning down over Wind Dancer's neck, Iliani was about to urge the horse to greater speed when suddenly and supremely unexpectedly, Thibert's hand reached across the distance and pulled on the horse's reins. Understandably Wind Dancer did not appreciate the conflicting signals, and he reared. A struggle ensued for a moment as Iliani tried to keep her seat, calm her horse, and jerk the reins from Thibert's fist.

When she had completed two of the three maneuvers, she turned to glare from Thibert's hand, still on Wind Dancer's reins, to his impassive face. Iliani was so furious she could barely speak, and it hadn't escaped her notice that during the fight to remain atop her horse and calm him, the remaining five men had encircled them.

Iliani took a deep breath, wondering what was taking place. She looked at each of their faces and was not fooled by their studied nonchalance. Beneath the relaxed mask of expression each wore, there was the steel of determination. Her anger grew. She finally looked back to Thibert.

"You will please explain." She did not have to say anything else, and in any event she was too angry to do so. Nor was she in the least appeased by Thibert's faint increase in color or seeming discomfort.

Thibert was uneasy. He had reluctantly received this task of guarding his mistress and had been about to balk vehemently when Jon had advanced menacingly upon him and asked if he questioned an order. Regaining his temper and his common sense, Thibert had denied it, which had promptly halted Jon's advance. He still did not know what had prompted Jon to explain, and while the explanation had soothed his pride it had not increased his desire for this particular duty.

Jon had told him it was a high honor Alaex bestowed upon him. Not all were counted worthy enough to guard the lord's wife.

Looking now into the lady's sparkling eyes, Thibert felt an intense resurgence of his original distaste for his assignment. Judging from the lady's expression, he was not going to escape the next few minutes unscathed—despite his merely following orders. Honor and worthiness were quickly losing their appealing value. He swallowed.

"I—you . . . the dense forest is ahead."

Iliani's eyes narrowed. "I am not blind, Thibert. I know where we are."

Thibert did, too, but he wished he were anyplace else. He tried again. His orders were explicit: she was not to enter the woods and he was not to tell her unless he had to. Even then he was not allowed to tell her why.

" 'Tis difficult to see to your safety in such a circumstance and with so few in number."

Iliani frowned as a burning thought began to form. If there was one thing she knew about Alaex's men, it was that they were fearless and nearly invincible. She had heard the rumors of their ability before, and since then she had come to see the proof of the statement that two of his men were worth five of another. She rode with six. On their land. In daylight. Thibert must be desperate to keep her from entering that part of the forest if he were willing to imply that he and his men were not fit enough for whatever could await them. Since fear could be ruled out, that left one overwhelming and unavoidable reason: Alaex.

First, Iliani thought with steaming venom, she could not leave without him. Then, after "the incident," when Alaex could ill bear her presence, she could ride only with a guard of six. Yet it was now obvious that even within those limits there were other limits.

Iliani's face smoothed and she smiled at Thibert, leaving him less at ease than ever. Without a word she turned Wind Dancer around and headed back for the hall. There was, after all, no benefit in wasting her "talent" on him. Nay, Iliani thought, setting a furious pace that was no match for the emotion churning in her heart. That reward only Alaex deserved, and she wanted to see that he got it.

Iliani never had the chance to give Alaex what she intended. It wasn't that her anger had died by the time they regained Fontwyn, not at all. If anything it was hotter. What checked her rage was the unexpected sight of new horses gathered in the outer yard. They had guests.

When Iliani entered the hall she was stopped as much by the sight of the tall, voluptuous blonde talking to Alaex at the lord's table as by the cloying scent that seemed to fill every corner of the room. Its sweetness was so great that for an instant Iliani thought every flower in Alfred's kingdom had been plucked and brought to Fontwyn's main hall.

Alaex and the blonde seemed immune to it. But, Iliani thought acidly, perhaps their immunity existed because they stood so close that any air between them was an impossibility. Or perhaps it was because nature was kind and after a few moments it had killed their sense of smell. In any event, she noted, her irritation growing, they seemed to notice neither it nor her.

It was one thing for Alaex to ignore her. It was another altogether for him to ignore her while paying close attention to another woman—in her face, no less. As a few more seconds passed and neither Alaex nor his guest seemed inclined to notice anything but themselves, Iliani's stubbornness asserted itself and she allowed it to lead her anger unchecked.

Thibert, who had come in behind her, took in the scene immediately, and as he already knew of his lady's pique he knew this did not bode well. One quick glance from her face, with its mounting anger evident, to Alaex and the woman across the hall, and he knew someone should do something. He coughed gently, making Alaex and the woman look up. Thibert closed the hall door and edged himself around Iliani, causing her to take a step.

That one step was all it took to free her feet and propel her forward. Normally Iliani was not awkward, nor was she usually so taken with physical appearance, but the woman's face was one to stop a herd of rampaging horses. It was perfection. Even from across the hall Iliani could find no flaw, which meant that Alaex, standing as close as he was, must be nearly blinded by it. Was it any

161

wonder he had not noticed her or her entrance, she thought dazedly, nearly forgetting her anger in her awe.

Slowly Iliani walked the rest of the way toward them, absently realizing that neither made a move toward her. The blonde spoke first.

"So this is Aeric's daughter." Her deep blue eyes flashed at Iliani before they turned innocently to Alaex. "The little girl you were honor bound to marry. I see your dilemma and applaud your honor, milord. Poor thing, she looks frightened, and why should she not be? She's scarce more than a child."

Those catlike words had, Iliani was certain, the opposite effect of what had been intended. She was not crushed by them. In fact, she was almost happy to hear them. They revealed the first visible flaw in the woman, only this was worse than having a crooked nose or rotting teeth or mean, beady little eyes. They showed an ugliness harder to conceal, an ugliness of the heart and spirit, and they shrank the blonde, who was at least half a head taller than Iliani, to a size somewhere beneath her knees.

The tension within her eased along with some of her anger, and Iliani smiled. "Since I am already known to our guest, may I be told who she is?" She directed her question to Alaex, completely ignoring the woman and her words.

Alaex's smile was tight. "Iliani, this is another of my wards. You heard mention of her when we paid our respects to the king. Her name is Brita."

The nod Iliani gave was a mere jerk of her head. "Aye. I do recall *his* mentioning her." Her inference was clear. Alfred had mentioned her, but Alaex should have been the one to do so. Yet a second later, Iliani could have bitten off her rash tongue as the tall blond woman looked from her to Alaex and a calculating sparkle entered her beautiful blue eyes.

The gleam in her eyes reminded Iliani of a ferocious predator who had just sighted its prey—wounded prey at that. The smile that spread across Brita's face was nearly as sickening in its falseness as its sweetness.

"I take it you did not know of me, either," Brita practically purred in her soft voice.

Trying to regain ground as well as protect herself against the assault she was certain was coming, Iliani forced herself to relax. "Should I have?" she responded, her tone just as sweet and as false.

The sudden silence was broken by Thibert's uncomfortable cough. Jon, who was standing on the far side of Alaex and his guest, and had gone unnoticed by Iliani until that moment, took a sudden and intense interest in the stones around the hearth.

Brita's eyes hardened for a brief moment, and then the rancor was wiped from her face, replaced with one of false camaraderie. "No, little one. No reason at all." She lowered her voice as if confiding a great secret while she linked her hand through Alaex's arm. "Men usually don't tell their wives everything, especially about some things."

Giving that insinuation a moment to settle, Brita continued as if she weren't deliberately needling her. "I knew not of you either." This time the venomous look she cast to Alaex was sincere, if well-disguised beneath the flutter of her obscenely long lashes. "In that I am not alone. Since I am certain he never will"—Brita rubbed her hand along the bulge of Alaex's muscled forearm—"I will tell you that there also were many others who did not know of you, and of whom you'll also probably never hear, who were disappointed to learn the news of Alaex's marriage."

Alaex disengaged his arms—a little too slowly in Iliani's opinion—as he leveled an inscrutable gaze at his ward. "That's enough, Brita."

Brita paused, obviously assessing how far she could go. Something she saw in Alaex's eyes made her retreat, but Iliani knew the war was not over, only delayed, and Brita's next words, a final barb, told Iliani not to expect the delay to be a lengthy one.

"Oh, Alaex," she chided in a falsely apologetic tone. "I did not call any names. Besides, they have all given up. You are safe, darling. A person can be forced into marriage only once, you know."

If Alaex was going to answer, Iliani did not give him the opportunity. Her eyes roved over the beautiful woman in front of her before directly meeting her gaze.

"Then I would say that makes him the most fortunate of men." Her meaning was clear.

The roles reversed. Thibert now took to an examination of the stones, and Jon coughed. Alaex, however, was beginning to look bewildered.

Iliani, her gaze still direct, experienced a new kind of rage as she stared at the blue-eyed creature who dared to taunt her in her own home in front of her husband. Her anger at Alaex was totally forgotten. She knew that her words, which to him could have more than one meaning, confused him. She smiled brilliantly, enjoying herself for the first time since entering the hall.

"As always, Husband, guests are welcome in our home."

That her welcome was clearly insincere caused Alaex's confusion to mount, but he wisely decided not to speak of that. Yet it impelled him to say something, to explain somehow, and he didn't know why.

"Brita needs to speak with me about her upcoming marriage."

"Oh?" Iliani asked sweetly in a tone that mocked the innocence of that reply. "Who is the un— *ahem* . . . excuse me." Iliani halted and then ended, "Fortunate gentleman?"

Now both Thibert and Jon took to coughing, and while Brita glared at them and Iliani continued to smile, the expression in Alaex's eyes, which he had shifted to them also, alternately begged and warned them.

Again Jon and Thibert were united in their response. They both ignored Alaex's silent warning and coughed out a garbled departure.

When the two men had gone, Brita, in the thinnest

voice Iliani had heard yet, said, " 'Tis why I am here. Alaex knows me better than any. He was a friend to my father as well. He must approve. There is an unworthy trying to force a marriage and I came to Alaex for protection, wisdom, and guidance."

Instantly Iliani's irritation returned. She didn't know which was worse, the cloying smell of perfume or this nauseating performance. If there was anyone in less need of protection, it was Brita. Iliani had no doubt she could handle the unknown suitor—if indeed such a man did exist—and a thousand others like him without pause. After a quick glance at Alaex to see how he received his ward's words, Iliani's irritation grew. Clearly he saw nothing amiss.

In disgust, Iliani wondered if all men were this gullible or if she was merely fortunate to have picked the only prize among them all. Brita had been as subtle as a stone wall. Couldn't he see what she was doing? Another glance and Iliani had her answer. Apparently not.

Under Brita's watchful unblinking stare, Iliani resisted the urge to clench her fists in frustration, unwilling to give her another advantage. The woman seemed almost snakelike, waiting for the right opening or sign of weakness so that she could strike.

Suddenly Iliani tired of the whole situation. She was not even certain how it had come about or why she should care what Brita thought.

In the perfect tones of a gracious hostess, she said, "Since there is such pressing business to be discussed, I will leave you two to your discussion. Excuse me."

With those words she sought her room, and for the first time since she had entered the hall, the three of them shared the same feeling. Iliani was relieved to be out of Brita's spiteful presence even as she wondered if she could be hung for tearing out each strand of her hair. Brita was relieved because with Iliani gone and with Jon and Thibert's earlier departure, she had Alaex to herself. And Alaex, without knowing why, was just relieved.

Chapter

→ 16 ←

It has been a sennight since Brita's arrival, Iliani thought as she again sat through one of the seemingly interminable suppers and indulged in what was becoming her favorite fantasy. As she stared into space, she twirled her dagger absently between her fingers while wondering how Brita would look with a permanent part.

Someone's loud laughter brought her from her reverie and Iliani's eyes met Jon's amused ones across the table. There was a muted twinkle in the eyes of Alaex's first in command, and after looking surreptitiously in Brita's direction and wiggling his eyebrows outrageously, he nodded slightly in clear and silent encouragement of Iliani's violent intent.

Iliani burst into laughter, which caused everyone to look at her. She didn't care. With a jaunty look she returned Jon's nod, oblivious to the stares of the others and Alaex's sudden scowl. She raised her cup to her lips to hide her growing smile, and after taking a sip she relaxed in her seat, deliberately ignoring Alaex's questioning look.

For the days that Brita had been at Fontwyn, Iliani had

maintained the facade of a gracious hostess. However, she didn't know how much longer she could sustain it. Perhaps if she knew when the woman intended to leave, she could endure. But Brita had the tenacity of a tick on a dog. She showed no signs of leaving, and as long as she played a game without openly revealing her true intent, Iliani was determined to do the same.

This nonsense had begun the night Brita had arrived and they had shared their first evening meal, which had been a grimly accurate foretaste of the agony of the days to come. Iliani admitted dully that the first meal probably would have gone better had she not tortured herself with thoughts of Alaex and his ward during the remainder of the afternoon.

Her success in drowning out the disturbing inner voice that taunted her had lasted only as long as it took to reach the solitude of her room. The doubts nagging Iliani refused to be dismissed merely because she wanted them so. While her fierce avowals that she should not and did not care what Brita thought were true, that also was not the cause of her misery. Her concern was that she should and *did* have a concern over the woman's wants. Brita wanted Alaex. That had taken no time to decipher, and given the recent decline in her and Alaex's relationship and Brita's obvious appeal, the dismal thought had occurred that Alaex might be inclined to find her preferable. Brita was definitely welcoming, and hadn't that been his requirement? If he wanted a woman to want him, he needn't journey far.

Iliani was acutely uncomfortable with the fact that Alaex might respond to Brita. Why, she did not know, or more truthfully, preferred not to face. Logically the situation Brita caused should have made her happy. For a certainty it would have solved what remained of her problems. Yet that logical knowledge solved nothing. If anything, Iliani felt worse since Brita's arrival. With those depressing thoughts buzzing in her mind, Iliani had gone below stairs for the evening meal.

Initially it hadn't been so awful. After their earlier

sparring, she and Brita seemed to agree tacitly to ignore each other. However, not long into the meal it was obvious they were the only two comfortable with that decision.

It hadn't been anything overt. The talk had seemed as loud as usual; the laughing camaraderie had seemed as warm as usual. Yet somehow it wasn't quite the same. The laughter had been harder and the talk louder, giving it a telltale air of falseness. Alaex, of course, had said little. Brita, on the other hand, hadn't seemed to notice. She had constantly tried to engage him in conversation. Could he pass the wine? How was his meat? Did he prefer salted fish or fresh? The questions had gone on and Iliani had wanted to expose the man who looked like her husband for an impostor. When had Alaex ever cared whether his wine was mulled or spiced?

Still unable to think of that episode without grimacing, Iliani pulled her thoughts from the past and wondered briefly how long *any* of them would be able to last under the strain. Inwardly she sighed and bolstered her resolve not to give the woman any more to chew on. It had been bad enough that earlier this evening, when her frustration was unbearably acute, she had stabbed her roasted boar as if she needed to kill the beast anew. Everyone had looked at her and then quickly away in embarrassment. Knowing she was close to a repeat performance, Iliani turned to Alaex and forced a pleasant tone.

"If you will excuse me, Alaex, I will retire now." Putting forth a good face was one thing. However, her patience had limits. For days she had been excusing herself from the meals as soon as possible. Tonight, with memories and frustration pushing in severely, she needed to escape faster than usual.

Alaex had not yet opened his mouth to respond when Brita said, "I am sure he understands, dear. When one is so tender in years, sleep is very necessary."

The truce was over. Iliani's smile lost all traces of genuineness. "True. Just as I'm certain he also understands that when one's age is not so tender, lack of sleep shows so much quicker."

Deafening silence followed Iliani's remark until someone chuckled nervously. All eyes, except Alaex's, who was watching his wife, were on Brita as she attested to the accuracy of Iliani's barb by raising her hand to her as-yet flawless skin. Her blue eyes narrowed as she realized what she did and they promised venom as she glared at the younger woman.

Jon broke the tension with a wry, "Now that we have discovered—and more than we desired—what milord knows, let me be the first to bid you good evening, milady."

Iliani's smile was less frosty, and when she turned from him to Alaex, it died altogether. The look of quiet speculation made her yearn to know his thoughts, but as usual since Brita's arrival, it was not the right time or place. Thinking that over and wondering when the woman's game would end, Iliani went upstairs.

Brita did not leave her to wonder long.

The hall had barely quieted when there was a knock on Iliani's door. Not in the mood to pretend sleep, as she had a strong suspicion who it was, Iliani called out brusquely, "Come in."

When Brita's tall, lithe body slipped in, Iliani was aware of a loosening in her chest, as if she had been waiting for this. After closing the door, the women stared at one another with an undisguised dislike as thick and impenetrable as the stone walls surrounding Fontwyn. Iliani did not indulge in pleasant formality.

"What do you want?"

Brita, despite her apparent dislike, seemed taken aback by Iliani's bluntness. Instead of the insult she intended to hurl, she said, "I would like to talk to you."

Iliani's silence was not encouraging, and when Brita continued, her voice was uncertain. "Come now, Iliani. There is no need for us to be enemies, nor to continue with this fruitless sparring. I have come to see that our wants are similar."

Disbelief was etched on Iliani's face. Her smile was slow and mocking. "Somehow I do not think so."

Gaining confidence, Brita laughed lightly. It was one of the rare genuine reactions Iliani had seen her make since she had come to Fontwyn. "If not similar, then definitely not opposite. It has to do with Alaex." She studied Iliani's face, waiting for a reaction. "I want him," she declared boldly. "You do not."

There it was, baldly out in the open, and Iliani felt a peculiar sense of relief at finally hearing the words. The dread she had been anticipating did not come. In a flash she realized why. While it was true that Brita was no less beautiful and it did not sit well with Iliani's confidence to have her for a rival, it at least explained the natural antagonism between them. It was a relief to know she had been neither insane nor wrong. Brita wanted Alaex. It had not been her overstressed imagination when she had thought that everything the woman had said and done since her arrival announced that. The only doubt that remained for Iliani was Alaex's inability to see it. She was certain his men did.

Although this was the first time Brita had said the words, she had shown it a thousand ways. She had been practically panting after Alaex, nearly drooling over him like a besotted hound, Iliani thought, warming to her metaphor. Controlling the pleasant urge to continue to compare the woman to a dog, Iliani focused on the very real problem she presented.

"What makes you think I do not want my husband?" she asked with quiet and commendable calm.

Instead of answering her, Brita stared at the large bed, of which Iliani did not fill half. Her eyes asked if she needed to say anything else. Iliani colored and looked away. Brita went on as if she had spoken.

"It need not be so unendurable. I know you want another. I know that Alaex interrupted your wedding feast. Neither you nor he wanted this."

Despite her earlier determination not to reveal anything to her, Iliani flinched beneath the assured ease with which Brita said the words. "Things are not at all times as they appear," she murmured, unknowingly repeating a phrase Alaex used often.

Brita's eyes hardened slightly. She had heard Alaex say the exact thing and she wondered if Iliani said it now on purpose. Her disquiet eased when she noted that it had not been said with confidence, nor was Iliani's expression filled with that emotion.

Deciding to ignore it, Brita returned, "And sometimes things are exactly as they seem. All I am saying is that they do not have to be like this. 'Tis not just the sleeping arrangements. 'Tis the look in your eyes," she said craftily, playing on the uncertainty she could see in Iliani's eyes and hoping that her words would cause her to reveal an even greater weakness. "They mirror your body's innocence. Love unfulfilled shows there, and the opposite is also true. Any woman who loves and has been loved cannot hide it."

Brita's words hammered into Iliani with a worldly sophistication she found difficult to refute. It was even harder to dispute them after that horrible night in Alaex's room. Still her heart refused to be quelled, and ignoring her mind's inability to find the words and logic to argue, it set up a protest that pushed away all traces of the apathetic acceptance that Iliani had been laboring under the past few days.

What did it matter what the woman thought she knew? Until Alaex gave her a reason other than masculine naïveté to think otherwise, Brita could argue until her voice failed her. She spoke from only one perspective: hers. Alaex had not. And neither she nor Brita had the right—a harsh lesson Iliani had learned through her own experience—to decide his life for him. It was unimportant that Brita had heard of her near marriage to Cam. By this time, Iliani supposed that there were few people who had not. All Brita had was common knowledge. She lacked the pertinent facts and the realization crystallized in Iliani's mind that she would be a fool to allow the woman to distort for her own purpose a truth everyone already knew.

Iliani looked back to Brita and caught the victorious expression in her eyes. Her resolve solidified.

"I think you should go."

"We have not dis—"

"Now."

Something in Iliani's eyes convinced her that retreat would be best, and Brita hurriedly left the room. When the door closed, Iliani fell back in the bed feeling as if she had just fought a major battle with an uncertain outcome. She did not lie back to sleep. She thought.

The hall was totally quiet as Iliani made her way to Alaex's room. While she was in no rush for a repetition of the last time she had been in his room, she had thought enough. She needed to talk. To him. And his room and the lateness of the hour should ensure them privacy from his ward.

Taking a deep breath, she raised her hand to knock on his door, only then realizing that the door was opened a crack and a sliver of soft candlelight slanted across her bare toes. Seeing that and deciding that Alaex must not have gone to bed, Iliani pushed the door open gently. She was about to call out to him when she saw him standing across the room before the hearth, and froze.

He was not alone. He was as unalone as a man could be. Brita was there, and they weren't talking. The blonde was plastered across Alaex's broad and *naked* chest. Iliani knew everything that Brita must be feeling, having recently known the wonderful intimacy of being in that position with Alaex. She even thought she could feel the heat of their embrace. Or maybe it was the heat of the rage that swamped her. She didn't know. Suddenly she could neither think nor breathe and it felt as if someone were driving a sword through her head, it was pounding so.

Everything happened quickly after that. One moment Iliani was standing in the door watching another woman kiss her husband, and the next she was leaping across the room, a snarl of outrage marring her features, and pulling them apart—using Brita's hair to do so.

Brita screamed, as much in shock as in pain as Iliani's relentless grip propelled her backward until she landed on her backside on the cold hard floor. Iliani's attack had been so swift and unexpected that Brita had stared blankly at Alaex, wondering what had happened, at the same time that she saw Iliani's bare feet beside her. When she raised her eyes to meet the sparkling violet ones of the girl she would not have thought possessed such strength, Brita halted and nervously swallowed her question.

The expression on Iliani's face was not triumphant, but her stance was warriorlike and her eyes promised more of the same should Brita so much as bat a lash. Even Iliani did not recognize her voice as she hissed, "Hear my words and heed them better. You have one hour to pack your belongings and be gone from here."

Finally realizing she still sat sprawled ignominiously on the floor, Brita hurriedly got to her feet. Wisely she took a step back from Iliani. However, that was the extent of her caution.

"You cannot ask me to leave. I am Alaex's ward. 'Tis his home. Only he can order me from it."

Iliani's eyes began to glitter. "Your pardon, *lady*," she uttered softly in a tone that showed that she found Brita anything but. "I must not have been clear. You see, I do not recall *asking* you to leave."

Her warning was clear. Brita looked toward Alaex and caught the tail end of a smothered smile. It was that smile coupled with the very real threat in Iliani's eyes that made Brita decide to go—at least for the time being. Further confrontation would be useless, and already she began to fear that she had done too much. Far too much, if the way Iliani fingered her dagger was an indication.

Loath to turn away and give her a tempting place to lodge it, Brita backed away from the two of them as quickly as she could.

It was Iliani who closed or, rather, slammed the door. She needed a further outlet for her rage, which she had erroneously thought would cool once the woman left. It didn't, and slamming one door didn't help, either. To calm herself, Iliani felt she'd have to slam every door in the hall, then cut, carve, and build more so she could slam those, too. Perhaps when she was done she would be merely angry.

Through the haze of her rage, she felt Alaex staring at her, and her anger shifted, finding a new target. Slowly Iliani turned to face him.

Unlike the smile he had allowed Brita to see, Alaex kept to himself any humor he found in the situation. He watched his bride, who he was certain would soon be his wife, approach him. When Iliani was in arm's reach, he grabbed and kissed her, effectively quelling the shower of angry words she had been about to pour on him.

She was still as a slab of stone within his arms, but that didn't stop him. He didn't care. He was too happy to care. However, when Iliani began to struggle, he released her.

"Did you truly think that what you started with another, I would finish?" she snapped, finally feeling the hurt beneath the anger.

"I started naught with Brita, Iliani," Alaex said softly, his eyes locked on hers. "She kissed me," he said simply, unaware of the burning sensation in her stomach at those few words. "In truth, your entrance was premature. Had you stood outside a moment longer, you would have heard me tell her the same as you: it was time for her to leave."

Emotionally, Iliani leapt at those words like someone struggling for air. Even with her doubt they seemed magically to soothe the greater part of her hurt and all of her anger.

Alaex saw the lingering doubt. "I do not lie, Iliani. She

kissed me. If you will but think on what you saw, you will recall that I did not return her kiss." He saw the uncertainty wavering in her expressive eyes, and Alaex pressed his advantage. Again he took her in his arms and this time she was less rigid. She felt too good just to hold, so he began to kiss her. Small, nipping kisses across her eyes, down her nose, feathering across her lips.

When Iliani began to respond, he pulled his lips away and began to rain gentle kisses down her neck, finding her pulse and drawing on it in a tempo and intensity that matched its heavy beat. Alaex didn't need to hear her sigh or feel her arms go around him to know that this time he had won, or that this victory was the sweetest of his life.

Iliani was no longer stiff in his arms. Her relaxed posture and the eager little kisses she was giving him told him that she believed, not forgave, him and he wanted her with a need that trembled on obsession. With a groan he captured her mouth once again and lifted Iliani in his arms and carried her to the bed. After extinguishing all the candles and leaving the room to glow in the light of the low fire, he joined her there.

Iliani had regained a portion of her senses and was about to speak when his lips joined hers again. As before when she had been in his arms, the words fled. All she knew was Alaex and the rightness and excitement of being in his arms. Soon Alaex had brought her senses to a fevered level where pleasure bordered on pain. Even the feel of her own clothing against her was an exciting torture. By the time he removed her gown, Iliani's desire was out of control. When he had removed his hose, she didn't know, but the remembered delight of his hard flesh paled against the reality of actually having him there touching her, wanting her.

Alaex's hand reverently touched her high firm breast, while the other cupped her face and smoothed her hair back from her face. Instinctively Iliani turned into that hand and kissed it as Alaex leaned down and gave her breasts similar attention. When she gasped from pleasure, he chuckled and turned from one breast to the other.

It was the beauty of the chuckle that did it, bringing back the memory of the last time when he had done something similar, and how that scene had ended. Iliani tensed, and immediately Alaex felt it.

"What is it?" he whispered, concern on his face.

"Nay," Iliani murmured, overwhelmed and apprehensive because of her memories. "No words, not tonight. Please."

Looking deep into her eyes Alaex saw her fear and understood. Yet for their first joining he wanted no fear of any kind. He lowered his head and grabbed gently on her full bottom lip.

"If we are not to speak, how can I tell you of my desire?" he asked softly. "I cannot believe you do not want me to say how exquisite it feels to know that you will finally be mine. How, without words, can I tell you of my pleasure?" His tongue gently invaded her lips.

By the time Alaex raised his head, Iliani felt as if she burned. It was fire Alaex had started with his words and had stoked with his kiss. Everything he did intensified it—the touch of his hand, the warmth of his desire, and the flame that burned muted yet strongly in his eyes as he hungrily gazed at her own passion-touched features.

The last time was forgotten. In the grips of a feeling she had never had before, Iliani grabbed his face and with a moan uttered, "You need no words. Show me."

Then she pulled him down and kissed him, returning and sharing the fire he had built within her. And that keen and powerful sharing was the most sublime moment of her life. Somehow in her heart Iliani knew there would never be another quite like it, and she didn't want there to be. What was passing between them was exquisitely special and even to attempt to replicate it would tarnish its memory.

When Alaex slid entirely over her, Iliani tensed slightly. She had an idea of what was about to happen, but that was it. However, before full-fledged worry could take hold, Alaex soothed her.

"I would give my heart for it to be otherwise, but there is some pain involved," he said, and it sounded as if he ached for her. He had laid his forehead against hers and his words were uneven due to the harshness of his breathing.

"I know," Iliani said gently. "Eadwina tried—"

Alaex raised his head and Iliani saw the twinkle in his eyes before he smiled. "I'll bet she did."

Iliani was positive it was another unique moment, and her breath caught as she realized how truly handsome he was. The warmth and beauty of his smile transformed his features, and Iliani could not help return it. That he would say and do something to set her at ease made her heart swell with an extremely tender emotion. In that moment she wanted him more than anything she had ever wanted in her life. It was desire past a physical need. It went further than the depths of her soul.

"Alaex?" she called, all traces of humor gone, seared away by the unquenched flame flaring between them.

Taking his own advice to forget the last time, Alaex looked into her eyes and was not disappointed. What he saw on her face tore a groan from his chest, and he felt as if he answered her call with his heart.

"Hold on to me, Iliani," he moaned deeply. "It only gets better from here." With that he entered her with a full lunge, ripping through the frail barrier that made her no longer a maid and, more poignantly, made her his. The only thing that kept Alaex from crowing with pure delight and plunging madly within her warm depths was the pain he could see on Iliani's face.

Iliani, who had not expected such a burning pain, had only gasped when he entered her, when in truth she had wanted to scream. However, when she looked fully into Alaex's face and saw his anxiety, all traces of the pain were forgotten. That done, it was easier to smile at him honestly.

Alaex's heart tightened at that smile. As Iliani's fingers traced his lips and she leaned up to kiss him, he gave her the deliciously wicked chuckle of which she was coming to love the sound and said, "I must amend my last statement. It only gets better from *here.*"

As he began to move inside her, Iliani found he was right. It did.

Chapter

⇒ 17 ⇐

"Alaex?"

"Hmm?"

Iliani could hear his smile and she smiled, too. She hoped that what she was about to say would not remove it.

"I would like to talk."

"About what?" His voice wasn't harsh, but it was definitely sharper, wary.

Iliani smoothed her hand along his chest, tickling the few hairs on his chest and teasing his tight nipples.

"That, Iliani," Alaex said in a voice caught between laughter and desire, "is not the way to start a conversation, at least not one with words."

Her hand stilled. It was an effort, though. Never having made love before, everything was keener to Iliani, and she was possessed with the near-overwhelming urge to keep touching him despite her desire to talk.

"Can we not do both?"

Alaex laughed softly. "That depends."

"On what?"

"On what you want to talk about," he returned, and spontaneously kissed the top of her head.

"I wanted to ask you something," Iliani began hesitantly.

Alaex fought to keep the tension he was feeling from his tone. "What is it?"

Iliani took a deep breath and blurted, "Why did we make love?" This time she felt him tense beneath her hand. "What I mean is," she hurried to clarify, "when I came to you before . . . well, that incident did not end as this one did. Yet I came to you to consummate our marriage. Why did you not want me?"

Alaex heard the pain in her voice, and his arms tightened. "I am sorry, Iliani, if I ever gave you the impression that I lacked desire for you. That would be one of the greatest lies ever told."

Iliani accepted that. Still . . . "That does not explain what happened. Truly, it makes it harder to understand the incident."

"Incident?" Alaex queried.

The shadows concealed the blush that suffused her face. "That's how I refer to what happened that night."

"Oh," Alaex responded in a thoroughly emotionless tone that he hoped served to cover his amusement. "It was different."

"In what way?"

All humor fled as Alaex recalled that night. This was the first time he had done so. He had been so enraged that the only way he had been able to function was to avoid all thought of what had occurred.

"You did not desire me, Iliani," he said, his voice roughening with memory. "Some misplaced sense of honor forced you here." Slight bitterness crept into his tone. "If that was all, then I did not want you."

Iliani swallowed, accepting that, too, and becoming aware of how he had felt. "Yet tonight—"

"Tonight," Alaex interrupted, rolling her beneath him, "you came to me without any thought of fulfilling honor's requirement. You trembled in my arms, not in fear but from desire."

"But desire was not the reason I came."

"Was it not?" he asked wickedly, leaving Iliani certain that he meant something else.

She frowned. "Nay, I came to talk to you."

Alaex laughed at her innocence and impetuously leaned down to kiss her. "Does it matter?"

Iliani was confused now, having lost her thought. Finally she said, "Nay. I suppose not."

"Good," he said, settling back on the bed. He was beginning to drift off to sleep when she called to him.

"Alaex?"

"Hmm?" he replied drowsily.

"About Brita . . ."

Alaex's eyes flew open. Immediately he pinned Iliani back on the bed, seeking her eyes. "Listen to my words and heed them better," he said, deliberately repeating what Iliani had told Brita. "There is no 'about Brita.' I did not say what I did merely to get you into my bed. Had you interrupted or not, I was sending her away."

Iliani caressed his jaw. "I believe you," she said solemnly, deciding in that instant to forgo her other questions about the woman. "I believed you then."

Alaex studied her expression and by degrees the tenseness left his. He was lying on his back again when an unpleasant thought occurred to him, and it was Iliani's fault. If she hadn't brought up the subject of Brita, then he probably would not have recalled Brita's words about Iliani's feelings for Cam. Then, he'd had no time to think on that. Brita had thrown herself in his arms after saying it didn't matter if his wife didn't want him, because she did, and then Iliani had almost immediately thrown her to the floor. Now, however, with his mind clear, the question came and stayed.

"Iliani?"

"Hmm?" she answered, having nearly gone to sleep herself.

"Do you love Cam?" Alaex felt like a fool for asking, especially after what they had just done, but he was wise enough to know that sex was not love. Therefore, the question was unavoidable. It burned a bitter path from his mind to his heart.

Its effect on Iliani was no less. She sat up abruptly and stared down at him. "Pardon?" she asked, thinking she couldn't possibly have heard correctly.

Alaex irrationally felt himself becoming angry when she didn't immediately deny it. "I know that you heard me, Iliani. All I need now is an answer, an honest one."

As quickly as the anger rose up in her chest, something beyond the clip in his words and the stiffness of his manner killed it. Slowly Iliani eased herself back beside him, her conviction strengthening when his arm came back around her. Although the muscles in them were tense, the gesture seemed almost compulsive. Iliani wanted to smile, certain Alaex was revealing more than he knew or desired.

"Aye," she answered gently, laying her hand on his chest. "I suppose you can say that. He means a great deal to me." Iliani stopped, uncomfortable with her feelings and her attempt to explain them. "In honesty, Alaex, what I feel I cannot so easily explain. There is loyalty there for Cam, for Edouard. They were all I had. Edouard and Eadwina were good to me. So was Cam. I know he can be selfish sometimes, but still I care for him because there are other times, most times, when he can be endearing." Iliani sighed. "Knowing his flaws and yet caring, is that not what love is?"

Alaex jerked her hand from his chest, although he did not remove his arm. "I would not know," he said tightly.

Now Iliani felt like laughing—not in amusement, but the sort of laugh that comes spontaneously when one feels good. And she felt great.

"Haven't you ever loved anyone?" she teased.

Alaex grew more rigid. For the longest time he said nothing, giving Iliani the impression he was not going to answer. Then to her surprise, he did. His voice was deliberately hollow.

"It has never been a question of whether I love, rather whether I am loved in return." With those torn words, he erased every vestige of amusement Iliani found in this situation. She knew there was more there than the words, just as she knew asking would bring nothing. She had already glimpsed that he was extremely guarded about his past. Maybe in time. After all, she had never dreamed he would say what he just had. Perhaps in the future he would. However, for the present . . .

Iliani rolled atop Alaex, not examining closely her deep-seated urge to soothe him. "I do not know of others," she began seriously and cautiously, "but I do know of Cam and me. What I feel for him is no threat to you."

When Alaex's mouth tightened, revealing his doubt, Iliani experienced faint exasperation until it occurred to her that his behavior was not different from the way hers had been when she had seen Brita kissing him. Remembering the rage—and the pain, she reluctantly admitted—made her want to explain fully. While grappling under the weight of that wondrous revelation, others came rushing in on her, stopping her from speaking.

Alaex's reaction to Cam explained a lot. Such as why he hadn't allowed her to see Cam before they had left Lourds Keep . . . and more recently, his seemingly absurd restriction against her going into the dense forest.

Because of Brita's visit, Iliani had never gotten to question him as to why Thibert would not allow her to enter that region of Fontwyn's forest. Now she felt no need to ask, certain she had her answer. It all made sense. On the day of Eadwina's visit, hadn't he accused her of knowing that Cam waited for her? He had also given her Cam's location, and although at the time Iliani had paid it scant attention, she now knew where Cam was.

Momentarily, though, she was puzzled, remembering Alaex's words to him the day of her aborted wedding. Why did he not do as he had promised and challenge him? True, Cam may not have directly crossed his path, but that did not seem as if it would be the reason. As improbable as it seemed, the only reason Iliani could think of was that Alaex refrained from confronting Cam because of her. Had he not just asked if she loved Cam? Even on the day he had come for her, she could see his restraint as he saw what Edouard, Eadwina, and Cam meant to her. Thinking of Eadwina solidified the notion. Her silent pleading, Iliani was positive, had kept him from being sharp and thus crushing the older woman. He had, while not exactly inviting Eadwina, tacitly agreed to allow her to visit. And in proof, he had not sent her away when she had come.

Aye, this man took a care for her feelings, and that knowledge raised a tenderness within her that rivaled her feelings of minutes ago. Instead of explaining, as she had originally intended, Iliani looked deeply into Alaex's eyes and then kissed him ardently.

When the long hot embrace ended, Alaex grabbed her head, and this time it was his eyes that probed deeply, eloquently asking why. Not yet ready to reveal what was not thoroughly clear to her, Iliani leaned down and gave him a soft, yet no less passionate kiss.

"If you recall the other night, you will remember that I said I wanted a family."

He nodded warily.

"I still do," she breathed, her tongue sensuously following the perimeter of his lips and then dipping between them, giving him an openly carnal and enticing invitation. "Are you willing to give me one?"

For a fraction of a second, Iliani read his determination to have an answer—a real one—to his questions. Knowing it was not fair, but not caring, she used the little he had taught her of his body so far and began to softly trail her hand down his stomach. As she reached her goal, she could see his desire for an answer give way to desire of a different sort.

She didn't need to do anything more. Alaex took over from there and proceeded to show her in undeniable terms that he was very willing to fulfill her wish.

The day was well along when Iliani finally awakened, and she was alone. The coolness of the sheets on the side of the bed where Alaex had slept attested to his having risen long ago.

Thinking of Alaex brought a soft smile to her lips. Remembering his obvious jealousy—hers she conveniently forgot—and the evidence of his consideration brought warmth to her heart. Recalling his passion made her yearn for his touch.

Feeling the self-protective need to shy away from close examination of her new feelings, Iliani merely accepted that things did not seem as insurmountable as they once had. What was ahead she didn't know; yet it seemed her relationship with Alaex had taken a better turn and now had possibilities. Refusing to focus on the negative sides, feeling that she had already given them more than their fair share of her thoughts, Iliani concentrated only on the positive ones. Everything felt new, as if life were just starting today.

Half an hour later she was still enraptured with life and on her way down the stairs to the main hall. She didn't expect to see anyone, because the morning meal was long since done. Therefore, her surprise turned rapidly into unpleasant shock as she saw the last person she expected to see.

Brita was seated at the lord's table. Iliani paused, uncertain as to what she should do. What had happened between her and Alaex had changed things for them; however, it had not changed her feelings about Brita.

As she stood there considering whether to go back upstairs or into the hall, she became aware of swift, clipped footsteps. Seconds later, Alaex came into view. Knowing she shouldn't eavesdrop was a far cry from not doing it, and with very little shame Iliani waited on the stairs to see what would happen.

"Are you ready?" His voice was implacable, not harsh.

Brita had stood when he entered. "Alaex, I—" She raised her hand with the intention of putting it on his chest, then stopped, sensing that such an action would be unwelcome. Although Alaex was a hard man, Brita had never before found him unapproachable. For the first time, she was uncertain with him.

As she lowered her hand to her side, she watched him consideringly. She had known him over five years and had loved him nearly as long. She had hoped for something—anything—from him in all that time, and even when he gave her no encouragement, Brita had never faltered in her certainty that one day he would return her feelings.

The discovery of his marriage had been a devastating blow. Yet, even had he told her of it himself, Brita doubted she would have believed it. Marriage to a child? Nay, she would not have believed, and most likely her father, who had wanted him for his daughter almost as much as the daughter wanted him herself, would not have, either.

Brita's father Nyland had been as much in awe of Alaex as most other men, intrigued by the warrior and the myth. It had been Brita who had seen through to the man. Nyland had not been a warrior of renown, only loyal. He had thought that with his daughter's marriage to Alaex he would gain some of what he could not attain on his own. However, Alaex had remained elusive and Nyland had died before seeing his plan realized.

Not one to be deterred by mere death, he had left Brita in Alaex's care as ward and upon his deathbed had frankly told her to do what was needed to ensure she married him. That had been a year ago.

Now as Brita watched the man her father had nearly revered and she had simply loved, she felt rage at the futility of it all. If Aeric had still lived, she probably would have tried to run him through. How dare he so thwart them all? Pushing that thoroughly irrelevant thought aside, Brita concentrated on Alaex. He looked different today. More handsome, more rested. There was an air of contentment, of almost tangible satisfaction, and Brita's nimble mind was able to draw a very accurate conclusion.

Brita actually had to step back, the pain she experienced was so sharp. She couldn't even be fully angry with him. Just as she had assumed last night, she had gone too far. She had pushed him into his wife's arms. Brita didn't have physical proof, but she didn't need any. Alaex had slept with his wife.

Jealousy burned hard and hot in her heart, making her want to weep, rant, rage, and inflict violence on the woman who caused her such pain. No wonder Iliani had yet to come down. Originally she had assumed that Iliani merely waited above stairs until her departure. Although that had seemed out of character with the fire the girl had previously shown, it was all Brita could conclude. Now she knew it was untrue. Iliani was most likely still abed, exhausted from Alaex's lovemaking.

Despite the iron will she exerted over herself to show none of what she felt, Brita's eyes chilled.

Alaex, who watched her carefully, saw the coldness in her eyes before she dropped them from his and said in a brittle voice, "Aye, Alaex. I am ready."

"The riders wait for you," Alaex said awkwardly, uncomfortable with the undercurrents he could feel but not define.

Brita took a few steps toward the hall doors and then came back. She couldn't go without trying. She had loved too long and powerfully. All, including Alfred and seemingly except Alaex, knew of it. They had laughed then; they were probably hysterical with mirth now. Yet she felt no shame. She cared not what they felt then or might be feeling now. She was desperate and she couldn't leave without one last attempt.

"Alaex, it doesn't have to be this way. We could—"

Suddenly Alaex understood everything he had not since her arrival. Worse still, he finally understood Alfred's pointed inquiries about Brita's knowledge of his wedding. Although he knew he had done nothing to encourage her, he felt the stirrings of compassion. Alaex tried to be gentle.

"Nay, we cannot." The words were soft, his resolve firm.

In surprise he watched tears gather over the frost in her eyes. His surprise grew as she continued on to him and then reached up and briefly kissed him on his lips. Then Brita turned and walked away, leaving a puzzled-looking Alaex staring at the tapestry over the hearth and an even more confused Iliani watching from the stairs.

Unlike Alaex or Iliani, as Brita thundered away from Fontwyn she was not confused. She was defiantly determined. She wanted Alaex and she would not give up. Five years was a long time to wait for naught. A grim set came to her lovely face. There were other ways.

Later that night, shortly after she and her entourage made camp, Brita excused herself. After relieving herself, she waited. Not long after, a warm hand closed over her mouth to seal her scream.

But Brita had no intention of screaming. She knew who it was. When she was spun around, her eyes quickly made out Cam's features in the growing dusk.

"You are not surprised," he said.

Brita shrugged and stepped back. She didn't fully trust Cam, but their alliance had been formed in mutual need. He had been the one to come to her and inform her of Alaex's marriage—not that she thought she cared about her feelings. He had thought their interests similar and best served if they banded together.

Cam's thinly veiled revulsion as he had said that her feelings for Alaex were no secret had not deterred Brita. His disgust didn't matter. Ignoring it, she made the agreement to assist him, while deciding then not to trust him.

Since then he had given her nothing to make her change her opinion, but that didn't bother her excessively. She didn't have to trust Cam or like him, only use him.

Finally she answered. "Why should I be surprised to see you? I expected you. I know you watch Fontwyn and so would know of my departure."

Excitedly Cam took a step forward, his eyes narrowing when Brita took a step back. "Since I have not surprised you, do not make me wait for what I want to hear."

Brita sighed. " 'Twill not be to your liking. I failed."

"You what?" Cam nearly shouted, forgetting himself. His eyes cast about and he expected that at any moment a guard would come crashing through the bush. After a few tense minutes passed and no one came, he visibly calmed himself. "What do you mean, you failed?"

"I mean that I failed," Brita hissed, her own anger, which had not been far all day, coming to the fore. "I was unable to entice him. It now remains for you to do."

Cam swung away from her, his thoughts racing. "How?" he said more to himself than to her.

"I do not know," Brita snapped, "but I tell you this, it had best be soon. Whatever went before, they have a true marriage now."

An ugly glitter entered Cam's eyes. "I will kill him."

Brita's heart lurched. "Nay, you will not. Besides," she said contemptuously, "you cannot. Cease foolish talk and think of something else."

Cursing himself for speaking that much of his thoughts aloud, since he knew of Brita's feelings for Alaex, Cam pretended to consider other options. Wanting to get away from her quickly and knowing he had spent too long in this spot as it was, he smiled and said, "I will try. Once I have achieved success, I will get word to you. Do not worry."

Brita was no fool and her feelings of distrust intensified at Cam's words. Aye, she knew he was no match for Alaex, but that was only in honorable combat. An arrow in the back or cowardly ambush knew no honor. The urge rose in her to ride back to Fontwyn and warn Alaex, but as her hands were not precisely clean, she let herself believe what Cam was saying. Besides, what else was there for her? Cam was her last hope. He had to succeed where she failed. She would do as he asked and wait.

Nodding to him stiffly, she left quickly, not turning her back on him until she was well within sight of the camp.

The moment Brita disappeared Cam's smile died. He knew she didn't trust him, but what could she do? Her involvement was nearly as great as his. Of course, she wouldn't be the one to kill Alaex, but that was a mere trifle because neither would he. That he would be the cause of Alaex's death was even less significant. There was no other way. He had tried.

In angry frustration he looked around the unremarkable wooded area and was assailed by a quick and fervent longing to return to Lourds Keep. But he knew he could not return, not without Iliani. She was his. She belonged to him. His father had always told him it was so. Alaex did not deserve her, and Cam grew tired of living as an outlaw, watching Iliani and Fontwyn from afar, watching what should have been his. He tired of the wait, and he would wait no longer. Unlike Brita, he could not go to Fontwyn to play on his and Iliani's past.

As he walked back to where he had his horse tethered, Cam recalled the angry words he had hurled at Alaex on what should have been his wedding day. Those words, though rash, were now fixed firmly in his mind as the solution.

Swinging himself onto his horse's back, he rode back to his camp, and a rich laugh, more chilling because of the lack of evil in it, escaped him. Aye, lovely Brita, that was the only way. What were the words spoken in the ceremony. " 'Til death us do part . . .?"

Cam would not have been so smug had he known that

Iliani had focused on that same phrase from the marriage vows on the day Alaex had come for her. Her reaction would have warned him about the ilk of his adversary. For while he thought those words were the solution to his problem with Alaex, Iliani had intuitively known they were nothing of the sort.

Chapter

→ 18 ←

Cam was not the only one with thoughts of Alaex. Iliani had been thinking of her husband ever since she had watched him that morning with Brita.

Strangely, she had not dwelled on the exchange she had heard between Alaex and his ward. Iliani hadn't lied to him last night when she had said she believed him. His action, when he had not known he was being observed, confirmed that she had been right to do so.

In the short time since Iliani's return to Fontwyn, she had developed and learned to rely on her instincts. Those same instincts that had told her Alaex spoke the truth now warned her that for Brita the matter was not finished. However, for Iliani it was. She did not have to concern herself any longer with Alaex's possible desire for his ward. She wanted to tell him that, but could not think of a way to bring up the subject without revealing what she knew and how she had come to gain her knowledge.

Their beginning was fragile and uncertain. There was no way she would damage it by having him think the real reason she had accepted his word was because she had spied on him to gain her proof. There had been enough distrust, and despite her lingering questions about the origin of their marriage, Iliani was aware of a tiny bubble of happiness forming in her chest. The feeling was so foreign, and given her circumstances, unexpected, that it had taken her a while to recognize it.

Once she acknowledged it, though, Iliani firmly decided to do all she could to make it grow into something more enduring. So instead of focusing on the things she still did not understand about her marriage, she steadfastly clung to the fact that things between Alaex and her were infinitely better than they had been. That undeniable fact grew each time she remembered last night and having been in his arms.

She was still flushing from a vivid and torrid memory when she entered the hall and unexpectedly encountered her husband. He seemed to be in a deep discussion with Jon, but when he casually glanced up to see who entered, and saw the flushed look on her face, his gaze softened and lingered.

Uncertain what to do, and feeling her face heat more under his warm perusal, Iliani walked over to the hearth near the table where Alaex and Jon stood, and picked up her embroidery. Usually she did her stitching earlier, but then Alaex was not usually in the hall at this time of day. Iliani found herself reluctant to leave his company, even if he was not talking to her. She was seated when he and Jon resumed their conversation.

"The additional length of wall should take no longer than a few months, unless you have changed your mind and want to reinforce the entire structure." There was a silence after Jon's words, and Iliani, certain that Alaex had heard him, looked up to see what was wrong.

To her surprise, Alaex was staring at her and Iliani found herself instantly ensnared by the subdued fire, potent as any caress, in his eyes. Her body reacted, and she nearly swayed toward him. The intensity of Alaex's stare deepened, encouraging her as they were both caught in the sensuality of the moment.

It was Jon's repetition of his question that broke the spell, making Iliani aware of her actions and surroundings. Her face quickly flushed with embarrassed heat and she pulled her eyes away from Alaex.

Alaex chuckled softly. "Nay, there is no need to redo the entire wall, only the western side." Alaex spoke to Jon but he continued to stare at Iliani, silently daring her to look at him again. He didn't glance at Jon at all.

However, Iliani did, and she was relieved that Alaex's lieutenant seemed unaware of what was happening as he was engrossed in studying the plans on the table before him. When she looked back at Alaex, Iliani glared a warning at him to stop, which Alaex blatantly ignored. His eyes moved from her lips to her breasts.

Iliani's indrawn breath at what felt as tangible as an actual caress was covered by Jon's query.

"With the additional length of the wall, do you think we will need to add three or four men to see to its defense?"

This time the prolonged silence made Jon look up from his drawings. He repeated his question, and when Alaex slowly looked to him blankly, Jon was forced to reiterate his query a third time.

"Four."

Jon frowned but said nothing and went back to his study of the plans. The moment Jon looked away, Alaex's eyes moved back to Iliani, who was now determined not to be caught in his sensual game again. She kept her eyes locked on the cloth in her lap.

After a brief period of quiet, she heard Jon ask, "Where?" and then repeat himself when again Alaex did not respond. However, when Jon looked up to see what was causing Alaex's unprecedented lapse in concentration, he finally saw what he had missed before as he followed his lord's gaze to Iliani's fiery profile.

Without a word, Jon rolled the plans and walked from the hall laughing.

Alaex did not notice Jon's departure, but Iliani did. She was about to tell him, when he gathered himself and turned as if he had been talking to Jon all along, only to realize the man was not there. When he looked back at Iliani, his expression was comical. His eyes dared her to laugh, but his own lips twitched revealingly.

Iliani burst out laughing, and Alaex took a step toward her, only to stop as Arthur entered the hall.

"Milord, if you have a moment, we need to discuss the renovation schedule for the hall's repairs. I passed Jon and he told me now would be a good time."

When Alaex's face colored, Iliani's mirth erupted again. It wasn't Alaex's glare that brought her laughter under control, but Arthur's clear confusion. Knowing that she couldn't dare meet Alaex's eyes again, with a few remaining chuckles Iliani excused herself, using the reason that she needed to speak with Gwyn.

Her smile was still in place when she found the servant. It lingered as she discussed a new weaving pattern with Gwyn, and it hovered as she oversaw the servant's chores. If anyone wondered at her unexplained joy, no one said anything.

Iliani noted the curious glances cast her way, but she didn't care. Putting their reaction from her mind, she moved about on feet that barely touched the ground.

As the day progressed, Iliani became aware of another source of happiness that had naught to do with what had taken place last night between her and Alaex. Although she couldn't say when it had occurred, the lightness in her heart left room for her to realize that she had stopped seeing Fontwyn as the place where Alaex had brought her. She was beginning to see it as her family's home and the place where she belonged.

Perhaps the feeling of belonging had begun when she and Gwyn had examined the tapestries and Iliani had remarked to the woman on the frequency of the use of the color purple within the hall. She was surprised to discover that the frequency was no coincidence. Purple had been a favorite color of her mother, for, according to Gwyn, the previous mistress had felt the color complemented her husband's eyes. When Gwyn had shyly added, "And now they complement yours, milady," Iliani experienced her first sense of connection to Fontwyn. The feeling of belonging, of being a part of something, whether tangible or not, was overwhelming.

Fontwyn was losing its sterile, unusual appearance and was taking on the characteristics of home. All those years at Lourds Keep, Iliani had done all she could to make herself believe that that place was her home. Marriage to Cam had been her way of legitimizing that desire. Iliani realized now that it had all been foolish and in vain. She had been unsuccessful in her goal of making Lourds Keep home because she had already had a home. Remembered or not, her home had been at Fontwyn, waiting for her return.

The more Iliani had thought about it, the clearer it became that her connection to Fontwyn had been happening gradually over the weeks she had been here. She had just been too occupied with other things—namely, her marriage—to notice.

The revelation was as keen as it was startling, and it intensified as Iliani rode along Fontwyn's paths. Even the land seemed different today, its beauty defined, its personality revealed. As she scanned the grass-covered ground and distant hills, Iliani learned something. As the hall had offered a fleeting glimpse of her mother, the land spoke of her father.

For the first time in her life, she felt closer to the man she'd known as her father and whom she had tried to recall for so long. Through the beauty of the land around her, she at long last came to see him.

Iliani was so affected by the emotion that she wanted to weep, especially when she had been unable to recall the numerous times at Lourds Keep when she had tried to envision her father or remember some small thing about him. Perhaps her failure was not based on scarcity of memory but the location. Her father had not been at Lourds Keep. He was here, in the massive stone walls of the hall, in the hidden trails of Fontwyn's forest, and the richness of its land.

Sitting astride Wind Dancer's back, viewing the expanse of Fontwyn's land from its highest point, that perception solidified. That it came at a time when she was so much at peace and entranced with the dark, ripe beauty of the land made tears threaten again. Not wanting the men to think anything amiss, Iliani turned and rode rapidly back to the hall, profoundly moved by the experience.

The nearer Iliani and her guard came to Fontwyn's massive stone walls, the higher her spirits lifted. True, the events of last night had neither blotted nor removed all of her questions, but they had brought changes that she would not have traded for anything on earth. When Geoff opened the gates and she and Wind Dancer thundered through, there was a serene look on Iliani's face as she entered the walls of her home.

And for the first time, Fontwyn felt as if it were just that.

Supper had been over hours ago and Iliani had bathed herself and washed and dried her long thick hair. The warm glow she had felt all day and that had grown during the evening under Alaex's even warmer gaze was fading. The hour was late and Alaex had not come to her, and she was plagued by questions. Should she go to him? Was that what he expected? The lingering uncertainty was rapidly eroding what good feeling she had left.

Iliani had long since admitted she wanted Alaex. She had thought, not so much from last night but from the events of the day, that he wanted her still. However, she was new at this wanting. Perhaps she had misunderstood his glances. Maybe she had seen in them only what she wanted. Perhaps . . .

Suddenly there was a discreet tap on the door. Rapidly smoothing her thick hair and straightening her robe, Iliani called out, "Come in."

Her disappointment was keen when Lucy's dark red head appeared in the door. "Aye, what is it?" she asked testily.

"Your pardon, lady," Lucy said, her face impassive. "I came to see if there was aught else you needed."

Iliani turned away, ashamed and angry that she had allowed her disappointment to show. Lucy had done nothing. In the last few days their relationship had been improving.

Walking over to the window to hide the upset her thoughts were causing, Iliani strove for a normal voice. "Nay, thank you."

Lucy nodded, aware of her mistress's distress. She was a good woman, that one—a little peculiar, but good nonetheless. She was like her father, Lucy thought with loyalty, and could Iliani have been privy to her thoughts, that sentiment would have pleased her greatly.

Unknown to Iliani, Lucy gave her one last sympathetic look and then turned to go, nearly shrieking when a dark shadow crossed her path. The door slipped from her nerveless fingers before she recognized the tall form of the new lord of Fontwyn.

Alaex ignored the woman's startled cry, and taking hold of the door, gently closed it and leaned back against the sturdy wood. He was watching Iliani, trying to gauge her mood, when she turned and saw him.

Joy burst through her and she almost ran to him, stopped at the last moment by her uncertainty. She marveled at the change a few moments made. Had he appeared seconds sooner, she would have felt no hesitation.

They stared at each other for agonizing moments, each waiting for the other either to move or reveal his thoughts. It was Alaex who finally broke the taut silence as the thought occurred to him that perhaps he had misread her warm blushes and intimate glances earlier today.

"Should I go?" he asked gruffly, recalling the gentle manner in which Iliani could shred his pride. After the sweet expectation of the day, he would be unable to endure such an episode.

Iliani had pictured his coming to her. She had wanted

it desperately. But now that he was here, why was it not going the way she had imagined? He had scarcely arrived and he was asking if he should leave. Without knowing how she knew, Iliani knew that the next few moments were pivotal. They would decide whether she got what she wanted or if she regressed to being alone. Suddenly alone seemed unbearable.

"Do you want to go?" she asked huskily, walking toward him with fluid sensuousness.

Alaex swallowed, chastising himself for hoping again. There was no invitation in her eyes or the sway of her hips or her words.

Iliani reached him, and he was still denying it. He was denying it when her arms slipped around his neck; however, denial and every other thought took flight when her hips brushed against his and her lips teased his. Her next whispered words sounded softly in his ears and echoed loudly in his heart. "That is not my desire."

Alaex melted and was freed from the icy feeling of rejection that had held him immobile. Although with her first touch he had lost the ability to think, passion-driven emotion took over and guided him. His arms closed around Iliani, locking her in his tight embrace and lifting her off the floor.

When he pulled away from the growing fervor of their kiss, he murmured, "Your bed or mine?"

Iliani's violet gaze was a perfect reflection of the passion in his. "How about ours?"

Alaex groaned and lowered his head again. This time when he broke the embrace, Iliani saw laughter in his eyes along with the passion. Ruefully he said, "Whichever that is, we'd best find it soon or the floor will win out over either."

Iliani smiled, unaware of how little she needed that inviting action. Her face glowed and as Alaex laid her on the bed and removed her robe, he saw that the glow was not just in her face. Her entire body seemed to radiate joy and happiness. This was no sacrifice here. This was passion in its unadulterated form. And as he lowered himself to her side to accept all of her generous offer, he thanked God for it.

Alaex's eyes snapped open and he was instantly alert. He couldn't tell what had caused him to awaken so abruptly, so completely, but he wasn't lulled by the undisturbed quiet. Something was wrong. He felt it. He was about to ease from the bed, automatically reaching on the floor beside it for his sword, when he heard it. The faint sound of someone struggling or in pain. The noise was so faint he thought he might have imagined it; nevertheless, he turned to assure himself that all was well with Iliani.

One look at her contorted face, revealed by the fire left burning in the hearth, and Alaex knew what had awakened him on the alert. The sounds, even though she now lay still, had come from her. Even now she grimaced and her head moved slowly from side to side.

"Iliani? Iliani, sweet, what is it?" he called softly, uncertain whether she slept or was in pain and had merely closed her eyes against it.

Unfocused violet eyes met concerned pale blue ones. Instantly Iliani's eyes cleared and her face smoothed. "What is it, Alaex?" she asked, echoing his words to her.

Alaex eased back down on the bed and pulled her into his arms. He sighed. "'Twas my question to you. You were moaning and your face bore the look of one in pain. Are you ill?"

Iliani relaxed against him. "Nay," she drowsily replied, ready to go back to sleep. If there was nothing the matter, she wanted to go to sleep. Sated from Alaex's vigorous and thorough lovemaking, Iliani had drifted effortlessly off, awakening only when Alaex called her name.

"Did you dream?"

"I don't think so." Iliani yawned, struggling to answer his questions and hoping he had no more.

"Are you certain?" Alaex persisted.

Iliani opened one eye and looked up at him. "As

certain as I can be. Even if I did, Alaex, what is your intent? Will you rush into my dreams and ease me from my torment?" she teased, trying to lighten his mood.

Alaex turned onto his side, facing her, his arms still around her. "If I could," he answered with a solemnity that Iliani didn't doubt.

She smiled. "My thanks, noble warrior, but your protection is unnecessary. No one here threatens me."

Iliani snuggled deeper into his side, and Alaex's arms tightened around her protectively. His heart clenched with the thought of anything ever happening to her, and to soothe his fear, not hers, he promised himself that as long as he drew breath, no one ever would.

Chapter

➤ 19 ◄

The hall was dimly lit, its shadowy darkness somehow both menacing and soothing as candle flame flickered unsteadily in the draft of the corridor. It was quiet, creating an aura of muted terror. She felt it. Yet even as the darkness frightened her, it beckoned. Just a little farther. She was able to walk through it calmly, for in some strange way it was familiar and she knew exactly where she was going. Unerringly she reached her destination and stopped. There it was as always and there was more light now, but the terror was greater. Then she saw why. He just lay there unmoving. He was dead. There was no blood, but he was dead. She was sure of it. Her dog had done the same thing when it was dead. They had put him in the earth and told her her mother was there, too. Would they put him in the earth? Nay! He shouldn't go in the earth! He shouldn't be dead, but he was. He lay there unmoving and she knew it.

Iliani awakened feeling refreshed yet curiously aware of a sense of unpleasantness. She took a moment to consider why that should be so, and finding no reason, she bounded out of bed.

Going through her ablutions as quickly as she could, she hurried to get below stairs. She wanted to get a glimpse of Alaex before he started his day.

Suddenly Iliani paused. Thoughts of Alaex brought a feeling of terror, and her hand slowed as it reached for the door.

" 'Tis nothing," she said aloud; yet she was unable to ignore the compulsion to turn back to look at the bed. Seeing that massive structure made her remember Alaex's concerns the night before, and the tight feeling in her chest eased.

"See what you've done with your talk of dreams and the like, Alaex," she continued. "There is naught to fear. For once, everything is going well."

Now as she watched the bed, a smile instead of a frown appeared on her features, and it remained as she shut the door behind her. It was going to be a wonderful day, Iliani thought, this time silently as she practically skipped below stairs to join the others to break the fast.

Iliani was not wrong in her feelings. It was a wonderful day, followed by another and yet another. The days began to pass in a blissfully uncomplicated blur and the nights went by in a delightfully sensuous haze.

Before her eyes, the many sides of her husband's personality were unfolding, and each discovery was more pleasant than the last. Alaex was turning out to be more than she had expected and better than she could have hoped. Beneath his seemingly impenetrable exterior was a man who was sensuously provocative and gently attentive. He might not have the words to express his feelings, but his actions spoke more than volumes of flowery phrases.

There was only one blot on Iliani's growing happiness. Each night after they loved, although Alaex would sometimes fall asleep immediately after, by morning he was always gone. Iliani found out that she had been wrong in her belief that he rose early. The truth was that he left after she went to sleep. After awakening once in the middle of the night, she had discovered that he was gone, and it was too early for rising. He hadn't returned.

Iliani tried to allay her worries over this by saying it was unimportant, but that was untrue. It was important to her. Although Alaex showed no irritation with her when she would see him later, his coming and going in the night began to leave Iliani with the disturbing feeling of being used. It made her feel like a convenience, not a wife, and to her it gave their relationship a transient air. She didn't like it, and she knew that she would be unable to endure it silently for long. Her endurance ended the fourth time it happened.

That morning when Iliani encountered Alaex, she could no longer dismiss her trepidations over him leaving her bed. With thoughts of why he would do such a thing plaguing her, her greeting was not as enthusiastic as it had been since their relationship had become physical.

"Good morn," she said quietly.

Alaex returned her greeting, watching her strangely before he added, "Did you rest well?"

Iliani stiffened. "Fine. Did you?"

Alaex stared at her without answering, sensing something was wrong. He was about to question her when Iliani said, "That's not completely true." Biting her lip in consternation, Iliani began to blurt, "Alaex, why—"

Her question was abruptly cut off as the men boisterously entered, going to their place at the table. Seeing that her chance to discuss his absence from her bed had passed, Iliani turned away and stopped suddenly when Alaex put his hand on her arm. She didn't look up at him immediately and Alaex did not wait for her to do so. Pulling her face to his, he lowered his lips to hers and whispered in a voice that conveyed regret and promise, "Later."

Later came much too swiftly for Iliani, for throughout the day she had been troubled by doubts as to whether she should ask him why even though he made love to her he still sought his bed elsewhere. Nevertheless it was too late for that consideration as she heard Alaex enter the room and close the door.

Iliani was standing at her favorite spot by the window, looking out. Until Alaex entered, she had not felt a need for a garment heavier than her chamber robe. Suddenly she was chilled and it took but a moment to realize that it was not from the temperature but from her nervousness. Her edginess was not lessened when Alaex remained silent, waiting.

He watched her a while longer, and then he started toward her, and Iliani clasped her hands together to still their shaking. There was always something about the way Alaex walked so purposefully that made her feel stalked. It was his way of concentrating on whatever was at hand. That purposefulness was there regardless of what he did, from sparring with his men to making love to her. When she was so unsure of him and unable to read his intent, being the focus of his intense attention was nerve-wracking.

When he took her in his arms Iliani expected him to kiss her, but instead he turned her back to him and pulled her into his warm embrace. They stood that way for a while, both staring into the night, and slowly Iliani's nervousness eased. It was as if she were seduced by the security of his arms and the peaceful and quiet nocturnal sounds.

"Can you tell me now?" Alaex's voice was whisper soft.

Strangely Iliani could. Without preamble, instead of asking why he left her at night, she said, "I want you to stay with me all night." Even though the words seemed naked in the silence, Iliani gave him no more of an explanation. If he stayed, it had to be because he wanted to and not for anything else.

Alaex turned her around, and Iliani had her answer. She did not know how he managed to look tender, loving, and slightly lecherous at the same time, but as he pulled her to him fiercely, he did. And in the hours that followed he showed her each of those emotions separately and in combination, leaving her breathless, extremely pleased, and happy that she had found the courage to ask him to stay.

When Iliani awakened the following morning, Alaex was not in bed. The curiousness of this occurred to her as she noted that it was not late and he should have been. She was just beginning to agonize over the possibility that despite her asking he had left anyway, when she saw the wildflower on the pillow next to her. It was beautiful, pale yellow, clearly one of the first early spring blossoms.

Iliani reached out to touch it, her vision blurring and her hand shaking, when she saw Alaex standing across the room in front of the window. In one of the sweetest and tenderest moments of her life, their eyes met just as her hand closed around the blossom. Their gazes locked.

Slowly Alaex walked over to her, not breaking their stare, and with a gentle hand touched her face.

"It made me think of you."

He didn't say anything else. But those few achingly sweet words were more than enough. Tears flowed down Iliani's cheeks. She didn't know what to say. However, one of the wonderful things she was learning from Alaex was that he didn't expect a word for every deed. So Iliani grasped his hand, pulling him to her, and proceeded to show him with all the vigor in her young body what she didn't have the words to describe.

They loved fiercely and passionately, without speaking a word, the heated poignant silence between them a communication all its own. After bliss had brought them back to the realm of mortals, they both slept, still joined and at peace.

When Iliani awakened again she was truly alone. Unhurriedly she reached out and pulled Alaex's pillow to her chest, all her previous worry gone about being left alone after they made love. The flower he gave her had done more than reveal his sentimentality. By giving it to her, Alaex was also letting her know that he was with her even when he was not physically present, and that at those same times she was with him. Iliani sighed, contented. Nay, her worries and doubts were gone. Through his touching sensitivity and the fire of his ardor, Alaex had burned away each and every one.

Later that evening as Iliani sat at the table after the evening meal, she was still marveling over the tender side Alaex had revealed that morning. She wanted to reach out and touch him, but being unsure of how he felt about public displays of affection, she turned away from him reluctantly and watched the servants clear the table.

She was surprised, then, when moments after she turned from him she felt Alaex grip her left hand, which had been lying on the table. Her shock grew when she turned, thinking he was trying to gain her attention, and discovered that Alaex wasn't even looking at her. He was deep in conversation with Jon about Fontwyn's defenses.

Thinking his touch an absent gesture, Iliani fought to control her reaction to it and ignore the fact that everyone noticed. Her discomfort increased when he began to play with her fingers while seemingly giving Jon all his attention.

Iliani, who seconds before had wanted his touch, now surreptitiously tried to pull her hand from his. Alaex might not notice or care that everyone watched with knowing smiles, but she did. However, the harder she tried to remove her hand, the tighter his grip became. Looking anywhere but at him, and avoiding direct eye contact with everyone, Iliani's dismay grew as she realized that despite their audience, she was becoming aroused by his touch. Alaex was rubbing slow circles in the center of her palm with light, sensuous strokes of his fingertips. She began to shift uncomfortably, and after trying once more to pull her hand away, she sat rigidly, hoping Alaex would soon end either his conversation or his torture. At a slight increase in the pressure of his middle finger in her palm, Iliani had to bite her lip to suppress her sudden groan. She lowered her eyes then, afraid that anyone looking would have seen her desire.

Again she tried to remove her hand, and again Alaex would not allow it. Iliani's thoughts were in a sensuous jumble and she was concentrating so hard on ignoring it that she did not realize that Gwyn stood over her expectantly. When she looked up into the woman's face, Iliani knew the servant had said something. Yet if her life hung in the balance, Iliani couldn't have formed a coherent answer, even if she knew what Gwyn had said.

Casting another quick glance at Alaex, Iliani saw he was still unaware of the havoc he was causing. In an attempt to be as nonchalant as he, she refused to ask Gwyn to repeat herself. So she tried for a neutral response and what she hoped was a normal voice.

"That will be fine."

The instant the words were out, Iliani knew her tone of voice was not the problem. Gwyn's expression was blank.

"Fine, milady?" she repeated dubiously.

At that moment Alaex squeezed her hand, and when she looked at him there was a smile on his face and rich laughter in his eyes, and Iliani did not mistake his message. This was wicked revenge for what she had done to him the day after they had made love the first time.

Alaex's voice was bland and his smile did not dim as he kissed her palm before releasing her hand. "A good cook Gwyn might be, Iliani, but I do not think even one of her talent knows how to prepare your request."

Iliani's face reddened and she was torn between mortification and laughter. She didn't dare look at anyone else, certain by the silence that they had heard her answer to Gwyn's question and Alaex's teasing response. Obviously Gwyn had asked—and Iliani cursed herself for not remembering sooner the servant's habit of asking at the end of supper her mistress's preference for the next day—what she would like for the evening meal tomorrow.

When Iliani found the courage to face Gwyn, the

servant's gentle smile eased a bit of her embarrassment. "What I mean," she murmured, "is that whatever you decide, I am sure will be fine."

Gwyn nodded and turned away, and Iliani rose to leave. As she looked around the table, there were traces of smiles on the men's faces, but no cruelty. They seemed both surprised and amused by Alaex's behavior and her reaction. The rest of her embarrassment faded.

However, when she reached the stairs, Iliani heard Thibert laughingly say to Jon, "If 'fine' is good enough for milady's evening meal, then I shall have a 'how do you do' to break the fast."

The rest of the men laughed good-naturedly, stopping abruptly when they realized Iliani had not entirely left and had heard them.

Iliani hurried to break the weighty silence. She didn't turn back, but with a perfectly normal voice she called over her shoulder, "Jon, tell Thibert that that is what 'milady' had planned for noon."

Their laughter resumed and the sound of it warmed Iliani as she climbed the stairs. For once the banter had not been flowing around her. She had been in it.

He just lay there unmoving. There was no blood, but he was dead. She was sure of it. He shouldn't go into the earth. He shouldn't be dead, but he was. He lay there unmoving and she knew it. She wanted to go to him, but she didn't. It was too cold and too dark, and she was much too frightened.

Iliani sat up abruptly and stared into the darkness. She was cold, chilled despite the perspiration that poured off her forehead and dampened her chest. Then she began to shake, or was it because Alaex was shaking her, calling her name?

She finally made out his form and some of the chill left her as she recognized him and where she was. Iliani threw herself into his arms, pressing as close as she could against his chest.

Alaex rubbed her hair soothingly, feeling the perspiration on her face and body, even though she shook in his arms. He was sure it was not from cold. The weather had been unseasonably warm and he had allowed the fire to burn lower than usual.

"Iliani, what is it?"

Her only response was to shake her head as her body continued to tremble. Gently Alaex eased them both back down into the bed. He lay quietly holding her, giving her a chance to become less agitated, calming her as best he could with gentle kisses, soft words, and light caresses. Eventually she quieted.

"What is it?" he asked again. "Did you have a nightmare?"

The terror of the dream had faded somewhat, and although now as Iliani thought of it she could find no logical reason for fear, it was there. It could be calmed but not dismissed, because although the dream was shorter this time, it made her remember what she had not: the dream from the night before.

"Tell me," Alaex cajoled softly.

Iliani's throat was dry and her voice sounded hoarse as if sore from silent screams. "There is not much to tell," she began hesitantly.

Alaex squeezed her gently. "Then tell me not much."

His calm tenacity was soothing, and Iliani's terror receded further. "All I recall is being in the hall in the dark and a man lying dead on the floor."

"What hall?" Alaex queried.

"This one."

"You are certain the man was dead, not just sleeping?"

Iliani forced herself to envision the dream. She shivered. "Nay. He is dead. I know it."

Alaex placed a soft kiss on her head. "Who is he?"

She was silent a long time. "I do not know."

Alaex sighed and kissed her again. "Then just forget it, Iliani. 'Tis a dream, naught else. You are safe here in your home and in my arms."

Iliani inched closer to his naked body and the warmth it provided. "I will try."

Alaex tipped up her face and lowered his head. The instant his lips touched hers, Iliani could feel the difference in this kiss from the others. Those had been meant to calm and soothe her. This one did nothing of the sort. It lit a fire in her breast and made her heart race with excitement instead of fear.

She knew he was trying to distract her, and for the next few glorious minutes he succeeded. However, when their passion abated and Alaex gently commanded her to rest, despite the satisfied feeling of her body it was a long time before Iliani's mind let her relax into sleep.

Chapter

⇌ 20 ⇋

When Iliani arose the next day, she tried to put the terror of her nightmare from her mind. She saw the wisdom in what Alaex had said. There was no need to worry. She didn't know who the man in her dream was, and aside from the darkness—an element present in most dreams—there had been nothing menacing about it.

Except the cold—and the fear.

Iliani quickly put that unbidden thought from her mind. There was much to do, and because of the particular loveliness of the day, she found herself anxious to start.

Whether it was the day's beauty that beckoned her or the terror of the dream that impelled her, Iliani did not consider. The sun shone brightly in a cloudless blue sky, and as can happen only in spring, everything looked new and crisp, burgeoning with life. Under such circumstances there was no room for unpleasantness, and the fears of the night that had seemed so vivid began to fade.

Iliani smiled to herself as she walked with an increased lightness in her step to the stables to get Wind Dancer. It was going to be a wonderful day for riding. Nearing the large structure where the horses were kept, she saw her guard already mounted and waiting. She smiled at them and hurried inside to get her mount, eager to be off and not wanting to keep them waiting any longer.

When the men had first started escorting her, they used to have Wind Dancer saddled and waiting, but the horse's recalcitrant nature with anyone but Iliani had soon discouraged them from performing this task. They didn't want to harm the beast or be harmed themselves. After seeing that she knew how, they left it to her to see to her horse.

Iliani approached the place where Wind Dancer stood, calling softly to the gelding. Its ears perked at the sound of her voice, and when Iliani moved in closer, the horse began to shift nervously.

"Easy, easy," she said, trying to soothe the horse. Wind Dancer was a high-strung, spirited beast, and he didn't like change. After the recent upheavals in her usually mundane life, Iliani sympathized with the feeling. However, much like the changes in his mistress's life, Wind Dancer had no choice in the recent changes in his venue.

For the past few days, while Alaex had set the men to working on the stable, Wind Dancer had been moved from his usual place. This change, coming not too long after having to become accustomed to a new stable, had made the gelding more skittish than ever. Instead of the stall where he had stood for weeks, today he stood where Alaex's large warhorse normally stayed.

Iliani approached him gently. "How goes it, my fine spirited beast?"

Seeming more nervous than ever with its new surroundings, the horse backed up a little.

"Come now, boy," Iliani crooned softly, advancing into the stall. "You know 'tis I, Iliani."

As the horse skittered a little more, Iliani moved to its side. She was about to pat his deep flanks when Wind Dancer pranced away again.

When the gelding moved to the side, Iliani saw the long, sharp, jagged wood protruding from the rear wall of the stall. But even if she could move the massive amount of horseflesh, it would be too late.

Wind Dancer took one final jolting step back only to be pierced by the wood. The horse, already nervous, screamed and reared with pain. Iliani, caught as she was between the side of the stall and the gelding's side, was knocked back, slamming into the side wall with a force that took her breath away. She was too dazed to move, and even if she could, it would be a dangerous thing to do in the confines of the stall with Wind Dancer rearing as he was. The blow having deprived her of breath, she couldn't scream, and with the flailing danger from the horse's hooves, she couldn't move.

Dread gathered in Iliani's heart as she knew it was only a matter of seconds until those mighty hooves crashed into her. Then she heard a shout and the sound of running feet.

Thibert, alerted by the unusual amount of noise, as Wind Dancer was usually quiet and docile whenever his mistress was near, had come into the stable. In an instant he took in the situation, called for the men as he grabbed a rope from the wall, and began to make a loop to throw around the gelding's neck. Fear for Iliani made him want to rush over to her. Yet he knew it would be exceedingly foolish to approach the horse in his already maddened state. The great beast barely tolerated them when it was calm. With it agitated . . .

All Thibert could do was pray quickly and fervently that Iliani did not move. The rest of the men had edged around the horse, Ethelward having made a similar loop in another rope. At Thibert's nod they both threw their ropes, and Thibert nearly swallowed his tongue when both ropes fell uselessly to the floor, having missed Wind Dancer's head.

The failed attempt to rope Wind Dancer made him more agitated than ever, and he was beginning to rear and turn. Again Thibert and Ethelward threw their ropes, and this time one after another, the loops went over the horse's neck as both men planted their feet and pulled. It was a wonder they didn't choke the beast to death, so tight was their grip as the continued terror of what the horse could do to Iliani's slight form seized them. They were perspiring with fear and exertion as they fought to keep the horse from turning.

After a few more struggle-filled moments, they succeeded in keeping the horse turned away from Iliani; however, no one went near Wind Dancer until his rearing had calmed into a few disjointed leaps. By this time Alaex had been told of the occurrence and had come bursting into the stable, nearly upsetting the beast anew.

"Iliani?" he called, barely able to see her dark head above the wall of the stall.

Iliani tried to answer, but now terror instead of a blow was stealing her breath.

"Iliani?"

Iliani heard his fear. Swallowing with difficulty, her breathing still shallow from fear, she was able to produce a croaking response. "Aye, I am unharmed."

Despite Wind Dancer's continued nervous shuffling, Alaex went over to the stall. When the gelding's ears began to twitch and it jumped, Alaex backed away. Then he went to the stall beside the horse and stood on the other side of Iliani, with the stall wall between them. Using the notches in the planks of wood to help him over, Alaex climbed atop while Thibert and Ethelward kept the horse's head turned through their unrelenting pull on the ropes.

Iliani was unaware of what was occurring, and so when Alaex's hands reached over and pulled her up, gripping her beneath her armpits to do it, she screamed.

The sound started Wind Dancer rearing again, and this time he turned toward it. Despite the men's grip on the ropes, there was no help for it. The animal was too powerfully enraged. It reared and Alaex barely got Iliani out in time before the beast's mighty hooves struck the wall where she had been standing.

With Alaex standing on the planks to lift Iliani over and Wind Dancer's hooves crashing against them, they gave way, causing them both to tumble to the ground. At the last instant, Alaex managed to land beneath her so that he cushioned her fall.

Iliani barely had time to register this, because with Wind Dancer still rearing and wood flying and splintering, Alaex rolled with her, taking her out of the danger. When he finished rolling, he lay on top and the wood struck his back instead of hers.

In mere seconds, which seemed like an eternity to Iliani, the horse had again quieted and the wood had ceased flying; Alaex, however, did not move from her. Caught between the hardness of his chest and the floor, Iliani again found it difficult to breathe.

After having moved Wind Dancer further away from the debris, Thibert and the others came over and stood around them. No one said a word, and still Alaex did not move, holding Iliani in a near-deathlike grip.

Iliani was beginning to think a piece of the wood had struck him on the head, making him unconscious. She struggled then to move, not because of her lack of air, but from her fear for him. It was her struggles that alerted her to the fact that Alaex definitely was not unconscious. His grip tightened more, and Iliani gasped painfully.

It was Thibert whom Iliani credited with actually saving her life. Finally taking in what was happening, he called to Alaex, and at last his voice seemed to press past the terror gripping his lord's mind.

"Alaex, I do not believe she can breathe."

It finally registered to Alaex that Iliani was not harmed but struggling beneath him, and some sanity returned. Quickly he got up from the floor, bringing Iliani with him. He relaxed his grip, but he did not release her.

Although he knew she was not hurt, Alaex found he could neither speak nor let her go. Each time he thought himself capable, he remembered the horror and his arms tightened.

She could have died. He finally found his voice. "Kill it."

Thibert turned away, instantly understanding. He did not halt at Iliani's impassioned, "Nay!"

His sword was drawn when she screamed again, "Nay! Alaex, please. He's hurt."

Alaex looked into her eyes, and the tears and anguish he saw shimmering in their violet depths swayed him.

"Hold!" he commanded Thibert without looking from Iliani's eyes. "Stay here," he said softly, going over to where Wind Dancer stood.

The horse was still nervous and skittered away from him. Thibert, despite Alaex's order to hold, still had his sword at the ready, looking as if he were prepared to battle a fierce dragon. Watching his face, Alaex found his first occasion to smile. Slowly he walked around the beast, and when he got to the rear of it he saw the wound. It was ugly and deep and a large piece of wood was still in the horse's hindquarter.

Alaex grimaced. While not fatal, the wound was undoubtedly painful. Yet the thing had to be removed, and given the gelding's temperament and the pain it was in already, it was not going to be an easy task.

"What is it?" a soft voice asked behind him, and Alaex turned abruptly, the horse forgotten. His gaze darkened.

"I thought I told you to keep away."

Iliani, rapidly regaining some of her spirit, smiled weakly. "He's my horse, Alaex. I need to know. Besides he is . . ." She started to say "calm," but one look in Wind Dancer's wild eyes and she knew differently. "Calmer."

Alaex grunted and came over to her. "Not for long, I fear."

"Is it so bad, then? Did he prick—"

" 'Tis more than a prick, Iliani," Alaex began gently.

"The horse near impaled himself on the thing. 'Tis fortunate that the wound is in flesh; however, the worst of it is that a part of the wood is still imbedded. He may yet have to be put to sleep."

Iliani's eyes widened. "But why?"

"Because," Alaex said, regretful that he had to hurt her, knowing how she felt about her horse, "the wood needs removing. The horse will not allow it without rebelling and it is already in pain, which will only worsen. You saw how he behaved before. If the wood is left alone, infection will set in and the only choice would then be to ease the beast's misery by putting it to sleep."

"Alaex, please," Iliani begged, knowing the truth of what he said and unable to accept it. It was a request that he find another way and Alaex was moved by her trust just as he cursed it for asserting itself now in a situation he could ill control.

Again he did not pull his glance away. "Thibert!"

"Aye, Alaex?" the square-faced man answered solemnly.

"We have need of the ropes again."

When Thibert turned to get them, Alaex said to Iliani, "This time, you will stay put."

Iliani was about to nod her agreement, sensing he was about to try to save her horse, but then she asked, "What are you going to do?"

Alaex sighed. "The wood must come out. Therefore, while Thibert and Ethelward hold the horse, I will pull it."

Remembering Wind Dancer's reaction before, Iliani paled. "Nay, Alaex, you cannot," she blurted, scarcely realizing that she contradicted him in front of his men. She loved her horse, true, but she . . .

Iliani's mind went blank, unwilling to complete that thought. All she knew was that she didn't want Alaex to die or to endanger himself unnecessarily.

"There is no alternative," Alaex countered, breaking into her thoughts, "except to kill him."

Wind Dancer chose that moment to back up, and

when he brushed his rear against the wall, touching his wound, he began to whinny and rear slightly.

Instantly Alaex grabbed Iliani and pulled her away. When he thought he had her at a safe distance, he said, "One or the other, Iliani. The beast suffers."

Alaex read her refusal to accept the horse's death. With another sigh, he squeezed her in silent admonishment to remain there and was about to turn away when Iliani grabbed his sleeve.

"Wait," she said softly. There was something else. She hadn't done it in a long time so she was uncertain it would work. Besides that, she didn't relish doing it in front of Alaex and his men. They would think her odd. Still, it was the best chance Alaex had if he were trying to save her horse, and Iliani could see that was his intent. She pushed aside her personal feelings and all the uncertainty from her voice.

"Let me soothe him, Alaex."

"How?"

Iliani flushed, but she had known he would ask. "By talking to him."

"Talking to him?" Alaex repeated with disbelief.

"Aye," Iliani averred, her gaze faltering slightly beneath his disbelieving expression. She hurried on before she lost the nerve and he lost his patience. "I know 'tis difficult to believe, and I cannot in truth fully explain it. I only know that by talking to Wind Dancer I have the ability to control him."

"So does any other master over his steed," Alaex countered.

Iliani shook her head. "Nay. This is different. Have your men not told you that he rebels when they come near? Have they not also told you that I can quiet him with but a few whispered words and then he will stand still as stone until I have done what I needed?"

Alaex could not deny he had heard of that astounding feat. His men told him everything.

"Aye, they have spoken of it. However, your talent was useless today. The beast nearly killed you."

"That is true, but by the time I saw the sharp wood, 'twas too late. After that I could not breathe, let alone speak. Let me try it. If he balks, I will accept your alternative because I do not want him to suffer, nor do I want you to be injured or killed trying to save him."

She saw him weakening. "Please, Alaex. I promise to be cautious and you yourself can tell me when to move away. I give you my word to obey instantly."

A rueful smile tugged at Alaex's full lips. "Instantly? 'Twould be a first, no doubt."

Sensing she had swayed him, Iliani smiled back and ignoring his astounded disbelief, confirmed "Instantly" without hesitation.

Alaex nodded, and the only thing that kept Iliani from hugging him was the fact that he turned so that together they could walk back to where Wind Dancer was standing in the center of the loose circle of his men. They stood near enough to keep the horse from bringing further harm to itself and far enough to keep it from harming them.

Iliani walked slowly through them, and Thibert was about to restrain her when Alaex's soft voice stopped him. "Nay." He walked beside Iliani until Wind Dancer, sensing his presence, began to shy.

Alaex stopped and Iliani continued, calling softly to the horse, and although he wanted to call her back and say to move away, he couldn't take advantage of her given word that way. However, he promised himself grimly, one move from that gelding of hers and it was over.

As Iliani took another quiet step toward her horse, Alaex and all the others were the furthest thought from her mind. She began talking softly to Wind Dancer, while praying she wasn't making the biggest and possibly last mistake of her life.

Iliani made eye contact with the gelding and still she crooningly whispered to it. In slow degrees, she saw Wind Dancer calm, and by the time she reached the horse he was perfectly still. She grabbed his head between her arms, and without a break in her glance or her words she closed the last bit of distance.

Alaex and the men watched in awe. After a few seconds of incredulous staring, Alaex realized that he had to move around to the horse's rear. Iliani couldn't break her communication with the beast, and from what Alaex could see he was as still as he would ever be.

The gelding paid Alaex no attention as he moved around him. Thibert and the others were so awed that they were motionless, so that except for Alaex's stealthy footsteps crunching the hay and Iliani's soft voice, there was no sound at all in the stable.

When Alaex reached the horse's rear, he still couldn't fully believe what was happening, but taking no time to dwell on it, he muttered brief thanks that enough of the wood was protruding so that he could grip it. He also added a plea that he not find himself in the next instant blown through the wall of the stable should the gelding not be as docile as he appeared. Then he reached out swiftly and grabbed the wood and pulled. Although Wind Dancer's flanks trembled, the horse did not move.

Alaex was still in shock at what Iliani had done when he came back around the beast and rejoined his men. Within moments he had returned to the horse's side with water and had the wounds cleansed and bandaged. It was only after Wind Dancer was comfortably replaced in a stall chewing on some hay that the tension eased.

As they left the stable, Alaex noticed the incredulous looks his men were casting at his wife. Although he, too, was amazed, he wanted to ensure that his men's minds were not working toward the unsavory. His own questions he would save for later. With a brief order for them to await him, Alaex escorted Iliani back to the hall.

They had taken a few steps and were beyond earshot of his men when he asked, "How were you able to do that?"

Iliani shrugged, very uncomfortable with the look he was giving her, not too unlike those of his men. "I do not know, nor do I understand it. It just is. I am—" She paused. "I am just able to communicate with animals," she finished lamely.

"All animals or just horses?"

Beginning to feel like the freak she always strove hard to convince herself she wasn't after such an episode, Iliani muttered defensively, "I have not been around *all* animals so I would not know."

Alaex heard the angry embarrassment in her voice. "I meant no offense, but you must allow 'tis unusual."

"Aye," Iliani replied shortly before going through the hall door that he held open for her. When he didn't follow her through, she turned questioning eyes on him.

"I shall be along anon. I want to check with my men that all is well."

Alaex walked away and Iliani said nothing. She knew what he intended. He was going to make sure that his men did not think her an oddity, or worse, a sorceress. Well, she was neither and she wished him success in his endeavors. It would be difficult to convince his men of something it looked like he didn't quite believe himself.

Chapter

→ 21 ←

A few days after the episode with Wind Dancer, there was another bizarre accident. It occurred the day before Alaex went to see Alfred and was more the disturbing because of the routine sameness that had fallen over Iliani's life.

She was on her way to speak to Arthur at Alaex's request. He wanted her to tell the servant that owing to his imminent departure he would not be able to meet with him, and that during his absence he did not want the work to proceed because he specifically wished to oversee it.

There was a portion of Fontwyn that even now Iliani had not toured. It was the level behind and below the main hall. As only the servants usually occupied it, before now she'd had no real reason to go there. For that reason and because it was unexpectedly darker than she had thought it would be, she walked with care.

Yet even proceeding with caution, she was unable to catch herself as she placed her foot on air instead of the step that should have been there. However, her shriek of fear and surprise was cut short and her fall was abruptly halted when Arthur, carrying a candle to light his way, appeared before her.

The elderly servant showed surprising strength as he gripped her gown with one hand, held his light with the other, and fought to keep them both from plunging headlong into the darkness. Although he kept her from completely falling, her momentum made her swing about and come down hard on her foot, which gave way and caused her to land harshly on her bottom with Arthur now standing on the stair above her.

Iliani's heart was beating so frantically that she was afraid it would leap from her chest. Arthur, when she cast a look up at him, didn't appear any calmer.

"Are you unharmed, milady?" he asked anxiously, and Iliani could not decide if fear or anxiety caused the breathless quality in his voice.

"I am a lot better than I could have been had you not appeared when you did. Thank you, Arthur. I believe you saved my life."

Arthur nodded his acceptance of her gratitude, his face flushed, and again Iliani could scarcely tell the source—her words or what had just occurred.

"May I ask, lady, what you are doing here?"

Iliani gave him a tepid smile. "I was coming for you, or rather to tell you that milord would not be able to talk with you about the renovations to the hall. He has decided to have the work stopped until his return from the king." She looked up at the stair that even in the near darkness she could see was all but gone, and when she spoke again her voice was wry. "But perhaps given the state of some conditions, he would rethink his decision."

Arthur followed her gaze. "I do not understand, milady," he murmured, puzzled. "I cannot recall it being thus before, and the dark . . ." He stopped to shake his white head, staring at the wall as if he expected to find the answer to what bewildered him there. Looking more confused than ever, he shook his head and then looked back to Iliani. "Can you walk back up?" he asked with concern.

Iliani was sure she was fine, but when she stood and took a step, she gasped with pain. Her left ankle would not support her weight.

"I was about to ease your fears, Arthur," she said with a pained expression. "It now seems I cannot."

Arthur understood. Stepping over the damaged stair, he disappeared and quickly returned with Alaex, who didn't ask what happened, as Arthur had obviously told him. Wordlessly he lifted Iliani, not setting her down until he laid her on their bed. He dismissed Arthur and set about to tend her injury himself.

As silent minutes ticked past, Iliani, aware of the grim set to his mouth, tried to lighten his mood. "I did not know you knew the art of healing," she remarked.

Alaex barely looked at her. His only response was a half grunt.

Realizing that his mood was set because he carried the accident to its possible hideous conclusion, and swallowing a huge lump of terror as she, too, contemplated what could have been, Iliani shoved the thought from her mind and made another attempt to get him to do the same.

"Where did you acquire your skill?" she asked lightly.

This time the grunt came with an answer. "A sprain is a sprain."

He sidetracked her with that response.

"Meaning?"

"Meaning that Bear has had similar injuries," Alaex said roughly, pulling the cloth he was using to bind her foot a little too severely.

Although Iliani winced from the pain, she couldn't help laugh. It was her chuckle that finally pulled his attention. There was a question in the gaze he leveled on her.

"I have known that some men treat their wives with less care than their horses," she chuckled. "I have also understood that some treat them better. But I am sure I am the only wife in Alfred's kingdom who gets treated the same." She collapsed in laughter and through her mirth saw a begrudging smile tug at Alaex's lips.

" 'Tis not really cause for humor, you know," he said referring to what had almost happened to her.

"I know," Iliani replied with sham solemnity, "and it could have been so much worse."

Alaex nodded sharply, all humor gone. While he was aggrieved that he had had to frighten her into accepting the harshness of what could have been, he was relieved that she finally understood the full danger. Now she would take more care. He reached out to take her in his arms, intending to soothe away any lingering terror.

"I am glad you recognize that."

Unable to hold it in any longer, Iliani's laughter rang out, and in surprise Alaex pulled back and looked down into her violet eyes filled with tears of mirth. "You could have been a foot soldier."

A week later, Alaex still carried the memory of her sweet laughter and smile in his heart. At odd times since he had been gone, Iliani's face with its various expressions had come to him, but it was the one of her trying to tease him from his worry that caused the most warmth and an occasional smile to flit across his face. It was no different now, except that in minutes he'd get to see the real thing instead of the memory he carried.

The visit with Alfred had gone well and the king had been pleased with Alaex's report of Fontwyn's strength and defenses should there be a need. Alaex's report had set Alfred's mind at ease. Frowning, he had told Alaex that although Ethan's report had been favorable it had also been confusing, as if the man were uncertain of what he saw and what was said. He had gone on to tell Alaex of Ethan's agitation and how it had grown when he had cursorily asked after Iliani.

On that score Alfred's curiosity had not been lessened, as Alaex had only smiled enigmatically and said nothing, leaving Alfred to think that the next time he wanted to know something, he'd find it out himself.

Recalling the king's confusion, Alaex thought of Ethan, whom he had not seen during his entire visit. Ethan no doubt was thinking not to undo the good thing Iliani had done by saving his life and had decided to wait awhile longer before letting himself be seen.

Putting Ethan from his mind to allow his thoughts to traipse along the increasingly worn and pleasurable path that led to his wife, Alaex smiled. Fontwyn was just beyond the bend and suddenly he could wait no longer. Sinking his heels into Bear's sides, he pulled away easily from the sedate pace of the rest of his men.

Jon, who had seen that smile and who had been glimpsing similar expressions on his lord's face throughout their trip, smiled to himself. He knew what caused it and had a fair guess as to the source of Alaex's sudden impatience to be home. Before he could raise his arm in the signal to follow, Alaex had disappeared from view.

Yet when Jon and the men came around the last bend before Fontwyn, the smile died from his face and his dark gray eyes narrowed first in disbelief and then in horror as he saw Alaex battling five attackers. In an instant he gave the order to attack and he and the rest of the men joined the fray.

Moments later the sounds of battle died and five bodies lay dead, their blood soaking the ground.

Jon frantically searched for Alaex, of whom he'd lost sight in the battle. When he saw him still sitting on Bear's back and viewing the carnage, he rode to him.

"What went on here? Who would dare to attack you so close to Fontwyn?"

Alaex looked down at the men's faces, none of whom he knew. "I do not know. They set upon me seconds before you appeared. My thanks, Jon," Alaex said distantly, and Jon knew that something else bothered him.

"What is it Alaex?"

"'Twas most strange," Alaex said slowly. "Their attack did not seem well planned. 'Twas as if I surprised them as much as they me. 'Twas that surprise that enabled me to hold them off until your arrival."

Jon smiled faintly. "I think it not. True, they did not fight well, but in number alone the victory should have been theirs."

"You are too flattering."

Jon snorted. "And you too modest."

Alaex looked away toward Fontwyn and ignored Jon's comment. "Let us ride with haste for Fontwyn. I do not believe it to be under attack, especially from the likes of such as these, but I will not rest until I see it."

With their new pace set, it was not long before they reached the stone walls of Fontwyn. All was peaceful. Seeing that, the men began to relax, allowing the tension from the battle behind and the expected one ahead to leave them. As they rode through Fontwyn's gates, they had even begun to jest with one another and praise Alaex for his skill in holding off "hordes and hordes."

Alaex paid little attention to their exaggerated recitations of his supposed feats as his eyes scanned hungrily for one person. Only when he caught sight of her did the tension leave his body.

Iliani had come to stand in the hall's doorway, having heard Alaex and his men return. It had been a long week without him—especially since the injury to her ankle had not healed as rapidly as she had hoped. She had half-jokingly told Lucy as she had changed the cloth that bound her ankle that both she and Wind Dancer were lame for a while.

Now as she advanced toward Alaex she had only the slightest limp. But it was not the remnant of pain that made her stop and gasp.

Iliani's eyes widened as she listened to the men jokingly refer to a battle. None noticed the blood pooling at Alaex's foot.

Alaex, who at first thought it was her injury that caused the discomfort, still had not noticed his own until he looked where Iliani did. Moving his cape aside, he looked with surprise at the wide and growing circle of blood on his side. He heard Iliani gasp again and saw her start for him with a hurried limp, and he raised his eyes, wanting to reassure her, but it was as if seeing his wound caused him to feel its effect. He began to sway from dizziness that he knew was caused by loss of blood, and when he tried to speak, his words were slurred and difficult.

Aware that one by one his men had ceased their laughter, Alaex tried to focus on his wife. He didn't want to worry her, but the matter was beyond his control. Just as Iliani reached him and screamed a warning, he passed out, sliding from Bear's back to her feet.

It was a nightmare—a waking one. That was the only way Iliani could think to describe the days that followed Alaex's return. She nursed him, not knowing if he would live or die.

His wound had been deep and ugly, and the frantic pace Jon had told her they set for Fontwyn clearly had not helped. When Iliani had screamed at Jon, asking how they could not notice that he was wounded, he had told her there was blood everywhere and as Alaex's mantle had fallen back over his side, there was no way to know.

"I'm sorry, Jon," she had tearfully apologized. " 'Tis only . . . 'tis only that—" Her voice had broken and she had begun to cry, looking at Alaex's pale face.

Realizing that she was upsetting Jon further and that it was not helping Alaex, Iliani had pulled herself together. Alaex needed her.

When Arthur and Gwyn had entered with water and cloths and Jon had cut away Alaex's tunic and shirt, Iliani had been determined to be the one to tend him. It was then that she discovered a previously unknown squeamishness. Her bile had risen as she cleaned and dressed the wound. It had continued to rise daily when she changed the dressing and viewed his progress.

Her days became an anxiety and pain-ridden ordeal. Between bouts of increasing nausea, Iliani fought back the tears and fright that Alaex would succumb to his wounds and die. There were times when her fear paralyzed her, even prohibiting her crying, and then there were other times—especially as Alaex seemed not to respond to anything—that all she did was cry.

One morning three days after his injury, Iliani sat bathing Alaex's body, trying to cool it from the fever that raged within him and then trying to soothe down his throat the tonic Gwyn had made for him. As she sat with his head cradled against her breast and her arm around his neck for support, her tears fell unchecked on his face.

"Alaex," she called, unable to believe that so big and powerful a person could be dying. Even at rest, his muscles bulged enormously and with a seeming vitality. Surely such strength would not be prematurely extinguished.

"Alaex," she repeated, her voice a grief-stricken whisper. "Please don't die. I do not know which pain I would feel greater, the sorrow of your passing or the emptiness of my life. You have brought a fullness to it, Alaex, that I did not know existed. You, who speak so few words, have filled my life with meaning.

"I have been unfair," Iliani continued, his cherished face blurring behind the curtain of her tears, "for I have not told you. Oh, God, Alaex, please do not die." Her weeping became harsher. "Everyone in my life has died before I have had the chance to truly love them, to tell them of my love, or to bask in the wealth of theirs. Do not you do the same.

"Alaex," she went on, wiping her tears from his face but not her own. "I will bargain with you. If you promise me you won't die, I promise you that at the first opportunity I will tell you how I feel, whether you return the words or not. I promise. Do you hear me, Alaex? I promise," Iliani whispered brokenly.

Gwyn entered the room then, and the old servant also became teary as she saw the distress of her mistress and the unchanged condition of her master. Calling to Iliani did no good. Finally Gwyn had to pry Iliani's arms from

Alaex so as to lay him back down. As she pulled Iliani up, the bandage dressed on Alaex's wound slipped, and when Iliani saw the ooze coming from it, she fell away vomiting.

Clearly upset, Gwyn did not know whom to tend first. Casting a quick glance at Alaex, she moved toward Iliani, who was still retching uncontrollably.

Although the cloth she placed on Iliani's forehead and the supporting pressure of her arms felt soothing, Iliani pushed her away, shaking her head. She didn't need Gwyn's assistance; Alaex did. Iliani had had enough of these episodes to know that there was little help for them.

Finally the retching stopped and Iliani took the cloth Gwyn had left beside her and wiped her face. When she could stand, she rinsed her mouth and moved next to Gwyn as the woman redressed Alaex's wound.

"Milady—" Gwyn began.

"Not now, Gwyn. Alaex needs me. I will worry about myself later."

"But—"

"I said not now," Iliani repeated sharply. She hated using that tone with the servant, but her emotions were spent. All her concerns were for Alaex. When he was improved, she would think about other things, and not a moment before.

Despite her firmness in front of Gwyn the day before, now as Iliani automatically bathed Alaex she found it harder to ignore her increasingly delicate stomach. She had never been plagued by anything like it before and she found it hard to blame her queasiness on the sight of Alaex's wound alone. She had seen worse. Iliani could think of no easy answer, and so she shrugged off her reaction with the thought that her response was different because this wound was attached to someone she loved.

A soft smile crossed her face as she reached out and smoothed back Alaex's thick blond hair, her love flowing over her as she made the gesture. She did not know when she had begun to love him. Despite the magnitude of her feelings, she was not foolish enough to think she always had. Nor had she fallen in love with him at first sight, which, as Iliani looked at his handsome face, she conceded would have been easy to do. There had been too much fear in the beginning for that. First fear, then suspicion, and then anger. Yet inexorably Alaex had broken through them all. Not with fancy words or eloquent speeches, but with a quiet intensity much more devastating.

Iliani's smile changed to a rueful one as she remembered the thunder in his voice when he was angry and she amended that his assault on her senses had not always been *quietly* intense.

Nevertheless as the days wore on and Alaex did not regain consciousness, Iliani found it harder to combat her growing despair, and as her thoughts lingered longer on their past she began to see his actions differently, even those done in anger. He had not acted with vengeance against those she held dear, despite his grievances against them. He had even apologized for his blazing loss of temper the night she had accused of him lying over her father's bones, going on to explain just how it had occurred that he was the one to actually give the order for the tapestry to be made.

There were other things. He had not killed her horse; instead he allowed her to attempt what he had never seen before. He had given her time to adjust to him, and last and most telling, although he had not forced her into his bed, when she came there he had held back nothing, taking her with an intensity that in memory caused her blood to flow thickly.

It was during his fifth day of unconsciousness, as Iliani bathed him, that Alaex began to groan, moving his head from side to side. At first Iliani had thought he was regaining consciousness, but when he began to talk she knew it was the delirium Gwyn had warned her might come.

"Nay, Aeric," Alaex said. His eyes opened and fastened piercingly on Iliani's. The expression in the fevered orbs was as hot as that of his body. "I will not learn. Of what use is it?"

Iliani tried to soothe him as he struggled to rise and continued to look into her eyes while speaking to her father. "I do not believe your words, old man, but I will accept your food until I am well enough to once again take what I need."

Mercurially his body tightened and the fire in his eyes blazed hotter. "Nay! I will not speak of her, and you press fortune sorely if you but ask again."

Then his body went limp and Alaex lay back and closed his eyes, leaving Iliani curious as to the identity of the "her" he spoke of. Since he was talking to her father, perhaps the woman had been herself. Alaex's next ranting disabused her of that thought.

"You pester as an old woman, nay, worse, Aeric, with your questions of she who bore me. Since 'tis clear you will give me no peace, I will tell you what I know of her." His voice this time was not as angry, more resolved.

In shock and with tears running down her face, Iliani listened as he told of his mother's abandoning him years after his father had disappeared. He told of how he did not know the man, only that he was of the upper class and his mother was not. After a while his father had tired of the uniqueness of dallying with someone beneath him and had repudiated his mother and left, leaving Alaex to bear the brunt of her bitterness and the shadowy stigma of bastard.

His father had left before he was born. He would not know him if he saw him.

Judging from the rage in Alaex's voice that even the delirium could not hide, Iliani thought that a good thing. Her tears continued to flow for his pain, revealed terrifyingly by the hurt he could not hide when he spoke of his mother's running off when he was only seven.

What made his pain more stark was that from his

words Iliani gathered that even when the woman was there, she cared for strong drink more than her son and had treated him brutally.

From there his tale became disjointed, but Iliani was able to fill in the spaces. She experienced a moment of amused terror as he recounted how he had attempted to lift her father's purse and Aeric had caught him. In the struggle Alaex had been wounded, striking his head hard against the ground. Instead of having him beaten or hanged, or both, Aeric had brought him home.

Iliani could tell from Alaex's raving that he had detested Aeric's being of the higher class and his animosity had doubled when he sensed that Aeric pitied him. Yet from what he didn't say, Iliani sensed the fear in him and she knew it had been that which had forced him to accept the very pity he detested. There was part of him, though, that still could not accept it, she thought sadly when she remembered his reluctance to speak of his past and the details of his relationship with her father.

Alaex calmed, once again lapsing into complete unconsciousness, and Iliani eased from the bedside. Ignoring the wave of dizziness and nausea, she went to stand at the window.

Now she knew. Alaex's ravings had answered some of her questions—such as why he would marry a child. He had married her to repay a debt, one that clearly brought him much humiliation if his confessed aversion to her father's sympathy for his plight could be believed.

Wondering where that left her, Iliani felt new tears trace down her face. Despite his situation, Alaex had been proud. That same pride that had made him resent Aeric's sympathy had pushed him to agree to marry his daughter.

"I wouldn't be surprised if he hates me," Iliani murmured in despair. "Each time he looks at me I must remind him of my father and an obligation of a painful past he wants only to forget."

Finally she fully understood the hurtful blow she had dealt him when she had gone to him that first time to consummate their marriage. Having learned his reasons for marrying her, she understood his rejection, knowing that she did not want him because of a sense of misplaced pride, as payment for a debt long owed. Iliani would rather endure the pain of his rejection a thousand times than one day of acceptance because he felt obligated. Yet, what to do? The damage was done.

The cowardly thought occurred to her that to avoid his remaining with her out of obligation, she could run away. However, just as quickly she realized that that was no solution. Honor had forced Alaex to come for her once and it would do so again.

"If leaving is not a solution, then what is?" Iliani whispered, her tear-dampened eyes looking back at Alaex. The instant she did, the love she felt for him surged to the front of her other jangled emotions and she gained strength.

For so long she had despised her situation. Now she was willing to admit it was a hatred based on fear more than anything else. She had focused that antipathy solely on Alaex, refusing to have her father share any of the consequence of the arrangement that he had brought about. She had refused to accept that this was to be her future—a destiny inherited from a man she had loved with all her heart, yet could barely recall in her mind. Cherished memory was all she had of her father, and she would not tarnish it with thoughts of his doing such a thing.

Nevertheless Iliani saw that that was no longer true. The same father she had barely known had not left her with only lifeless memories. He had left her much more. He had left her a living inheritance.

Her father's method might have been wrong, but he had not been. Alaex *was* worth loving. Aeric had known that, had looked beyond what Alaex was, and had seen his heart. It was scarred, aye, but not shamefully so. It bore its marks much like a warrior wears wounds from battle: as a symbol of his courage. There was fierce agitation and turmoil in him, but there was nothing to fear in that. It made his love, when he gave it, all the more precious, and Iliani knew beyond a doubt that if he gave her a chance she could soothe the unrest in his warrior heart. She knew she could give him what that horrid woman who had birthed him had not; what that base and cowardly father who had sired him had denied him; and, finally, what her own father had attempted. She could love him, and whether he loved her now, when she already was swamped with that feeling for him, did not matter. He would, and that was all there was to it.

Chapter

→ 22 ←

Iliani?"

The voice was a hoarse croak, but Iliani heard it. Quickly she went over to the bed where Alaex lay and looked down into his pale blue eyes. For the first time in days they were clear, showing no effect of fever.

As Alaex stared into Iliani's concerned face, he struggled to make his mind as clear as his vision. That was no easy feat, for he recalled nothing after seeing her come toward him in the outer yard today. Or was that yesterday? Suddenly he was uncertain, having the disconcerting conviction that more time had passed than he knew.

Alaex shifted slightly and became aware of the dull ache in his left side. Dropping his eyes from Iliani's he looked down, feeling the dressing beneath the cover.

"I am wounded?" he asked amazed. "How did this happen?"

Iliani was not surprised by his question. Gwyn had warned her that sometimes when someone was unconscious for a long time, he might forget things for a while after waking.

Without thought, partly because over the past days she

had become used to touching him freely in any manner she chose, Iliani leaned down and rubbed his forehead, smoothing his hair back from his face.

"There was a battle," she said in gentle reminder, studying his eyes. "Do you not remember?"

Alaex's confusion was due as much to Iliani's soft touch as to her explanation. His frown deepened as he thought that a lot must have happened when he was unaware, because he could not recall her touching him so before. Before what? His mind struggled to find an answer, but the effort of thinking made him tired.

"Tell me of it," he said finally, neither confirming nor denying his recollection.

Absently Iliani stroked his head and face. "You were riding ahead of your men," she began softly, repeating what Jon had told her, "and were attacked by five men. When the rest of your men reached you, you were able to prevail. However, you became uneasy because you thought Fontwyn might have been under attack. Riding here swiftly you discovered naught amiss, never realizing that you had been wounded."

Her fingers began to move in slow circles in his hair, soothing herself as much as him, as Iliani strove to keep the remembered pain from her voice. "When I came out, I saw the blood dripping down your leg, pooling on the ground beneath your foot. After moving your cloak and revealing the wound in your side, you slipped to the ground unconscious."

Iliani took a deep breath. "Jon and Thibert brought you here and since then I have cared for your injury."

In her nearly dispassionate recital, Iliani gave no clue of the things she had discovered from him or herself. Yet Alaex had the peculiar notion that something momentous had occurred. Or had he been dreaming? He couldn't recall, but inexplicably he felt looser, freer, unburdened.

"How long have I been unconscious?" he asked suddenly.

"One week."

Alaex frowned.

"You truly remember none of this?"

"Not as yet," he replied, feeling as if he should. He knew by the way Iliani looked at him and touched him that something had happened that he should recall. She was still petting him, and Alaex wondered if she knew it.

He swallowed, trying to ease some of the dryness in his mouth, and became aware of his thirst. "May I have some water?"

Iliani moved away to pour water into a cup, and despite his thirst Alaex regretted his request. It was the first time since he'd awakened that she'd stopped touching him.

"Are you strong enough to manage on your own or should we do as we have been?" Iliani asked, standing over him.

"What have we been doing?" Alaex's expression was skeptical.

"I have been holding—"

"I think we should continue with what we were doing," he interrupted, sidestepping the issue of his strength. He was for anything that required Iliani's holding him.

Iliani eased down beside him, and as she had been doing for days, she raised his head and shoulders, anchoring them against her breast and supporting them with her arm. As she brought the cup to his lips, which were cracked and chapped from the fever, she was surprised to see that he was smiling, but Alaex said nothing until after he had taken a long swallow of water. He would have drunk the entire Thames if it could have kept him where he was.

"If this is the service I have been receiving, 'tis no wonder I lay abed so long."

Iliani smiled, and it was her first real one in days. She was saved from responding, however, when Gwyn entered. When she saw Alaex was awake, a broad smile lit the servant's face.

" 'Tis good to see you awake, milord."

Alaex said a weak "Thank you" when what he wanted to say was that Gwyn should leave. When she had come in, Iliani had eased his head back on the bed. He wanted it where it was.

'Tis plain I'm not dying, he thought in amusement as he lay still, allowing them to examine his wound. No one who was dying thought of the softness of his wife's breasts or the gentle stroke of her hand. The imagery was so vivid he actually flinched, making his wife and servant look at him. After studying his impassive features for a moment, Iliani turned back to his wound and Gwyn moved away to get clean cloths.

With chagrin Alaex realized where his thoughts were leading and what part of his body was following. Trying to squelch his body's natural reaction, he prayed that the examination would be over soon, but it was already too late. Seeing he was losing the battle, he stared intensely at Iliani.

Engrossed in watching his wound, Iliani was unaware of his growing discomfort, which had nothing to do with his wound. Her concentration was centered on examining him until out of the corner of her eye she saw a movement. At first she stared disbelievingly, then she turned her stunned gaze to Alaex. She was torn between horrified amusement and anxiety. When Alaex raised his brow and a slow, insouciant smile slashed attractively across his lips, Iliani forgot everything else.

Her attention was jerked away from him when she heard Gwyn gathering her supplies. Swiftly Iliani jumped up and walked over to the old servant. In a near choking voice she said, "I think that's enough for now. I'm sure milord is tired and needs his rest."

Gwyn looked at her in puzzlement, her confusion growing as her mistress seemed determined not to allow her a better look at the master. Without anything further, she left, uncertain as to what was happening.

When the door closed Iliani rounded on Alaex in laughing consternation. "That was not well done of you."

His response was impenitent and unabashed. "I can assure you, madam, that the matter was beyond my control."

Iliani shook her head, trying to be stern and failing. "You'll get no more sympathy from me."

At Alaex's questioning look, she said, "It has just occurred to me that any man who could do such a thing is not going to die."

Alaex smiled lazily. "At least not yet."

After redressing Alaex's wound, Iliani quietly left the room. Despite the clarity in his eyes and the strength in his voice, Alaex was still weak. After having his wound cleaned, and eating a few mouthfuls of food, he had drifted back into a deep sleep.

For the first time in days, as Iliani moved down the corridor, her thoughts were not consumed with the state of Alaex's health. After his display and the wound's healthy pinkness, which she had noticed when she changed his dressing, Iliani was positive he would be up in a few days.

Nay, Alaex's health did not bother her. She could not, however, make the same statement about hers. Now that her fervent concern for Alaex eased, her previously ignored worries for her own health surfaced. The disturbing nausea was not relenting. Alaex's wound had looked less grotesque today and still her stomach reacted squeamishly. Ruling out Alaex's wound as the cause, she tried to find another reason for her state. Her nausea couldn't be the result of what she ate, because since Alaex's injury she had barely touched food. Also, with the increase in her queasiness as time passed, her desire for food lessened. So when Iliani descended the stairs in search of Gwyn, the advice she needed was for herself, not Alaex.

Iliani found Gwyn in the small yet well-kept room at the rear of the hall where foodstuffs and the supplies Gwyn used in her healing were stored. Stepping into the tight, airless room, Iliani was about to call out so as not to startle Gwyn, when she was assailed by dizziness. It was the strongest sensation she had experienced since the onset of these attacks, and Iliani leaned against the wall, shutting her eyes and swallowing heavily.

Strong, gentle hands eased her down to a crate. "Breathe deeply, milady, in through the nose, out of the mouth."

Even if Iliani hadn't seen Gwyn's competence this last week in her care of Alaex, she would have obeyed. While she instinctively trusted the quiet authority with which Gwyn spoke, the stronger reason was that at the moment she felt so sick and frightened, she would have done just about anything. When she opened her mouth to ask Gwyn if she had any idea what could be the matter, the room tilted alarmingly, and she didn't need Gwyn's calm order.

"Nay, milady, do not try to talk," she said, sitting beside Iliani. "Just breathe. Put your head down between your legs. This will pass. I promise you."

Iliani did as she was told, feeling so miserable that she wondered if she were dying. However, as time passed she found the easing of dizziness that Gwyn had promised, and her hope grew. Perhaps Gwyn knew what ailed her and could tell her what to do, or could give her something to make the feeling, or whatever it was, go away.

"Better?" Gwyn asked in that composed manner of hers.

Iliani opened her mouth tentatively, having learned a lesson from the last time she tried to speak. This time there was no dizziness, and the nausea receded further.

"Aye. What is it, Gwyn?" she blurted hurriedly, before the dizzy feeling returned. "Am I dying?"

Gwyn smiled broadly. "I do not think so."

"But you do know what's wrong with me?" Iliani persisted, satisfied when Gwyn nodded.

"Milady, do not think I am being impertinent, but I must ask you a personal question."

Iliani hesitated, then nodded slowly.

"When last did you have your woman's time?" Gwyn

asked gently, making Iliani color. She hadn't expected the question to be quite that personal, and she was surprised to find she could not readily remember. It seemed she hadn't since coming to Fontwyn.

Nay, Iliani corrected herself, thinking about it. That was not so. The first month here she had, but that had been her only time.

"About two months ago," Iliani finally whispered, wondering how she could have ignored something like that.

Gwyn seemed to expect that answer. "Have your breasts been tender, fuller?"

The color flew high in Iliani's cheeks again as she considered this, too. She looked down at her breasts, which had always been a modest size. They *did* seem a bit larger. Raising a hesitant hand, her embarrassment deepened, but she touched one of the soft mounds.

"Aye," she murmured, raising fear-stricken eyes to the older woman.

Gwyn hurried to calm her. "'Tis no cause for worry, milady. Based on what you have told me and what I have seen, I would say you are with child."

"With child?" Iliani echoed blankly as if she had never heard the words before.

"With child," Gwyn repeated, once again smiling. "The little one will probably be here by year's end."

Iliani put her hand on her stomach as her world began to spin again. A baby? She was going to have a baby? She was suddenly cold and then hot.

"My thanks, Gwyn," she said absently, rising to leave the room before she started laughing and crying hysterically in front of the servant.

Iliani just made it through the door before the tears started. She wanted to laugh; she wanted to shout. In a haze of happiness, she recalled her promise to tell Alaex of her feelings at the first opportunity. Now there was this. As she walked toward the main hall, she wondered how he would take this double shock.

* * *

The rest of the day passed in a happy blur. Iliani could not stop smiling, and that evening as she ate in their room with Alaex, who was propped up in bed, he noticed it almost immediately. Although he was tired, he fought back the fatigue, intrigued by the sparkle in her eyes and the winsome curve of her lips. He waited until Iliani had removed their dishes to remark on it.

"There is something different about you this evening."

"In what way?" Iliani asked. She had been aware of his increasingly probing stares while they had eaten.

Alaex paused. "In truth, 'tis more than this evening. Now it only seems enhanced. I first noticed it earlier when I awoke." His voice deepened. "It was a beautiful thing to see when I opened my eyes."

"Thank you," she said. A secret smile that said she knew something he did not played about her lips.

"You are welcome," Alaex said hesitantly.

"Is there something wrong?" Iliani asked, her fear for his health returning quickly to douse the happy sparkle in her eyes. "You are not in pain, are you?" she asked worriedly, sitting beside him on the bed.

Although he was, Alaex shook his head. The discomfort from his wound was not worth mentioning. He could see she had worried about him enough. Raising his hand, he brushed it gently against her face. The soft warm touch felt so good that Iliani closed her eyes, and so missed the tender expression that entered his. With slow insistent force, Alaex pulled her in to him and after assuring herself that it did not press on his wound, Iliani relaxed against his chest.

The touch of his hand did not compare with being folded in his arms. That had felt good; this was exquisite.

Long moments passed as Alaex continued to hold her quietly. He had almost drifted to sleep when he realized Iliani was crying.

After the expression in her eyes, her sparkling mood throughout supper, and the shared contentment of holding each other, he was surprised at this sign of distress.

"Iliani," he demanded gently, "what is wrong?"

"Nothing," Iliani answered, crying harder.

Alaex tried to tip her face to his, but she resisted. "Have I been asleep that long that tears are now a good thing?" he teased.

"Sometimes," Iliani said, ignoring his jest. She had been trying to think of a way to tell him about her love and her pregnancy, but each time she thought of it she would become overwhelmed with emotion and couldn't find the words. Deciding to take it a step at a time, Iliani raised her face to his.

"Alaex," she queried, lifting up to look searchingly into his eyes, "have you ever wanted something so badly that you were afraid, because the depth of your desire was frightening, making you think it could never be yours?"

Stunned as much by her question as by her tears, Alaex shook his head slowly. He wanted to agree with her. He wanted to say that he understood that kind of desire, but life had taught him early the futility of wanting for anything aside from what it decided to bestow upon you.

Iliani saw his desire to see things the way she did, and she cursed herself for belatedly forgetting what he had revealed when he was delirious. Suddenly it became important to her to wipe away his vision of hopelessness. She felt a compulsion to show him that as surely as food fed the mind and body, hope fed the soul and heart. Life without hope was empty, and it was that sort of emptiness she glimpsed deep in Alaex's eyes. It was the emptiness that Iliani yearned to erase and thus help him see life in more possible terms. Instead of shifting the conversation away from talk of wants and desires, which had been her intention when she had seen the haunted look in his eyes, she decided to continue.

"I have," she said solemnly. "I suppose that makes me fortunate, although until now I would never have thought of myself that way."

Alaex stared at her, waiting.

"Alaex, I have some important things to tell you. Yet

because of certain episodes in our past—yours and mine—I know that you might find one difficult to accept. So I feel the need to explain something about myself first. I hope that my explanation will help you to understand my previous behavior better, but more important, that it will help you to understand and believe the truthfulness of what I have to say."

When Alaex maintained his silence, which was neither discouraging nor receptive, but somewhere precisely between those two extremes, Iliani momentarily faltered. She saw that her words about acceptance, belief, and truthfulness were raising his inherent skepticism. Knowledge of his past bolstered her lagging confidence that his mistrust was not a deliberate rebuff, and it eased some of the pain of his reaction.

Iliani ignored the slight residual pain that even knowledge could not completely erase. "All my life," she began, "while growing up at Lourds Keep, I wanted a family. Do not misunderstand. Edouard and Eadwina were good to me. They treated me as if I was one of their own. Still it didn't feel the same. I cannot say it was they, for I was the one making the distinction." Iliani paused, searching for the right words to make him understand her without thinking her to be selfish. Compared to him, she had had so much more. "No matter how pleasant the surroundings," she continued slowly, "being a guest—even a very welcome one—is not the same as being at home. Being included is not the same as belonging. Do you understand?"

This time Alaex did, but she had kindled his curiosity, so after a brief nod he waited wordlessly.

"From as far back as I can remember, I have wanted a family of my own, a place I could call unmistakably my own. Perhaps it was because with both my parents dead I felt I had nothing truly mine. I do not know. I only know that scarcely a day passed when I didn't long for that with all my heart. It was a surprise, then, to discover that I do not long for it anymore, and that the reason I do not is because of you. You have helped me to find my true home."

Iliani gathered her courage to say the rest. "That said," she uttered, her eyes locking onto his and her voice trembling slightly, "I need to tell you of a bargain I made with you while you slept."

Alaex's brows furrowed but still he stayed silent, waiting for her to finish.

Taking a breath, Iliani went on. "You see, for a while—several days, actually—I thought you might die, and that made me realize something that I had been hiding from myself. However, once I recognized it, it made the pain of the possibility of your death more acute. Just as I was finding my home, I had to face the fear that you could die as my mother and father had, without my getting the chance to love them or tell them of my love."

He knew what she was going to say, and Alaex sucked in his breath sharply, ignoring the pain it caused to his wound. His entire body tensed as if preparing for a blow. His expression now was devoid of everything—discouragement, reception, any discernible emotion at all. However, this time Iliani was unaware of his reaction as she rushed on, reaching out with unsteady fingers to trace his lips. "So I bargained that if you lived, I would tell you that I loved you."

Although her voice had gained strength near the end of her speech, Iliani had not gained confidence. A hope that she had barely acknowledged was shining, along with the love she had professed, in her eyes as they probed his.

Although Alaex had sensed what she was going to say, hearing the words made him speechless. He saw the hope—and the love. A lifetime of cynicism aside, he now knew it was that emotion he had been feeling in her touch all day. He didn't know what to say. The most natural and fitting thing would be to say he loved her, too, but he didn't know if what he felt was love. Silently he cursed his past for never having taught him what love was. It had so deprived him of it that even accepting it was difficult. He was uncomfortable accepting something he was unsure he could return. It felt as if he had amassed a debt he would never be able to repay.

He had suffered the same discomfort with Aeric. Now he faced it again with Iliani, except this time the guilt was more intense. With Aeric he had accepted his limitations; with Iliani he wanted to overcome them, and as always when faced with a question of an emotional nature, he was at a loss how.

While he fought himself for an answer, Alaex kept his eyes locked on Iliani's. Therefore, he knew the instant she realized that he was not going to return the words. Cursing himself now, he watched the hope in the sparkling violet eyes before him die, and her hand fall from his face to rest by her side. Yet to his amazement, as he continued to watch, the love remained.

With an agonized groan, Alaex pulled her head back down to his chest and placed a tender kiss upon it, only then acknowledging the fear beneath the guilt. Although he did not yet know what he felt, he did not want to lose her love because somehow he knew—as he thought of all she was—that one day, if such a thing were possible for someone like him, he would love her.

Iliani's tender words of consolation to him when he should have been consoling her drove that certainty even deeper into his heart.

"'Tis all right, Alaex," she said softly, making the decision then not to speak of the child and hoping he wouldn't recall she had wanted to tell him more than one thing. His unhappiness and guilt were so strong, Iliani felt them. "I did not say the words to force you to repeat them. Force has no place here. I just wanted you to know. Do not feel obligated to return them or feel sorry that you cannot." Iliani tried to disguise the pain in her heart with humor. "You did not die, and so kept your side of the bargain; I was honor bound to keep mine."

His response was a convulsive tightening of his arms

around her as he marveled at her incredible sweetness. Then Alaex slowly raised her chin, lifting her face for his kiss, which promised a future that he lacked the words to express. The promise in that kiss mercifully gave back what his silence had taken away.

Through that one melting embrace, the hurt Iliani felt when he did not return her declaration was eased because he gave back something else equally precious. He gave back her hope. While it was not love, it was enough for now.

Chapter

→ 23 ←

Although Iliani had lost her nerve to tell Alaex of the babe when she confessed her love, she did not intend for so much time to pass before she found another suitable opening. Or at least one *she* felt was suitable. Time was racing against her and she knew that right moment or no, she would have to tell him soon before he found out some other way or the babe introduced himself at birth.

Knowledge, however, was a far cry from action, and the days went by with her finding neither the nerve nor the opportunity to tell him. After poignantly feeling his guilt when she declared her love, Iliani didn't want to increase it or place more pressure on him by telling him of the child. It occurred to her that because of his past a child might be very special to Alaex, and that knowledge worked against her. Even with warnings tolling in her head about pride going before a fall, she couldn't bring herself to tell him and have his affection for her come because of the babe.

Iliani still cherished the promise in his kiss. If that promise was going to be fulfilled, she wanted it to be because of her and not the birth of the child. As much as

Iliani wanted children, and Alaex's child in particular, she lamented the timing of her pregnancy. And time was running out.

Although she was no longer as nauseated as she had been, her figure had definitely changed. Her waist was thicker and her stomach had a gentled roundness that Alaex would certainly notice the first time he took her to bed.

During his convalescence, despite what had happened the first day he'd awakened, there had been no intimacy between them. But over the past days that had been changing. Iliani could tell from his increasingly heated glances that Alaex desired her. What would she do then?

The situation and possible solutions were taken out of her control in an unexpected way.

As Iliani had become more comfortable in her role of mistress of Fontwyn, she had taken on the responsibility for its internal workings. As the need arose she made changes. One change was in the haphazard schedule for mending, washing, and other such chores. Because of the chaotic schedule there was always a need to perform these tasks. That was now different. Washing was done on one day, mending on another. The other schedule had exhausted the servants because there was always an article of someone's clothing to either wash or mend.

It had taken a while for the men, including Alaex, to become accustomed to the new arrangement. In the beginning there had been confusion and Iliani had amusingly noted a stain here or a rip there as certain ones had forgotten which day was which, but she did not relent. Eventually the men had come around, and with the servants' load made easier, things went smoother. Iliani still glowed with pleasure when she remembered Alaex's praise for her efforts.

He won't be praising me for long, she thought as she picked up his clothes and hurried to find Gwyn, cursing herself for her tardiness. Since Gwyn knew of her condition, when Iliani had begun to sleep longer in the mornings, the woman had kindly arranged for her to be undisturbed.

Today was the latest she had slept. As she rushed down the stairs and considered the time, Iliani tried to ignore the guilt she felt at the unintentionally awkward position in which she had placed the servant. Every morning Gwyn looked hopefully at her or expectantly watched Alaex, clearly waiting for him to announce his impending fatherhood. Every evening after a day with no such announcement, Gwyn would stare at Iliani harder and longer.

Trying not to think of the meaning behind Gwyn's stares, Iliani reached the bottom of the stairs. With the clothes piled high in front of her, she didn't see the person in her path until they collided. Shifting her bundle and peeking around it, Iliani's eyes met the disapproving dark brown eyes of the woman she had just been thinking about.

"I was coming to bring these to you for washing," Iliani said quickly, her guilt increasing. "Since you did not disturb me and kept the others away, I felt that the least I could do was save you a trip."

Gwyn silently reached out to take the clothing, her expression unaltered. Iliani knew no servant at Lourds Keep would have dared to look at her or any other member of the family that way, but here at Fontwyn things were different. To the servants at Lourds Keep, once the chore was done the members of the house they served ceased to matter. At Fontwyn, the servants fussed and scolded, and it was not impertience. It was care.

Iliani had grown used to Gwyn's mannerisms, and she had discovered that when Gwyn voiced a dissenting opinion, she was usually right. Having a fair idea of the reason for Gwyn's expression, and fearing that this might be another time when the woman was right, Iliani wanted to avoid it, but it was no use. With her usual forthrightness Gwyn stated her thoughts.

"Milady," she began, "you cannot continue to do this."

Iliani sighed. She felt much like a child caught in mischief by its mother.

"I know."

Gwyn's gaze sharpened. "You know the danger—?"

At the word danger, Iliani's eyes snapped to hers. "Danger?"

Now Gwyn sighed with the realization that her young mistress had no perception of the possible danger one wrong step could cause a woman in her condition.

"Lady, you are with child and must have a care. First, you should not be lifting, and certainly you should not be lifting and carrying. Above all, lifting and carrying while coming down the stairs with your view blocked is—please pardon, milady—foolish."

Gwyn flushed and waited for a reprimand. When none came, she continued, her tone gentled as she explained. "You could have lost your footing and fallen. Many babes are lost that way."

Iliani's eyes widened as she fully understood the foolishness of what she'd done. She was about to thank Gwyn for her cautions when she looked past the servant's shoulder and saw Alaex quietly standing there.

She did not have to wonder. Unless he was deaf he had to have heard every word.

Their eyes met and locked. Iliani wanted to look away from the inscrutability of his expression, but Alaex would not allow it. She forgot Gwyn was there as time passed and they stared.

Confused as to what was happening and why her mistress looked frozen, Gwyn turned around. She froze, too, when she saw Alaex.

No one spoke. Finally the silence was broken by Alaex's clipped footsteps as he came over to Iliani. When he reached her, he released her guilty gaze long enough to dismiss Gwyn.

"You may go, Gwyn."

Alaex turned back to Iliani, and Gwyn had gone only a few steps when he called out, "And my thanks." The servant turned back, puzzled. But she only nodded to Alaex before walking away.

As Iliani watched the servant leave, she wished she could call her back. True, she could not detect any anger in Alaex's voice, but she still didn't want to be alone with him. Not after he had found out about his child this way. Gwyn might be confused; Iliani was not. Alaex had thanked her for telling him—in a way—of his child, and Iliani's heart sank even as it increased its tempo. She felt trapped and there was nothing she could think of to say. Now that the situation was beyond her control, she sickly acknowledged that there was no justifiable explanation. Her defenses crumbled, leaving only the unconscionable truth that for weeks she had kept something from her husband he had every right to know.

Iliani was struggling to find a way to apologize when Alaex spoke. "How long?"

"Nearly three months." Her voice was strained.

"You have known for three months about—"

"Nay, Alaex," Iliani hurried to explain. Her offense was bad enough without his thinking that. "I have known only a few weeks."

"Weeks?"

Somehow when he repeated it like that, it didn't sound less condemnatory. A sound at the back of the hall drew their attention, and when Iliani looked back to Alaex he seemed to have grown more distant.

"Here or in our chamber?"

Iliani wanted to stay where they were, but if someone came in, as they were likely to do at this time of day, the situation would be a thousand times worse. Since she didn't trust herself to produce a voice that didn't squeak, Iliani turned wordlessly and started up the stairs.

Halfway up, Iliani had a change of heart about facing Alaex in either place. Progressively she slowed her steps until they were all but a crawl, and it still seemed that she virtually flew up the stairs. Alaex said nothing about her exaggeratedly slow pace, merely matching his to hers. As usual, his air of relentlessness increased Iliani's trepidation. By the time they reached their room her nerves were screaming, and it was an effort of will to keep her hands from trembling.

Alaex seemed calm, but when Iliani took a closer look she saw that it was not calm but control. He closed the door and waited, saying nothing. He didn't need to. It seemed that even the silence accused her.

Having had enough of it, Iliani ventured, "Have you nothing to say?"

Alaex smiled, and Iliani's stomach clenched and she wished she'd remained quiet. She hadn't seen that particular smile of his in weeks.

"I was thinking that you were the one needing to speak." A little of his anger cracked through the calm.

"Alaex, I know how this must seem—"

"Do you?" he asked, his voice like iced silk.

Iliani swallowed. "I think I do."

"Then after you have explained everything else, you can explain that also. Nay, Iliani," he said, a little more of his anger showing, "for this do not wait. Explain to me now how it seems. Explain to me why I have to learn *accidentally* from a servant that my wife is carrying my child."

"I did not mean for you to find out this way," she said regretfully.

Alaex snorted. "That was clear. Except I don't believe you meant for me to find out at all."

Iliani shook her head, stung that he would think that. "That is not true. I wanted to tell you, but—"

"Go on," Alaex encouraged coldly, when she closed her lips over the words she had been about to speak. "You wanted to tell me but . . ."

Iliani bit her lip. She couldn't reveal that she wanted to tell him but that her pride wanted him to want her first. Nay, not want, love. Alaex wanted her. She would have to be dead not to know that. She looked quickly at him and then away.

"You were saying?"

Starting to feel cornered, and forgetting the apology

she had been trying to form since they were below stairs, Iliani felt her own anger stirring. Instead of answering, she fired a question of her own.

"What would you have me say, Alaex?" she asked hotly. "That I should have told you? Done. I should have told you. That I regret your discovering it this way? Done again. I regret your finding out about your child this way."

Alaex stared at her, unable to believe she was trying to make him the villain. "Why?" he questioned, refusing to be deterred.

"Why what?" Iliani snapped, although she suspected what he wanted to know.

Alaex's voice was still. "You have not told me why you didn't tell me."

"I couldn't."

"Why not?"

Iliani clenched and unclenched her hands, and Alaex's pale blue eyes dropped to watch that gesture. When he raised his eyes back to hers, he had stilled further.

"I cannot believe the conclusions I am reaching, but I can reach no other." Alaex stared at her a few agonizing, nerve-wracking moments.

Whatever his thoughts, Iliani knew that they could not be good, but his words still caught her unprepared.

"You said you wanted a family. Have you changed your mind?"

Her anger, which had been welcome because it minimized her own feeling of guilt and fortified her against his questions, disappeared beneath this one. Iliani shook her head and walked toward the window.

"Alaex, let it be, please."

He was silent so long that Iliani thought he was willing to do that. Therefore, when his voice finally came, the cold distance in it was even more unsettling.

"Have I ever told you about my m— the woman who bore me? Nay," Alaex answered his own question so unemotionally that Iliani actually felt fear. "I have not. I do not like to think of her, let alone speak. She gave me life and a name and nothing else. Because of my father's lack, she hated me. Is it to be that way for my child as well?"

Iliani turned to look at him and nearly died at the lifeless expression in his eyes. She forced her words out.

"Why would you—?"

"Why would I not?" he returned harshly. "From what thing am I to derive the feeling that this pregnancy makes you happy? The guilty and anxious expression on your face? Your reluctance to share with me something I had a right to know?"

The sarcastic emptiness in his voice ripped into her. "I would have told you," Iliani said, helpless beneath the crushing weight of her regret and the pain she had caused him.

"When? What was the difficulty in telling me at all?" he shot back. "You never had such restraint before in telling me what you felt."

Alaex was referring to the many times Iliani had stood up to him. Iliani, her emotions raw, thought his scathing remark was targeted at her telling him she loved him.

It hurt, and unthinkingly she snapped back, "That was it! I had told you too much already."

Iliani regretted her outburst long before she saw Alaex's reaction. He froze, and then an ugly understanding dawned in his eyes.

"So it *is* my lack. Just as it was with my mother. Because she loved someone who did not return her feeling, I bore the consequences of her hate. And since you have professed love for me, which I treated with honor and value when I did not belittle it by lying merely to return the words, you felt justified in keeping the news of my child from me."

"That's not true!" Although Iliani denied it because he was not exactly right, he was close enough to the truth to make her face color guiltily.

Alaex saw it and his temper exploded. "Just because

you *love*," he sneered, "does that give you the right to lord it over others? Does it give you the right to cause pain to another?"

His mind was working furiously and drawing all the wrong conclusions. The problem was that Iliani's was working too slowly. She had no idea how things had gotten this bad. It was almost as if he did not rage at her or fling his contemptuous questions at her. His anger with her seemed to be merging with another, deeper one, and Iliani finally made the connection. This was part of the rage he'd felt for his mother, a rage that had been buried beneath what should have been unendurable hurt.

Iliani recoiled from her thoughts. It was enough that she had made a mistake. For that she was sorry. However, while she was more than willing to try to make up to him for what he had lacked as a child, she adamantly refused to pay for it. Still, the shield of his unrelenting anger was formidable, and Iliani had to dig deeply for courage to go on.

"Alaex, listen to me," she said quietly, resolutely. "I will try not to treat you as if you are about to run out of my life, if you will try not to treat me as if I am a heartless woman who takes out her misery on the nearest available innocent."

Alaex started and then he frowned, only just realizing what he had said. The fire in his eyes still blazed, but his expression altered to one of confusion as he looked at Iliani.

His pained confusion was as clear to Iliani as if someone had written it for her to see. She knew her answer confused him because he believed her unaware of his past, and her heart went out to him. However, she still did not trust the look in his eyes.

"What I mean," she clarified softly, "is that for a long time when I was growing up at Lourds Keep, I felt resentment for my father. It was so deeply buried I did not recognize it. That ignorance did not keep me from acting on it. I was afraid that those closest to me would leave as he and my mother had. I do not know how long it took to rid myself of that fear. In truth, I don't think I have, because at odd times it still overtakes me and I feel its effect even with you. When you were wounded and I thought you might die, the feeling returned. I was terrified, but I was angry too."

Iliani paused, not wanting to reveal what she knew of his mother. "Whatever went on with you and your mother," she said carefully, "has as little to do with me as what occurred between me and my father has to do with you. I shall try not to make you pay for his deeds if you will try not to make me pay for hers. Agreed?"

After a long time, some of the fire died from Alaex's eyes. He nodded curtly.

Finding some encouragement in that, Iliani now felt more confident about approaching him. She walked slowly over to him and placed her hand lightly on his chest. "I did not intend for things to become so out of control," she said gently. With a sincerity he could little doubt, she added, "I am sorry for keeping the babe's existence from you."

Without waiting for a sign from him that he either accepted or rejected her apology, Iliani's hand crept around his neck. Just before she pulled his lips to hers, she whispered softly, "And I will never, ever use what I feel for you or whatever you may come to feel for me as a weapon against you." That said, she pressed her lips to his and sealed her vow with a heated kiss.

Although Alaex's mind reeled as much from her words as from her kiss, he did not allow her to be the initiator for long. Swiftly he brought his arms around her and his lips began a tantalizing assault on hers. They teased and cajoled, and when Iliani opened her mouth to allow him access, his tongue began the same beguiling game with hers.

Iliani groaned, pressing herself against Alaex's hard form, suddenly realizing that he was not the only one in need. She had missed this—the closeness, the sharing, his caresses, his kisses, and the knowing pleasure his hands gave her body.

By the time Alaex lifted her to lay her on the bed, Iliani was whimpering with desire. When he bared her body in the bright, unrelenting sunlight, she felt no shame. She did not attempt to hide from his hungering gaze, nor did she look away as he slowly removed his clothing.

Completely naked, Alaex stood beside the bed, looking his fill and allowing Iliani to do the same. His heart ached at what his eyes beheld. It seemed that in his thirty-two years he had never really looked at a woman before this one. What he saw in Iliani's eyes made the beauty of her body that much more exquisite. His hand reached out to touch her, and he was stunned to see that it trembled. When he would have pulled it back to cover that unmanly reaction, Iliani reached up and clasped it, using it to pull him down to her.

Once he lay beside her, instead of kissing him, as Alaex expected, Iliani did something much more endearing. Her eyes, filled with a tenderness that nearly wrung tears from him, never left his as she took his hand and placed it on the tight, gently rounded mound of her stomach. *Then* she kissed him, and the aching sweetness of it stole his breath, causing his heart to beat in heavy, painful strokes. Gently Alaex moved his hands to cup her face, pulling back so he could see the searing emotion he had felt.

Iliani did not disappoint him. In the same way she had not shielded her body from his hunger, she did not hide her feelings from his quest. What he saw within the compelling violet depths that stared unblinkingly back at him made Alaex feel both weak and strong. However, there was no conflict in his desire. Iliani's inflamed gaze increased it a thousandfold until Alaex wanted her with an ache past bearing.

Lost in her own blind ardor, Iliani feverishly ran her hands over his body, learning him through each new stroke and caress of her fingers. She couldn't get close enough. She couldn't feel enough or touch enough. Groaning mindlessly, she took his hand and placed it on her breast, needing to be touched as much as she needed to touch.

Unable and unwilling to resist such a sensuous invitation, Alaex caressed the high, firm mound and then he pulled his lips away from hers to nuzzle it in his mouth. Iliani's cry of pleasure pierced through to his heart and sharpened his desire.

Pressing her onto her back, Alaex lifted his head, wanting to see her uninhibited reactions as his fingers continued their assaulting caress on her breasts and body. His eager gaze devoured every moan, drank in every sensuous groan, as if her reactions were the sustenance he needed for life.

And unknown to him, through his touch he revealed more than he was shown.

Iliani wanted to weep with the beauty of what he was making her feel. Alaex had never once told her he thought her beautiful, but from the magic of his hands she felt it. What he never said, he made her feel.

It was as if he spoke through his gestures, and these gestures and touches repeated the promise of his kiss given weeks ago. With his ardent mouth and hot hands, he promised her everything he could not say.

Soon his kisses and caresses brought Iliani to a writhing state of need, and it was only then, with her desire at its pinnacle, that he joined his body to hers. Since he could not promise love, he gave her everything else with each thrust of his body. The mindless pleasure of it was so acute that Iliani felt as if every second of her life had been preparing her for this one moment in time. She was past desire, past want, when her body shattered into a million climactic pieces, her pleasure doubling and returning again and again as she recognized that Alaex, too, had reached this ultimate perfection.

Chapter

⇒ 24 ⇐

It was cold and dark and she was so afraid. Although she knew she could find her way to him as easily as she had found her way here, she didn't move. She was afraid to move. There was a terrifying reason why she was not supposed to move. And it had to do with him—the man lying there on the floor. It was because of him she shouldn't, but she couldn't remember why. She just knew she should not be discovered. He wouldn't like it. Although he may be dead or dying, he wouldn't like it. Dying? Could she help? She began to cry, not because of the fear, the dark, or the cold, but because no matter how much she wanted to go to him she couldn't, and it was her own fault. Despite her being unable to remember what it was, she knew she had done a bad thing.

"You said you wouldn't think about it," Iliani muttered to herself. She was so engrossed in her attempts to run from her thoughts that she forgot her promise.

Unthinkingly Iliani applied her heels to Wind Dancer's side. The gelding, who had been chomping at their restricted pace, needed no further urging. In a blink he complied with her order, and before she knew it Iliani left her escort behind.

She heard Thibert's shout at the same time she realized what she had done. Reining in Wind Dancer, who seemed to have healed from his injury with no permanent damage, Iliani waited for the rest of her guard to catch up. The gelding snorted, not liking her new command, and from the disapproving look on Thibert's face as he drew near Iliani knew he had not liked her old one.

Any hope she had of avoiding unpleasantness evaporated as Iliani realized that there could only be one explanation for Thibert's disapproval: he knew of her promise to Alaex to ride at a sedate pace. Looking at Thibert's set features, Iliani wanted to scream in frustration, seeing the possibility of future rides diminish. She knew that Alaex would receive a full recounting of her lapse.

Without a word of defense on her behalf, because she knew it would be useless, Iliani turned Wind Dancer around and headed back to the hall. Thibert said nothing, and for that he earned her gratitude and, perversely, her increased rancor. Part of Iliani was happy he did not question her as if she were a naughty child. The other part, which was just itching to pour invective on his unsuspecting head, wanted him to say something. One word would have done. However, after glancing in her face, Thibert wisely held his tongue and they started back in silence.

As they paced their mounts back to Fontwyn, Iliani ground her teeth in annoyance. She regretted breaking her word, and for that she was angry at herself. She was, however, also angry at Alaex for making her give it in the first place.

Riding with the wind in her ears always helped her to think. It cleared her mind and brought her peace. With the increasing horror of the dreams, she needed to find that kind of peace—which she certainly was not going to get riding as if she were an old woman, Iliani thought irritably. For God's sake, she was pregnant, not mortally ill.

As suddenly as it surged, Iliani's anger ebbed. It was pure defense anyway, and useless. There was nothing to be done. She knew that Thibert could not be coerced from his duty to report everything to Alaex, and she also knew that her pride would not allow her to make the attempt even if a sweetly worded explanation would work, which in this instance it wouldn't. It would only make the situation more awkward, as Thibert would feel that it wasn't for him to hear her explanation. Alaex's men did not interpret orders; they followed them. If they did not, they were no longer his men.

The same rigid code Alaex asked of them he demanded of himself and had even come to expect of her. In any other situation—meaning one in which she was at fault—Iliani would have been flattered by Alaex's expectation. It was more than an honor that he was willing to take her word. It was a rarity beyond mention. Women might be treated with honor, but as if they *had* honor? Never. Honor was considered the exclusive domain of males.

When looked at that way, Iliani felt double remorse for her unthinking act, which was exactly what it had been. She sighed as she saw the stone wall of Fontwyn in the distance. Unthinking or willful, she had broken her word and she did not think Alaex, given his strong feelings on this issue, was going to care why.

He did not. Alaex, whose face had tightened as Thibert had given his account, had vacillated between waiting until his anger cooled before confronting his wife, seeking her out immediately to shake her senseless, and striding off to the stables to kill that ill-tempered beast she rode. After a few minutes in which his anger rose instead of cooling, he contemplated doing all three. Thibert's attempt to offer excuses had not helped.

"She was repentant immediately, Alaex," he put forth hesitantly. "I could tell that. It seemed she just forgot.

However, the instant she remembered, she reined in the horse, and offering no word of protest or rationalization, she merely turned him back to Fontwyn."

"There was no rationale," Alaex coldly retorted.

Uneasy with doing something he had never done before—making excuses to Alaex—Thibert was not encouraged by that taut answer. It was the memory of the look in his lady's eyes that made him want to continue.

Hoping, nay, praying fervently that he was not about to lose his tongue or something else he equally valued over what he was about to do, Thibert ventured, "Perhaps I was mistaken about the true speed . . ." His voice drained away as Alaex's eyes narrowed.

To both his and Alaex's amazement, he tried again. "Perhaps, 'tis much like learning a new maneuver in drill. It takes time to master the technique," he said in a hopeful voice, pleased that he had come up with that example. His pleasure sizzled and died beneath the increased heat in Alaex's gaze.

"One more 'perhaps,' Thibert, and 'twill see you cleaning chamberpots for the next moon. Understood?"

There was no way he did not, and deciding that he had done all he dared for his lady, Thibert rapidly retreated.

Alaex stared after him until he closed the hall door. Without realizing it, he was already allowing himself to be soothed by Thibert's argument—not the ludicrous one about his being mistaken about the speed—truly that was enough to raise his ire again—but the other. It could be that Iliani had forgotten. If she had, he could not blame her for that. It was just that this situation was too important for forgetting. She could have killed herself and the babe.

That thought made his eyes glitter again, and all of Thibert's well-intended efforts were forgotten as Alaex decided on an action. He would seek his wife. *Now.*

While Thibert stumbled through possible excuses, Iliani herself was wondering what she could or would say to Alaex when he came. And he was coming; Iliani had no doubt. Just as fulsome dark clouds brought inevitable rain, Alaex's wrath would swell and grow until it impelled him to rain down his shower of rage. Despite his perhaps wanting to do otherwise, he would be just like the bloated clouds, unable to hold back.

Iliani wracked her brain for an explanation that would shelter her from the worst of it, and discarded one thing after another. Her only viable plan was that perhaps she should pretend to be asleep when he came. Alaex would not disturb her then, and perhaps his anger would cool.

Iliani was not proud of it, but she would do it. She had moved only one foot toward the bed when the door swung open and Alaex strode in aggressively, his eyes pinning her midstride.

Swinging the door shut, he moved a few steps into the room, looking from Iliani to the bed. "About to seek rest, madam?" His query sounded more like an accusation.

Beneath the weight of it, Iliani lost the battle to control her telltale blush. Instead, trying to gain back ground she'd just lost, she walked casually over to one of the two chairs flanking the fireplace and sat down.

Instead of answering his question, which really wasn't one, she said quietly, "Thibert wasted no time, I see." There was a fair amount of accusation in her own voice.

Alaex started to say something, then changed his mind. When he did speak after looking at her for a long time, his words were neutral despite his anger, which was still evident.

"What happened was reported, aye." After a few taut moments of silence he asked, "Have you naught to say?"

Iliani shook her head, nervously smoothing a nonexistent wrinkle from her gown.

"Why not?"

She shrugged. "I am positive that I cannot add to what Thibert has related."

Alaex snorted. "I am sure you can. Your tale would

not be thick with conjecture. Of the two of you, I was hoping *one* was actually there."

He aroused her curiosity with that. "What does that mean?"

Alaex's mouth twisted in fleeting wry humor. "It means that it was the worst report I have ever been given. The man either did not know his mind, did not trust his eyes, or was not there. Maybe your horse spooked. Perhaps you did not gallop as quickly as he assumed. Perhaps you had forgotten your word. 'Twas sickening."

Iliani's lips began to twitch as she pictured Thibert offering those highly implausible excuses. She looked away from Alaex, her heart warming. Thibert had reported her action, but had done what she had not. He had offered explanations or possibilities to mitigate her guilt, bless his square face! If it were near her Iliani would have kissed it, and the only thing that would have stopped her would have been the image in her mind of Alaex's scowl of displeasure—much like the one he was wearing now.

Leaving thoughts of Thibert, Iliani concentrated on Alaex. Knowing what he waited for, she said simply, "Thibert was right."

"About what?" he demanded.

As she said the words, Iliani couldn't meet his piercing gaze. "About forgetting. I did. I recalled my promise at about the same time Thibert called to me."

Alaex folded his massive arms across his chest. "It seems you two agree on that." His stance, despite the position of his arms, became looser, less aggressive. "What happened?"

There at last was a real question, not an accusation in the form of one.

"My mind was elsewhere," Iliani offered lamely, knowing that in some ways that was worse than forgetting. "I was trying to sort out something that bothered me. Unthinkingly I did what I always do at such a time. I sank my heels into Wind Dancer and fled. It was only after a few gallops that I remembered that I had promised not to do that because of the babe."

Instead of the further chastisement she expected—for Alaex rules were rules—Iliani watched in surprise as the anger faded from his eyes and his stance loosened the rest of the way.

"Do you want to tell me of it?"

"I just did," she replied, mistaking his meaning.

Alaex smiled gently. "Nay. I meant the other. The thing troubling you."

Irrationally Iliani was besieged with fear. For whatever reason, she didn't want to tell Alaex of her recurring dream and the lingering terror it brought. The terror was worse than the dream, lasting long after she awakened.

"'Tis not of great import," she hedged.

The smile on his face dimmed. "Iliani?"

She should have been warned by his tone, but Iliani was so preoccupied with the sudden onslaught of the remembered terror of the dream she paid no attention to the tension in his voice. Her response was an absent "Aye?"

"Do you remember how I feel about lies?"

That pierced through her memories and Iliani's eyes widened. "I have not lied to you."

"Do you want this child?"

"Aye. You know—"

"Would you do aught to endanger it?"

The dispassionately methodical way he was firing questions at her made Iliani take note of what she should have before. It also brought the feeling that he was building a trap. Even knowing that, she couldn't see it.

"Nay, I would not. I have told you this, Alaex," she said, hoping that her uncertainty, which was based on trepidation and not dishonesty, could not be heard.

"If that is so—"

"It is, Alaex, I vow it," Iliani said, her panic over his manner increasing.

"If that is so," Alaex continued as if she had not interrupted, closing his trap with irrevocable finality, "then you will explain to me how the thing that caused you to forget your well-being and that of your child as well as your promise to me could be of little import."

By the time he finished speaking, some of the tension in his voice was replaced by returning anger, and Iliani was stunned. His logic, she lamented, was indisputable. If something weighed heavily enough on her mind that it had caused her to behave that way—and it had—then it must be important to her—which it was.

She had to tell him. There was no other choice. Despite her overwhelming fear of doing so, Iliani could think of nothing else to do. She had known all along it would come to this. If she were honest with herself, Iliani knew it was the certainty that she would have to confide the entire situation to Alaex that had caused her feeling of inevitableness and foreboding. Whether Alaex would understand her fear was not the issue. She couldn't tell him of it without telling him what caused it.

As Iliani wrestled with her tormenting thoughts, she forgot Alaex watched her. Seeing her anguish so vividly, Alaex was beginning to think she would not say anything, and despite his desire to know what happened, he was not going to force her.

"Iliani—"

"I was mistaken," Iliani said softly, never hearing him call her. "It was not that it did not matter. I knew I would feel foolish in the telling of it, and so I sought to avoid that."

"I would never make you feel foolish."

"I dreamed again," she murmured, not realizing until she said it how difficult the words actually were.

Alaex's interest immediately perked. "The same as before?"

"Aye," Iliani replied, then, "Nay."

"Which is it, Iliani?"

Baffled by the edge in his voice, Iliani admitted helplessly, "Both. 'Twas the same as before. I now recognize the place as this hall. 'Twas night, dark and cold. I was afraid." She began to shudder with remembrance and gooseflesh started to rise along her arms. Absently Iliani hugged herself and began to rub her arms beneath the sleeves of her gown.

"Go on," Alaex encouraged softly, the edge in his tone blunted.

"There is not much more than that," Iliani replied, her voice reflecting her inner tensions. "I saw the man lying there and he was dead."

Alaex's stare intensified. "Was there anyone there?" he asked sharply. Too sharply, Iliani thought, staring at him perplexedly.

"Nay." She shook her head. Then because his manner was making her more jumpy than the dream itself, she asked, "Why do you ask?"

Alaex shrugged, and a sharp tremor of apprehension slithered down Iliani's spine. Either her mind, sharpened by her own intense concentration for answers, was giving her insight into what existed, or her nerves, already sensitized from the remembrance of the nightmare, were making her see what did not. Whichever, Iliani did not believe his sudden—and she was somehow certain, forced—air of unconcern. It mattered to him and if he could ask questions, she was entitled to answers too.

"Why, Alaex?" she persisted.

His eyes slid from hers. "You mentioned fear. I wondered if you were being threatened. Since you have already said the man on the floor was dead, the threat could come only through the presence of another."

Again his logic was sound. Then why did it ring, if not false, then not completely true? There was something else. Iliani knew it. She felt it.

Alaex interrupted her musings. "'Tis a pity you are so plagued by dreams of the night, Iliani. Especially at a time such as this, I would prefer that you had no worry at all. However difficult I know it must be for you to do it, you must put it from your mind before it causes you more damage and pain. It does you no good to fret over the possible death of someone you do not know."

Iliani heard the question in that statement; however, her awareness of that faded quickly as something more overwhelming occurred to her.

The thought crystallized so clearly and suddenly, it made her gasp. It had entered unbidden, as if her subconscious had applied itself to her problem, and only after reaching a solution would it allow her to glimpse its working by showing her the result.

Iliani did not wait for Alaex to ask the question. "Whatever else remains debatable, his identity is not," she said in a curiously strained voice. "He is my father."

Chapter

→ 25 ←

In the aftermath of her revelation, Iliani felt the rush of many emotions too numerous to identify, and none of them pleasant. It seemed to her that Alaex took her declaration no better. He definitely looked as if he had received a blow.

"Your father?" he repeated quietly. "I thought you told me you could not recall him."

Iliani nodded, confusion etched on her face. "I did. I mean, I couldn't. Nonetheless, Alaex, I know that he is the man I see dead." The stifling and frightening feeling of terror overwhelmed her, overshadowing all other emotions, refusing despite the best of her will to be controlled any longer.

Seeing the fear expressed so torturously in her lovely face, Alaex could not stay away. In three long strides he reached her, pulled her in his arms, and held her tightly against his chest.

"What's happening, Alaex?" Iliani voice was muffled against his chest, but he heard her clearly. "Why am I seeing this? Was I there when my father died?"

Alaex tensed. "What did Edouard and Eadwina say to you?"

"They refused to talk about it. All I ever knew was that my father died when I was five." Iliani was so afraid and confused, she didn't note that he hadn't answered her question.

For a long time he said nothing at all, and neither did she. Both were lost in their own thoughts and the unexpected tension.

When Alaex did speak, the strain was evident in his voice. "I know you probably think 'tis easy for me to say, but do not worry. What is happening, although terrifying, is natural."

Iliani tried to pull back from his arms, but Alaex tightened his hold, keeping her face against his chest as he continued, his words less stilted.

"The few memories you have of Aeric are here at Fontwyn. Although I could have wished they did it in a milder way, those memories are resurfacing. 'Tis unfortunate," he said, kissing her on the top of her head, "that they have begun with the worst. Soon, though, Iliani, I promise that will fade to be replaced by happier ones. I remember being here with your father then. It would pain him no end if he knew you dwelled on such darkness."

Iliani allowed his words to soothe her because she very much wanted relief from the tension and the terror. She forced herself to relax within his arms and sighed as Alaex's fingers began to rub gentle circles on her back. However, despite how good his hands felt, they brought only partial relief. They relaxed only her body. Iliani's mind still worked furiously, refusing to cease or even slow its quest for answers. As Alaex's hands drew more tension from her, she focused on his words about knowing her father.

"I know this is a peculiar request, considering he was my father, but you were older. Your memories of him are clearer because you would have known him better." She paused. "I have never asked about your past because I know how deeply you dislike discussing it, but will you share a bit of it with me? Only the part that pertains to me," she rushed on before he could object. "I want to know of your time here. More specifically, I want you to tell me of my father."

Alaex looked deeply into the violet eyes so like those of the Aeric he had known, and he knew that he would be unable to deny her. The decision to talk came easier than he thought it would, and slowly he nodded.

Not wanting to release her, instead of reseating her and taking the other chair in front of the fireplace for himself, Alaex led her toward the bed, not missing the sideways glance Iliani gave him. He read her thoughts, and even as his mouth turned up in a glinting smile that bordered on wicked, he managed to say innocently, "We will talk."

Not fully trusting his words and definitely not trusting his smile, Iliani lay down beside him. Once Alaex had settled himself in the bed and gathered her to his chest, he asked softly, "What is it you want to know?"

Iliani hesitated. She couldn't ask how he met her father. After tending him when he was wounded, she knew the answer and she didn't want him to either lie or become angry. Nor did she want to make him uncomfortable. She was tense enough for both of them. Also, there might come a time when he discovered that she knew and she would not like to be caught out in the tale.

"Tell me what he was like," she said, and although she couldn't see his face, as it was above her, she sensed he was pleased with her request.

Alaex was. He had experienced a moment of dread when he thought she would want to know how he and Aeric met. Telling her of that would have left a gap furlongs wide in his story, as he was positive Iliani would have wondered how he had come to be in such a state. Even if she never asked, he would feel as if she did every time she looked at him, and he wouldn't be able to endure the uncertainty. Because he did not trust himself or his reaction, Alaex preferred not to delve into his past. Therefore, Iliani's simply phrased request was a huge relief. It enabled him to inject the right carefree note in his voice as he answered her.

"Your father was a remarkable man, truly one of honor. However, I am sure this is no new revelation."

Iliani, who had become more uneasy during his long silence, nodded.

"I am equally certain that that is not what you want to know," Alaex teased gently, his soft chuckle melting over her. When he began to speak again, the humor was gone, but it was replaced by respect and near awe.

Through Alaex's quiet words, Iliani learned of the man her father had been, not the lord. Alaex's reminiscences revealed Aeric's warmth, his sense of justice, and the remarkable fact that her father had been a jester with a huge sense of humor. He had loved books and learning, his home and estate, but mostly he had loved his wife and his daughter.

"That," Alaex said softly, bringing himself from the past, "is all. There is no more I know of to tell."

Iliani was silent, going over in her mind everything she had just learned. In these last hours, she felt as if she had finally got to know her father and she was aware of a previously unrecognized anger that no one had thought to share these things with her before. Her image of her father would never be complete. That fact was unalterable. Too much time had passed and he had died when she was too young. However, the information she now had added a warm color to an otherwise vague picture of the man who had been her father. It answered unspoken questions that had lain unresolved for what seemed an eternity in her mind and heart.

She had needed to know these things. She had needed to know that it had been Aeric's love of learning and books that had brought him to Alfred's attention. That it had been this that lay the seed for their friendship, which was ended only by Aeric's death. There were other facets of his personality revealed as well—facets commonly taken for granted when someone is present but rare and precious when he is gone.

According to Alaex, Aeric had had a zest for life and all things living. Iliani was amazed to discover that Aeric had loved animals, and it would not be far-fetched to think that her own love of animals had probably been inherited from him. Aeric's laugh had been deep, his loyalty—another trait they shared—unquestioned, and his love unwavering and strong.

Aye, she had needed to know these things, Iliani repeated to herself. Hearing them seemed to heal a thirteen-year-old wound.

At last she had learned of her father, and her love for Alaex grew because he was the one who had given her this priceless gift. Iliani no longer blamed Edouard and Eadwina for their silence. They had done what they thought was right. In their way they had made Aeric known to her. There was proof of that in Edouard's having her educated, although such a thing was a rarity for men and practically unheard of for women. In honor of his friend, though, he had had it done.

Her anger faded and Iliani felt nothing but gratitude. Although she never knew her mother and her father died when she was young, she felt fortunate. Her father's love had lasted beyond his death. First, he had provided for the child she had been by giving her Edouard and his family. Then he had provided for the woman she would become by giving her Alaex to love for the rest of her life. To Iliani both were gifts beyond measure.

"Iliani?" Alaex called, breaking into her thoughts. "Have you fallen asleep?"

"Nay, I was only thinking."

"Care to share your thoughts?"

"There are too many," she said, shaking her head. Before Alaex could respond, Iliani raised herself up and leaned on his chest, her gaze fastening on his. "I will simply give you the shortened version."

Seemingly from nowhere, as keen as it was sudden, Alaex felt as if his body was on fire. He didn't know if

Iliani did it deliberately or if she was totally oblivious to the effect her intense stare was having on him.

"And that is?" he managed huskily.

Iliani's lips moved closer, but her eyes never left his. "Thank you." In the time that followed, Alaex's "You're welcome" was all she could have hoped for.

The darkness was gone, but the cold and fear remained. She could see his face now, quite clearly. He hurt. Was it her fault? He seemed to be looking at her. Was he hurting because she had done a bad thing? She shouldn't be here. Papa had sent her to bed. Maybe he didn't hurt. Maybe he was mad and he lay on the floor with it. She had done that once. Her dog had licked her face and she had gotten up. Should she do that for Papa? Should she lick his face? When her dog had done it, it had tickled and made her stop being mad. Maybe it would do the same for him.

She started to go to him and then she stopped, noticing the spots for the first time. They were thick and red and they were everywhere—drops of it were on Papa's face. Maybe that was why he frowned. He didn't want that on his face. She would not lick it, but she could wipe it off. She started toward him again and this time she stopped because of what she heard. Someone was coming! The fear returned. She had to hide. She had to hide! She had to—

Iliani sat rigidly upright in the bed, as disoriented by the bright afternoon sun streaming in through the window as by the dream from which she had awakened. Her breathing was shallow and quick and it was a long time before she controlled it. Her hands, which were clenched tightly, were sweaty once she forced herself to open them. Her heart was pounding so fiercely that it actually hurt. It was only after she felt the tears on her cheeks that she knew she was crying as well.

Slowly, as if every muscle in her body pained her, Iliani swung her legs to the floor and got up. She put on her gown without really noticing what she did. When she moved over to the window, her steps were weighted, as if she had not fully awakened.

But she had. She was as awake as anyone could be who had dreamed they saw their father covered in blood.

As Iliani stared out the window, allowing the late afternoon breezes to cool and calm her, her disorientation began to fade. The day's events began to come back to her: the ride, her argument with Alaex, his telling her of her father, their making love. She must have fallen asleep after that, and no wonder. Alaex's tender yet fierce lovemaking had left her feeling blissful and sated. Then had come the dream.

Iliani shuddered. "So much for the better memories," she said to herself bitterly, recalling what Alaex had said. This was ten times worse because she now knew who the man was. It was her father.

Not given to superstition, Iliani did not believe that there was life beyond the grave. However, she was as terrorized by the consistency of the dreams as she was by their substance. Nay, she didn't believe her father was trying to tell her something, but her mind certainly was. It had just chosen a horrifying way of doing it, and despite its persistence Iliani still couldn't figure out its message. She needed help for that, *but not from Alaex.*

The certainty of that feeling made Iliani uncomfortable, especially as she could find no reason for it. Something inside had just said it without offering her any further insight into why. Shrinking back from her unease, Iliani rationalized that her need to keep Alaex out of this was because she had spoken to him already and nothing had been resolved. To speak of it further would only worry him when maybe, in this instance, someone else held the key.

Rapidly Iliani considered the other people involved who knew her and her father. There weren't that many, just Edouard, Eadwina, and Cam. For some reason, she didn't want to tell Edouard. He would worry worse than Alaex, Iliani thought, remembering how distressed Edouard would become when she tried to recall anything about her father. Nay, it couldn't be him. Cam had known her father, but he was somewhere in the dense forest of Fontwyn, and going to him was impossible. Alaex would never understand or permit it, even if she got the courage to ask. To ask, she'd have to explain why, and that was a disaster Iliani refused to think of.

That left Eadwina.

Iliani's mind rebelled at that solution, even as it recognized Eadwina as her only feasible option. Eadwina had known her father and she was the only one of the three Iliani felt she could ask without sounding a major alarm. The only drawback was that the same innocent exuberance that made Eadwina the best choice because she would not be anxious also made her the worst choice to accept as far as getting a real answer. Iliani sighed, hoping that the strength of her argument would outweigh the weakness, because she had to do it. She couldn't continue under this cloud of uncertainty and fear.

Chapter

⇨ 26 ⇦

"Alaex, I have a request."

Iliani winced at the serious note in her voice. She had practiced all afternoon what she was going to say to Alaex, and the one thing she had constantly admonished herself to do was to keep her tone light. She knew Alaex heard her tension when he froze, his tunic half on and half off. He finished removing it and stretched the stiffness from his muscles before answering.

"What is it?"

Taking a second to calm herself and get her voice under control, Iliani said, "I want to ride over to Lourds Keep to visit Eadwina."

Alaex walked away to put his tunic on the chest. He kept his back to her.

"When?"

Something in his manner did not allow Iliani to take his response as assent. "Tomorrow," she answered, unsure of how he was taking her request. Trying to stem the growing awkwardness, Iliani continued quickly. "I will not be gone long. I intend to return to Fontwyn before dark, and I am willing to take my guard with me."

Alaex finally turned to look at her. But it seemed he was doing more than that. He seemed to study her.

"I believe," he said slowly, "that I once assured Eadwina that you were not a prisoner here. Need I convince you of the same?"

Iliani frowned. "I don't understand."

"Agreed. Neither do I," Alaex returned. "You seem ill at ease, Iliani. Why?"

Quickly Iliani made the decision not to deny her discomfort. "I am uncomfortable," she admitted. "I know how you feel about Edouard and his family and I try to respect your feelings. But you have to understand that I do not share your view. When it comes to them, we see things differently. If I spoke nervously, it was because I feared you would refuse my request out of hand."

"Have I been so unreasonable?"

Iliani did not miss the edge in his voice, and too late she recognized the unfair implication of her words. Alaex had never tried to change her mind about her relationship with Edouard and his family nor interfere with it.

"I am sorry, Alaex. I spoke without thinking."

His stillness did not give any indication whether he accepted her apology, and taut moments passed as they stared at each other. When Alaex walked over and caressed her face, Iliani let out a long, low sigh. When he bent over and kissed her, she almost forgot her request.

Her eyes were clouded with a soft passion when Alaex released her. He still did not mention her apology, but as he ran the pad of his thumb caressingly over her lips, Iliani knew it was all right. His gesture told her she was forgiven long before she heard him say softly, "Enjoy your visit."

The next day as Iliani and her guard rode to Lourds Keep, she thought of the remarkable ease with which Alaex had consented to her request. His only objection had been the number of men riding with her. She would have to ride with a guard of twelve instead of six.

Iliani did not think that was necessary, but she knew Alaex was only considering her safety. His desire to protect her was endearing, and so without protest she had given in to his added stipulation.

With her thoughts still on her enigmatic husband, Iliani was aware of an easing within her as she looked ahead to the gates of Lourds Keep. Whatever his stipulations or possible misgiving, Alaex had allowed her to come. His consideration of her feelings spoke more than any words, strengthening her hope that in time all would be well with them. They had not mentioned love since that time when he was recovering from his illness, but his actions were encouraging her to think that if there was no love, there was deep care.

"Iliani! How happy I am to see you!"

Pulled from her thoughts by Eadwina's birdlike voice, Iliani was surprised to find that while she had been thinking of Alaex, she and her guard had gained Lourds Keep. Focusing on the woman standing below her, Iliani's smile was natural and genuine. Eadwina might be a birdwit, but her warmth and presence had a way of making Iliani smile for one reason or another.

No sooner had Iliani dismounted than she was enveloped in Eadwina's firm, plump embrace. "Why are you here, pigeon? Is it a visit or are you still having difficulty adjusting to your fierce husband? You haven't left him, have you? Truth, I do not know if 'twill make me happy or nay. He did look the sort to not take such a thing well. Except, Iliani," and she lowered her voice, letting Iliani know she was about to be scolded, "when next you attempt to leave your husband 'twould be much more successful if you did not bring his men with you."

Eadwina stopped her chatter long enough to remark on Iliani's stunned expression. "You did not think I had noticed you were upset, Pigeon? Well, fie on you! I did. I notice lots of things, lots and lots of things that I do not say. That's what's wrong with the world, if you ask my opinion, and of course you haven't, but you shall be-

cause I'm certain that's why you are here." She stopped
again, a chubby ringed finger tapping on her chin. "Now
where was I?" she murmured almost to herself. Then the
clouds lifted from her green eyes and her face seemed to
brighten. "Uh, aye, there I am, or was, until I became
distracted. 'Tis terribly easy to do," she added as if
revealing something momentous, and shook her head as
if trying to focus. "But to hand, I was saying how
everyone feels the need to comment on everything and
that's what's wrong with the world. There! I have said
it!"

Again Eadwina's eyes clouded. "Except now that I
have, I realize that my comment on everyone's need to
comment makes me just as bad as they. Is that not so?"

Forgetting Eadwina's outrageous presumption that she
was attempting to leave Alaex, Iliani laughed and hugged
her, hoping to ease the woman's spirit as she admitted to
herself the fruitlessness of what she had intended. She
loved Eadwina with all her heart, and coming here for a
visit was one thing, but expecting to find an answer to
settle her fears . . . that was unrealistic and only served
to show how desperate she had become.

Deciding that it would hurt Eadwina's feelings if she
should turn around and leave after having only just
arrived, Iliani followed her inside Lourds Keep. It had
been several months since she had been in the long
angular hall, but little had changed. It was still well lit
from the large square windows lining the right side of the
wall, and the rich dark red wood of the lord's table that
stood beneath them gleamed dully in the bright sunlight.
As always, Edouard's chair sat in regal and stark dark
splendor at the center of the table. He had once told
Iliani he preferred it thus because it allowed him an
unhindered view of the hall, from the gallery in front
and above it to the double doors to the left of it and the
wide high hearth to the right of it.

When Iliani looked toward that fireplace, she saw a
silent, lean figure there with outstretched arms.

"Edouard!" she cried happily, going toward him.

Iliani only glimpsed the welcome on his face before being wrapped in his strong grip. It was a long time before Edouard released her, and then he did not let her go completely, instead looking her over from head to toe. His gaze was not only searching, it was apprehensive.

"Are you well, Daughter?"

Iliani blinked at the unexpected moisture in her eyes, overwhelmed by his words and the feelings she sensed in them.

"Aye, Edouard, I am," she said, hoping to ease the lingering worry she saw in his gaze. Watching him as closely as she was, it was not difficult to see the definite signs of fatigue and stress. There were circles under his eyes and he had lost weight. "And you?" she asked with soft concern.

Edouard released her the rest of the way. "I am better than I have been," he answered truthfully. "That day you left was one of the worst of my life. I never thought to see you again."

Iliani thought she heard quiet censure in his tone. "You are always welcome at Fontwyn."

Edouard's face constricted. "I cannot go there. I haven't been since your father—" His lips compressed, and his voice became hard. "I will not while he—"

"Please do not," Iliani interrupted, unwilling to have him say anything about Alaex. She understood his pain over her father's death and his disappointment owing to his unfulfilled desire to have her marry Cam, but that was done now. In truth, Iliani was still uncertain as to whose tale to believe about her father's wishes, but she loved Alaex and she could forgive Edouard if he had been mistaken, so that was an issue she tried to place behind her.

"Very well, I will not," Edouard said sourly, "but I will not have them in my house." He pointed to her guard, who had followed her inside. "They may await your departure out there."

Iliani looked to Thibert and saw his face tighten. He

didn't need to say the words. She was in his care and that meant she stayed in his sight, and mercy on any who tried to change that. Edouard's face when Iliani turned back was just as unyielding. She pleaded with him silently, and when he looked away from her coldly, Iliani knew he would not budge.

His words confirmed it. "He sends guards. Who here wouldst harm you? You have more to fear with h—" He broke off, seeming to recall her words, and finished with, " 'Tis an insult plain."

Seeing there was no hope for it, and truly concerned for Edouard should he not desist, Iliani turned again to Thibert. "Please wait outside for me. I shall not be long."

Thibert was about to object when Edouard said, "You have just arrived. What nonsense is this that you cannot stay?"

Iliani looked at him with sadness. Of all the things she had expected, this was not one of them. "If my husband's men are not welcome, that means he is not. If he is not, you make it impossible for me to stay. I refuse," she said with firm softness, holding up her hand to forestall either Edouard's retreat or objection, "to make you go against something you feel so strongly. Therefore, I will stay only a moment while my guard waits outside."

Turning to Thibert once more, Iliani assured him. "I will be out shortly. Please wait."

Her unhappiness was obvious. Thibert could see it from across the floor and he cursed the stubborn old man for causing it. He had no right to make her choose. Iliani had spoken eloquently of her support for her husband and his men. It was that which made Thibert decide he would not make it harder for her. After a curt nod to her, he and the men left.

When the door closed there was a slow, insulting clap from the corner of the hall where the stairs to the gallery were. Iliani, Edouard, and Eadwina, who had been silent during the interchange, turned to it.

Only Iliani was surprised to see Cam there. As far as

she knew, he was still camping in the forests of Fontwyn. To her surprise she was not as happy to see him as she would have thought.

Cam pushed away from the stairs and advanced to them, his eyes never leaving Iliani's face. "What, no warm welcome for me?" He said the words as a jest, but there was an underlying coldness in them that made Iliani unable to accept them as such.

Without waiting for her to answer, Cam, still with his eyes on her face, said, "Father, Mother, will you leave us alone for the few moments that the lady here has graciously spared us?"

Finally Eadwina spoke again and Iliani could have cheerfully throttled the woman. "Oh, I understand, Cam," she bubbled happily. "You two have not seen one another in a while. There are things to say. Do not berate her overmuch, Cam dear, Iliani has not been happy."

Each of Eadwina's three listeners took her words differently. Iliani was comically chagrined, belatedly remembering that Eadwina had told her she noticed her discontent. If Eadwina *had* to begin to follow a thought, Iliani would have given much for it not to have been that one, and not now. The look on Edouard's face was quietly hopeful, and some of the ice left Cam's eyes to be replaced with mild interest.

Before leaving, Eadwina and Edouard gave her a kiss, the latter squeezed her arms saying, "When you left that day, I lost my son too. Now he has returned and so have you. There is a sign in that, I think."

Iliani pulled back, saying nothing. The only sign was in what Edouard wanted to see.

When he and Eadwina disappeared, Cam studied her a long time and Iliani, noting the cool, cynical expression in his eyes, developed an abrupt and alarming feeling of regret that she had thought to come to Lourds Keep at all. However, she tried to push the notion away as nonsense. This was Cam, after all, and this place was her home. There was naught to fear here and naught to fear of him. Had he not camped in the forest of Fontwyn to watch after her and ensure no harm befell her? He would not do to her that from which he had tried to protect her.

Relaxing a bit, Iliani spoke, as it seemed that Cam was reluctant. "How fare you, Cam?"

Cam studied her pale, beautiful features a little longer, then he shrugged. "Well enough for a man who has lived the past months in a forest."

"Oh."

"Is that all, Iliani?" he queried. " 'Oh'? Wouldn't you like to know which forest? Aren't you even slightly curious why I would do such a thing?"

There was anger in Cam's voice, and Iliani's alarm rose again, making her rue her decision to send Thibert away. Cam was behaving strangely. It seemed as if he were angry but trying to conceal it, a thing he had never been able to do successfully. Growing up with him, Iliani knew that Cam had always been unpredictable and violent when he felt he was wronged, but he had never directed that side of his personality toward her before. Praying that this would not be the first time, she answered him, deciding at the last moment against telling him that she had known where he had been.

"If you want to tell me, then I want to hear," Iliani said neutrally. The instant the words left her mouth she knew that that was not the right response either.

Cam's eyes narrowed and his fists clenched. It was almost like looking at a stranger with a familiar face. Iliani had never seen him like that before. And that was before he spoke.

"Don't you dare patronize me!"

Iliani swallowed, involuntarily taking a step back while trying to ignore the anger blazing in Cam's eyes and denying the hatred she thought she heard in his voice. "I am not doing that."

Although her voice was calm, there was fear she couldn't hide in her eyes, and it was that fear which calmed him. Cam held himself rigidly, forcing a composed demeanor he was far from feeling. His days in the forest and his frustration at the lack of success in ridding himself of his enemy might have taken their toll, but he wasn't stupid. All was not lost, at least not yet.

This was Iliani. She didn't think badly of him and he knew he had to keep it that way. As soon as the inconvenience of her husband was removed and they were married, he wouldn't care what she thought. In fact, he might just let her see what he was hiding and more, he thought, struggling to keep his eyes from narrowing with irate repugnance as the memory resurfaced of what Brita had told him about Iliani's activities. That she would dare to sleep with that filth while he had endured hardship in the wilds of Fontwyn's forest enraged him and was a wrong he could not let go unanswered. For now he would wait, but Iliani would pay.

Cam smiled with the thought of his revenge, receiving double pleasure because he knew Iliani had no idea what was behind his amusement.

But Cam underestimated her. Iliani was no fool. Even without knowing its source, Cam's smile made her heart beat heavily in warning. Too much was happening that she did not understand. It was as if everything said and done was only topical with a murky and malevolent undercurrent. That alone made Iliani decide that she preferred not knowing what brought that smile to his face.

"Is it true what Mother said?" he asked as if only just remembering Eadwina's words. His eyes were piercing. "You are unhappy?" The thought of her in Alaex's arms made his eyes glitter. "I would not have thought it so."

"Why is that?" Iliani ignored his questions and responded to his statement, again feeling that more was being said than the words implied.

Cam lowered his eyes and stepped away from her. "Just a thought."

Whatever game was being played, Iliani wanted no part of it. Her voice was firm. "The thought is wrong."

When Cam swung back to face her, the expression on his face before he cleared it made Iliani remember her unease. The apprehension made her soften her tone, but it did not keep her from saying what she knew needed to be said.

"Understand me, Cam, I do not mean to belittle the times we have shared by saying that it was a mistake for me to come here, but it was. I see now 'tis too soon for everyone."

Without realizing she was doing it, she compared Alaex's respect for her feelings for Edouard and Cam with Edouard and Cam's reaction to her husband. Alaex never tried to poison her against them. They, however, seemed determined to not rest until they had turned her against him. It was so unfair.

And it doesn't have to be, she thought sadly, turning to go. Iliani was no longer afraid, only confused. She was so upset that when Cam reached out and grabbed her arm, her fear didn't immediately return.

However, all it took was one glance from his hand to the fevered brightness in his eyes, and Iliani's dread returned. It was more forceful than it had been before and it completely overshadowed her confusion.

"Nay, Iliani, do not go. You cannot," Cam beseeched. Despite the conciliatory tone in his voice, his thoughts were not kind. That she would reduce him to pleading was yet another thing for which she would pay later. Now he needed to build on the wary confusion he read so clearly in her eyes. His next words were calculated to do just that. And in his fervent desire to convince her, Cam also convinced himself that they were true.

"I love you. You are mine and belong to me. You have and always will."

Cam's impassioned words made Iliani waver in her resolve to be away from Lourds Keep as quickly as possible. Until that moment, she had been certain that he, like her, had agreed to the marriage only because it had seemed to be the cherished wish of both their fathers. She had never thought that what was between them was anything deeper. Believing his words and now viewing his disturbing behavior as a result of his love, Iliani felt truly sorry, because although she understood, she felt helpless to prevent his pain. She had never loved him that way. She would have married him, aye, but she never felt for him a fraction of what she felt for Alaex. If that was how he thought about her when there was no hope of it being returned, Iliani genuinely pitied him.

Cam saw the pity and he thrust her arm away. "I do not need your compassion. Were I you," he sneered nastily, his enraged pride causing him to forget his resolve to keep certain facets of his personality from her, "I would save it for myself. There will be need of it, I promise."

Absently rubbing her upper arm where he had grabbed her, Iliani's eyes searched his. "What do you mean?"

He shrugged. "All were keeping it from you, trying to spare your sensibilities." His dark brown eyes scraped over her. "They seem hardy enough to me."

"What are you speaking of, Cam?" Iliani asked again, although an inner sense warned her that she really didn't want to know.

He told her.

"Aeric did not die because his heart had given out," he said bluntly. The statement was all the more brutal because of the casual way he said it.

Iliani could scarcely produce a voice. "What are you saying?"

"I am saying that he was murdered and the murderer was never punished, although several people knew who it was."

The warning screeched louder than ever, and Iliani finally heeded it. "I do not want to hear any more," she mumbled, turning to go to the door.

Pushed past his limits and angry at himself as well as her as he belatedly realized how much irreparable damage he had done to his cause, Cam called after her. "I think you should. After all, 'tis not every day a man murders another, gains the dead man's property, and marries the man's daughter."

The cold, heartless words slammed into Iliani's back

with the force of a thousand blades, freezing her with their implication and calculated cruelty.

"Liar!" she gasped, rounding on him. She would have struck him, but Cam had not moved from his spot.

"Am I?" Cam asked with a calm Iliani found sickening considering what he had just said and the amount of pain it caused. When he shrugged insolently as if he did not care whether she believed, the pain twisted deeper.

Without answering his question, Iliani again started for the door, knowing she couldn't stay any longer. She had only taken two steps when Cam continued in that revoltingly dispassionate voice.

Don't listen, Iliani, her inner voice pleaded. *Just keep walking.*

It was no use. Her footsteps were not loud enough to drown out the sound of his words.

"I will not say I have not lied from time to time to gain my ends, or that I would not do so again in the future should the need arise. But in this instance I need not. The facts present themselves, standing with no assist from me. Aeric took in street filth—"

Despite the best of her will Iliani stopped, nearly trembling with the need both to go and to stay if for naught else but to launch herself at Cam and silence his painful words. She did neither, but stood in frozen pain and let his words tear through her defenses to shred at her heart beneath.

"A boy with no name or scruples. He ate from trash, so I heard, and stole anything with a shine. Your father took pity on him. 'Aeric of the Lost Causes' he was called behind his back, and that was truly fitting here. His cause lost him his life, his land, everything."

Iliani could think of nothing to say to combat so vicious a lie, and for the first time in her life she did not allow herself to hide from what Cam's words revealed. Not about Alaex, but about himself. How could she have thought him only a *little* selfish?

All through the years of growing up at Lourds Keep,

she had overlooked or ignored the faint glimmers of his dark side. Yet even those shadowed glimpses had given no clue to the extent of the evil she now saw. And he was evil. Anyone who could say such horrible things for the purpose of causing another the keenest pain could be nothing but. Cam's aggressiveness did not so much as leave her the opportunity of thinking that perhaps he had said what he had out of misguided concern for her welfare or in an attempt to warn her.

Finally Iliani turned to stare at him across the distance, and it was more than disbelief that caused her eyes to search his. Despite her pain, years of better memories that refused to die in an instant caused her to try to find something in him that would be redeeming. Iliani searched for any sign of remorse in him and, moreover, any flicker of evidence that he lied.

Because he had to have lied.

However, as Cam held her stare, Iliani saw evidence of neither remorse nor guilt nor anything else that would mitigate his revelations and her discovery. All she saw and felt, as if it pulsed from him, was unrelenting malevolence, and his rancor was not solely for Alaex. It included her as well. It was so strong, so powerful, it made Iliani wonder how she had missed it before. The signs of it had always been there. Numbly she turned and walked through the doors, knowing she would never return to Lourds Keep as long as Cam was there.

She mounted Wind Dancer in the same numbed state, ignoring Thibert's concerned look. Having given up on finding anything noble in Cam or his actions, Iliani concentrated on what was important, all she had left.

He's lying. He's lying, she chanted to herself to negate Cam's accusation against Alaex. Iliani repeated those two words nearly the entire way to Fontwyn, but no matter how often she said it, she couldn't sweep back the darkness, chase away the cold, or calm her fear. These elements all came back with a permanent vengeance. But this time she wasn't asleep.

Chapter

⇢ 27 ⇠

It has been a week, Iliani."

Oddly, Alaex's words, though implacable, did not disturb the aura of peaceful contentedness around them. They had just made love and it had been as tinglingly sensuous and throbbingly devastating as always. As Iliani lay in the curve of his arm, the only element that eluded her was the sated and satisfied sleep she usually succumbed to when it was over. Alaex's soft statement made her miss it more than ever. Still, Iliani lay quietly, hoping that Alaex would think she slept. He dashed her hope with his next words.

"I know you do not sleep. We must talk."

Giving up pretense, Iliani tried distraction. She leaned up and kissed him with enough energy to pull his mind away from thoughts of talk, but not enough to belie her claim of fatigue.

"Alaex," she murmured against his lips, "I am tired, and you, milord, are the cause." He could not miss her implication. "Therefore, because of that and quite possibly the babe, I can barely keep my eyes open."

Iliani stopped herself from asking if it could wait. She

knew what his answer would be and she didn't want to give him the chance to say it.

Sliding back down beside him, Iliani made what she hoped was a convincing yawn, closed her eyes, and lay still once more. She was just beginning to relax when she heard Alaex's soft chuckle.

"Well done, Iliani. I was spared naught in your arsenal of weapons."

Iliani's eyes snapped open. Although she knew she would regret it, she answered. What good was silence when he knew she did not sleep? "'Arsenal of weapons'?"

"Aye," Alaex averred, "your weapons. Admittedly I know little of matters of the heart, but I recognize warfare in all its forms. Congratulations, Wife. You use your weapons well and to good effect. First there was your rather lively bed play. Nay, nay," he hurried on, his grip tightening when Iliani would have arisen. "I enjoyed it, just as I enjoyed your kiss of a moment ago and was amused by your need to rest because of the babe."

He actually did sound amused. His amusement did not last, though. It disappeared with his next words. "'Twas most amusing when one considers you have scarcely slept in a week. There are faint circles beneath your eyes to prove this. I have given you a week to reveal to me of your own accord what happened to upset you when you visited Lourds Keep. I was trying to be more . . ." He hunted for the right word. "Sensitive. My wife told me I should learn to be so, and I was trying to see things from her part. In everything since my entrance into her life she has felt she had no say, no freedom, no will. So I allowed myself to feel a measure of guilt over this, saying to myself that here at last is an opportunity to try to be more 'sensitive.'"

Alaex went on without giving Iliani the opportunity to speak. "I have tried it, Iliani," he spat out in distaste, "and I like it not. I take your 'sensitive' to mean spineless, allowing you to have your way despite my knowing better otherwise. It seems to be a ploy to allow you to hide from me things you should not."

By the end of his speech he sounded disgruntled, and Iliani wanted to smile even though he could so arrogantly assert that he knew what was best for her and that his patience with being "sensitive" was apparently at an end. Alaex would see sensitivity that way, but he had misunderstood what she meant. She had only wanted him to be aware of and consider her feelings, not alter his personality to the point where he avoided a situation. Iliani merely wanted him to temper how he handled it. Unable to suppress her smile any longer, she told him that.

"So I have been sensitive by allowing you to keep your own counsel?" Alaex asked dubiously.

"Aye." Iliani nodded.

Alaex sighed. "Verily, I do not understand these things, as I have said before. Is there a limit of time for making such an allowance before becoming *insensitive?*"

"I don't know, Alaex. That would, I suppose, depend on you," Iliani admitted honestly.

"'Tis done," he declared promptly, and she felt him relax beneath her. "I have reached my limit. I know something troubles you and I know it occurred when you visited Lourds Keep. You will now tell me what I do not know—what happened and who is the cause."

He certainly did not wade in, this husband of hers, Iliani thought wryly. Nay, Alaex plunged into the water whole souled. One day she would have to caution him against such action lest he cleave his head in two upon an unseen rock because of having misjudged the water's depth. For now she felt only relief. He was right. She had stewed long enough.

When Iliani had first left Lourds Keep she had not been able to think straight. As furlong passed furlong, her mind had slowed its frantic buzzing and she was able to see Cam's words differently. Instead of looking to Alaex to disprove them, she had turned her thoughts to making Cam prove them, and Iliani had calmed somewhat with the knowledge that he could not. 'Twas just like the myth that surrounded Alaex's fighting ability. Over the months that Iliani had lived with him, all she had seen was a man, a strong one, an agile and skillful one, but a man nonetheless. Never in action or word did Alaex try to portray himself as aught else. However, Iliani knew that she would be unable to convince Cam or any others of that because they believed the myth. They *wanted* to believe it. Just as, she had become surer as the distance between her and Lourds Keep grew, Cam now, or always had, wanted to believe that Alaex had done the horrible thing of which he accused him.

Iliani had frowned in distaste with that thought. Cam wanted to believe Alaex a murderer, and therefore to him Alaex was and no proof was needed. He had no interest in proof because he was not interested in justice. It did not really matter to him that her father might have been murdered or that she might have experienced pain from the fact. Iliani saw that her possible reactions—aside from blaming Alaex and running from him to Cam—were of no account. The only thing that mattered was his wants. And he had wanted her.

Cam had said he loved her, and perhaps he believed that. Iliani no longer could. Love was not selfish. It did not seek its own advantage at the expense of another.

When she thought of it Iliani could have wept with the irony. Alaex had never said he loved her, but conversely, he had never hurt her. Cam proclaimed his feelings loudly, yet he had wounded her grievously. The only reason he had mentioned her father's possible murder was to achieve his own ends, not to see a wrong righted. What chilled Iliani was the knowledge that if the logic were pointed out, Cam would see nothing wrong with such selfish reasoning.

He seemed to see nothing amiss with the fact that neither he nor those others he also claimed knew the truth had permitted thirteen years to pass without doing anything. If he or they had had any shred of integrity, an effort would have been made to bring Alaex to Alfred's justice, but it hadn't. Cam hadn't. He had done nothing because the possible crime hadn't mattered, only how the information could be used for benefit. Iliani hated that and Cam's use of love as a justification for his cruelty worse than she hated his lies.

Rubbing Alaex's chest gently, Iliani relived that horrible day and found that her feelings had not changed. Not about Alaex and not about Cam. She wondered briefly if Alaex knew what people thought. She wouldn't be surprised if he did, but she would not mention it now. If he didn't know she didn't want to hurt him, and if he did she did not wish to be the one to reopen old wounds.

"I tried to put it from my mind," she finally replied softly, knowing he still waited for an answer.

Alaex rubbed his hand along her spine. "Apparently it would not go far."

Iliani shrugged against the truth of his words, especially since she had just envisioned the day clearly. "Apparently not."

There was a long silence. Then, "Iliani?"

"Aye?"

"You still have not told me what *it* was."

Blast him! Iliani groaned inwardly. There was tenacity and then there was Alaex. She had run out of ploys subtle and overt.

"It was too ugly to speak of it."

Alaex sat up abruptly and even in the near darkness—with the increasing warmth of the days the fire was not kept burning intently—Iliani could see the blaze in his pale blue eyes.

Sensing Iliani's apprehension, Alaex tried to tamp back his rage. Her answer would determine his success.

His voice was conversationally cold. "Did he touch you?"

Iliani knew what he meant and quickly she said, "Nay." A split second later she was confused. She had answered automatically, without thinking, but she had replied from the knowledge that Cam was there. Alaex could not know that. Cam had entered after Thibert had left. Confused as to the "he" to whom Alaex referred, she asked curiously, "Who?"

Alaex's brow lowered. "Cam. Who else?"

Iliani could not contain her surprise. "How did you—?"

The smile he gave her was lopsided. "Iliani, I may be a warrior, but I do possess a shield."

"And that means?" she prodded, more confused than ever.

"That means that 'tis unnecessary for me to ward off blows with my head. Therefore, I have a brain left to me and I use it." The smile left his face. "Edouard's actions, as you know, have been relayed to me. Your response let me know that he upset you, but not unduly, at least not enough to cause you the sort of disturbance I have seen. Therefore, he is eliminated. Eadwina, birdwit that she is, other than chattering you into deafness, does not possess the capability to cause you distress. That eliminates her, leaving only Cam. I know he is no longer in the forest. I assumed he went home, although I did not concern myself with his time of departure and your visit until you began to behave strangely."

Now that Alaex knew Cam had not attacked her, he calmed. " 'Twas he, was it not? What did he do?"

As always, his ability to sift through possibilities and logically reach an accurate conclusion amazed her. "Aye, 'twas Cam." Iliani studied Alaex's face, seeing concern, warmth, and reduced anger. Trying to keep it that way, she chose her words carefully.

"Alaex, have you ever entered a battle for which you felt prepared, only to have the unexpected happen, thus devastating your defenses such that even if you prevail it is at a loss to yourself?"

Alaex nodded warily.

"That is much like what occurred with Cam and me. I thought I knew him—even his bad points. Then I watch him sink to a greater low." There was confused pain and anger, too, in her voice. "I stood and heard him say things like 'you belong to me' and that I should stay there with him as if you or our marriage did not exist and deserve honor. He didn't think of me, Alaex, or what I might feel about the things he said; 'twas all for him."

Putting his arms back around her, Alaex laid them both back against the bed. "Was there more?"

Iliani hedged. "Was that not enough? Naturally after my refusal, his ire grew and temper became nasty." She splayed her fingers across his chest to keep him there. "I said 'nasty,' not physical." Iliani sighed. "Between his and Edouard's behavior, the trip was a waste. I regret going and I regret more the knowledge that I cannot go back." An underlying sadness was in her voice. "You know how very important belonging is to me, Alaex. It always has been. I worked hard to create the feeling of belonging when I was at Lourds Keep. Last week I realized just how illusory it was. You either belong in a place or you don't. Both Cam and Edouard treated me as if I betrayed them. Edouard I think I can forgive in time. Cam I cannot."

Alaex kissed her gently, not to invoke passion but to soothe her. He heard her distress and he decided to let the matter lie. There was naught else he could do. He couldn't change Edouard's opinion and he was not hypocritical enough to try to change Iliani's about Cam. As the moments passed and he knew that this time Iliani's stillness was not a ruse, but that she had indeed fallen in a fitful sleep, Alaex continued to try to find a way to distract her from what had happened at Lourds Keep. Just before he himself succumbed to sleep, his arms tightened around her as his mind closed in on a possibility.

The next day Alaex sought Iliani out in the kitchen where she was discussing the day's chores with Gwyn. He walked in just as Iliani asked, "Should we salt the meat first or clean the tapestries?"

"Neither."

Both Iliani and Gwyn looked at him. It was Iliani who spoke.

"They must be done, Alaex. Unsalted meat spoils faster and accumulated dust in the tapestries will soon get into the throat," she explained. Then when it occurred to her that she had never seen him in the kitchen before, and certainly never at this time of day, Iliani asked, "What do you here, milord?"

Alaex's eyes sparkled, making him look like an excited child. "I have come for you."

"For me?"

"Aye. 'Tis my understanding that there is a merchant's fair to attend and a picnic lunch to be eaten and I, despite the arduousness of such a chore, have volunteered for it."

The smile Iliani gave him was warm and bright. Here was yet another facet of her husband she was seeing for the first time. Alaex playful? Disbelieving or not, she could not resist his manner.

"Since you volunteered for it," Iliani teased, "I shall not stand between you and your duty. Never let it be said I kept a man from so difficult a task."

Alaex looked down at the floor. "I cannot," he mumbled, and it was all Iliani could do to keep from bursting into laughter. Now he looked like an abashed child. Casting a quick glance at Gwyn to see how the servant was taking this behavior of Alaex's, Iliani's lips twitched at the smile on her face. She looked back to the top of Alaex's dropped head.

"Ahem, why can't you?" Laughter was definitely in her voice.

"On the cause that I volunteered you, too." Alaex peeked up at her and it was too much. He sounded like a seven-year-old.

"'On the cause that . . .'" Iliani repeated and then collapsed in laughter, unable to finish. Through her mirth she heard Gwyn give a chuckle or two herself.

"Well, sir," she said as her laughter died down, "I hope you now realize the folly of volunteering for someone else."

"You won't aid me?" he asked hopefully.

Although still amused, Iliani was about to refuse and explain that she really did have quite a bit of work to do, when Gwyn spoke.

"Go, milady. What needs be done here I can do or I can get Sarah or another of the village girls to help me if Lucy has not the time." The usually serious expression on her face was gone, and her lips twitched with unexpressed mirth. "I would hate to see such effort wasted."

Iliani shook her head. "So would I." She turned to Alaex. "Very well, you have yourself a volunteer. When do we leave?"

Alaex's smile was brilliant. "Now."

Chapter

→ 28 ←

In a very short time, Iliani found herself riding Wind Dancer beside Bear as she and Alaex started out for their day of recreation. Although she likened Alaex's manner to that of a child, in her own excitement over the unexpected outing Iliani now felt like a child herself. Even if they did nothing else, being out with Alaex was treat enough. Truly, Iliani did not particularly want to attend the fair. There would be people there, and she preferred to keep Alaex to herself. But Alaex insisted and off they went.

The fair turned out be wonderful. It had been set up by traveling merchants. Because of the Viking raids, and raids of other sorts, it was difficult for merchants to peddle their wares. Banding together this way increased their safety and their sales, and people were inclined to come for the recreation as well.

Iliani enjoyed herself immensely, but she was happy that they didn't linger long. Alaex bought her hairpins with amethysts on the ends and a beautiful gold, amethyst, and diamond brooch of a lion rampant. Its weight alone signified its worth.

Not too long after, she found herself listening to the lazy slapping of the river against the bank and lying on a blanket under an enormous tree that she was certain had been there since the founding of Rome. The spot was beautiful under the clear blue of the sky. It was perfect for a picnic.

In little time she and Alaex had managed to finish most of the huge lunch that Gwyn had packed for them, not saying much as they ate and enjoyed the scenic view. Even when they put aside the considerable amount that was left of their meal, their conversation remained random and desultory, but this didn't diminish the day or the beauty of the occasion. Soon though, the warmth of the day and the pleasantness of heart and mind had them both beginning to drift off to sleep.

It was the scratching sound that did it. Iliani awoke tensing. Her head was still lying in Alaex's lap and the subtle pressure he exerted on her side told her to stay put. He obviously had heard the sound too.

Iliani may have lain quietly, but her heart was beating an awful racket, making it almost difficult to hear anything else. Then the noise came again, closer, louder.

In the next instant there was a blur of activity as Alaex reached out to apprehend someone, forgetting that Iliani's head still lay on his lap. She stopped it from slamming into the ground, but the delay of making certain she was unhurt cost Alaex his prey. By the time Iliani had righted herself, both Alaex and the would-be assailant had disappeared in the thick bushes.

Iliani heard the sounds of struggle, and although she wanted to go and see how Alaex fared, she had already seen what had happened when she was around to split his concentration. Better that she wait here. The sounds of the skirmish were dying down and Iliani stood to see what would happen next.

She was staring so hard that when Alaex first appeared, Iliani could feel only relief that he was unharmed. It was another moment before she noticed he still exerted himself. The reason for his exertion was clear. In his arms he held a boy no older than seven or eight winters, and the lad still struggled.

"You will hold!" Alaex commanded, using a stern and authoritative tone. The little boy heeded neither his words nor his tone. In fact, his struggles increased. His little face was red with the effort, and although Alaex held his arms and legs, his body bucked and his hands and feet moved rebelliously.

Alaex began to look frustrated and the boy was relentless. Iliani tried to diffuse the situation.

"A friend of yours?"

The glance Alaex gave her was at first exasperated, and then, as he found the humor in the situation, amused. "I do not know. He will not stay still long enough for me to find out."

"Perhaps if you put him down," Iliani suggested, her humor growing as the last of the tension due to fear dissipated.

Alaex was shaking his head before he answered. "Nay. True you already carry my heir, but I do have other uses for that of which he would deprive me."

Iliani laughed, then sobered immediately at Alaex's outraged look that she could find aught for humor in that. She coughed. "Then set him down at arm's length?"

Alaex glared at her to let her know that her humor, which was still evident despite her no longer laughing, was not appreciated. Gingerly he set the boy down—at arm's length as Iliani suggested and keeping a tight grip on his hands as he thought necessary.

Once the boy was standing, he looked smaller than ever to Iliani. She did not know if the sudden strong emotion she felt was because she carried a babe herself or was based purely on the sight of tousled brown hair, frightened dark blue eyes in a grubby chubby face, and even grubbier clothes of the little boy before her. Whichever, Iliani wanted to understand. Clearly the boy had been attempting to steal, but she wanted to hear his side of it.

Iliani got down on her knees and instead of ordering it as Alaex had done, she softly suggested, "I really don't think you should continue to do that."

No one was more surprised than she when the boy stopped and stared at her. Alaex, taking no chances, did not release his young prisoner. Finally the boy, his tone filled with uncontrollable curiosity, asked, "Why?"

"Because," Iliani said without a hint of sarcasm, "your bravery has been proven. You have battled the great beastie."

A trace of a smile appeared on the tiny round face. Then it quickly disappeared. "I was still ketched." He sounded disgusted with himself and Iliani did not dare laugh.

"True, but look yonder to your victory. He is huffing and puffing as if he fought the greatest of adversaries, and—" Here she lowered her voice as if confiding a great secret. "He is not without a mark or two from your battle."

Hesitant dark blue eyes flicked over Alaex's great height, noting the tear in his braies and the scratch on his cheek. The boy's smile was bolder now. It was what Iliani had waited to see.

"So you see, you have no need for fear. You can quite handily defend yourself."

"I am not afeared," he contradicted, and his voice was stronger.

Alaex looked down at Iliani incredulously. Then he felt the boy relax in his grip. He was about to relax his hold when the child tensed again at Iliani's next question.

"How are you called?"

Tears appeared in the eyes before her and Iliani could see he hated them, but one or two fell because he was unable to wipe them, as Alaex still held his hands above his head.

"If we are to talk, then I must call you something. Is that not reasonable?"

The boy nodded curtly, yet he volunteered no information.

"I am called Iliani," she said gently. "He," she added inclining her head toward Alaex, "is called Alaex. And you are?"

"Alfred," the boy said in a low voice.

"Why that's a wonderful name."

Alfred's face perked up at that. "Me mum called me for the king." Suddenly as if realizing what he just said, Alfred looked horrified and Iliani rushed to reassure him.

"There is no need for fear, Alfred. No one will hurt you or your mother. In fact, since you've shown such strength and have so honorable a name, I will take your word if you give it."

Alfred said nothing, but there was curiosity in his eyes.

"If you give me your word not to fight or run away, I will ask Alaex to let you go. Do you promise?"

Iliani read the indecision on his face, especially after he quickly glanced up at the awesome length of Alaex's body. He swallowed audibly and Iliani watched him gather himself in hand and then nod slowly.

Alaex did not wait for her request; he let go of Alfred's hands the moment the boy nodded, although he kept a wary eye on him. Alfred, for his part, kept an alert eye on his former captor. When he looked back at Iliani, she didn't miss his longing glance as his eyes passed over the food.

Struck by an impulse, she asked, "Would you like to join us for the meal?"

This time his answer was not hesitant. "Aye, lady." Without waiting for a further invitation, he plunked himself down on the edge of their blanket. When Iliani piled the bread, cheeses, and fruit in front of him, he looked first at the food and then at her, adoringly. He was so taken with the bounty before him that he jumped only slightly when Alaex sat down beside him.

For the first time since commanding him to hold, Alaex spoke directly to Alfred. "Even for a man such as yourself, that is a mighty meal for one bite." Alaex's expression was carefully bland. "If, however, you would like to take some home with you—to finish at a later time—you may."

Alfred's face lit up poignantly. "Really?"

Alaex nodded. "Fighting men must keep up their strength. 'Tis useful in protecting their own."

Iliani watched Alfred's small chest puff with pride, and she wondered at Alaex's purpose, but the boy seemed to understand. He told them, "Me mum has been under a bit. She needs me."

There was a wealth of unspoken meaning in those tight little words, and unexpectedly Iliani felt tears start in her eyes. It was Alaex who broke the silence by asking quietly, "And your father?"

Alfred sniffed and Iliani's heart ached for him. She could see the effort he exerted to keep his composure. He was trying so hard to be an adult and strong. "He took to fever and died."

Instantly Iliani saw the picture: a widow, her young son, and hardship. Then the woman becomes ill, and where there was hardship now there was destitution. Alfred hadn't been trying to take those things Alaex had purchased for her at the merchant's fair. He had wanted the food. Somehow Alaex had known that and that was why he had offered to let the child take the food back home. She saw, too, that in doing that it had also been a good way to find out if he had a home.

Now it was Iliani who watched with wonder, marveling at her husband's insight and touched by his kindness.

He ate from trash and stole anything with a shine.

Cam's words echoed harshly in her mind, but instead of revulsion or pity, they brought understanding. Of course Alaex had understood Alfred. He had once been just like him, except his parents had left, not died or fallen ill. Remembering his rantings and what they had revealed of his lacerated pride at feeling that Aeric had pitied him, Iliani's heart swelled with warmth and love. Alaex had been trying to spare Alfred that, making it seem that the boy was manfully filling his responsibility. Thinking about what he had done, Iliani felt awe at his fellow feeling for a boy who was naught but a stranger to him. And again she echoed her father's feelings: this was a man worth loving.

"Alfred," Alaex called, his voice disrupting her thoughts. He had to wait for the boy to swallow a huge chunk of meat before he got a response.

"Aye?"

"Where do you live?"

"In the village, where the fair is." Alfred pointed a dirty finger.

Alaex nodded. "Then you and your mother reside on Fontwyn land and are subject to its lord and its law."

All the color washed from Alfred's face. "Aye." He was silent a moment. "But please, sir, do not take me to him. He's some fierce. I knowed 'twas wrong doing what I done. Ye and yer lady taked my word afore. If I gi' it agin, that I'll not steal, will ye promise not to take me afore the lord of Fontwyn?"

Alaex frowned and Iliani could see that his expression wasn't soothing the child. "Alfred, why do you fear the lord of Fontwyn?"

His blue gaze moved to her, and when he pushed away the remainder of his food it told of his fear. " 'Tis too large he is," Alfred croaked.

Iliani hid her smile of relief. At least it was no worse. Just a child's fear.

"Alaex is large," she said, pointing to him.

"Not so large as the lord." Alfred showed every sign of disgust at what, Iliani clearly saw, was to him her girlish ignorance. "Have ye not heared of his strength and the way he won them battles? When he is mad his eyes shine red and hard," Alfred related, warming to his recital. "With his one arm, he smited armies, and he can, acause he's as tall and as thick as this tree!"

Neither male in her company appreciated Iliani's humor.

"I am not," Alaex said sharply, causing Alfred to close his mouth when he was about to say something else.

"Ye are the lord . . . of . . . Fontwyn?"

Iliani thought he looked about to faint. Alaex's curt nod did not help; however, he did mercifully add, "And you have naught to fear from me. I do not harm children."

"But me mum—"

Alaex held on to his temper. "Nor do I inflict harm on helpless women. You may depend upon it. I asked you where you live," he went on in an even voice, "not to seek vengeance, but to discover if a law of Fontwyn applied to you."

"What law?" Alfred didn't know it, but he asked the question for both himself and Iliani.

Alaex studiously avoided Iliani's curious stare. He cleared his throat. "The law that the oldest male can be called to the hall for duty when there is need. As I know this takes from your other responsibilities, at the end of each day a day's supply of food is given him."

The fear evaporated from Alfred's eyes. But the child was smart. "There is sech a law?"

Alaex raised a brow. "Am I not lord of Fontwyn?"

"Aye," Alfred said slowly.

"Would I not be the best one to know of its laws?"

This time Alfred's "Aye" was more confident.

"Good," Alaex said. "For now, I shall not detain you. However, you may take what is here as payment for work you will do on the morrow. I will see you then."

Alfred's face was shining as he gathered up the food and then quickly disappeared through the bushes. Iliani pulled her eyes away from where she had last glimpsed him to look at Alaex, who still would not meet her gaze.

"A law?"

Alaex nodded, and Iliani noted the rise in his color. She would not relent.

"He will be given a duty?"

Alaex nodded again.

Iliani moved closer. "How long has this 'law' been in effect?" She was near enough to pull his face up to hers and her shameless grin openly challenged him.

Alaex's pale blue eyes began to twinkle. "I would call it a 'long' law."

Iliani drew back slightly, a frown between her arched brows. "A 'long' law?" she repeated, certain he wasn't referring to its duration.

"Aye." Alaex grinned. "The law is in effect as *long* as it is needed."

She couldn't resist the impulse any longer. She loved him so much. And as Iliani placed her still laughing lips on Alaex's, the ugliness of Cam's words slipped further from her mind.

Chapter

→ 29 ←

From the day of the fair, time passed for Iliani in a glorious haze that banished Cam's ugly words further with each day's end. At first his words receded from lack of proof. Then they retreated more as Iliani began to accept what she was learning about Alaex. He revealed himself in minute ways. When she considered not hearsay but his deeds—most recently, his kindness to Alfred, as, true to his word, he found a chore for the boy to do that was light enough for a child but work enough to make him feel he earned the food he happily carted home each day—she refused to believe that a man capable of such deeds could do what Cam claimed. Another, more compelling reason to believe in Alaex was simple: she loved him.

The days passed no less wonderfully for Alaex. He had never known happiness such as Iliani brought him. Each day she added a new measure of joy to his life. He couldn't see enough of her or hear enough of her voice. He wanted to be with her when he was not, and when he was he wanted to stop time. Although he was not ready to admit to love—that was too irrevocable a step—he did admit without reluctance to the power of the nameless emotion he felt. Never having been religious, mostly because he had never been taught about God, Alaex now found himself believing in the possibility, and he prayed his thanks to a god he had not known was there. *This was enough,* he told Him. *If You never gave me anything else, this would do.* It was so much more than he ever had before, he felt rich beyond measure.

Yet old fears die hard, and as Alaex acknowledged his, he recognized his hypocrisy. He had told Iliani to let go her dreams because they no longer had the ability to hurt her. They were things of the past. He knew he was able to speak so freely because she was unaware of *his* past and therefore could not turn his words against him. His feeling of hypocrisy eased when he noted that she no longer seemed to have the dreams, but his demons of the past refused to be exorcised so easily.

Alaex was bitterly aware that lying not too deeply inside himself was the fear that all his happiness was temporary. That thought was as irrational as it was amazing. Hardship he had accepted and borne stoically with relative fear. Now that he had all he could ever ask, the fear was disproportional. He tortured himself with imaginings of losing what he had miraculously received. Since he did not know what he had done to get it, Alaex felt at a loss how to go about keeping it. Adversity could be met, challenged, and overcome. What the devil was he to do about blessings? Somehow it seemed that just saying "thank you" was not enough. He found himself plagued by these things and the need to always be reassured, and yet he could not bring himself to ask.

Conversely, then, as the days wore on, summer ripening in all its verdant glory and then giving way softly to the calmer, fiery beauty of autumn, as his happiness increased so did his irritability.

One autumn evening Alaex decided he could endure it no more. As he watched Iliani move through the day, still graceful despite the growth of the child, he decided that this was the night he would put an end to his torturous misgivings.

Iliani was aware of Alaex's disquieting stare throughout the day. She would feel his eyes fix consideringly on her, but she could not read his expression. Nor could she think of anything that could have caused it. Nothing unusual had happened. The day was passing with a normalcy that bordered on uneventful. Yet as Alaex continued to stare, Iliani's unease grew as she tried to decipher the source of his displeasure.

Once as he had watched her, her heart clenched painfully as the fleeting thought occurred that his dark stares might be because of her increased girth. Perhaps he found it unattractive. Before Iliani was able to banish the thought her hands moved to her stomach, and to her chagrin, Alaex's eyes followed, narrowing. He did not even look away when she looked at him. After tense moments, she was the one forced to break the stare.

With scenes such as this throughout the day, it was no wonder that the evening meal that night was a disaster. Alaex's brooding cast a pall over the usually festive event. Even his men were giving him frequent curious glances. Jon and Thibert tried to engage him in conversation, but Alaex's unencouragingly short answers had dissuaded them from making any further attempts.

When Iliani thought the men were engaged in other conversation, she tried to get him to talk. "Is there anything the matter?" she asked softly.

Alaex's answer to her was as brief as the ones he had given Jon and Thibert. "Nay."

"Are you well?" she asked, and although she thought it unlikely, she added, "Your wound is not still bothering you?"

Alaex looked puzzled, then his brow cleared. "The wound has not pained me for some time."

Something is. However, Iliani only thought the accusation. She couldn't bring herself to say it. Besides, the men chose that moment to turn their attention back to them and Iliani didn't want them to see her discomfort. So she said nothing.

The remainder of the meal was an uncomfortable ordeal. For the first time in a long while, Iliani excused herself early. She needed to think, but mostly she needed to get away from Alaex and his brooding stares.

Later as she soaked in her bath, Iliani tried to relax away the unexpected tension brought about by Alaex's perplexing behavior. She knew he had been having difficulty with what he felt; therefore, she had tried to leave his feelings alone, saying nothing of love, just trying to build a happy home. With the looks he had been giving her that day, she now second-guessed that plan of action. He had seemed happy and then . . . then what? She lost the thought from there.

Sighing, Iliani laid her head back against the rim of the tub, closing her eyes. The water was beginning to do its job, and she felt herself loosening. Unfortunately her mind was doing the same, and Iliani was having difficulty holding on to her thoughts.

When he slipped in, she never knew he was there.

Alaex watched her quietly, and if he but knew it, both his heart and soul were in the hungry gaze he leveled on his bathing wife. As he looked, he felt as if he were dying inside of want for her. There was so much he wanted to say, so much to express. Yet he knew if he opened his mouth, naught of what he felt would come out. He would feel and quite possibly look the fool.

A self-derisive smile crossed his face. Most of his life he had heard the rumors that circulated about him, of his prowess with weapons, of his skill as a strategist. It had made him what one silly gushing female had said: "a legend." He would trade the legend in a flash to be naught else but a man, one who could dig deeply within himself and tell of the things closest to his heart, if indeed that organ did exist within him.

No longer able to resist the lure of his wife's long neck appealingly decorated with wisps of curls that escaped from the haphazard pile of her massive night black hair,

Alaex took a step forward. The firelight gilded her skin with a healthy glow, and with the water glistening on it provocatively, Alaex wanted nothing more than to pull her from the bath and to himself. She would need no linen. He would be her wrap. She would not need the fire. He would provide her warmth.

All these thoughts and more ran through his head, yet when he stood above her he did not reach out, did not touch all the beauty his eyes beheld and for which his body hungered. Instead he knelt silently and whispered, almost as if to himself, "Are you happy, Iliani?"

That was her first inkling that he was there, his deep voice washing over her with the same smoothness of the warm water caressing her body.

Iliani was not startled by his voice. Alaex's deep and mellow voice had been so soft and low that it barely disturbed the quiet, and since she had been trying to concentrate on him, it had at first merely insinuated itself into her mind. However, when the voice was accompanied by a gentle massaging touch against the back of her neck, her eyes opened languorously and were immediately seized by the intensely piercing blue gaze directed at her.

Then his question registered, but it was too late because it was the look in his eyes that robbed Iliani of what little breath shock had left. Alaex was kneeling beside her bath, his face in full view of the fire behind them both, and what she saw set off an immediate reaction in her body. Iliani's heart began to beat faster and then slow to a throbbing pulse that made her feel her blood in every part of her body.

Words defied her. Iliani was not conscious of her nudity, and her previous apprehensions about how he might have been viewing her rounded shape vanished. Alaex held her mesmerized by the sheer want that seemed to almost tangibly radiate from him. Even if she could, Iliani did not want to answer his question—at least not the one he asked with his lips. It was the one in his eyes that haunted her. The one that continued where the other had stopped. The one that asked, "Are you happy *with me?*" That was the question ringing through every fiber of her flesh, making her ache to chase it away.

Slowly she raised her hand to his face and ran her fingers softly over his beloved features. Still without speaking, she brought the other up to join it and then pulled his face down to hers.

This kiss was unlike any other she had given him or they had shared. It did not begin with a slow burn. From the instant their lips met it was a conflagration beyond control, fed voraciously by Alaex's hunger and Iliani's desire to quench it in all ways.

Iliani could not tell if her groan or his wafted into the air as their embraced deepened, and Alaex did not care as his arms came around her and pulled her close to his chest just as he had envisioned, with total disregard for the fact that she soaked his clothing. With one arm around her back, his fingers submerged beneath the water and brushing lightly against her buttocks, his other hand freely explored her, kneading her breasts, taunting her senses, and creating a seemingly unquenchable fire that entered through his touch and vibrated excruciatingly even where he did not.

When Alaex lifted her and carried her to the bed, Iliani did not feel the coolness of the air as she should have. Alaex was her fire. Breathlessly she told him that, and wondered briefly at his enigmatic smile. There was not time to think about it for long, as her body began to shiver not from cold, but from heat. Alaex broke their kiss as he set her down on her knees on the bed, although his hands continued their fevered exploration of her body.

This time Iliani knew whose groan filled the air as she meltingly and inexorably leaned into Alaex. It was hers and it was imbued equally with desire and desperation. Her hands would not stop moving over his body and their fevered quest was soon satisfied as Alaex peeled off his clothes and Iliani's fingers found the hot skin they had been seeking. Where her fingers ventured her lips trailed, kissing him, teaching him, pleasing him—loving him.

Iliani's mind was afire. She was functioning on the plane where only the physical mattered. It became more than a sense; it was communication she didn't cheapen with words. As her lips followed in the burned path her fingers made along his body, they said, "I need you, Alaex." As her hands caressed, exhorted, and coaxed, they said, "I want you, Alaex." And as her body strained increasingly toward his, seeking him with mindless intensity, it screamed her love for him.

As Iliani lay back on the bed pulling Alaex with her, she was only vaguely surprised to find that her body had already dried. There was no real astonishment because she felt as if the fire within had become a living thing, burning past every inhibition, sizzling everything in its path. What chance did a few drops of water have when she herself felt consumed? The fever raged greater and hotter when her lips again fastened on Alaex's, and when they broke apart, finally the words came.

"I love you, Alaex."

It was the first time Iliani had spoken her love to him since he had been ill, and it was what Alaex unknowingly had been seeking. Long ago he had begun to suspect that she alone might be able to still the lonely wailing in his soul, and now, as their lips met and the tension eased from his heart, he knew he had been right. Perhaps Aeric had known that, too, or had hoped it would be so.

Feeling wetness against his face, Alaex pulled back from Iliani, his eyes locking onto hers. "Tears?" he asked huskily, wiping at the moisture on her face with a forefinger. "Why?"

Iliani swallowed and her tears flowed faster. In a fraction of a second everything she loved about him, the good and the bad, flashed before her. In that brief instant she relived every moment, every kiss, every touch. She couldn't say what she felt, why she cried. How did one describe the indescribable? How could she tell him about something of which she had only dreamed but he had turned into a reality? Yet he had done more than that. It was as if he looked into her eyes, past her soul, and read her desires. In fulfilling them, instead of giving her a mere physical existence, he gave her the unspoken fantasy of her heart and her dreams were the sweeter for it.

For the first time Iliani fully understood Alaex. She wanted to say these things to him, but she didn't know how. All she could do was feel them, experience them, and hope that she gave to him a fraction of what he unstintingly lavished on her.

The tears were still in her eyes when she tightened her arms around him, bringing him close again, planting a small yet ardent kiss on his lips.

"I just love you, Alaex, that's all."

Alaex rose slightly and slowly began to enter her body. What little of his control remained evaporated like a drop of water in the midst of an inferno when Iliani added achingly, "Please love me back, just a little."

The answer burst in his head like a thousand suns and smoldered in calm acceptance in his heart. Alaex lost all control. Iliani's words and the emotion he could feel and see within her eyes freed him, blasting away the restraint of a lifetime. At the same instant he came inside her, his heart erupted and words spilled from his lips.

"I do, Iliani," he gasped, "and not just a little—more than I have the words to say."

The words were out and as Alaex felt Iliani's body convulse and tighten around his, felt the wetness of her tears on his chest, his own arms tightened around her and he knew he had never meant anything more.

Chapter

→ 30 ←

'Twill not be long, Iliani, only a day or two. Alfred needs those regions checked. He would do so himself when he travels through, but that is weeks hence and he does not care to leave it that long. There has not been much Viking activity, but the last years have left him unwilling to ease his vigil. I do not blame him."

Iliani, who sat on the bed in their room watching him prepare for departure, nodded. "I understand, Alaex. The Viking menace has seemed relentless."

Alaex paused in the act of cleaning and checking his sword. The blue eyes he raised to Iliani's were interested and teasing. "What know you of the 'Viking menace'?"

Tucked away as she had been all those years at Lourds Keep, which in truth had seen no immediate threat from invaders, Iliani could understand his jesting question. "I heard things," she said defensively, and when Alaex's gaze grew more dubious, Iliani colored slightly and sought to change the subject. "Why does Alfred send you? I thought he had messengers he used specifically for this."

Alaex laughed. "Normally he does."

It took a moment for Iliani to concentrate on what he said. She was captivated by the sound of his laughter. A rare thing that. It had a warm and deep tone and it made her smile. With effort, she brought her mind back to the topic.

"Why does he not send one of them?"

The residual smile disappeared from Alaex's face. "I shall not be gone long, Iliani. I do this for Alfred now because your time grows near. I would not wish to leave you later. You have promised to introduce me to someone I very much would like to meet," he ended lightly, his sparkling eyes straying to her stomach.

Absently Iliani rubbed her stomach. "That is not my concern. Perhaps 'concern' is too strong a word. I was curious. If Alfred has messengers, why not use them for this?"

The laughing twinkle was back in Alaex's eyes. " 'Twas Ethan's turn."

Iliani's eyes widened in instant comprehension and her lips began to twitch revealingly.

"I see you begin to understand," Alaex said, attempting a tone of seriousness and failing as Iliani began to chuckle. " 'Tis bad of you, Iliani," he scolded teasingly, "to laugh at an emissary of the king."

Disregarding the fact that he was doing the same, Iliani replied with mock seriousness, "I was not laughing, merely smiling . . . a lot." She barely got the words out before her laughter erupted at the picture of Ethan as she had last seen him, practically running from Fontwyn.

Alaex grinned at her. "To the nonce Alfred probably wonders what we did to his man."

" 'We'?" Iliani asked, remnants of humor still on her face. "As I recall I did naught, although I fully understand why you go in his stead."

"And why is that?" Alaex asked, trying to sound stern and forbidding and accomplishing neither.

Totally ignoring the droll warning that flashed within Alaex's eyes, Iliani went on impenitently. " 'Tis only fitting. One should always replace what one breaks, and you, Alaex, broke a perfectly good messenger of his."

Struck by the humor anew, Iliani began to laugh again, her mirth increasing when she heard Alaex laughingly mutter, "Impudent wench."

Alaex left at first light the next day and by noon Iliani already missed him terribly. She had not realized how deeply she had come to rely on his presence or the simple knowledge that he was somewhere around. She still felt his presence and there was comfort in that as she walked the outer yard for exercise. Even with the minimized threat of Viking invasion, Alaex had increased the hall's defenses. There were more men on the wall and the rest were at drill practicing as if their leader were there.

Iliani looked over to see Thibert instructing a new young warrior, whom she had not seen before, on the proper way to parry and then disarm an opponent. The young man was either nervous or inept because he could not seem to hold his sword. Iliani smiled, knowing Thibert would hold his patience. Alaex's men were like that, as was he. His rule was not to lose patience but to make the person try again and yet again.

Turning away to continue her walk, Iliani put the scene from her mind, knowing that by evening the young warrior would either know how to execute the maneuver or be unable to lift his arm from trying.

A cool breeze, one of the first she'd felt, caused her to shudder. It had been a remarkably mild summer, making one think that the following seasons would be no less so, but that breeze made it feel closer to winter than early fall.

Not having brought a wrap, Iliani was about to go back to the hall when she saw Arthur standing in the door of the stable. He was clearly upset. Changing her direction, Iliani started over to him, and although she could not be certain, she thought his face reflected both relief and chagrin as he watched her approach.

"What is it, Arthur?" At close inspection the old servant looked worse than he had from afar. He didn't answer immediately, making Iliani repeat her question more sharply as worry entered her voice. "What is wrong?"

Even though Arthur looked at her, he seemed not to see her. Gradually his eyes focused on his mistress. He would have given anything not to have to tell her this, but the lord was away. He was about to speak when Ethelward came from the stable and nearly collided into his back.

"Did you call Thi—?" He stopped abruptly when he saw Iliani standing there.

"Call Thibert for what?" Iliani asked in a tone she hoped they would understand to be one that would not stand evasion.

When the two men hesitated and exchanged anxious glances, Iliani's patience, spurred by increasing fear, evaporated. Since whatever it was that caused such a disturbance was obviously inside the stable, before they could stop her she pushed between them and entered.

Iliani didn't know what she expected, given Ethelward's and Arthur's reactions, but at first look everything seemed normal. Wind Dancer was in his stall, the other horses in theirs. The stall to the left of her gelding's was empty, but that was as it should be. Alaex kept Bear there, and he had gone on the mission for Alfred.

Suddenly her eyes swept back to the stall on the other side of where Bear usually stood. No horse was there, but it was not empty. There was something, or rather someone, in it. A foot was visible. If she hadn't been looking for something amiss, she might have missed it.

Iliani started toward it but was halted by Arthur's hand on her shoulder. "Do not, milady. 'Tis not a sight for your eyes. The man is dead."

There was a draft behind her and Iliani knew that Ethelward had gone to get Thibert. "Who is he, Arthur?"

"One of the workers—you know, milady, the men

hired to work on the hall and such. Harold, I believe he was called."

Thibert and Ethelward came rushing into the stable, and immediately Thibert assumed control, trying to get Iliani to leave. She refused. A man had died, and while it was not pleasant she would not be shunted aside as if she would faint at any moment.

Seeing her determination, Thibert relented and asked, "Will you then stay here and not come any closer?"

Iliani was happy to concede that. She didn't want to see the man or his wounds, if he had any. She was about to ask if he did, when Ethelward answered her question.

"The blade is through the heart," he said looking down at Harold.

"Do you recognize it?" Thibert asked.

"Nay. Was most likely his," was Ethelward's calm response.

Thibert frowned. "Why say you that? Do you know this man or something of him?"

Ethelward shrugged. "No more than any other, I suppose. 'Tis truth if he were not so deep in his cups just last eve, I probably would not have recognized him at all."

"What happened?" Thibert's tone said he wanted a complete account.

"The man had obviously drunk much wine, so much so he could scarce walk. When I asked if he needed assistance to his own hearth, he said nay. Then he muttered about being unable to either return to his home or stay here."

Thibert's frown deepened.

"I said he was drunk," Ethelward explained. "I understood him no more then than you do now. He kept babbling on about his work here not being complete."

Arthur spoke. "Why, 'tis not so. Near all the work is done."

Thibert turned to him. "You knew him?"

"Nay," Arthur denied. "Only of his assignments.

Milord hired him and he did small tasks wherever needed. The man did not talk much, but he worked—mostly in the kitchen, on the wall, on the stairs that needed repair, and here."

Iliani could sense Thibert's frustration. That information was not particularly helpful. The man could have been any one of a dozen men from the village or even a passer-through. From time to time a traveler would hire on at an estate to earn coin to continue his journey.

Thibert turned back to Ethelward. "Do you know why the man was so deep in his cups?"

Ethelward paused, then he said slowly, "He seemed to be afraid of something. I passed it off as the usual drunken fear, but now that you ask, he said he had tried to do as the lord had asked, but he failed twice. 'Twas why he could not leave until he completed it, but he was afraid to stay and just as afraid to go."

The situation wasn't getting any clearer. "Are you certain the man's work was done?" Thibert asked Arthur.

Arthur did not hesitate. "Positive."

Thibert sighed. "Then I can only see this as an unfortunate accident. The poor man was drunk and he fell on his blade. We will see that he is buried and find his kin if we can. There is naught else to be done."

Naturally at the evening meal the thrust of nearly all conversation was the death of the man called Harold. He had no family—none at Fontwyn at any rate—that any could recall. The consensus echoed what Arthur had said. Harold was quiet and industrious. No one knew aught else of him.

During most of the meal, Iliani's mind, like most everyone else's, was occupied with the questions surrounding the discovery of Harold. It was near the end of it that snatches of a different conversation caught her attention. Thibert was talking about training the newer men.

"I cannot remember whether I was so inept," he was saying to Ethelward, "but I doubt it. Alaex would not have tolerated it despite his rule of patience. I was ready to forget that rule about patience myself, because surely the man had tested mine to its limits."

"He did not seem so bad," Ethelward offered.

Thibert snorted. "You did not have to train him. When I came back from the stables, I was almost relieved to see that he had deserted. Wherever he ends, I hope 'tis with an enemy and not an ally. 'Twould be like having a self-destructive weapon in their camp. 'Tis better than a spy any day, I'd wager."

Ethelward laughed at Thibert's undisguised repugnance for the man's abilities or lack thereof, causing a begrudging smile to cross his friend's face. No more was said about it after that and the conversation shifted again. Neither man noted that Iliani had heard them. She smiled in irony as she recalled the young man she had seen earlier with Thibert. After hearing Thibert's remarks, she quietly answered her own previous question, deciding that the cause of the man's failure had been ineptitude and not nerves. If that were so, it was probably best that he sought his fortune elsewhere. It was not a common thing for a man to leave after so short a time, but it was not unheard of either. Given all that had occurred in the few hours since Alaex's departure, Iliani put it from her head.

The other occurrence was not so easily set aside, and Iliani found herself still thinking about it as she readied herself for bed. With her thoughts filled with the dead worker, Iliani was glad that Alaex would be returning tomorrow or the day after. It was very unsettling to say the least to have someone found dead within the walls of Fontwyn. It did not matter that the person had no family that any knew of, or that he was a virtual stranger. Iliani did not want to have to handle this situation by herself, and with Alaex's return there wouldn't be the need.

Death always made those left living feel uncertain. Unexplained and questionable death made the living feel insecure, vulnerable. With Alaex's return would come a measure of security. Even though Iliani knew that such a thing could happen with him there, she also knew that just his presence would make her feel safer.

"Aye, Alaex, hurry home," she whispered to herself, pulling off her gown and shivering slightly from the coolness and her dark thoughts.

A short while later, Iliani was still trying to dismiss what had occurred. Yet try as she might, it remained in her thoughts. Something bothered her and it was not just the man's death. For some reason, Ethelward's words plagued her. He had said that Harold had muttered that "he had failed twice." Failed what? The work on the hall was nearly completed and done very well. At what could he possibly have failed twice? What could have been the task he was assigned that failure could have tormented him to the point of fear and then quite possibly to take his own life? According to Arthur, Harold had worked in the kitchen, on the wall, in the stables, and on the stairs. There was nothing left undone in any of those places.

Like an irritation in a place difficult to reach and thus soothe, the words that had been said in the stable played again and again in Iliani's head. It was as if they stirred something else, meant something much more important that she should not have forgotten. Faint recollection stirred in the back of her mind. She could not fully grasp it, but it troubled her. There was something significant she was overlooking. It had to do with Harold and his failing twice and his chores in the kitchen, the stable, and the . . .

Barely pausing to throw on her chamber robe, Iliani ran from the room and down to the main hall. Lucy was there doing a final cleanup from the meal.

"Your father," Iliani asked a little wildly, filled with panic that could only be stilled after Arthur answered her question. "Where is he?"

Her agitation did not allow Lucy to respond. "Get him. Now. Quickly."

The servant hurried away, and when Arthur came in shortly, his breathing quickened, Iliani knew he had hurried.

"Is it the wee one?" Arthur asked before he reached her.

Thrown off temporarily, Iliani paused to wonder what he meant and then realized that he and Lucy both probably thought she was in pain from the baby. If what she suspected was true, then even the pain of labor, which she had heard was great, would not compare.

Shaking her head to ease Arthur's anxiety and praying that his answer would ease hers, Iliani asked, "Arthur, the man who died, Harold, on which stairs did he work?"

Arthur frowned, clearly trying to see why that answer was so important to his mistress. Not knowing why she asked, and unable to answer any other way than truthfully, he said, "The stairs leading to the cellar."

Automatically Arthur put his hand out to steady his mistress, who didn't swoon but looked as if she might. Her face had lost all color.

"Are you well, mistress? Is there aught I can do?" Arthur asked, his face lined with concern.

Iliani had already turned and was numbly walking away. "Nay, nay," she answered absently. "Naught at all."

By the time Iliani reached her room again she was shivering and trying desperately to deny what she was thinking. There had to be something else, some other reason why Harold's words had bothered her. Someone, a "lord," had hired Harold to do something. He'd attempted it twice and failed, making him afraid for his life. Yet for what he had been hired to do at the hall, his work was successful. The kitchens were done. So were the wall, the stable, and the stairs. It had to be something else. The only thing Iliani could think of—a thought that recurred despite her desperate attempts to push it away—was that twice there had been accidents, once in the stable and once on the stairs where Arthur told her Harold had worked. Both times she ... could ... have ... died, Iliani thought with painful slowness. Both times she didn't. *Harold failed twice.*

Shivering more than before, Iliani slipped into bed without removing her robe. There had to be another explanation. She was thinking too much. She was tired. She was insane. Iliani would settle for it being anything but the persistent thought that someone, a "lord," might want her dead.

Chapter

→ 31 ←

Papa was hurting and she had to do something! She had to help him! She began to cry. What to do? Slowly she walked over to him, her tears still flowing. She thought she heard someone coming, but after stopping a minute she swallowed her fear. She still had to help him. Maybe that's why the person was coming. Maybe they wanted to help, too.

The floor was cold and wet. The red stuff was on her feet. It made her more afraid, but she kept going. Finally she touched him and he turned. He looked at her. He cried, too. His tears made funny lines in the red dots on his face and when he tried to speak, he coughed instead and more red stuff got on his face from his mouth. He tried again. His voice did not sound like Papa's deep, booming voice. It sounded sad—little. It added to her fright, his voice and his words.

"I was wrong. Do not trust him . . ." The rest of the words were covered by his coughs, and the sounds of footsteps growing closer, harder, faster.

Papa heard it, too. He looked frightened as he tried to peer beyond her shoulder and he tried to push her away.

But he wasn't strong enough. Finally, he said another word, calling a name. "Alaex."

And the fear was worse than ever.

Iliani groaned herself awake.

"Nay," she kept mumbling, "not that. Not now. Oh, please." Her pleas were to no avail, because even when she was fully awake the dream and all its ugly implications stayed with her, making Iliani feel as tired as if she had not been to bed at all. She definitely did not want to sleep anymore, yet she could not bring herself to rise either.

For a long time she just lay in a miserable huddled ball in the middle of the bed. Part of her mind was trying to convince herself she was being irrational; the other part, which unfortunately was the greater one, had no intention of listening.

After the dream of last night and the happenings of yesterday, she could no longer think of the fear as something born of twilight, vague and shadowed, which could easily be reduced to naught beneath the bright light of morning. It was tangible and present, demanding answers before it would recede, and just because she didn't want to accept the plausibility of her thoughts did not make them less real.

That bit of rationality caused quiet tears to course down her face, or maybe they had always been there, a sorrowful continuation of the emotion of the night. Iliani did not know. All she knew was that her pain was great. It was like a stone weighing against her chest and she felt as if she were choking beneath it.

With extreme effort, Iliani found the strength to get up from the bed, which was beginning to feel as if it, too, was constricting her. The source of that feeling was easily discovered when she stood up and looked down at herself. She had slept the night in her robe and it had twisted and bunched.

Iliani couldn't so much as smile at the disheveled picture she made. Smiling and those other things that made for happiness belonged to someone else. She felt as if she'd never smile again.

Straightening her robe automatically she crossed over to the stand where the basin and water ewer were and went through an abbreviated and reflexive ablution. Then she sat in one of the chairs before the fire and stared at it intently as if the flames held the answers to her problems.

Yet even as she did it, Iliani knew it was useless. The fire was a source of warmth, and owing to the coldness of her thoughts, which seemed to spread their ice to every part of her body, she needed it more than ever—but answers? Nay, answers could be found only in the place from where the coldness originated: her mind. She knew things now she could not ignore; she remembered things now she ought never to have forgotten.

Those weren't dreams that plagued her at night. They were memories. Iliani knew that for a certainty.

Suddenly she froze. Why did it seem that even that knowledge was not new, that she had heard it somewhere before, and not just in the distant past? Iliani grew even stiller as she tried to recall where or from whom she heard that thought.

Alaex.

He had said that to her when she told him of the dreams. He had called them *resurfacing memories*.

Iliani wanted to swoon and howl at the same time. How could she have overlooked that? On the heels of that came other thoughts previously shunted aside. She had specifically asked Alaex if she had been present when her father died, and he had not answered her. Yet he knew. She clearly remembered her father saying his name. Or was he calling him? Or trying to tell her something?

The frustration of indecision was back, and before its companion panic could set in, Iliani forced herself to calm down and consider what she knew. There would be leagues of room remaining for what she did not. Fleetingly the thought came to her that this was naught else but overreaction to the discovery of the dead man yesterday. But no matter how hard she tried to convince herself of that, she knew it was flimsy and she was grasping.

Iliani stood up and began to pace as feverishly as her increased girth would allow. Looking down at her stomach as if only just remembering her state brought another moment of panicked terror as she thought of the baby—Alaex's—and she determinedly pushed that from her mind.

"Later, Iliani, later," she admonished herself. "You have enough in your trencher for now."

Resuming her pacing, which was no match for the speed of her thoughts, Iliani resolutely put aside the excuse that her growing conclusions were based on an overwrought state due to the discovery of the dead man. What she had thought were dreams but were instead reawakening memories had started long before the man's death. The only assumption she had made was that Alaex had been there with her when her father died. She did not recall seeing him. Her father had merely called his name. He had been talking, that was all. Perhaps he had been trying to tell her . . .

Iliani's blood chilled as she recalled Aeric's words: "Do not trust him." He had coughed then and the first thing he had said after that was Alaex's name.

Papa had cried, Iliani remembered, her own tears starting again with the memory. He had said he was wrong. Was he wrong about Alaex? Did he finally see what everyone else saw when it was too late? Was she falling into the same pattern? As with the father, likewise the daughter?

Everyone else—people who had more knowledge and experience than she—saw Alaex as dangerous and untrustworthy. Could it be she saw only what she wanted because she wanted to so fiercely?

Iliani nearly staggered back down in her chair as, unbidden, Cam's words came back to her. He had told her to save her pity. He had said everyone knew that

Alaex had killed her father. The reason was clear to him: to get Fontwyn and her. It made no sense, though, if Aeric had already promised her to him in marriage. It dimmed the prospect of his wanting her for herself and supplied a distasteful answer to her long-ago question of what could induce a grown man to bind himself to a child, but it did not make him a murderer. Why should he kill Aeric? If anything, he would be grateful—

Her thoughts stopped dead as she remembered Alaex's rambling when he was ill. He had nearly hated Aeric for pitying him. While she had assumed that he had had a change of heart—*aye, just as you believed he loved you for you,* her mind interjected derisively—perhaps he had not. He had snarled his acceptance of her father's generosity until he could again "take" what he needed.

Iliani's heart cried out that that was not evidence, but her mind was determined not to be silenced anymore. Relentlessly it brought back her suspicion of the night before, that someone, a "lord," wanted her dead. If Alaex had killed her father and he knew or suspected she was beginning to remember, would he not want her dead, too? What of her accidents? And the fact that Ethelward had said that Harold seemed afraid because he had failed his lord twice. All knew Alaex was the lord who hired him and that his failure could not be the work. The work was done. There was naught else. Harold had said he had failed twice . . . and both times, her accidents had occurred after following Alaex's instructions. Wind Dancer had been moved because of him, and *he* had sent her to Arthur.

Iliani felt as if she were going insane, and she knew that if she told anyone else without proof, with only overwhelming coincidence, they would agree with her estimation of her sanity. Perhaps her father had not been trying to warn her about Alaex. If that were so, then she was making herself miserable needlessly. If he was, there was naught she could do without proof. She was Alaex's wife, and although the people who either hated or feared him might believe her, Iliani knew it was not enough. He would need to be brought before Alfred's justice and Alfred would not believe it. And if she could consider—however painful the thought—that Alaex had tried to kill her because he suspected she knew of his part in her father's death, what would he do with the accusation in the open?

The situation was one Iliani saw no way of winning. Either way she was going to lose Alaex, because she could not stay with him with these doubts and he would not stay if she accused him outright.

For a weak moment, Iliani tried to put her doubts aside, but there were now too many. They gained strength not just from what others said but from Alaex himself. He had said he would take from Aeric. He had been the one who caused her to be in both situations where her life had been in serious danger.

And most tellingly, Iliani now remembered, the danger had begun after she had revealed her dreams to him, or what she had thought were dreams. He had become extremely tense and had asked sharp questions about who else was there, and when she could name no one, he had called her dreams reawakening memories.

Unable to sit any longer, Iliani rose and walked to the window, staring sightlessly as the rising sun bathed everything in its orange-tinted glory. Without exception, there was no time in her life she could ever recall being this afraid—not even when Wind Dancer's hooves had threatened her or when she had nearly plummeted down the cold hard stairs.

Iliani felt paralyzed with it—nay, worse. She could not go back to ignorance; she did not want to proceed forward to knowledge-based certainty; and it was impossible to stay where she was. So where did that leave her? She couldn't question Alaex. For the first time since his departure, she was glad he was absent. Even though she could not see her face, Iliani was certain that the anxiety was there for all to view, and Alaex would not be gone forever. He would return this evening, or at the latest, tomorrow morning.

Iliani knew she had to make a decision by then, find some answers, but what and how?

"I tell you, milady, 'twas all so long ago, I cannot remember clearly," Gwyn said, casting a worried glance to Arthur that Iliani did not miss.

Iliani had called them both to her room. After many hours of thinking, she knew she needed to talk to someone. Bias alone ruled out Edouard and Cam. Eadwina was not considered. Besides, none of them had been there. Gwyn and Arthur had been. She could ask them about the night her father died, without raising ugly suspicions that might make their way back to Alaex. They might, or so Iliani had hoped, see it as natural curiosity.

Seeing the look they both had on their faces, she was not as sure as she had been before. Iliani sighed knowing it was too late to back out.

"Gwyn, Arthur," she implored softly, looking from one to the other and reaching out a hand to them both, "I know my questions seem strange. But 'tis my father I seek to know about and I do not care how unseemly it appears to question servants. I was a child. You were not. You were there. Just tell me what you know of the night he died."

Both Gwyn and Arthur seemed to hesitate, and Iliani, sensing their concern, rushed to reassure them. "Whatever you say shall not be repeated. I give you my word."

Arthur looked from his mistress's pleading expression to his wife's dubious one. He understood what Gwyn was trying to say without the words. *The mistress is upset. We cannot add to it.* As clearly as if he heard those words, he also heard Gwyn warn him to have care for their lady's condition.

It was uncanny, but Iliani could tell they communicated and she almost envied them their relationship and the security it must bring to their world. Hers was shattering into a million seemingly irreparable pieces.

"We do not wish to distress you," Arthur said when he

finally looked back to Iliani. "I feel 'tis my fault what happened."

Arthur looked so contrite that Iliani's head began to spin as she tried to decipher his meaning. "What do you mean, Arthur? What is your fault?"

"Your condition—I mean your upset," Arthur amended, flushing at what his slip of the tongue implied.

Before Iliani could assure or question him, Gwyn spoke, a remnant of annoyance with her husband in her tone. "What he means, milady, is that he ought never to have let you see that man, that Harold, yesterday."

Iliani shook her head. "I did not see him."

"Well, you shouldn't have heard of him either," Gwyn said tartly, sparing an accusing glance for her husband. "What with your condition—"

"My condition is fine," Iliani stressed. She was about to add that Harold had nothing to do with her questions, but that was not true. If not for him and Ethelward's words, she would not have started thinking and, in turn, putting things together. The part of her that wanted to run back to before Harold's body was found was angered by the occurrence and its ensuing revelations. However, the part of her that wanted the truth was outraged that she had allowed things to float by without ever truly questioning them.

Well, no more! Whether she wanted to hear or not, Iliani was determined to find the truth. Only then could she accept happiness with Alaex. If the discovered truth stripped her of that . . . well then, 'twas neither real nor deserved in the first place and she would have lost naught.

Only her heart.

Ignoring that, Iliani repeated again, this time to Gwyn since it seemed she was the binding on Arthur's tongue, "I am fine, truly. Please. I want to know of the night my father died."

After a long time, Gwyn nodded. "We were not here, milady. There was an ailing woman in the village. Arthur had come with me. The hour had grown late before she showed any signs of improving. Because of that we passed the night there."

Arthur took up the tale. "When we returned to the hall, we heard of it. We, like the others, could not believe it. Your father had seemed fine the night before at the evening meal. He had been laughing. His health had seemed much improved."

"How was I?" Iliani asked stiffly, her question catching Arthur off guard.

He paused, a frown between his white brows. "You were not here, milady. Lord Alaex had already taken you to Lord Edouard."

Iliani took a deep breath and strove for a natural tone. "And Lord Alaex, how was he?"

Arthur's pause was longer and he looked at Gwyn, who said for him, "Lord Alaex was Lord Alaex. One never knew what he felt—much like now, except for recently with you, milady," Gwyn added quickly.

There was no news there, and although Iliani knew Gwyn had added that last to soothe her, her intention fell short. Doggedly she went on, cursing the tautness she could hear creeping into her voice but unable to ask the question any other way. "Was Alaex with my father that night?"

Both servants dropped their eyes and they didn't have to speak. Iliani knew he had been. Their quiet screamed that he had been. She was about to dismiss them when Arthur offered, "'Twas no different from many other nights. Lord Alaex often sat with your father and they argued—"

Gwyn's and Iliani's eyes snapped to him, the horror in them expressed for different reasons. Gwyn's was caused by disbelief that Arthur could say something so foolish; Iliani's was caused by the sudden rush of hopelessness that would not be held off any longer.

Very aware of the expression in both women's eyes, Arthur hurried to explain. "Milady, 'twas naught. Your father and Lord Alaex argued all the time."

The expression on Gwyn's face eased. Iliani's despair

did not. It couldn't because it had just occurred to her why the two were so reluctant to speak. They had either heard or believed the rumors of Alaex's part in her father's death. There was no other explanation for it. Like her, having affection for him, they were trying to avoid the coincidence of Alaex being alone with her father the night he died. They might be able to, but Iliani no longer could. It was the last in a long line of coincidences and it was one too many. She knew what she had to do.

Chapter

⇒ 32 ⇐

Alaex hated traveling at night. The only thing worse was traveling in the rain and cold at night. It was raining and that had caused the temperature to fall. All that kept it from being thoroughly miserable was that the rain was not heavy. It was a fine mist, albeit a steady fine one. Still, it was the sort that after a while seeped into your bones until you were colder inside than it actually was outside.

Several times he thought about stopping for the night, and each time the warmth to be found at Fontwyn beckoned him onward. Then he would ride a little longer and convince himself that since he had come so far, it was senseless to stop now.

His men said nothing, stoically following him. Perhaps they, too, thought it senseless to stop after so much time. Or perhaps, Alaex thought ruefully, they were not blinding themselves as he had the penchant for doing. Most likely they were unafraid to admit that there was *someone,* and not something, warm that beckoned them homeward.

Alaex smiled in the dark as he thought of Iliani. He

had been gone nearly two days. *Two days,* he marveled. He had never counted time before. Days, weeks, months, and years used to flow into each other and on any given one of them, he would have had difficulty declaring which it was. Yet, since he had discovered the wonder of loving and being loved, it seemed he now noticed everything. There was not a second of a day that he did not notice, and each one was special. Every passing hour was more precious than the one before. He found it hard to believe that through one person the entire world could open for another, but that was what Iliani had done.

It was very strange to him because he had always considered himself a strong person for what he had endured and survived. He had been and was still proud of that, but he used to take particular pride in the fact that there was nothing soft in him. He had felt it was that which had made him better than his enemies.

Now, he admitted that he had been wrong. Here at last he had found true strength, and it was not something he had inside. It was something that had been given to him. Iliani had gifted him that through her love, and Alaex recognized that. Aye, it took strength to survive adversities alone, but he acknowledged that there was a certain amount of cowardice in staying that way.

There was naught in love to fear. With the right person it only made you stronger. The gentle strength of love could take what was once iron and make it steel.

Embarrassed realization of how far afield his thoughts had gone made Alaex color slightly and cast a sheepish glance at Jon, who rode beside him. Jon's eyes were ahead and Alaex realized that even had he looked, he would not have been able to see enough to discern his thoughts. Relaxing with the assurance that he had not been seen in that unprecedented emotional lapse, Alaex sternly gained control of himself. He, too, turned front, only to have his pulse leap with what he would have previously called undue excitement as he made out the blurred edges of Fontwyn Hall in the distance.

Had he looked to Jon again, Alaex would have seen

that his man now watched him with a soft smile playing about his lips. Alaex saw nothing but Fontwyn and its warmth, not from fire but from Iliani's smile. He missed the quick glance and silent order that Jon gave the men. However, it did register vaguely that when he dug his heels into Bear's sides, he did not pull away from Jon or the men who rode behind them. Unlike the last time when his desire to see his wife had overwhelmed him, taking away his common sense and making him ride in advance of them and subsequently fall to attack, this time they stayed with him all the way to the gates of Fontwyn.

"Where is she?"

Arthur and Gwyn's concern, shown by the worried glances they exchanged, did not appease Alaex even a little. It was late, much later than he had thought. Nearly everyone in the hall had been asleep. With boyish eagerness, Alaex had bounded up the stairs to see Iliani. He hadn't been able to wait to see her, touch her, hold her. He had found rather unpleasantly that he would have to wait to do all three. Iliani was not there.

If he had leapt up the stairs, he nearly flew down them, holding rein over himself only long enough to summon the servants. When they had come, Alaex wasted no time on preliminaries, asking his question abruptly and coldly. He had no time for their concerns; he was too busy grappling with his own. He focused on Arthur.

"I do not know, milord." Arthur swallowed heavily as Alaex's eyes narrowed threateningly. "We thought her asleep. Until you asked, we had no idea that milady was not where she should be."

Alaex began to pace, furiously ruling out one possibility after another. He had forgotten Gwyn and Arthur were there until Gwyn called to him.

Annoyance at her call and worry he could not conceal were in his pale blue eyes as Alaex stopped his pacing and faced the servant. The near ferociousness of his stare robbed Gwyn of her ability to speak immediately, especially as what she was about to say she was certain would not please the raging lord of Fontwyn.

Gwyn cleared her throat. "'Tis something you should know, milord. Milady was distressed. She asked us"— she indicated herself and Arthur—"questions about her father's death. 'Twas the first she had ever done that."

Alaex froze, and although Gwyn did not like his new expression any better than his old one, she stood her ground. As to revealing to the master what Iliani had asked, she felt no guilt at all. Iliani had promised that she would not speak of it. She had not asked the same of them.

"Did she dream?" Alaex asked sharply.

Gwyn threw a baffled glance Arthur's way. "Dream, milord?" she echoed. "Nay, she was awake."

"I meant before," Alaex clarified impatiently.

"I do not know. I do not think so," Gwyn said.

"What did she ask?"

This time Arthur answered. "She wanted to know about the night he died, who was here and who was not. We told her what we could. I even apologized. It did little good. She was not eased," Arthur ended sadly.

"Why did you apologize?"

There was nothing to like in the tone Alaex used to ask that question. It demanded an immediate and thorough answer. Arthur gave it unhesitatingly, knowing that it mattered little. If he did not, Alaex would hear of it soon enough from his men.

Arthur's explanation only confused Alaex. Iliani was not so featherbrained that the accidental death of a man would cause her to run away.

Once the thought occurred, Alaex turned on his heels and ran back to the stable, cursing himself for a million fools. Now was not the time for questions. Answers could come later. Iliani had run away. He knew that, even though he didn't want to face it or the possible reasons for her behavior. There was no other possibility. Abduction would have meant struggle, either with her or definitely with his men. There was no sign of one. Also, abduction would have meant a ransom demand, of which there was none. Therefore, Iliani had set out on her own.

His theory was confirmed when he saw that Wind Dancer was not in his stall, and he cursed himself for not noting that earlier. No one else could handle that horse like Iliani, and definitely not quietly so as not to alert others. No one else would dare go near the beast, especially on a night like this.

As his last words replayed in his head, Alaex practically threw his gear onto Bear's back. Even Iliani could have an accident on such a night. There was no time for delay.

The urgency seized him, making Alaex nearly a madman. He knew she needed him. Somehow he felt it. He only prayed that neither he nor that knowledge had come too late.

Nearly two hours later, after having lost her trail and doubling back to retrace it, Alaex found her. And the sight he saw nearly caused him to add his own wailing roar of rage, pain, and fear to those of the other night creatures around him. Iliani lay crumpled on the ground, her head against a thick stout branch. Wind Dancer was there not three feet away from her.

Jumping from Bear's back, Alaex ran over to her and checked for injury. He did not bother to call out. Iliani was not sleeping and he knew it. His mind blanked away from the thought that she might be dead, and doggedly he searched for what caused her to lie so still on the cold damp ground.

When he rolled her over gently, Alaex found it. His hand came away from the back of her head and he knew before he looked that it was blood and not damp from the rain. He was about to move her when he felt her stomach muscles harden. Despite his desperately fervent prayer that it be anything else, he knew what caused it. Iliani was having the baby.

Alaex's frustration was so great that for a moment he

pounded the damp ground beside his unconscious wife. He was no midwife and Iliani needed care. If he rode with her back to Fontwyn, she might die and he was certain the baby would. It was coming early as it was. Yet if he waited and tried to deliver it himself, his ineptitude might kill her and his child, and if not that, then the blow to her head might worsen.

For a few precious minutes more, Alaex agonized over what action to take. Suddenly like a gift from God, calm overtook him and he made a decision. In battle one never worried about the men to come, only the warrior before you. If you vanquished him there would be the opportunity to challenge the next. If you did not your concern would be for naught, because all it took was one strike of the sword to make all other worries small or nonexistent.

The challenge before him was the baby. He would deliver it. Then he would ride as quickly as he could to get both the babe and Iliani back to Fontwyn. Getting her home and dealing with the blow to her head were distant challenges. There was no time to lament that he had brought neither his men nor Gwyn with him. He was aware only of being grateful for the rain that he had previously cursed, for it had made Iliani's direction visible by the tracks Wind Dancer had made and he had followed. That was all he had the room and the time to think of.

Iliani was still alive, and as best he could tell so was his child. How long they remained so depended on him.

Using the water pouch on Bear's saddle, Alaex cleaned the dirt from his hands as best he could. He didn't know why he did that. It just seemed smarter to touch her and his child with clean hands instead of dirty ones. With a quick grip he tore away strips of her gown to have something in which to wrap the child.

The moon shone brightly, and while it was not as much light as Alaex would have wished, it at least enabled him to see what was happening. Iliani groaned faintly and immediately Alaex looked at her face thinking she was regaining consciousness. She was not. However, when her stomach contracted again and she winced slightly, Alaex wondered if the pain was so fierce that even in her unconscious state she could feel it.

His child gave him no more time to ponder it, because shortly after Iliani's stomach relaxed, it tensed again. It continued to repeat the process until a few moments later, Alaex's son slid from his mother's body and into his father's waiting hands.

A howl filled the night, but it still was not Alaex's. It was his son adding his sound to that of the night, and Alaex thought he had never heard anything so delightful, or loud. The intensity of the babe's wail didn't matter; his son's bellows echoed what Alaex felt in his heart.

Alaex's hands shook as used his dirk to cut the cord and then wrapped his son in the strips of material he had torn. He laid the babe inside Iliani's cloak while he examined her. Although she bled, it did not seem excessive to him. As carefully as he had wrapped their son, Alaex bound material around Iliani's head and between her legs.

When he turned back to the babe, it had stopped crying. Now he was making tiny little suckling noises. Picking him up, Alaex laid him on Iliani's chest, smiling slightly when the wrinkled little face immediately began to root around for the sustenance it instinctively knew was there.

Not sparing a moment to help his son in his quest, Alaex used another strip of torn material as a sort of security binding and tied the baby into place. Then he lifted them both and the three set off on a frantic pace for Fontwyn.

Chapter

→ 33 ←

The first thing Iliani was aware of was pain. There was a sharp piercing pain in her head, making her not want to move her head or open her eyes, and there was a steady throbbing pain in her stomach, making her not want to move anything else. She wanted to open her mouth and ask why she hurt so, but confusion set in and she couldn't remember where she was or why she thought that there wouldn't be someone to either hear or respond to her question.

Then Iliani became aware of other things—the softness beneath her and the cool comfort of the linen covering her. She was lying in a bed. Iliani's confusion grew even as she accepted those things that shouldn't be. She was not able to remember why, but she knew they were out of place. The surface beneath her should have been hard, damp, and cool. Not soft, dry, and warm.

As Iliani lay struggling against those contradictions, she heard people speaking in hushed, muted voices. The soft tones let her know she was not alone.

She wanted to open her eyes, but the pain made her quickly change her mind. So instead she tried to listen more carefully to see if understanding would come that way; however, straining to hear hurt nearly as much as trying to open her eyes, and through the ensuing confusion one shred of understanding occurred to her. She had to relax.

Tension caused the pain in both her head and her stomach to mount unbearably. Without meaning to Iliani groaned, and while she tried to relax she heard the sounds of footsteps drawing closer.

Shortly afterward she felt a mercifully cool cloth against her forehead and the piercing pain eased somewhat. The voice that spoke was low and gentle, familiar.

"Easy, milady, easy. I know there is pain, but you must not fight. 'Twill only worsen if you do."

"Gwyn?" Iliani's voice was a dry, rasping croak.

"Shh, shh, 'tis I," Gwyn said softly, then cleared the rest of the confusion crowding Iliani's mind. "You are home and safe. Do not try to talk. You must rest."

The old servant's admonition was unnecessary. Iliani had never known what an effort it took to speak, and the cost of forcing out that one word was not one she cared to repeat. But she was so thirsty. Her tongue felt as if it were the size of her head and growing. At least one of her discomforts should be assuaged, and since it appeared that the pain was going to remain a while, then something had to be done for the thirst.

Iliani was gathering her meager strength to ask for a drink of water when she felt herself being gently lifted. All thought of thirst disappeared as the pain turned white hot and she nearly screamed.

"I know, milady. I know it hurts, but you cannot drink otherwise," Gwyn soothed. "I am sorry."

Trying her best to ignore the pain, Iliani took a few strength-sapping sips of water from the cup Gwyn held to her lips. She wanted to drink more, but she was too weak. Iliani also wanted to ask questions; however, that, too, seemed a task beyond her. As the burning pain in her head cooled slightly, she decided to take her blessings one at a time. Questions and their answers could wait for later. Right now, sleep would not.

When Iliani awakened again, it was day. Whether it was the same day or several days later, she didn't know. This time, however, the pain in her head was bearable and the throbbing in her stomach had become a dull ache. She wasn't as disoriented as she had been before, and she knew where she was, remembering what Gwyn had told her. She was in her bed at Fontwyn Hall and the quiet was absolute, making her think that this time she truly was alone.

Slowly Iliani opened her eyes, cautious in case sudden movement would bring a return of the near-blinding pain. The first thing she noticed was not the rather disheveled state of the room, attesting to the fact that she had lain abed for more than a day. Nor did it register that despite what she had thought, she was not alone. Gwyn sat near the fireplace with needlework in her hands. Nay, she noticed none of that. The first thing— the only thing—Iliani noticed was that her rounded stomach was gone. While it was not board flat as before pregnancy, it definitely was not the size of a woman carrying a seven-month babe.

Regardless of the pain, and sickly aware that that was the cause of it, Iliani gripped her stomach as fast tears rolled down her face. She didn't want to ask, but not knowing was unbearable. Once she heard the words, she could then quietly grieve to insanity.

"The baby," Iliani began, finally looking in Gwyn's direction and ignoring the huskiness in her voice, which in itself spoke of prolonged lack of use. "What happened to my baby?"

Gwyn hurried over to the bed and looked down into Iliani's clear, yet pain-filled eyes. "Milady, do not. 'Tis all right, truly."

Iliani, knee-deep in a pain much worse than the one in her head, did not hear. She had thought she needed the words to begin the grief, but that was not so. All that was needed was the emptiness in her womb where there should not have been.

Aware of nothing else, Iliani began to moan and cry harder. When she refused to listen and began to beat at her stomach, thrashing her head from side to side, Gwyn leaned down and grabbed her by the shoulders, pinning her to the bed.

Under normal circumstances Gwyn would never have grabbed her mistress in such a way, afraid she would cause her more pain, but Iliani was doing more damage to herself than Gwyn would ever have done. And it was all for naught.

Nearly yelling to ensure she was heard, Gwyn said, "The little lord is fine. He sleeps."

Iliani's eyes were fastened unblinkingly on the dark brown ones of the woman above her. Her tears still flowed, but her fighting ceased.

"You do not lie to me, Gwyn?"

Gwyn smiled to reassure Iliani and reinforce her words. "Nay, milady, I do not. The little lord sleeps soundly, and despite his early arrival, he is large and quite healthy."

Now Iliani's tears flowed for a different reason. Sensing that, Gwyn relaxed her grip.

"He? 'Tis a boy?"

"Aye." Gwyn nodded. "If you promise not to excite yourself further, milady, I will get him. 'Tis truth, you were far worse than the babe."

Iliani's answer was instantaneous. "I promise."

Gwyn chuckled softly and left, returning moments later with a wrapped bundle. Before Gwyn neared, Iliani's arms were reaching for her child. It was as uncontrollable as it was instinctive. She ached to hold him and see him, and to know for herself that he was well.

As Gwyn laid the sleeping baby in her arms, Iliani's tears flowed harder, and because of them she still couldn't see him. Blinking rapidly to clear her eyes, she got her first glimpse of her son and thought that never had there been created or seen such a beautiful sight.

Just as Gwyn had said, he was large and looked much like babes she had seen from women who had not delivered early. His color was good and the top of his head was covered with golden blond hair that reminded her of his father. Iliani was just accustoming herself to that when the baby yawned and opened his eyes to look at her.

His hair might be Alaex's, but his eyes were hers, blue-violet as they stared back at her and a tiny frown appeared between his hairless eyebrows. He seemed to be studying her as intently as she studied him, and that made Iliani laugh even as her head throbbed with discomfort.

"Do you think he sees me, Gwyn?" Iliani asked, unknowingly giving the same first response of nearly all new mothers.

"I do not know," Gwyn answered, "but I would wager he knows that here at last is his mother."

Gwyn's words caused Iliani to stiffen with renewed memory. Suddenly everything came back to her, including the reason for her frenzied flight to seek Alfred. She had intended to go before the king and sue for justice. True, he might like Alaex, but Aeric had been his friend also and Alfred had seemed honorable. She had thought he would do the right thing, the fair and just thing. And if Alfred had been able to assuage her misgivings—despite her fears and suspicions, Iliani was still aware that she lacked proof—then all the better. She knew that the latter had been her secret, selfish hope, and she didn't try to rationalize it. There was a part of her that felt the burning desire for justice and there was another part, equally as fervent, that wanted that justice to cost her no more than she had already paid. She had lost her father. While that was harsh, it had been so long ago that acceptance had nullified pain. She had grown up with the *idea* of a father, not the reality.

Alaex was not an idea. He *was* reality. Her reality. Iliani's love for him had become her entire existence, and it had manifested itself in her heart and in the physical being of the son she now held.

Aye, it might have been selfish, but even now Iliani still hoped for something that would erase the blight of suspicion that hung over Alaex's head.

With the baby's premature arrival, she knew that her questions were going to be delayed, if ever addressed at all. The situation, however, was still bleakly the same. She could not ask Alaex. First, he would not answer. Iliani knew him well enough to know that. Besides, if the positions were reversed and she were innocent, she might not be inclined to answer such an insult either. Second, and worse, he might leave, thinking she had besmirched his honor once too often. He would see it as unforgivable. Again, if innocent, Iliani could only agree.

There was no way to accuse him *politely* of murdering her father or attempting to murder her. There was no way to ask such a thing without giving the gravest offense. Since her chances of getting to Alfred were severely reduced, the near future seemed bleak despite the healthy birth of her son.

"What is it, milady?" Gwyn questioned anxiously. "Do you not believe what I say about the baby's health?"

Iliani shook her head. "Nay, I believe you, Gwyn." Silently she continued, *'Tis only my husband I seem to have difficulty believing.*

Unaware of Iliani's continued thought, Gwyn eased a bit. Unfortunately her next words to Iliani did not invoke a similar feeling.

"And 'tis certain I am that milord does not blame you for the early birth."

Iliani's eyes snapped up. "Alaex? Where is he?" Suddenly her head was filled with questions she should have asked long ago. "How did I get back here?"

"Milady, remember your promise to remain calm," Gwyn reminded gently. "The danger is past. You need only to rest to reach full recovery."

"I remember, Gwyn, but answer my questions, please," Iliani said with a calm she did not feel.

Gwyn studied her mistress's blank face and ignoring that, instead focused on the desperation beneath the calm in her voice. Taking a deep breath, she said slowly, "The night you left, Milord Alaex returned late. 'Twas rainy and cool."

Iliani nodded. "Aye, I recall."

"Well, 'twas late when he came in and discovered that you were not here. I can tell you true, milady," Gwyn said, giving a little shiver, "I have not seen him in a state such as that, so fierce he was. His fierceness seemed to grow when he realized that none of us knew where you were."

Any censure Iliani thought she detected was set aside. There was nothing in Gwyn's eyes to give evidence of disapproval, only concern. She merely seemed to be stating what happened, and her only visible reaction was that of trepidation over Alaex's response.

"Before we could fully explain," the servant continued, "milord was astride that hideous beast of a horse he rides and out the gates, his only words a shout for Jon to secure this place."

Iliani's heart grew heavy. "So Alaex found me." She didn't wait for Gwyn to nod her assent, remembering the night and Wind Dancer's increased skittishness, and that while concentrating to keep the horse calm, she had not noticed the low-lying branch. It had knocked her from the horse's back and she had struck her head. She hadn't known anything else until she awoke with the screaming pain in her head.

Looking back at the babe, who was once again asleep, Iliani asked, "When was he born?"

"More than a week past."

Iliani hid her reaction to that. Not only had she had her son without knowing it, but she had also obviously severely injured herself. There would be questions for her, but she had no answers she was ready to give.

Instead she said, "In any event, I thank you, Gwyn, for his safe birth and care."

There was no mistaking Gwyn's surprise. "You may thank me for his care, milady, but I did not birth him."

"Then who? . . ." Iliani's voice faded and again she didn't need an answer from Gwyn, but the woman gave it.

"Milord did. He came thundering back with you wrapped in his arms and the babe tied to your breast. The men were still standing about chafing at their inability to follow him. We were all relieved to see him return and then we saw what had happened to you."

Gwyn didn't say more, but her shudder was eloquent.

"Where is Alaex now?" Iliani asked again, looking up again when the servant didn't answer immediately.

"I do not know," she finally replied. "He talked with Thibert, Jon, and the others and then after assuring himself that you rested and had not slipped into unconsciousness again, they rode out."

Iliani's heart lightened somewhat. Alaex's absence wasn't much of an opportunity, but she took it.

"Gwyn, I need your assistance," she began hurriedly. "Before Alaex returns—"

Iliani got no further because at that moment the bedroom door opened and Alaex's massive form filled it. His pale blue eyes instantly sought Iliani's. Hers fell away and suddenly Iliani began to shake.

There was no time left and she had no plan. One look in his eyes and she knew that she desperately needed one. She didn't doubt that he had heard what she started to say to Gwyn.

When Gwyn looked down to her, worry returned to her face. "Are you all right, milady?"

Iliani could think of nothing to say, but Gwyn answered her own query. "I knew 'twas too much. Rest now."

Iliani lay back, the pain in her head that she had ignored while she spoke to Gwyn coming throbbingly back to her attention. She shut her eyes, but she did not rest and she knew Alaex knew it.

"Take my son," he said to Gwyn.

Was it just her or did his voice seem vacant?

Without mincing words or pretending that he had not heard, Alaex said, "There is no need for my wife to tell you whatever she intended. Now that I am here, she can say it to me."

Iliani swallowed, because beneath those calmly spoken, seemingly innocent words were threat and promise. And she heard them both.

Chapter

→ 34 ←

An awful silence stretched between them after Gwyn shut the door, taking the baby away as Alaex had bidden. Afraid of him and even more afraid of herself, Iliani kept her eyes closed. She didn't think Alaex would believe she had fallen asleep, but she could think of naught else to do. Talking to him was not high on her list. Answering the questions she knew he would have wasn't on the list at all.

With a heart that beat heavier with each sound, Iliani heard him step toward the bed. When Alaex stood beside her she knew it without opening her eyes. Just as she also knew he stared down at her intently. It was that knowledge that caused the telling color to rise in her cheeks. Knowing he could not possibly miss that, Iliani opened her eyes.

As she had thought, he was standing over her, staring. What took her by surprise was the faint smile twisting his lips. Alaex did not leave her to guess the cause of his mild amusement.

"Better," he said, his words as sharp as his predatory

facade of a smile. "I always find it more rewarding to see my opponent's eyes."

Despite the pain in her head, Iliani struggled to sit upright, leaning against the massive headboard of the bed. While she straightened the covers around her, she asked in what she hoped was a casual voice, "Opponent? Why do you persist in using terms of war?"

The question answered itself. Belatedly Iliani recognized the belligerence she had been unable to keep out of her tone. Alaex did too, and although her tart response proved his point, he chose to be perverse.

"Oh? Then I was mistaken?" he queried with feigned confusion. "Strange that after having been in so many, my nose would fail me now."

He was baiting her. Alaex would not allow her to pretend sleep nor would he permit her to avoid the issue between them. Instead, through subtle taunts, he was setting the scene for the confrontation. Iliani knew this as clearly as if she were privy to his thoughts. Yet even knowing this, she could not hold her tongue.

"So many what?" she snapped. "In what way is your nose failing you?"

The baiting humor left his face. "Battles, Iliani. There is a scent in the wind just before one, as if the earth knows what is about to take place and is crying out its protest. The scent, once perceived, is not forgotten. 'Tis unmistakable, and this room reeks of it."

Iliani's eyes escaped his. "You were correct the first time," she said flatly. "You are mistaken."

Alaex sat down beside her and they both noticed that she flinched. He allowed that revealing action to stand between them a few agonizing moments. Then he said, "Do I really need to ask?"

Nervously Iliani bit her bottom lip. Her head really did pain her. She decided to tell him that. She just was not up to playing mouse to his cat.

Looking fully at him, she took a deep breath. "Alaex, my head pains me. I prefer not to talk."

At first he did not acknowledge that she had not

answered his question. "I am certain it does," he returned blandly, but his tone was at variance with his gaze, which was sharp, piercing. "Such a bump as you have usually does bring pain. So then let us compromise. I will settle for what you were about to tell Gwyn when I returned. Your head did not bother you enough to prevent that."

Even through the softness of his words, Iliani heard the thread of unyielding steel. Obviously she *was* going to play whether she wanted to or not.

Iliani could no longer meet his gaze. As she averted her eyes, she tried to think of a way to end this distasteful and tense interlude without telling him any more than she felt she could. There was no way she would tell him that she had been about to ask Gwyn to help her keep him away by not revealing that she had awakened so fully. Gwyn would have been curious, but Iliani had been certain that she would have adequately handled her questions. With Alaex she was under no such delusion. She was not prepared to answer any of his.

"'Twas naught worth repeating," she responded evasively.

"Agreed," Alaex replied tightly, his voice growing harsher. "But as you have not said it once, 'twill not be repetition."

Iliani's temper slipped slightly. "Leave me be, Alaex! If you were so interested, then you should have stood longer outside the door. Then you would have heard it all! You did not, and I do not wish to reintroduce the subject. 'Tis not necessary! If you cannot accept that, supply your own ending as you will!"

In a flash Alaex's face underwent a subtle change. The implacability remained, but his expression no longer challenged. "What is wrong, Iliani?" he asked with a directness that said he, too, tired of games.

"Naught."

"Where were you going when you fell from Wind Dancer's back?"

"Nowhere," was her stubborn response.

This time when Alaex's expression altered, it became the one Iliani had not seen since her first days with him. She sensed it was not just her refusal to answer his questions that caused its return. Whatever its cause, it was terrifying. She had nearly forgotten the sheer menace he could exude. Yet as easily as others breathed, Alaex seemed to revert to that other personality, letting her know it was never far from the surface.

For his part, Alaex was unaware of what his face revealed. He was fully preoccupied with the fire in his mind. He had not been mistaken. Iliani was once again afraid of him and that frightened him. His fear, in turn, cocooned itself in anger. He had thought they had gotten past all of this. Everything he had done since bringing her to Fontwyn had been with the hope—sometimes ignored, sometimes denied—that she would come to see him as he was, not what he was reputed to be. He thought he had succeeded. Failure now was unacceptable. She had given him her love, and it seemed she had given it to Alaex the man, not the myth, not the person whom past circumstances had made him appear.

Alaex acknowledged now that that was part of the reason he had not shared his past with Iliani as yet. Aye, there was the issue of pride, but there was also the fear that she would see him as the sum total of his past and find him lacking and unworthy. He tried to convince himself that that was unwarranted, but as he had long since admitted, fears die slowly if ever. Iliani mentioned love, not worth. Perhaps if she knew it all, she would think him unworthy of her love.

Reluctantly he admitted that he probably should have told her of it before this, but she had given him her love and he was afraid she would take it back. He did not see love as an irretrievable gift. No experience in his life had ever taught him it was so. To his mind, it could be retracted, and Iliani's flight, her fear, and her actions now only proved it. She was trying to withdraw from him, but he refused to let her. However, he didn't know how to stop her, because he had no idea what had caused her disillusionment and flight in the first place.

All these things ran through his mind, yet only his anger showed on his face. Whereas in another man the next words would have been soft and persuasive, Alaex's words, despite their substance, were clipped.

"Iliani," he said, drawing nearer only to stop when she drew back. Again his expression altered and his voice was rougher when he continued. "'Tis well you know that 'tis not my fortune to have been blessed with an easy tongue. If 'twas something I did or said that has given offense, will you not tell me?"

Iliani saw past the anger in his eyes and at the moment her heart would have softened, she saw other things: Wind Dancer's hooves flailing at her, her near-headlong flight down steep stairs. She heard things, too, to which she had not properly listened at the time they were said. Edouard halting just short of saying that she was not safe here with Alaex. Cam's outright accusation that Alaex had murdered her father. True, Cam might be what he was, but that did not mean he lied. Remembering his face, Iliani was certain he believed what he said. To him it was truth, and all she could fault him for was his saying it to hurt and not to enlighten or warn her. Yet even had there been no Edouard, no Cam, the last voice she heard was the most condemning. It was her father's. In her reawakening memory she heard her father admitting his wrong and warning her not to trust Alaex.

She might have been able to discard some of these things, and for a long time she had, but all of them? How could she stand beneath the weight of that? How could she scream at all of them that they were wrong and she alone was right?

Iliani again looked away from Alaex, her lips compressed so tightly together to keep the words inside that they made a mean line across her face. As she did, she recognized that the situation was unbearable. If she could neither accuse nor acquit because there was not enough proof one way or the other, the only thing left was to seek refuge and justice with Alfred. He was the only one who would be able to resolve this. He would be able to sift through whatever lies or, worse, half-truths that had been spoken to find the reality lying below. She had lost her opportunity to get to him on her own, but perhaps—as long as he did not suspect her true thoughts—Alaex would take her.

It was desperate and most likely doomed to failure, but it was all she had. She just could not wait until things resolved themselves. Forcing herself to meet Alaex's gaze again, Iliani began to put her feeble plan into action.

"I am sorry, Alaex." Her words sounded sincere, because they were. She was sorry. "I do not mean to upset you or make things difficult." Again another truth, but with the cynical look that crossed his face, Iliani decided it was best for her to stop there. Still sticking to the truth, she changed direction. "I see you do not believe me."

Alaex's voice was harsh. "Should I?"

Iliani managed a small smile. "Probably not from your view."

"And if I saw it from yours?"

There was a question difficult to answer. Taking advantage of the fact that she had already flinched from him twice, Iliani said, "You would see fear based on indecision."

A cautious look entered Alaex's eyes. "About what are you undecided?"

"I have a request and I am dubious of its being granted." Iliani did not make him ask. "I needed to see Alfred. 'Tis where I was going. I went alone because I knew your men would not take me without specific word from you and I did not think you would give it." That was as close to a lie as she would come.

"Why would I not?"

"You would want to know why and when I would not say, you would have refused."

Alaex did not hide his surprise. However, he had one of his own. "'Tis because of your father, is it not?"

She was so astounded by his matter-of-fact statement that Iliani did not know what to say, so she only nodded.

Tentatively Alaex smiled in compassion. He lifted his hand to touch her jaw with that same tender emotion, but uncertain as he had not been in a long time, he allowed his hand to drop back to the bed.

"Arthur and Gwyn told me of your questions the night you ran—left for the king." Alaex studied her face a long time. "Why did you think to hide that from me?"

Warnings went off in Iliani's head, warring with her growing need to sob out all her misery on his chest. She had not missed the look in his eyes or the compelling movement of his hand, and despite everything she wanted his touch.

Ignoring that look and her response to it, Iliani concentrated on strengthening her unlikely plan. She could not back out, nor would she change her strategy. The truth, or as much of it as she felt safe to tell, was best.

"I did not—do not wish to hide it from you. He was my father, Alaex. I was the one with the questions; therefore, I was the one needing the answers. Edouard never talked about him. Alfred knew him. It seemed the logical place to turn."

Sensing he was about to object, for the first time, Iliani used the things she had learned while tending his wound. "Have you never had something in your past that you had to make peace with yourself before you could share or discuss it with someone else?"

Iliani kept her face bland, refusing to show her satisfaction at the look on his as her question pierced its mark. For good measure, though, she thrust against the tender spot once again, casting aside her guilt feelings at doing so. She had no choice, she reminded herself firmly.

"Would you not resent it if someone tried to force you to speak of it or reveal it before you were ready?"

When Alaex finally nodded slowly and reluctantly,

Iliani released her first easy breath since she had seen him in the doorway.

"I'm glad you understand. I was wrong to set out as I did, but I thought I had no choice. I realize now that I do. Since I cannot go to him, would you send word to Alfred asking that he stop here when he comes through?"

Alaex did not answer for a long time. When he spoke, instead of answering he asked a question of his own, admitting his own hypocrisy as he did so.

"Then will you tell me of it?"

Iliani nodded. It was easy to do so, because after talking to Alfred, Alaex would know one way or the other.

In the weeks that passed after her discussion with Alaex, Iliani healed from her head injury and from birthing her son, whom they decided to call Aeric. That decision had been made when one day Iliani had casually mentioned to Alaex her desire to name the babe for her father, and after quietly thinking, he had agreed. After giving his agreement to her request, Alaex had stared at her long and hard, making Iliani extremely uncomfortable.

It was not the first time she had felt that way. For weeks Alaex had been giving her long considering looks, and for just as long Iliani had tried to ignore them.

There was an unacknowledged tension between them that she naturally understood, and it seemed that Alaex dispassionately accepted. Despite her believing that and all her efforts to remain unaffected, Iliani was becoming disconcerted by his lengthy stares. She tried to act as if nothing out of the ordinary was happening. There were days she felt better about her success at that than others. Her injury and Aeric's subsequent birth had been an unexpected boon. Iliani had been able to use both to avoid much, especially intimate contact with Alaex.

Initially she had sensed that he had merely wanted to stay with her during the nights. Iliani was certain he had known that nothing physical could have taken place between them. If things were different Iliani would not have cared; she would have welcomed it. As it was, she couldn't allow that and then later, when physical intimacy was no longer prohibited, tell him that she could not or did not want to. This way, with Alaex in his own chambers because of the injury to her head and the birth of their child, the situation could simply play itself out. And Iliani intended it should until she spoke to Alfred. If her fears were realized, physical closeness would be one additional pain she could do without. Although it was becoming harder to avoid Alaex's questioning glances, which betrayed his mounting impatience and pained confusion, Iliani knew it would be impossible for her to bear the increased pain that such intimacy could bring if ugly suspicions turned into even uglier truths.

At odd times when the guilt the looks raised within her was more than she could bear, Iliani found herself silently promising him atonement. "I will make it up to you, Alaex. I vow it. Only for the sake of the love I feel, which is being tortured enough by doubts, it must be this way for now."

After those same moments, she would issue a fervent prayer that he would be around for her to make atonement. Iliani was still unsure how Alaex would respond to her thoughts if he were innocent. It seemed that either way she proceeded there was going to be pain in her future. The only difference was that one held out a slight hope of happiness after it ended and the other offered gaping and endless despair.

"Alfred will be here in a week."

Iliani looked up into Alaex's eyes as he stood in the door of the room they had turned into a nursery for Aeric. She tried not to flinch from the chill in his voice. Alaex's voice had been getting increasingly colder as the days went by and Iliani pretended not to notice his attempts to draw closer to her. However, in contrast to the growing frost in his voice, there was a steadily increasing fire burning hungrily within his eyes.

As she watched him now, his eyes left her face and moved down to Aeric, who still suckled at his mother's breast, unaware of the strong undercurrent existing between his parents. The look of unconcealed yearning on Alaex's face made Iliani draw in her breath sharply. The heat from his glance made her feel as if her entire body was exposed to the fire of his gaze instead of just one breast.

Under the direct blast of his desire Iliani felt weak, hot. Desperately she licked her lips, unable to suppress a groan when Alaex's eyes followed her tongue.

Alaex heard it. As if that tiny hungry sound was all the permission he needed, he came forward, walking like a man who functioned on pure instinct alone.

Warnings clamored in Iliani's head. She had come so far. There was only one week more. Then one way or another this nightmarish existence would be over. She opened her mouth to stop him, but he was too close. It was too late.

Alaex's lips closed over hers, and all her protests and arguments fled. Even her thinking ceased as Iliani was seduced. His kiss fed a hunger she didn't know existed and persuaded her to give up her fight, which was more against herself than it had ever been against him.

When Aeric moved restlessly between them, Iliani thought she might have had a reprieve, until Alaex's mouth fastened on the breast his son had just left. The fire of Iliani's response was instantaneous. She knew she was lost. She had no more will.

Salvation came in an unexpected way. Aeric, with the innocence of a babe totally oblivious to all needs and circumstances but his own, burped loudly. The sound was deep for one so young and so at variance with the intensity of passion tightening around Iliani and Alaex that they both stopped and smiled. When they looked down at Aeric, the babe was smiling, too, pleased with himself and uncaring that some of his meal was now running out of the side of his mouth into his ear.

Iliani wiped her son's face, relief flowing through her

body, replacing the passion. She had come extremely close to abandoning everything for a moment in Alaex's arms.

Alaex, too, seemed to see that moment was lost. When he pulled back, his expression was shuttered as he watched Iliani cover herself. The shaking he saw in her hands was in her voice also.

"'Tis just as well that our son called us to our senses. Now is not the time."

"'Twould seem it never is." He didn't make her try to answer that cryptic statement but placed a soft kiss on her forehead, and giving Aeric similar attention, he quietly left the room.

Iliani stared after him and her resolve nearly broke again. She wanted to call him back. She had to bite her lip to keep from doing so.

Alaex disappeared through the door and still Iliani sat staring at where he had last been. Again it was Aeric who brought her back to her surroundings as he began to fidget in her lap. Iliani lowered miserable eyes to her son and saw what caused his dilemma.

Obviously he didn't like having his mother's tears drip unrelentingly on his face.

When Iliani prepared for bed that night, she did what had become a habit: she counted time. One week, Alaex had said. Alfred would be here in a week. Then she completed the other part of the ritual: she told herself that she could last until he came. After the scene in Aeric's room, she needed to believe that more than ever.

Having completely healed, Iliani was unprepared for the enemy she found within. She no longer thought it was just Alaex wanting her. It was much worse. She wanted him, too. His obvious desire combined with her own yearnings made a formidable adversary. Theirs had been a physical and very passionate relationship. Her body remembered and her heart reinforced the memory by refusing to set aside—even temporarily—her love for him.

Tonight was worse than any other because her mind chose to relive their torrid past, heightening her desire until it seemed both mental and physical. Iliani tried to stem the passionate memories that plagued her, hoping that if she controlled her mental desire, the physical desire would soon ebb. As much as she tried, she could neither stop nor ignore the memories. Each memory fired a greater heat for the next, until the scene in Aeric's room seemed as inevitable as it had been uncontrollable.

Her body had seemed to have a mind of its own then as it did now, and its desire flailed her with a flame-tipped tongue. Iliani bit her bottom lip and hugged herself tightly, nearly grimacing in pain, her want almost unbearable. Her breasts tingled and the fire burned a hungry path from there to her loins. No longer able to hold it inside, without volition a moan escaped her and even to her ears it sounded passion starved and sensuous.

Iliani wanted to rip off her gown, her skin had become so sensitive. Instead she took a deep, settling breath. Quiet seconds passed agonizingly by as inch by burning inch, she forced the fire in her body to cool. When her desire softened from unbearable to merely acute, Iliani blew out the candles, crawled into her massive bed, and reminded herself that she could endure this.

I can, she thought vehemently, sliding beneath the cool linen, *because I have to. I have no other choice.*

For a change, her dream was pleasant. It was sensuous and passionate and allowed her to vent her considerable pent-up passion harmlessly. In it Iliani could feel Alaex's hands on her breasts. When they moved away they were no less arousingly and realistically replaced by his lips. She arched into him and gave herself over to the dream. Here in her dreams she could love without pain, without questions, and without any guilt brought about by perhaps loving unworthily or unwisely. She betrayed no one or his memory by what she gave here.

The sensations grew keener, more powerful, but for once Iliani allowed herself to let go, having no fear of passion's impact. She dreamed and it was safe. She was safe. She knew she had to be dreaming because she had worn a gown to bed and its mere softness had chafed against her sensitive skin like the coarsest material. Yet now she was gloriously, deliciously naked as her body floated in a sensuous pool of unbelievable beauty and intensity.

Iliani could feel every inch of Alaex's hard body against her own. Greedily she opened her eyes, wanting to see in her dreams what before she had only felt. And when she opened her eyes, the illusion shattered and she knew it was no dream.

She called his name—whether in prohibition or encouragement, Iliani did not know. Whichever, it was too late. Alaex's hard body plunged into her heated one and Iliani could no longer think. She had not asked for this, had done her best to avoid it, but it was happening and Iliani would not—could not at this point—play the hypocrite and pretend she did not want it. The intensity of her want was past desire. She arched up to meet each thrust with a force that should have thrown Alaex from her. She bit, clawed, and suckled on whatever part of his body she could reach.

Iliani knew what awaited her on the other side of desire, and it was as if that knowledge fed her fervency, increasing her passion until it was beyond measure. Her first climax brought her cry; her second, her scream, smothered by Alaex's devouring lips; and her third, oblivion.

It is always difficult to make the ascent from oblivion, but for Iliani the journey this time was sheer torture. Her trip there and back had brought her more than incredible physical release. It had brought mental release as well: one that also brought her the proof she didn't have before, and didn't want now.

In that moment of total abandon she had seen Alaex's face not as it had been straining above her in the throes of passion, but as it had appeared menacingly above her thirteen years ago. *He had been there.* But unlike her and Aeric, he had not been crying. The expression on his face had been as unreadable as it had been menacing. His words had been clipped and condemning. He had said he was sorry and that it was his fault.

Iliani shivered as she remembered that she had run away from him screaming. Odd how history repeated itself. That was exactly what she wanted to do now.

Chapter

→ 35 ←

The next day Iliani moved about in shock and dull acceptance. Her last bit of hope was gone, shattered in an instant of mind-freezing passion and heart-chilling clarity as memory rushed in where there had been none. And the pain was fierce. She wanted to weep, to pull her hair and howl like a demented berserker, but after the many tears spent in the early morning, she did neither. She merely moved through the day on reflex alone, ignoring or genuinely not seeing or caring about the looks of concern cast her way.

Her only care was her certainty that she could no longer wait for Alfred's arrival. Before last night's revelations she had thought she could. The events of last night, both physical and mental, had altered that opinion. She couldn't wait.

It was nearing evening when her unuttered prayers were answered with the watch's announcement that many riders approached Fontwyn. Since Alfred was the only one expected, it appeared he was arriving early. At least a part of Iliani prayed it was so. The other part would not give up its trust—one she was painfully aware no longer had any substance in reality.

As the riders drew near, Iliani's misery grew instead of lessened. No matter how much her mind told her to be happy about Alfred's early arrival, that soon this living nightmare might be at an end, she couldn't. She wanted to be happy that after all these years there would be justice for her father, but again she could not. The only thing she had, and it brought merely a veneer of contentment, was that despite the personal suffering it was bringing her, she did not close her eyes to truth. At least not anymore, she amended bitterly.

Iliani bit her bottom lip in agony, closing her eyes against not that pain, but the one within. Truly, it was an act of mercy that Alfred approached, because the turmoil she felt inside was tearing her apart.

A few moments later Iliani found that her turmoil was not yet at an end. The riders were identified. It was not Alfred who approached, but Edouard. Iliani was so surprised when Lucy came to tell her of it, she was unable to respond. She nodded stiffly to let Lucy know that she had heard, and turned away.

For once she was unconcerned how her reactions would be viewed. There was no room for such a worry in her troubled thoughts. This new information made Iliani feel as if either she alone or the rest of the world had gone insane. Edouard *here? Now?* When for thirteen years he had refused to come to her?

Iliani had understood and respected his pain. Her father had been his closest friend. After a time she had ceased to ask. That request, like her attempts to visualize her father's appearance, had seemed to cause pain and naught else. When she stopped doing the former publicly and continued to do the latter only privately, it had seemed to make everything easier for everyone.

As difficult as that had been, having grown up under those unspoken prohibitions then had seemed easier than accepting Edouard's presence at Fontwyn now. For

Edouard to be coming after so many refusals before, something must be terribly wrong.

And that was the knowledge from which Iliani shied. She could not bear yet another problem. She was already drowning beneath the situation between her and Alaex. Anything more would be a stone around her neck from which she felt she'd never surface.

Iliani heard a footstep behind her, and since she had not heard Lucy leave, she thought the woman had remained. In a tight, drawn voice she snapped, "I heard you, Lucy. The master of Lourds Keep approaches. Now please, leave me."

"I am not Lucy, and I have left you alone long enough. I will not leave."

The deep, quiet, *masculine* voice made Iliani swing around, her wide violet eyes connecting instantly with Alaex's blue ones. It took the greatest effort of Iliani's life not to shake and babble hysterically. It was all too much.

When she had awakened this morning Alaex was gone and she had been grateful. Her tears had been partly gratitude for not having to face him and partly self-pitying misery for the time when she would. Cowardly, she had spent the day in either her room or Aeric's alternating between fear that Alaex would come to her again that night and dread that he would not.

It was time for the evening meal and Iliani had no wish to leave the sanctuary of her room. But the room was no longer a haven. Alaex was there, and by his own mouth he was not leaving. He had to. Iliani knew she couldn't bear it if he stayed.

Struggling for control, Iliani returned Alaex's stare, waiting for him to reveal why he was there. For a long while he said nothing, allowing the oppressive silence to grow painfully. When he spoke in a quiet and flat tone, his question made Iliani long enviously for the previous silence.

"Why are you afraid?"

Iliani squared her shoulders, ready to deny her fear.

However, Alaex's soft warning froze the lie within her throat.

"Do not."

Flushing slightly, Iliani looked away from him. She hoped that her fervent desire for him to leave was not as evident as her fear, as she murmured, "Edouard approaches. Should you not be there to meet him?"

Alaex gave a slow shrug. "Since he comes without invitation, if I am not there upon his arrival, 'tis of no consequence. He can wait. What needs take place here cannot."

"What do you mean?" Iliani managed to squeeze out.

It was impossible for Alaex to miss the wariness that not only shone in her eyes but radiated from her body. However, to prove it he took a step forward and was not shocked to see Iliani take an equal step back.

"That," he said flatly.

Iliani cursed her instinctive cowardliness. Before he could advance closer and let her reaction reveal more, she turned away from him and walked over to the window. Keeping her back to Alaex, she hugged herself and still striving for calm, replied, " 'That' was naught."

"Was it?" Alaex asked in a deliberately offhanded manner. Then just as deliberately, he took several steps toward her and Iliani realized her tactical mistake. There was nowhere else for her to turn. He had her trapped. She was forced to stand her ground.

He stood so close she could feel his heat, and it was all she could do not to tremble. Alaex would think her action was motivated by fear, and he would be only partly right. Iliani did fear him, but even more she feared her reaction to him. Last night was a mistake that she could not repeat.

"Aye. What is it, Alaex?" she asked, trying not to shrink back from him. When he didn't answer or move away, Iliani gave him a quick sideways glance. " 'Tis almost time for the meal and if this can wait, I would prefer it."

"Hungry, are you?" he asked softly.

Until that moment Iliani had not considered eating, and she was positive Alaex knew that. He spared her the need to think of something to say.

Alaex smoothly stepped back and made a gallant sweep of his arm. Although surprised, Iliani jumped at the respite, already planning how to avoid such a situation in the future. Eagerly she latched on to Edouard's visit. He was not the king, and as much as she dreaded the possibility of any ill news he might bring, his visit might supply her with the opportunity to avoid Alaex.

Iliani was walking to the door deep in plans when Alaex's soft voice relentlessly crushed every one of them.

"There is always later."

If he noted her flinch, again he spared her by saying nothing, and silently they went below stairs to eat a meal it was clear neither wanted and to entertain a guest neither had invited.

Given those circumstances, the evening meal was not the disaster it should have been. Edouard had not brought bad news, at least nothing of which Iliani could make use. And once Iliani considered that Alaex was not going to allow stalling, she fatalistically accepted that it was just as well, and turned her attention as best she could to Edouard, who said he had come because of Eadwina.

"Is she ill?" Iliani asked anxiously, her voice high and sharp. "Should I go to her?"

Edouard's eyes narrowed on her, but his stare was nothing compared to the look Iliani felt Alaex give her. Edouard, his curiosity at her reaction evident, said lightly, "Nay, Iliani. Her concern is for you." The lightness in his tone disappeared. "Why did you not tell us of your pregnancy? Eadwina did naught but fret, especially when she discovered the babe had come early. We asked then if we could come to you, but your h— Alaex thought it best we wait. We have waited, Pigeon, nearly two months of waiting. Eadwina could not bear it any longer and so here I am, unannounced and uninvited."

Iliani was reeling from what Edouard revealed, and she did not miss the censure in his tone. It was clear he had seen Alaex, and Iliani did not need to be there to know that that visit had not passed pleasantly. But when? She had no knowledge of this. The tentative inquiring glance she gave Alaex was enough.

Alaex twirled his cup between his long strong fingers, a fixed look on his face as he answered Iliani without looking up. " 'Twas while you were recovering."

Iliani wanted to ask more, remembering the day when Gwyn had told her that Alaex and his men had gone riding off. Gwyn had not known their destination. Now that Iliani had a fair suspicion, it raised more questions. She did not have the opportunity to ask them.

"Aye, you were recovering, or so we were told." Edouard's facile manner slipped a little. "When no further news came, I had to come. Tell me you forgive me?" he asked Iliani.

The fact that he should have and did not ask Alaex's pardon was apparent. Iliani noticed it immediately. On the outside it appeared that Alaex had not, but Iliani was not fooled by his calm facade, certain that that was all it was. The myth might not be true, or not *all* true, but didn't Edouard know that Alaex was a dangerous man? To insult him in Lourds Keep was one thing; to do it in Alaex's home, whether he wrongfully attained it or not, was another.

Iliani tried to divert the tension. Her efforts were not so much for Alaex, but if she had any hope of leaving with Edouard, Alaex could not be infuriated with him.

"I am sure we both understand," Iliani supplied diplomatically.

Alaex looked up, surprise in his eyes. Iliani managed to give him a weak smile, and had she not been playing a part she would have warmed beneath the astonished pleasure in his gaze and placed a hand on his. As it was, she barely managed a smile and watched helplessly as his expression cooled beneath her halfhearted encouragement. Just before he finally looked away, Iliani saw that he knew that what she had said had not been said for him.

His expression became harder than ever, but thankfully the meal ended shortly afterward. The men, both Edouard's and Alaex's, filed out to seek their entertainment or rest. Iliani rose to excuse herself as well. Aeric needed her.

"Please excuse me. I must see to my son."

Edouard's smile brightened. "Ah, aye, little Aeric. I have not had the pleasure yet of seeing him. Does he look like his namesake?"

"He has Father's eyes," Iliani answered quietly. Then, uncomfortable with talking about Aeric's looks, because actually despite his eye color he looked exactly like Alaex, she added, "I will bring him to you in the morning after we break the fast."

"If he is still here," Alaex said unmistakably.

Iliani started, thinking that if Edouard left before she had the chance to put forth her petition to leave with him, all would be lost.

Alaex was not looking at her. Edouard was, and he saw her alarm. He stood and walked over to her, gently escorting her to the stairs.

"Do not fret, Pigeon. I have come to set matters aright. Things have gone too long unresolved. It matters not to me what your . . . what Alaex says. I can assure you that by morning all will be well. There will be no more strife."

His words were reinforced by the determined gleam in his eyes, and while Iliani appreciated what he thought to do, she doubted his success. If he thought a few words would make peace with Alaex, he was mistaken. Besides, appeasing Alaex might be premature as well as unwarranted. If after Alfred heard what she had to say he agreed that Alaex had had something to do with her father's death, then there would be no need for peace. In any event, though, if Edouard did make some kind of peace, it might make her plan to leave with him easier.

Kissing him lightly on the cheek, Iliani said, "Thank you and good night," before running up the stairs.

She went straight to Aeric's room. He was awake and waiting for her. Already, in just two months, he had grown so much. His chubby little arms and legs kicked as he watched her approach. When Iliani picked him up, she was overwhelmed with love. Aside from what she had come to feel for Alaex—and regretted—she had not known it was possible to love another person so much. And the love she had for Aeric she didn't regret at all. It brought her joy just to look at him, and when she held him and he gripped her fingers with his, the feeling was indescribable. The time she spent with him was the most precious in her days, and when she considered the loneliness and misery that might lie ahead for her, its value grew.

All too soon Aeric had been fed and changed, and as babies do, had fallen back to sleep. Reluctantly Iliani laid him in his cradle and let herself out of the room, leaving the door cracked open so that if he stirred she would hear it.

Iliani took a few slow steps across the hall to her room, but remembering Alaex's promise, she hesitated to enter. There would be no escaping him this time and Iliani knew he'd tolerate no more evasions. Her time had truly run out, and she felt desperate and cornered.

Without consciously deciding to do it, she turned and started back toward the stairs. Besides trying to avoid the trapped feeling she would have in her room, she needed to speak to Edouard before he and Alaex came to the inevitable harshness that seemed to spew every time they met.

As she moved quietly down the candlelit hall to the stairs, Iliani was expecting to hear voices raised in anger. However, as the wind blew briskly through the hall, causing the candle flame to leap and flicker and create distorted images on the walls, there was only quiet.

Inexplicably Iliani's heart suddenly began to leap apace with the flickering of the flame. Her steps slowed as something in the silence below made her anxious. Realizing the cause of her anxiety, Iliani stopped, uneasy as to why the quiet should disturb her more than the sounds of anger she had expected.

Absently she began to rub her arms against the brusque and startling chill of the hall as she again started down the corridor. The quiet seemed so complete that Iliani expected the main hall to be empty.

It was not. When she was halfway down the stairs, Iliani was so stunned to see Edouard and Alaex there talking, she again stopped abruptly.

Neither one noticed her, and although Iliani knew she shouldn't, she moved deeper into the shadow of the stair to hear what they said. Their conversation was not that remarkable.

Edouard was doing most of the talking. He was telling Alaex how, in what little time he had been there, he had seen the extent to which Fontwyn had prospered under his leadership. The fields he had passed were ripe and fertile, and the people were happy and content. The hall itself had not looked better, Edouard went on as he looked about. Not even in Aeric's day could he recall it looking so well, he was saying.

Iliani's gaze shifted to Alaex to see how he was taking Edouard's praise. For all the attention he gave it, Edouard might not have been present. Iliani's heart went out to Edouard for his attempts. She knew what it cost him to be here and to say those things. Even now he was telling Alaex he was wrong.

"Fontwyn has prospered and it has a strong, healthy heir," Edouard said. "For the sake of Aeric, whom we both loved, and Iliani, whom we love, could we not bury the animosity between us?"

Finally Alaex stirred. He looked a long time at Edouard, but he did not nod until Edouard added in a rough, tight voice, "I will not hold your relations against you if you will promise to do the same."

Iliani was puzzled by that cryptic statement, but she didn't think about it long, because Edouard was beaming at Alaex for his slight unbending.

"Let us drink then to new beginnings, shall we?"

Alaex's second nod was no more enthusiastic than his first, but Edouard's smile grew. He poured wine in a cup and held it out to Alaex. Then he poured some for himself. His eyes sparkled and his smile widened as he raised his cup.

"To the future."

Suddenly, Iliani's anxiety turned to terror. There was something about Edouard's smile while holding the cup in his hand. Instead of making her happy, it frightened her. Without warning, she ran down the last few steps and straight for Alaex. The surprise on his face stopped him from taking a sip from the cup he held to his lips. His surprise doubled when Iliani knocked the cup from his hand and the red wine flew everywhere.

It was all over the room, the table, and the floor. Some of it—a few red dots—had splashed onto Alaex's face, making it look just like her last memory of her father's face. Iliani's heart slammed in her chest as, in a rush that made her knees buckle, she remembered everything. She gripped the table for support.

It had not been blood. Oh, dear God, it had not been blood!

It had been red wine. Stiff and trancelike, she turned to Edouard, who still held his cup suspended. In a voice so strangled even Iliani could not recognize it as her own, she spoke to Alaex, stared at Edouard, and began to weep.

"I saw him murder my father." Iliani couldn't say any more after that. Her voice failed her and she cried piteously.

Alaex, at a loss as to what to do or say, and not fully understanding what was happening, instinctively moved

to take her in his arms. He stopped when Edouard snapped, "Iliani, what the devil are you saying? Aeric's heart gave out. Everyone knows that!"

Since Alaex did not hold her, Iliani held herself and rocked and moaned. All those years she had lived with and loved her father's murderer. If these past months of suspecting Alaex were torture, the knowledge of the lying *years* she had spent loving Edouard like a father was unendurable.

Iliani could not look at Edouard anymore. She looked instead at Alaex, not that she could see him very clearly behind the tears that flowed. Her pain was doubled for because of Edouard she had lost her father and nearly lost her husband, and had Alaex not found her when he did she would have lost her son.

Alaex had regained himself and was about to take another step toward her when Iliani held her head back and screamed. And the sound was the worst thing Alaex had ever heard in his life. All the battles, all the wars, all the screams of the wounded and dying put together did not compare with the sound coming from his wife's slender throat.

At her tormented shriek, servants came running and Jon, who had just entered the hall, stood frozen. No one took note of the wine on their lord's face, their mistress's hand, and the floor and table. Iliani had their unswerving attention. There was no mistaking her agony, yet no one seemed capable of breaking the spell it wove to approach her. In its unrelenting magnitude it held them transfixed, and as they watched her, more than a few had to blink back rapid tears of their own.

The seconds played themselves out in a taut silence that was complete and unbroken, leaving only the torment, which seemed to fill every space and corner as it seeped unrelentingly from the slender woman who held herself so torturously erect.

They all felt for and watched her, and it seemed that Iliani was unaware of them all as she once again fastened her gaze on Edouard, whose expression, like that of the others, was of concern—only of a different sort. His apprehension stemmed from growing nervousness.

They were right. Iliani was unaware of it. She heard nothing else, saw no one else, as layer upon layer of memory unfolded. What her five-year-old mind had been unable to comprehend was now tormentingly clear. She saw that night as if it were taking place before her again, and in the seeing she relived everything: fear, cold, confusion, and pain. Trying to find comfort in a situation that mercilessly gave none, she was hugging herself so tightly that it hurt.

"You were here," she croaked at Edouard, crying heavily yet not bothering to wipe her tears. "I saw you. I had wandered down the gallery after Papa had put me to bed. You two sat and as I came nearer, I heard you arguing. It was about Cam and me, and, although at the time I did not understand what it meant, about marriage. You smiled at him, Edouard," Iliani accused in a childlike voice as she wept brokenly, "just as you smiled at Alaex. Then you drank. Papa looked strange and I was so frightened. I wanted to run to him, but I was afraid, thinking he'd be angry because I was not abed as I should have been. He flung his cup and there was wine everywhere, and when he fell to the floor, you left him there.

"When I finally went to him, he was barely alive. He couldn't call out for help and I didn't know what to do. All I could do was cry. He cried too. Did you know that, Edouard? He *cried!*" Iliani hissed and angrily wiped at her nose with the back of her hand. "Then he tried to warn me, but I misunderstood. For years, in my heart, buried beneath the memory, I feared the wrong man."

Iliani again sobbed uncontrollably, then stopped talking and vaguely she realized that there were other arms holding her now, stronger ones. She missed Alaex's grim nod to Jon, but when Edouard began to struggle, she looked to him. To her astonishment, he was crying too.

"Iliani, Pigeon—"

"How can you call me that—now?" Iliani managed to

whisper, revolted. Didn't he realize that what he had done and the pain it caused was almost like losing her father again? Now he dared weep and to try, by calling her the affectionate name he had used during her years at Lourds Keep, to wring some pity and understanding from her? Iliani's rage returned full-bodied and pure. Her heart clenched painfully and her tears nearly blinded her anew as she looked at the pleading expression on his face.

"Don't call me that! You have no right!" she snarled. "Don't *ever* call me that again!"

Edouard did not give up. "You don't understand. Aeric was an accident, a moment of anger regretted every day since. I *have* loved you, Iliani, and have tried my best to make it up to you. I *have* been your father. I have cared for you. You stand there now," Edouard gasped, tears rolling down his face, "in the arms of a man of no more worth than unturned dirt, when it should be my son here, his arms around you."

Alaex had heard enough. If not for Iliani's state and the presence of the servants, he would not have left Edouard to Alfred's justice. If naught else but for the pain he caused his wife, Alaex would have gladly killed him. That, in combination with his own pain at the loss of Aeric, and he could not stand the sight of Edouard. Feeling his control begin to slip as his rage fed on his and Iliani's pain, he motioned Jon to take him outside.

Edouard, however, was beyond control. He fought, his face turning an ugly red as he spat, "Iliani, listen to me! Had I killed him here tonight, it would be no crime! 'Twould be justice! He is the one who is guilty. Do you know what he accused? If you did, you would understand why I had to do it! Why else would I come here after all these years? I had to! Don't you see? He said terrible things about Cam! My son is not a murderer, attempted or otherwise! Cam would never harm you and he would fight fairly! He would not need to take dishonorably what birthright had given him and should have denied others."

There was no mistaking Edouard's contempt and for whom it was intended. Despite Jon's grip, which tightened as he, too, caught the slur cast upon his lord, Edouard's increasing rage gave him the strength to break free. Instead of running for the door, however, he ran toward Iliani.

That was enough for Alaex. Pushing Iliani behind him, he removed his sword with a lethal swish from its sheath. It pointed with unwavering threat at Edouard's throat and Edouard halted abruptly, not mistaking its threat or the murderous rage in Alaex's eyes.

"Do not stop, old man," Alaex hissed tauntingly. "You dare to speak of justice? Come closer that I may give you that which you deserve, and know that when I find your son he will get his just reward. You may depend on it." Contempt and rage filled Alaex's voice. "'Tis a pity one did not know of the cowardly plans of the other. Perhaps had you and your son worked together, you might have had success. You, at least, succeeded in your attempt at murder, but only because you fought a man whose very life was dedicated to peace. Cam does not, and even should he succeed now that he has been found out, be assured that if I die, I will not die alone as Aeric did."

Edouard seemed barely to register Alaex's words. He looked from Alaex's hot eyes to Iliani who stood behind him. Iliani's face was tear-streaked and full of loathing, and seeing that, Edouard's shoulders slumped.

"'Tis over," he said, defeat in his voice.

Still no one else said anything. No one moved, and no one noticed the new arrival who had stood quietly, watching. When he spoke, surprise registered on nearly all faces except Jon's, because he had entered to announce the man's arrival, but had forgotten his announcement when he heard Iliani's heart-wrenching scream.

"Those are the first words you have spoken, Edouard, with which I agree," Alfred said coldly from his position by the door.

Chapter

→ 36 ←

The king did not stay, and based on his reasoning, neither Alaex nor Iliani tried to convince him otherwise. Alfred felt that what had occurred was enough. He would not make Iliani, or Alaex, for that matter, have to endure knowing that Edouard was there. Nor did he want to mete out Edouard's sentence at Fontwyn.

"This hall," Alfred had said, "has seen enough of misery and death. I will not plague it further with this." So he had left early the following day and all were glad to see him go.

Iliani stood on the walk behind the protective wall atop the hall and watched Alfred and his men—and those of Edouard who had chosen to join with the king after learning what their leader had done—disappear. It was cold, but not brutally so. Even still, as the wind blew there was a briskness to it that identified the day as one belonging to early winter, and on the walk there was little protection against the elements. Nevertheless Iliani stayed. Arthur had told her long ago of her father's penchant for coming up there and walking the walls. He

383

had found it refreshing and calming and Iliani could see why. She got the same feeling standing there and looking out over Fontwyn's landscape as she did when she rode Wind Dancer.

Her mind was clear of most of her disturbing thoughts. The fact that she had been up there for a long time and still had discomforting thoughts attested to her state.

Last night had been terrible. Iliani could think of none worse—except possibly what was shortly to come. When she considered the wrong she had done Alaex, what she felt honor bound to say to him, and his possible reactions, her mind congealed into a lump of frozen horror.

There had been no time last night for talk. Besides that, she had been barely coherent by the time Alaex had led her from the room and Edouard's presence. Her tears would not stop. Iliani would not have thought it possible for one person to cry so much. Alaex had said nothing. He had held her and understood, which in turn had only made her cry harder, because he truly didn't understand. He was offering her a comfort she knew she didn't deserve, especially from him. Thinking that had not made her tears recede, and finally Iliani had cried herself into an exhausted sleep.

This morning, after seeing to Aeric and bidding the king farewell, she had escaped to the roof to watch Alfred leave and try to sort out the horrified jumble of her thoughts. Until now, she had accomplished only one thing. She had watched the king and his men disappear. Her other goal seemed to elude her. The harder Iliani tried, the farther away it seemed.

A strong wind blew then, lifting Iliani's thick black hair and blowing it to one side. Iliani turned her back to it and allowed it to mold her gown to her body, but she didn't retreat from the bite of the wind to the warmth of the hall.

"No matter how hard it blows, 'twill not take you with it."

Iliani started slightly at the sound of that deep quiet

voice. She did not turn. After a few seconds, Alaex came up behind her, his body acting as a shield against the worst of the wind. When he put his arms around her, he felt Iliani flinch but did not mention it. Gently he nuzzled through the hair at her neck until his lips found her skin. Placing a soft kiss there, he murmured, " 'Tis over, Iliani. You must let it go."

Tears gathered in Iliani's eyes. She would not have thought it possible after the amount of crying she did last night. It was a struggle to control them and not collapse again into a spasm of weeping. With determination Iliani bit her bottom lip and placed her arms over Alaex's. Her fingers began unconsciously to massage the strong muscles in his forearms, and with each pass they made the tightness within her chest began to ease.

" 'Tis not over yet, Alaex," she admitted softly. "Once it is, 'twill not be my choice to hold or let go." She was thinking of his reaction and his possible rejection of her once he knew how she had felt. Just thinking of it made her shiver.

For a moment Alaex ignored her enigmatic words and tried to turn her toward the stairs and the warmth of the hall. When she resisted he did not insist; instead, opening his cloak, he enfolded her in its warmth.

Iliani no longer felt the cold, and although she knew it was wrong, she leaned into him and borrowed not only his heat but his strength as well to help her bear the hurt she knew was going to worsen once she spoke the words. Yet when she parted her lips to say them, her voice croaked in fear and the words would not come.

"Say it, Iliani," Alaex whispered. "Things are never as bad as we think. They only worsen in the silence."

Hoping that his feelings would be the same after he had heard *her* words, Iliani took a deep breath. "I am such a coward, Alaex. Instead of just saying what must be said, I will tell you of things I feel relate to it so that when I admit my wrong, 'twill not seem as wrong as I know in my heart it is."

Alaex's arms tightened a bit. "If you were truly a coward, you would not have said that, thus weakening the effect. It weakens the strength of the claim if one admits from the start that one is making an excuse."

Iliani could hear the smile in his voice, but instead of making her relax, it made her nervousness increase. Tiring of torturing herself with what might be, Iliani braced herself, and forgetting her plan to tell him the other things that might help him to understand, she said bluntly, "I thought you had killed my father."

When Alaex's arms tightened more, Iliani held still, trying to disregard the notion that he might fling her from the roof in his anger. Either way she felt she was going to die because the grip he had on her was making it impossible to breathe. Nevertheless Iliani refused to call out, and after a few tense seconds, the steel bands of his arms began to loosen.

Then, the worst of her imaginings coming to the fore, Iliani thought, *Now he'll leave. He will drop his hands altogether and walk out of my life.*

As the taut seconds passed and Alaex neither left nor loosened his arms completely, Iliani realized she had underestimated him. It came to her that Alaex waited, and fleetingly the coward in her tried to deny her knowledge of what he waited for.

'Tis enough. Say no more, it pleaded. *He is still here. Take what blessing there is in that and flee.*

Yet Iliani was finding more inner strength than she knew she possessed, and backing away from that dishonorable thought, she admitted the rest.

"I also thought you had tried to kill me."

Her words were met with more silence that revealed neither Alaex's feelings nor his thoughts. His arms didn't tighten any more, but he was so still that if not for the beat of his heart behind her and his arms around her, she would not know he was there.

Iliani lost track of how long they stood that way when his voice, with a note of strain, came quietly.

"Is there more?"

Ignoring the two tears that slipped from her eyes, Iliani shook her head.

The silence didn't last as long this time.

"I think there should be," Alaex said in that same quiet tone. "Should you not at least tell me why—give me something to mitigate the horror of thinking that my wife thought me a murderer?"

"I was wrong," Iliani burst out, finally hearing the pain beneath the stillness. "I was confused. In all these years, I had never been back at Fontwyn; I was afraid. You had taken me from all I knew and I didn't know you or this place. That, along with the things I had heard of you, made everything seem hopeless.

"Then, when I began to dream of the night my father died, the confusion mounted and so did the fear. 'Twas not long after that I recognized it was returning memory. The memories only came back in bites and morsels. I did not remember Edouard in them. In truth, I did not really remember you until the day you came for me. I never associated the fierce warrior of whose reputation I heard so much with the young man who for a time lived with my father. At Lourds Keep no one mentioned that time. They barely spoke of my childhood, my father, or my life at Fontwyn.

"It made it easy to forget, and I must have buried everything about Fontwyn and my time here—especially about that night. Much later, one memory that came back was the moment just before you entered the hall. I recalled my father telling me he was wrong and warning me not to trust. He called your name. I realize now he must have been calling to you, but I did not know it before. I remembered only your look of guilt and your admission of blame."

Iliani fell silent, but she didn't need to say any more. Some of the pain eased from Alaex's heart as he saw how she had come to her conclusions. He remembered her pain-ravaged, tear-streaked face the night he had come upon her and Aeric. Finally he understood why she had run from him screaming.

Alaex remembered other things, too. He recalled how after she had left, he had held Aeric and Aeric had gasped out Iliani's name and then Edouard's. He remembered how he had thought Aeric had done that to try to tell him that that was what he wanted—for Iliani to be raised by his friend. It was the only reason Edouard had gotten her. Although he would not have called it love, Alaex had felt strongly for the child. With Aeric dead, she was all the warmth and happiness he had had left. He would have died before letting her go, but if it was Aeric's last wish . . .

Aye, Iliani had not been the only one in error. He, too, had misunderstood gravely—entrusting Aeric's daughter to the man who had killed him—and he had been older. Iliani had been only a child of five. A little more of the pain eased.

"I *was* guilty," Alaex finally said softly. "I had left Aeric here alone. We had fought, and in my anger I had ridden off, leaving him here alone. When I returned, I found you both."

Despite everything that had happened and they had learned, there was still a trace of guilt in his tone. Yet before Iliani could comfort him, before she could even decide if he would accept such comfort from her, Alaex spoke again, and some of the strain was gone from his voice.

"And the other? Your thinking I tried to kill you?"

"The accidents," Iliani whispered, her tone filled with unspoken remorse and self-condemning guilt. "'Twas you who had Wind Dancer put in that stall, knowing how unruly he could be. 'Twas you who asked me to give Arthur the message when you had never made such a request before."

The dark clouds that had enveloped Alaex's mind when Iliani had uttered those terrible words began to scatter. He was beginning to see that her opinion was based on misunderstanding and circumstance and not some flaw she detected in him. This time, when his arms tightened there was again support in them.

"Do you recall that day when you awoke and were about to ask Gwyn something before my return?" he asked gently.

Iliani nodded. He had gone to see Edouard.

"I went to Lourds Keep, but not to see Edouard," Alaex stated, contradicting her thoughts as if she had spoken aloud. "I went for Cam." There was no mistaking his emotion now. His anger was evident. He had not said, "to see"; he had said, "for Cam."

"The man Harold who died here—his death was no accident. Originally I found the tale of his death unbelievable, but there was little to say otherwise, so I let it be. Then on one of the patrol sweeps, Jon and Thibert came upon a few men in the thicker part of the forest. Before they could ask what their business was, two had drawn swords to attack and the third ran. The fight did not plague them, but the other man's running away without an attempt to aid his cohorts did, because even in that fleeting time, Thibert thought he had seen the man before. It was only later while he drilled with the new men that it came to him. When he came to me and told me that the man had been here as a recruit but had deserted, I saw naught of import. Yet when he said this had happened on the day when Harold was found dead, I found the coincidence too large to ignore. The man's nervousness then and his rapid flight from my men later, Harold's fear, and the men's being discovered near the area where I knew Cam had his camp made the short hairs of my nape rise in warning.

"I had suspicions but no proof. However, the suspicion grew when I arrived at Lourds Keep and Cam was gone. Eadwina was agitated. When I asked for Cam, before Edouard could silence her and make her leave, she babbled that Cam had left hurriedly. Why would he do so? Why would he disappear so suddenly unless warned by the man who fled? I told Edouard of my thoughts that Cam had planted the man here and that murder had been his intent, and I let him know my intentions, and then as naught could be furthered by remaining, I left."

The timbre of Alaex's voice changed. "I still have no proof, but when I find Cam, one way or another I will have my answers."

Iliani was confused. Although loath to agree with Edouard on any matter, she shared his opinion that there was no reason for Cam to kill her. "So you believe Cam was responsible for putting Harold here and causing the accidents? Why? Why would Cam want to kill me?"

"On that point I have had to revise my thoughts," Alaex replied in a steely voice. "I do not think 'twas you, but me. 'Twas just unfortunate that you were caught in it. Think, Iliani. Harold worked in the stables. He knew where I kept my horse. What he did not know was that your horse would be put there that day. Again, Harold worked on the repairs inside, most notably, the stairs. Each day *I* went down to Arthur. It was only coincidence that on that day I asked you to go in my stead to keep the man from waiting. Can you not see that both times it should have been me? And both times he would have—"

"Failed." Iliani completed Alaex's thoughts, shock in her voice as she remembered Ethelward's words about Harold's upset with his two failures. This was indeed another way to view it.

Alaex gave Iliani a moment with her thoughts and then went on. "If Harold had told Cam of his attempts and failures and perhaps even his growing distaste for his task, his life would have been worthless. Thus the fear of which Ethelward spoke. Why else would that man show up one morning—the same day Harold was found dead—and disappear before that eve? Why would the same man be in the vicinity of the place where Cam and his men used to be? Nay." Alaex shook his head. " 'Tis too vast a coincidence."

Iliani could see that, but having just been proven so very wrong for her belief in overwhelming coincidence, she tried to speak rationally.

"Aye, 'tis a large coincidence, but as you have said, you have no proof."

"What of his threat to me on the day I collected you?"

Iliani paled, remembering. She had forgotten that, and worse, Cam was still free. Wouldn't his twisted desire for revenge worsen when he heard what happened to Edouard? Yet somehow, despite her unease over that future possibility, none of it seemed as important as what would happen between her and Alaex here and now. Whether she fully believed that Cam was responsible for the accidents, Iliani did completely believe that Alaex was not. What of them?

"What do we do now, Alaex?"

Alaex heard her concern and misunderstood its source. "I will find him. Do not fear. He will never be a threat to us again."

"Will there be an 'us'?" Iliani asked softly, stiffening in his arms.

She took him aback with that question and the tension he could feel in her body. Her question also made him search himself for an honest answer.

As one tenderly probes an area where one has had great pain, Alaex searched for the hurt, only to find it gone. It had evaporated, leaving only the faintest echo that it had ever existed.

Slowly he turned Iliani in his arms. When she faced him, he cupped her face in his hands, his cloak falling away. Iliani shivered with renewed chill, either from the weather or from what she was hoping she read in Alaex's eyes. Her heart jumped with each word he spoke.

"I love you, Iliani; that has not changed. Love cannot be vanquished by fear, especially by the fears of a five-year-old child. For a time they ruled the mind of the woman, but did they ever reign in your heart?"

Iliani lost sight of his beloved face for a moment, her eyes were so filled with tears. She found the voice to answer him, and although her answer was choked, it was unhesitating.

"Nay."

Alaex smiled and Iliani's heart nearly burst with happiness in her chest.

"Very well then," he said softly, wiping at the tears that traced down her face, "I will not take offense. 'Tis not your mind I fear, but your heart, because from its fullness," he murmured, lowering his head, "come the only words that are worth heeding."

His lips closed over hers and the wind whipped her hair and billowed his cloak around them, but in that glorious moment in which the magic begins as overwhelming love is unleashed, neither one felt the cold.